*St. Martin's Paperbacks Titles
by Cheryl Anne Porter*

HANNAH'S PROMISE
JACEY'S RECKLESS HEART
SEASONS OF GLORY
CAPTIVE ANGEL
WILD FLOWER

Wild Flower

Cheryl Anne Porter

St. Martin's Paperbacks

WILD FLOWER

Copyright © 2001 by Cheryl Anne Porter.

All rights reserved. No part of this book may be used or reproduced in any manner whatsoever without written permission except in the case of brief quotations embodied in critical articles or reviews. For information address St. Martin's Press, 175 Fifth Avenue, New York, N.Y. 10010.

ISBN: 0-312-97716-6

Printed in the United States of America

St. Martin's Paperbacks edition / March 2001

St. Martin's Paperbacks are published by St. Martin's Press, 175 Fifth Avenue, New York, N.Y. 10010.

10 9 8 7 6 5 4 3 2 1

Combine class and intelligence with elegance and grace—and you'd have Glenda Howard, my editor. Glenda, you're a joy to work with.

Chapter One

The imposing National Penitentiary, hunkering with a glaring facade, stared blindly through unseeing eyes of iron-barred windows toward Tahlequah, the capital of the thriving Cherokee Nation in the Oklahoma Territory. Stone-built and stone-solid, its bruised, grayish-white colors those of a gathering storm. Three stories tall and square. Impenetrable, impregnable, isolated deep in the heart of the hilly and wooded land. Law-abiding red-skinned citizens skirted the edifice. And commerce rightly conducted its daily business at a discreet distance.

At the end of the Civil War, with the return of men hardened by fighting brother-against-brother, the tribal council had possessed the foresight to expect trouble. A whole lot of trouble. While most Cherokee men returned to peaceful lives, there were those not so willing to forgive their enemies. And even less willing to forfeit their killing ways. Sadly, the council had been proven correct in their fears. And so, with the small regional prisons full and a greater deterrent to lawless ways needed, the fathers had approved the prison. Construction was begun, and it was completed two years ago, in 1874.

The forbidding jail now housed the most dangerous and hardened prisoners in the Nation. Out back of the imposing structure, in a stark courtyard, sat a constant and hulking reminder to those who would break Cherokee law. A permanent scaffolding for the rapid carrying out of a sentence of hanging. With the new prison and its history of no successful escape attempts, there was no contingency, no type of prisoner, the council hadn't anticipated.

Until now, and except for this prisoner.

Isolated in a narrow cell on the otherwise empty third floor of the jail was the tribe's worst nightmare. A murderer and a thief. Unrepentant. Mocking. Wild. A black-haired, blue-eyed half-breed devil. Scornful of Indian ways and laws. The worst kind of outlaw. A bad seed in whose veins flowed the tainted blood of a white father. Indeed, a list of crimes as long as a man's arm accompanied the raging twenty-year life of this Cherokee.

Still, sadness flowed like blood throughout the Nation. This one lost soul tried theirs. Even so, the community was divided in their loyalties. This prisoner inspired either much love in The People's hearts or hatred of the worst kind. No one in the Nation, it seemed, had been allowed to remain lukewarm. A citizen was either for or against. But in the end, one truth shouted to be heard. No one had been able to redeem this lost soul, despite relentless religious training. And despite the best schooling in the Nation, in an education system the envy of surrounding tribes and white communities alike.

Still, at the risk of the peace that usually reigned throughout the wooded land, and with no other choice given them by law, with the evidence against the prisoner as plain as the mocking call of the blue jay, the uncomfortable verdict had been pronounced. Guilty of murder. Two months ago, the sentence of hanging had been handed down. But no one had wanted it carried out, rapidly or otherwise. There had been protests and appeals made, all of them futile. Principal Chief Thompson and his Executive Council of the sovereign Cherokee Nation, men equivalent in power and stature to the neighboring United States President and its Senators, and bound by the dictates of very specific laws, had finally ruled. No pardon would, or could, be forthcoming. No exceptions, no precedents, would be made.

Tomorrow, then, there would be a hanging. This act would not only mar what promised to be a beautiful spring day, but it would also sit heavily on The People's consciences. But with no choices left, the Cherokee Nation carried out its daily business on this, the late afternoon of the day before. Still, in the halls and offices of the Cherokee capitol building, no one seemed to want to look anyone else in the eye. They didn't say it, either, but the wish was palpable. Could no one do anything to save them from having to carry out this death sentence . . . against a young woman?

Not too far away from the capitol building, across dusty streets and around several city blocks, up on the third floor of the penitentiary, a Cherokee deputy sheriff tapped with his heavy key ring on the iron bars of the cell door. He spoke in his native tongue to the lone and condemned prisoner housed on this floor: "Taylor, get yourself up. Someone is here to see you."

Taylor Christie James, notorious half-breed outlaw, horse thief, and killer of men, abruptly sat up on her narrow cot that was pushed up against a wall on one side of the cell. Her heart raced. Could this visitor be Monroe Hammer—finally? Taylor's nerves were raw with anticipation, even though, by pretending to nap, she'd given no outward sign of being the least bit concerned with her imminent hanging tomorrow. *This better be him,* came the angry thought that capped two months of dashed hopes and fearful doubt every time a visitor for her hadn't turned out to be him.

After all, it was because of her love for Monroe and her loyalty to him that she was in here. She hadn't talked. She'd stuck to their story. She'd gone to trial and then to jail for him. He'd told her not to despair or to doubt. He would get her out, one way or another, so they could be together. They would go far away from here, and they would be free. Taylor wanted—needed—to believe this visitor here for her was him. Because she'd sure as hell tired of the long line of preachers and tribal notables who'd all evidently felt a need to minister to her today. Angry . . . and scared . . . that none of the visitors so far had been who she'd so desperately hoped they'd be, she'd sent them all packing in short order with either derisive laughter or hard and disrespectful words.

This better be him. It was the single chant in her mind today. Taylor swung her legs over the cot's side and gripped the thin mattress. She stared down at her stocking feet.

Through the black-velvet waterfall of her long hair, which hid her face from her guard, Taylor allowed herself a grin that said she still believed, even at this late hour, that Monroe Hammer would come for her. If she was right, then all hell was getting ready to break loose. Not deigning to look the guard's way—she didn't figure Rube had changed any in the past few hours since he'd belatedly remembered to clear away her lunch tray—she rubbed at her eyes and shoved her hair back over her shoulders.

Stretching her limbs, with her heart pounding against her ribs but her voice purposefully no more than a bored yawn, she finally glanced over at the guard and spoke in her native Cherokee. "Who's here to see me, Rube? Another preacher wanting me to repent of my sins so I can die with a clear conscience? Or so The People can kill me with a clear conscience is more like it. Tell him to go away and inflict his fear of hellfire and brimstone on someone who isn't already destined to feel it tomorrow. Tell him I don't want to see him."

"It is not a matter of want. They are here, and they will see you."

They? Taylor shrugged, keeping to herself the prick of worry that she might be wrong after all. She was expecting only one man—Monroe. Just then, a sudden spate of activity behind Rube captured her attention. Stepping into view and flanking her guard were three men. Three armed men. Taylor inhaled sharply, her eyes widening with alarm. Their faces were covered with bandannas, like white outlaws used. Then one of them slowly waggled his raised gun from side to side, as if trying to surreptitiously signal something to her. Taylor studied the man, noting details like his height, the way he stood, and his twinkling dark eyes. Finally, she recognized him—and fought her own reaction, afraid she'd give him away. He wasn't who she'd hoped he would be—but this man would do. He was her heretofore law-abiding Uncle Ned. And he'd brought reinforcements.

With her heart fluttering with excitement, but again careful to keep any sign of recognition of these men off her face, Taylor swung her attention back to her guard, only now noting that his holster was empty. "Rube, you didn't let a lynch mob in here to get me, did you?"

"No." His answer was simple and serious, as always. "But these men, with their drawn guns, have made known their plans. They will take you with them. This thing they are doing is wrong, Taylor Christie James—just as what you did was wrong."

Taylor was bored with Rube's continual sermonizing. "I shot a man who tried to steal my horse. But do you see that horse thief anywhere? No. Instead, it's me who's been sitting in this stinking jail with only you as company for the full two months it's taken the High Sheriff and the Principal Chief finally to get their nerve up to hang a woman."

Rube's tanned and leathery face set in hard lines. When he spoke, his voice remained maddeningly patient and judgmental, like that of some Old Testament patriarch. "It was not easy for our council to decide to hang a woman, Taylor. You know this. But you also lie, my daughter. The horse was not yours. You and Monroe Hammer stole it. The man came to you, wanting to take back his property. And he was shot in his back. He is not here now because he committed no crime. And because he is dead from a bullet, as are three other men you killed before this last one. So tomorrow, as it has been decreed, you will hang for these offenses."

"No, I won't." Mention of Monroe—as much as his not being here—inflamed Taylor's anger. She spoke through gritted teeth. "Look around you, Rube. There are three men here with guns drawn that put the lie to your words. They say you are wrong. I won't hang—not tomorrow or any other time."

She nodded in her confederates' direction, centering her attention on her uncle, Ned Christie, her mother's much-younger brother and a tall young man of twenty-four already influential in tribal matters. While Taylor was thrilled and relieved to see him, she was still surprised. But maybe Monroe had sent them. That made sense, now that she thought about it. The guards were no doubt on the watch for Monroe today, so he'd sent these men in his stead. That was a good plan. But why Uncle Ned? He may be her only hope of not hanging tomorrow, but he was also a family man. It was said that one day he would be chosen to serve on the Executive Council of the Cherokee, a position that could lead to nomination for Principal Chief. But not after today—not if he got himself hanged for helping her to escape.

A rare moment of remorse assailed Taylor. She entertained the notion of telling him not to do this, not to risk everything for her, a soul already doomed. In fact, she opened her mouth to speak her mind—

But Ned waved some official-looking papers he held in his other hand. "Right here is your official pardon, Miss James, signed and sealed by Principal Chief Thompson himself. So, are you ready to go? Or do you like it so well in here that you prefer to stay and chat with your guard?"

Her official pardon? Hardly. Taylor tilted her head at a questioning angle. It was true. Ned *was* up to something here, something beyond her escape. Obviously any prisoner officially pardoned didn't need a band of masked and armed men to escort her out of the prison. The papers were perhaps a forgery, meant to embarrass Principal Chief Thompson, a political rival Ned had never liked. That had to be it. Taylor shook her head and chuckled. Ned had his own plans. What became of him, then, was not on her head. All she knew was that, thanks to him, she was about to be a free woman.

With that realization galvanizing her into action, Taylor excitedly jumped up from her cot. Dressed in her usual shocking manner—a man's shirt and buckskin trousers—she ran to the barred cell door that separated her from freedom. Clutching at two of the close-set cold bars, she pressed her face against them and, though whispering, carefully avoided saying her uncle's name, just in case Rube overheard. "It is good to see you. I was afraid I would die here."

Her uncle chuckled and traded glances with his two friends, both of them upon closer inspection known to Taylor, despite also having the lower halves of their faces covered. John Wolf and Tom Keen. They'd been children together, these two men and Taylor. The three of them had, in their summers, run the hills and forests and streams of the Nation together. And now, here they were. Even if, by all appearances and for all she knew at this point, Monroe Hammer had forgotten his lover, these men had not forgotten their friend. Taylor's gaze slipped to their hands, noting that they still had their guns aimed at the unarmed Rube.

"Don't harm him," she heard herself commanding aloud. No one could have been more surprised than she was. Why should she care about the man who was a deputy sheriff, her ever-present guard and self-appointed spiritual tormentor? But still, for whatever reason, she did. . . . She cared.

Ned winked at her. "I see you've made friends here. But still, we figured we better come get you before the council can execute you tomorrow. Now, get your belongings, girl. We don't have all afternoon."

A sudden and exciting realization struck Taylor, sending a thrill of triumph streaking through her. This was a jailbreak. Had she dared laugh out loud, had she not been afraid of alerting others to the men's illegal presence here, the sound would have been a mocking, incredulous one. Because no one had ever escaped, except through hanging, from the new jail. Until now. Until her. She would be the first . . . if everything went well.

Just then, her Uncle Ned urged Rube, a bowlegged and leathery-skinned full-blood, to unlock the cell door. Taylor stepped back. As the key clanked into the heavy lock, she ran for her boots. In an instant, she had them on and was pushing past Rube as he was shoved into the same cell that until this moment Taylor had thought would be her last resting place before the grave.

John shoved a long black coat and a veiled hat into her arms. "Put these on." Confused, Taylor stared at the coat and hat. John added, "They're your disguise. So we don't have to shoot our way out of here. There's not anybody in the Nation who doesn't know your face, girl."

Realizing the truth of that, Taylor nodded, sticking the hat on her head and tugging the coat on and buttoning it over her clothes. The heavy door clanged shut behind Rube. Just as Taylor had done a moment ago, Rube now clutched at the metal bars. "Don't go, Taylor. This will only make things worse for you."

That was absurd. Gone was her earlier spate of sympathy for the man. Taylor struck an attitude of defiance, propping her fisted hands against her hips. "Worse? How? You and your kind were going to hang me tomorrow, old man."

Rube firmed his lips and shook his graying head. "You are our kind, too, Taylor. The white man's blood in your veins does not change that. You are of The People. But if you leave like this, your life will never be your own. The deputies will hunt you down. And they will shoot you, Taylor—like an animal. And all for a thing you did not do." Taylor's breath caught—he couldn't know that. He couldn't. "Your escape will bring shame to your family," Rube continued, his voice ringing with conviction. "Tears will fall from your mother's eyes to have had such a bad daughter as you."

More afraid than she'd ever been in her life—Rube spoke as if the things he said had already happened—Taylor called her emotion anger and spoke harshly. "Hear *my* words, old man. I am *not* of The People. My white father brought shame to my mother. And he left her alone, with only me, her half-breed bastard daughter, to remind her of her broken heart. And I tell you another thing—no one is going to shoot me or hang me. Because they're not going to catch me. Not ever again." She began pulling the heavy veil over her face.

"Maybe not our deputies. And maybe not soon. But the day will come, Taylor," the old man said cryptically. "You mark my words. The day will come for you. And you will have to make a choice. And that choice will be marked with the blood of those you love the most. Your life or theirs. The decision will be on your head and in your heart. This thing I have seen and it will come to pass."

His words were tantamount to a curse. With the three men ominously silent behind her—a curse on her would extend to them for their helping her—Taylor could only stare at Rube as foreboding ate at her. Her throat felt as if an unseen hand were closing around it. She swallowed and raised her chin.

"You are trying to scare me, and you know nothing. I am not afraid."

But her voice, lacking her earlier conviction, put the lie to her words. She was afraid, and she did believe him.

"I speak the truth," Rube countered. "I know the old ways, Taylor. And I talk with the spirits of the ancient ones. They have said this thing will be so."

Just then, her uncle pushed past her. "I've heard enough." Into the cell with Rube he threw the papers he'd brought with them. Like injured birds with broken wings, the papers fluttered helplessly and fell to the floor. "You keep your words to yourself, old man. Those are Miss James's papers. They bear the Principal Chief's signature. Only because you refuse to carry out our chief's orders—"

"I have refused nothing because he has given no such order." Rube now turned on Ned. "You take me for an old fool. There would be no need to hide your faces from honest men if these papers are as you say."

Through the black veil, which to her suddenly seemed funereal, Taylor saw the hesitation in her uncle's eyes, felt the stirrings of his friends behind them. She had to do something, say something. She couldn't allow the men to waver now. "No, Rube, it is as *he* said!" she cried, pointing at her uncle. "Those papers are legal."

Rube held her gaze. "These papers are not what they seem, Taylor. If they were, would they take my gun and lock me up?" He then skewered Ned with his dark-eyed stare. "Why do you have your gun drawn, Ned Christie? No one here threatens you or your friends. But know this—if you do this thing, you will be wanted men from this day forward."

Taylor heard Ned suck in his breath. John and Tom stirred and muttered. Taylor looked up at Ned, who was a good six or seven inches taller than she was. Would her uncle change his mind and put her back in the cell and leave without her? But Ned's attention was focused on the guard. "Tell your warden that no jail can hold a Christie." With that, Ned grabbed her arm and pulled her along after him. "Come on, Taylor.

Why do you stand here listening to that old woman? We need to get you away from here."

For some reason she couldn't fathom, Taylor took one last look at Rube before she and her uncle and his accomplices turned the corner that would take them out of Rube's sight. With one hand clutching at his shirt over his heart, with his face deeply red, as if he was in pain, Rube stretched his hand out to her. His dark eyes were imploring. "You will know a sign, Taylor. Look for it. It will be your spirit guide, and it will protect you, my child. If you do not believe, then you cannot be saved."

Saved? A sign? What did he mean? She didn't believe in signs or spirit guides. Those were only in stories the old ones told to entertain or frighten children. But Taylor suddenly realized that she had her hand out to him and was tugging against Ned's hold on her. Some deep and wounded emotion inside Taylor's heart had her crying out for the old man and the salvation he promised.

But then, too late, she was pulled around the corner. In her heart she knew that with that act, the die was cast, her fate was sealed, along with that of those she already loved . . . or would come to love. From this day forward, because of her choices, no one who came into her life would know happiness. Or peace. Or a long life.

Taylor couldn't believe it. They'd got clean away from the prison without once being challenged. So maybe Rube didn't know anything, what with his talk of choices and of innocent blood being on her head. Because her escape had been ridiculously easy. Once they'd been around the corner, out of Rube's sight, Ned and John and Tom holstered their guns and removed their bandannas. Again they were respectable citizens. As such, they'd simply walked Taylor out of the building, right past guards who'd been on duty, as Ned explained to her, for about fifteen minutes. Apparently Ned had planned it this way, around a change in shifts. It was perfect. The guards on duty when the foursome emerged hadn't been there earlier when the three men had first entered the prison. So the second-shift men had no idea that the black-coated, stooped, and veiled old lady from the Baptist mission hadn't been with them when they'd entered.

It was a brilliant plan. Sitting in an open carriage drawn by two horses, with Ned at the reins, he and Taylor had calmly ridden away at a stately pace. John and Tom had flanked them on horseback. And it had worked.

Taylor waited until they were well away from Tahlequah and out among the surrounding forest of hickory, oak, and elm before she threw off her disguise and whooped her pleasure. Ned brought the carriage to a halt. Taylor threw herself into his arms, hugging him fiercely. "You did it. You came for me, and you got me out."

Ned hugged her back and laughed with her. Then Taylor stood up in the carriage, her arms out-flung as she breathed in deeply. "Aah, fresh air. Freedom, Ned. Freedom. I can hardly believe I'm no longer in that musty cell with only Rube for company." Happy and smiling, she abruptly sat down, turning to her uncle, a blacksmith and gunsmith by trade. "How'd you do it? How'd you get in the prison?"

He shrugged. "It was simple. We didn't come in together. Or use our real names. I signed in as a representative from the Principal Chief's office. I said I had official papers you had to sign. John came in a few minutes later and said he was a reporter from the *Cherokee Advocate* here to get the prisoner's final words. And Tom—" Ned stopped and turned to Tom, who was still on horseback. "Who did you say you were?"

He grinned and tugged his hat up, revealing a tan face and dark hair. "I said I was the dead man's brother, come to forgive her. The guard was new and overwhelmed with all the official visitors Taylor has already had. He said the people in and out of the prison today were like busy ants, coming and going. He didn't question me closely, just waved me through."

Taylor grinned and shook her head at their ingenuity. Her heart swelled with gratefulness for their loyalty to her. *Loyalty*. Where was Monroe? She hesitated to ask about him, knowing the bad blood between her uncle and Monroe over Taylor's relationship with him. The last thing she wanted to do at this moment was start a fuss with Ned.

"We're lucky no one is required to sign out," Uncle Ned was saying. "Or the number of names on the two registers wouldn't have matched." The men nodded their agreement.

Taylor added hers to theirs and then asked a question of her own: "There is something I don't understand. With your stories having gotten you safely inside, why did you pose as a gang of outlaws for Rube?"

Ned sobered. "Because those papers I had weren't official papers for your release, Taylor."

Taylor looked from one handsome Cherokee face to the next. "I didn't figure they were. What were they really? Something to embarrass Principal Chief Thompson?"

The men exchanged uneasy glances. Taylor's heart began thumping leadenly. The papers had nothing to do with the Principal Chief. "Tell me," she demanded.

It fell to Ned to speak. "They were just . . . papers I put together to get me inside the prison. I couldn't use them on Rube because he'd want to read them to verify our story. We couldn't risk it or take the time for him to do so. We could have been discovered at any moment, as it was."

What he said was true. But he still wasn't telling her something. Taylor just knew it. "Then why'd you throw them in the cell with Rube if they were worthless?"

Her uncle exhaled and ran a hand over his clean-shaven jaw. "They weren't worthless, Taylor. They are very important. My hope is he will read them and turn them over to those in power. But we also went in masked so he wouldn't know who we are. That ought to slow the deputies down. They can't begin their search until they know who to look for."

"But the sheriff and his deputies are smart men," John Wolf interrupted. All eyes turned to him. Taylor recalled how at one time, when they'd been much younger, she and John had been sweet on each other. "We still don't have a lot of time, Taylor. The sheriff will begin with questions to your family and friends."

She nodded, knowing what lay behind his words. The men needed to separate and go their individual ways in order to establish their alibis. And she needed to get as far away from here as she could. "One thing." Taylor looked at her Uncle Ned. "Rube knew who you were. He even called your name."

Ned's expression clouded. "I know. But I never told him he was right. It's only his guess."

"A guess, yes. But a true one." Just as she had been earlier, Taylor again felt wooden with fear for Ned. The deputies were relentless in their pursuits, how well she knew. And now they'd be after him. He could become a wanted man, an outlaw. Just like her. Suddenly it seemed that Rube's curse was starting to come true. "I'm grateful for what you did for me." She included John Wolf and Tom Keen in her attention. "But I'm afraid for you now."

Ned gave her arm an affectionate squeeze. "You're not to worry about us. We can take care of ourselves. It's you we must worry about." His expression became grave, as if he dreaded her answer before he'd even asked her anything. "Tell me, Taylor, where is it you will go now?"

She looked down at her hands and then at her uncle, meeting his gaze. His black eyes hardened. He knew, she supposed, what her answer would be. "I will go to Monroe Hammer."

Ned's jaw clenched. Neither John nor Tom said a word. "You cannot," Ned said. "Monroe Hammer is . . . dead."

Taylor's heart froze. She felt ill and clamped a hand over her mouth. She stared at her uncle. That was why Monroe hadn't come for her. He couldn't. "What happened?" Her voice was barely a whisper of sound.

Her uncle gripped her wrist and leaned in toward her. "Listen to me well, Taylor. And do not interrupt. Monroe Hammer was *not* coming for you. He'd already taken up with another woman." Taylor jerked against her uncle's hold on her. He tightened his grip, never looking away from her eyes. "Listen to me. There is not much time. Two nights ago, Monroe was drunk and bragged about how he'd killed that man whose horse you stole. Bragged about how he let you go to prison and even to death for him. He was a coward. His words got back to me. I confronted him . . . and then I killed him."

A cry escaped Taylor. Her uncle jerked her arm hard. "Hear me. I put a knife to his throat and made him write his confession. And then, we fought and I had to kill him. I didn't want to, Taylor. I wanted to bring him in with his words and have you freed legally. But that was not to be. Without the man being alive to say the words on those papers were truly his, I did what I had to do. I broke you out of jail and left them Monroe Hammer's words to consider."

Taylor felt as if she were dying. She couldn't stop the keening wail that tore from her. Ned immediately clapped a hand over her mouth, forcing her to look at him. "Monroe Hammer was a worthless man, Taylor. He had no honor. He was a coward who hid behind women's skirts. And now, with his death on my head, I will become a wanted man. But the confession I threw in the cell with Rube could take this death sentence off your head, Taylor. Or not. Because Hammer's confession might not be believed. It may be that no one except you would believe the words of a liar and a cheat and a killer."

With Ned's hand still clamped over her mouth, all Taylor could do was stare back at him. Ned's expression became hard and ugly. "Tell me why you went to jail for him, Taylor."

With that, Ned finally took his hand away from Taylor's mouth and let go of her arm. As he'd spoken, a hot, wicked anger had overtaken her, replacing her grief and making her deadly calm. "Monroe never asked me to go to jail for him. I was the one who was caught for the death of that man. Not Monroe. There are those who would say I have no honor. But I do. And so I would not cry and beg for my own life, only to have the man I love lose his for my cowardice. But now, he is dead. And you did it. He would have come for me. He would. I know it. And so I will never forgive you. I hate you." Taylor all but spit her words out at her uncle.

"Hate me all you want, Taylor." Ned's stare was level, as was his voice. "I risked everything I have to see you free and alive, my niece. Monroe Hammer was *not* coming for you. So don't waste time grieving over such a man as he was. And know this: I did what I had to. Only time—time you didn't have and still don't—will tell if Hammer's words will be believed. What I did, right or wrong, was because of my love for you and my sister. I have given you another chance, Taylor. Use it wisely."

Taylor stared at her uncle. Then she looked to Tom and John, her childhood friends. They would not lie to her. "Is what he says true? About Monroe?"

Their silent nods spoke for them. She wanted to curl up and die. The man she loved—or thought she'd loved and who had loved her—was dead. She'd given him her loyalty and her body. And he'd never intended to come get her out of jail. He'd been going to allow her to die for his crime. And he'd already taken up with another woman. It was too much to take in. She had no time for grieving, as her uncle said. Something hard formed in Taylor's chest around the aching hurt balled up there. In this place, then, deep in her heart, would she keep her grief. Her uncle was right—she had little time and far to go.

"I will go home," she decided, speaking it in the same second as she thought it. Her chin came up. "I will go to the cabin of my mother."

Chapter Two

Taylor watched Ned exhale as if relieved. John and Tom also shifted in their saddles and made approving noises. "This is good," Ned said. "Your mother is anxious to see you. But you can't stay there, Taylor. We can't even risk being seen taking you. If Rube has already alerted the other guards, then they could even now be organizing the deputies to begin the hunt for you. They will go first to your mother's home."

Despite the hurt and hate in her heart toward her uncle, Taylor determined to keep a cool head so she could think in a practical manner, even if it meant taking his advice. "You're right. What you say is true." Her mind cruelly showed her an image of her mother's log cabin surrounded by the deadly efficient deputies and of a gunfight that could end up with not only Taylor dead but also her mother. She put her hands to her head and shook it, trying to dislodge the awful scene.

Ned grabbed her wrist and her wide-eyed attention. "Taylor, from this day forward, you must think in a way that keeps you at least one jump ahead of your pursuers. You are convicted of killing a man. I know you didn't do it. And so do John and Tom and your mother. But that's all. To everyone else, you are an escaped prisoner. I don't know what will happen to the confession I gave the law. They may just throw it away. You can't stay here until we know what they do with it. Remember, no matter what, we broke you out of jail. Your lot is now ours. So you must think what it is you will do from here. While you do, Tom and John and I also need to talk about what we're going to do."

With that, Ned let go of her and jumped out of the carriage. The other two men dismounted. With Ned, they stepped away from where Taylor sat and stood in a knot, their backs to her, and spoke together in low and worried tones.

As instructed, Taylor stayed where she was and tried to digest everything Ned had just said. But her mind shied away from everything except what her plans should be from this day forward. First, she would go home . . . because she always went home. No matter what her escapade or how much trouble she got into, she always went home to her mother, her fiercest defender. In fact, that was how Taylor had known something like Ned's showing up today at the prison to break her out was going to happen—because her mother hadn't come to see her on what was supposed to have been Taylor's last day on Mother Earth.

So, there it was. She would go home, say good-bye . . . and then she would leave. Go away. Disappear. Maybe forever.

Her heart and head swimming with woes, Taylor exhaled, only now suspecting the monumental price her freedom would exact upon what remained of her short life. And it would be short. She'd known that always. She wanted to cry—not for that reason, but for all she'd already lost in her life. Her youth, her homeland, her innocence. Taylor's chin, though it quivered, came up a determined notch. "I know I can't stay at home, Ned!" she called out to the man. Three pairs of deep-set black eyes looked her way. "I will go to my mother and let her know I'm free. And then I will . . . go."

Looking grim, Ned exchanged glances with his friends and walked back to the carriage. Standing beside it and reaching over to her, he took Taylor's hand in his, rubbing it as if it was cold. She realized it was. She was still very angry with him but didn't pull her hand out of his affectionate grasp. "My beloved niece, you sound like a child. You are not at all the hardened killer of your reputation, are you?" His gaze roved lovingly over her face. "But I see it on your face, in your eyes. You will do what you must."

For Taylor, his words were like the dying winds at the end of a spring day. Just as they settled back to the earth, so had her future. She was being cast out. Her newfound freedom meant banishment from all she loved. From the hills and bluffs and cliffs of the Nation. From the flowing streams and the forests thick with ash and oak and cottonwoods. Never again could she see the native redbud trees burst forth in spring with pink blossoms. Or hear the redbirds and the blue jays and doves sing. Never again could she attend the gatherings at the campgrounds for the tribal celebrations. Never again would she see Tom or John. Or her uncle and his family. But worst of all, never again could she see her mother.

Taylor looked from one to the other of the men. It was true. They were asking her to leave. She accepted this. How could it be otherwise? After all, if she hadn't been with Monroe when he killed that man for his horse, then none of this . . . not the trial, her imprisonment, or her jailbreak . . . would have occurred. It was as Rube had said. Their blood—Ned's, Tom's, and John's—was on her head.

"All right," Taylor said, pulling her hand away from Ned and striving to sound as hard as people said she was. "You have done enough. I will make my own way from here." She stood up in the carriage and made as if to get out.

Ned clutched at her wrist, stopping her. She turned to look at him. Lines of unhappiness creased his face. "I'm sorry for what I had to do, Taylor. I'm sorry it must be this way."

She swallowed past the growing lump of emotion in her throat. She wanted to hate him but couldn't. "So am I."

Ned didn't seem to want to let her go, though. He still held onto her. "You'll need things, Taylor. You can't go as you are now, on foot and unarmed."

"I won't stay that way for long. I'll soon get what I need from home." She watched his face, saw by his expression that he was about to caution her. "I'll be careful," she said first. "When I get home, I'll stay hidden until I make sure no one is around. If all is well there, and quiet, then I'll say my good-bye and leave. But if there are deputies about, then I will go as I am."

She tugged her wrist out of Ned's grasp and jumped easily out of the open carriage. Ned surprised her by taking her into his embrace and holding her close. Taylor's hurt and anger toward him evaporated. She realized she was clinging as tightly to him as he was to her. Barely able to stand this silent leave-taking, she pulled away, turning to Tom and John. In turn, they hugged her briefly and gave her their good-byes and best wishes. She thanked them and turned to walk away.

Not once did she look back.

Taylor was deep in the forest. Thick, low-hanging branches pulled at her clothing as she brushed by. The day's light waned, casting her in dark shadows. Carefully, aware of every sound and listening for the pounding of horses' hooves and the cry of men's voices, Taylor pushed her way homeward . . . for the last time. She knew in her heart that she would not see this land again. She had lived her life in such a way that now made it impossible for her to stay.

But she was no longer without a plan. She would live in the white man's world . . . where Indian laws or crimes were not recognized. So, once she left the Nation, and because Cherokee law was not respected or upheld by the United States government, Taylor knew she would be deemed guiltless of any crime. Every Cherokee knew that while the white lawmen frequently made forays into the Nation to hunt for white criminals, the Indian deputies could not pursue an Indian criminal onto white land. Nor could the Indian deputies arrest a white criminal for mischief on Indian land.

Yes, the white man's dismissal of Indian law was unfair, at the very least. There was no doubting that. But now Taylor intended to use that same imbalance to her advantage. She wouldn't be the first Indian to do so, either. But still, she could hardly believe it. Her, Taylor Christie James, living in the white world. Right now—and she hated the realization—the white man and his ways were her saviors. For years, in school and because of the missionaries who came into the Nation, she'd been taught the white language and customs and manners. Her mother had insisted on it, saying that the white ways were the ways of the future . . . of Taylor's future. So Taylor knew their religion, how they dressed, and the way they looked at the world.

Still, all of their ways seemed strange and foreign to her.

But thanks to her father's blood—this was the first time she'd ever been thankful for being half-white—she had blue eyes and much lighter skin than the full-bloods. Two months in a prison cell certainly hadn't tanned her skin any darker, either. In short, she could pass for white. Such a notion had Taylor shaking her head as she skirted a tree stump and avoided a broken branch underfoot. It was strange to think that only in the land of her father . . . a man she barely remembered, a man who'd abandoned her and her mother when Taylor was nine years old . . . would she not be a wanted woman. Only there could she regain her legal innocence and have a chance at life. Only there could she hope to outrun and, she hoped, outlive Rube's curse.

In what seemed like only moments but was perhaps longer, given Taylor's immersion into her troubling thoughts . . . especially those that kept reminding her of Monroe Hammer's desertion and betrayal of her . . . darkness blanketed the earth. Pulling herself back to the moment, she stopped and looked up. Revealed to her through a break in the interwoven branches were the stars, twinkling pricks of light overhead. The night was cloudless, the moon full. The earth under her feet was dank and musty-smelling. The forest about her teemed with life. This was a land and a way of life she understood.

But it was no longer her land, or her way of life.

Allowing for no sentimentality or regrets at this late date, Taylor walked on. With the moon's reflected light guiding her, she steadily picked her way through the tangling underbrush of the hickory forest also thick with oak and elm. She listened to every sound, pausing, heeding it, and then assuring herself, before she moved on, that what she heard were woodland noises and not the furtive movements of a posse. More than once, some small creature startled her by suddenly scurrying away from her advancing feet. An owl hooted, wanting to know who passed by. Taylor spared it only a glance.

Guided by unerring instinct as much as familiar habit—this terrain was her home ground, the earth of her childhood wanderings—Taylor stopped for nothing, pausing only to brush

back a low-hanging branch here or to ford a stream there. She
hadn't eaten since lunch, and most of that meal she'd left
untouched. Her belly complained now of its emptiness, but
there were no berries or wild greens to be found for gathering.
And she had neither the time nor the weapon to secure meat
. . . and no desire to be detected because of the campfire she'd
have to make to cook her kill. So, except for the occasional
mouthful of clear and cold stream water that she drank from
her cupped hands, she did without. It wasn't the first time.
Nor did she believe it would be the last.

It didn't matter. All that mattered was seeing her mother
and then leaving before she brought the law to the door and
more trouble to her mother's heart.

Finally, Taylor reached home. Stopping at the edge of the
woods, with her mother's cabin only a matter of feet away in
the small clearing, with moonlight splashing it with the bright-
ness of day, Taylor suspended emotion, not daring to give in
to the giddy excitement she felt at being this close to home.
What she wanted most to do was rush to the cabin and run
inside and be with her mother. But instead, and wisely, she
paid heed to what her senses were telling her.

Her eyes showed her nothing was moving outside and that
a light burned inside . . . where a silhouette suddenly passed
by the curtain-covered window. Taylor tensed, her mind proc-
essing what she'd just seen. Only one shadow. A woman's.
Her mother. Taylor exhaled the breath she'd been holding. As
she listened now, her hearing detected no leaves rustling as
they would if stealthily moving feet stirred them. No sounds
that would come from men hiding outside, sounds like a sudden sniff or a low cough, came to her ears.

But then, and startling in the silence, carried the low
whinny of a horse and its nervous stamping of a hoof. Taylor
jerked in the direction of the sound—the horse corral behind
the cabin—and realized it was only her horse she'd heard. Red
Sky, a long-legged paint, had caught her scent. He stood at
the fence, his ears pricked forward, his great dark eyes reflect-
ing moonlight as he stared directly at her. A grin came to
Taylor's face.

Soon, my friend. Soon will we ride against the night and away from this place with its many memories, she told her horse in a silent communication. But then, she noticed something about Red Sky that had her grin fading. He was saddled and bridled already. Taylor knew her mother had to have done so. Because Taylor had trained Red Sky not to allow anyone but her or her mother to approach him, much less handle him.

So, why had her mother done this? Taylor looked from the horse to the cabin. Was it in anticipation of Taylor showing up and then making a quick getaway? Or was this a trap? Had her mother been forced, perhaps by deputies hiding inside with her, to saddle Red Sky only to make Taylor think what she just had? Did these deputies believe she would be foolish enough to not proceed with caution and get herself captured?

Taylor focused again on her surroundings and had to admit things certainly looked innocent and normal. Her nose told her that a wood fire was burning in the fireplace inside the cabin. In the moonlight, she saw the smoke curling above the stone chimney. No doubt her mother was cooking her supper. Taylor's mouth watered. Her stomach growled its protest. But still she didn't move. She remained pressed against the rough-barked trunk of a scrub oak tree . . . and waited a few moments longer, long enough for anyone who hadn't yet made a telltale sound to do so.

Despite her grim alertness and acutely honed senses, Taylor's next thought had her grinning. Perhaps the best evidence that no one was in hiding out here except for her was that she hadn't yet tripped over some gunman. Not that she was arrogant enough to take anything away from the Cherokee deputies' tracking skills, but hers were every bit as good. Well, except for that last time, when they'd caught her. But even then, it had only been by a fluke that they had. She remembered that day well. Desperately dirty and aching from being on the run and sleeping in caves or simply on the ground, and while Monroe had gone to steal their supper from someone's chicken yard, she'd finally succumbed to the need for cleanliness.

And so it had been that she'd been bathing in a stream

when they'd caught her . . . naked and unarmed, her drying clothes and her weapon on the ground at their feet. Taylor burned now with remembered anger at the men's crude jokes and catcalls, at their lusting looks as she'd emerged, chilled to the bone, from the cold water. Remembering their sudden silence at the picture she'd made, then the rough groping and handling of her they'd subjected her to on that day, now narrowed her eyes to slits. She knew in her heart that only because she'd given them no satisfaction, only because she'd shown no fear, no emotion at all, only because she'd stood tall and proud and silent, had she not come to a worse fate at their hands.

She believed that in the face of her stoic pride and her level stare, they'd abandoned their taunting of her and allowed her to dress. But perhaps their suddenly respectful behavior toward her had more to do with her warning the men that there was no prison that could hold her, that she was Monroe Hammer's woman, and that one day she'd be free—and when she was, she and Monroe would find every man who'd dared to put his hands on her, and they'd fix each of them in such a way that he'd never again have the desire to touch any woman . . . and have no reason to do so. Apparently they'd believed her, because they'd abandoned their game with her at that point.

Also on that day, she'd sworn silently to herself that once Monroe got her out, she'd never be taken unaware like that again. And now, here she was upholding that two-month-old pledge to herself. Of course, Monroe was nowhere around. Taylor tamped down the sudden emotions that assailed her. Hurt. Anger. Loss. Betrayal. *No. He is dead.* And he deserved nothing from her. Nothing.

At this point, tired of the waiting and watching, and equally tired of her thoughts, Taylor called herself certain that she and her mother would be alone for their reunion. Still, to remain safe, Taylor had to behave as if the worst had already happened, meaning Rube's predicament had been discovered, since it was now past time for the supper tray to be brought up to the third floor. So, Taylor reasoned, only one of two things could have already happened. Either the deputies had been here and could still double back, hoping to catch her. Or they weren't here yet but would soon show up. Either way, Taylor didn't have long to say her final good-bye.

Knowing that, she made her move. Scurrying low to the ground and on a zigzag course, sticking to shadows when she could, she hurried to the side of the cabin. Edging along the rough bark of the cut logs that comprised the one-story house, she inched toward the covered front porch and lightly jumped up onto it. Sticking close to the wall, stepping around a wash-tub and butter churn, she felt for the door as she kept a lookout around her, trying to see everything at once and yet, she hoped, hopefully missing nothing.

Just then, the front door opened, startling the breath out of Taylor as she froze in place, her back against the wall, her heart thumping frantically. Into the shadowy, flickering light cast onto the porch by the cook fire stepped her mother. Ten-nie Nell Christie turned to Taylor, as if she'd known all along that she was there. She smiled, showing strong, white teeth. "It is OK, my daughter," she said. "The deputies have gone. But they could return at any moment."

Knee-weakening relief cascaded over Taylor's nerves . . . relief that the deputies were gone and relief that the one open-ing the door had been her mother and not an armed lawman. When she could, Taylor pulled away from the wall. Then, as if she'd only stepped out a moment ago, perhaps to bring in firewood, as if she hadn't been imprisoned for murder and wasn't supposed to be hanged tomorrow, Taylor adopted a pose of bravado and wanted to know only one thing: "How did you know I was out here?"

Equally collected and calm–appearing, her mother shrugged as she stepped back, making way for Taylor to step inside ahead of her. "You make too much noise. I heard you."

A scoffing sound erupted from Taylor. "I made no noise. You taught me better than that."

"I would have said so, too. And yet, here I am and I have caught you. You are not yet better than your teacher."

Grinning, Taylor continued to feign nonchalance as she en-tered the cabin. But then she turned, and with her mother's back to her as she closed and latched the door behind them, Taylor dropped her pose and filled her eyes and her heart with the sight of this most beloved of women to her. With mounting dismay, with her hands fisting at her sides, and laying the blame squarely at her own feet, Taylor noted that her mother was thinner, that her clothes seemed to hang on her. And her hair . . . when had it become this gray?

Just then her mother pivoted, swirling her long skirt about her legs, as she faced Taylor. No evidence of strong emotion marred her mother's countenance. To her, such displays were unseemly. Tennie Nell, a striking woman of high cheekbones and dark flashing eyes, with her dark gray-streaked hair braided, chuckled and confessed. "What you said outside is true—you made no noise. It was Red Sky who announced your presence with his whinny. I have saddled him and, as you taught him, he awaits you at the gate."

Taylor smiled. She'd been right. Her mother had anticipated her arrival. Further evidence was the already packed saddle-bags and the neatly tied bedroll that rested against the wall by the door. Taylor's gaze went to the items and then back to her mother's face. Silence fell between them, sobering them both. Taylor pulled in a long breath, feeling the emotion-filled tight-ness in her chest as she did.

She watched her mother's gaze roving over her figure. Tay-lor could see a glint in her dark eyes. Tears? Or the reflection of the glowing fire she faced? "They have not fed you well in their prison of stone," Tennie Nell said abruptly, angrily. "You are thin, like the reeds along the water's edge. I have prepared food you can take with you. It is already packed and is enough to keep you for a few days. But right now you can have some bread and some chicken. It will hold you until you stop later."

With that, and not awaiting Taylor's answer, Tennie Nell brushed by her daughter, not pausing to touch her in any way. Aching with knowing this might be the last time she ever saw her mother, Taylor turned to watch her heading for the rough-hewn dining table by the fire. Atop it, in chipped china bowls and a small woven basket, was the food she'd mentioned.

Feeling lost and alone, like an abandoned child, Taylor watched her mother's precise movements, her rigid posture, as she gathered up the meal. Taylor was no longer sure she could swallow the food. With her hands fisted at her sides, with her love for her mother an unspoken and aching lump in her throat, Taylor longed only for her touch. She wanted no sustenance other than that of the soul . . . the comfort of her mother's arms around her. She wanted only to be held, to have her hair stroked, and to hear again the soft murmuring words of reassurance she remembered from her childhood.

But that could not be, Taylor feared, because she had brought too much hurt and shame into this house to ask now for forgiveness. This then, to stand alone and yearning, untouched and unforgiven, was her sentence.

Such thoughts as these kept Taylor standing where she'd been since entering her mother's house. She looked around her. This cabin, this warm and tidy place, was no longer her home. She didn't belong here. This was the worst of all fates. To be inside the home but outside the loving circle of its warm shelter. Maybe forever. Still, not one sound or protest issued from Taylor. Her mother's silence matched hers. Tennie Nell was not a hard or unfeeling woman. Taylor never thought of her mother's behavior in those ways. Because she knew this reticence, this holding back, this bone-deep aching sense of loss that kept them from saying or showing anything they felt, was their way, the Cherokee way.

These were the blank faces The People turned to the white man—and to each other when emotions threatened to overwhelm. Tears and wailing were signs of weakness, a loss of face and pride. Taylor knew all that. And yet she had almost succumbed to it with the news about Monroe, a man she now realized she was beginning to hate. Still, she prided herself on her tough hide, on her inscrutable countenance, her unrelenting disdain. Except where her mother was concerned. And so, nothing had ever hurt so much in Taylor's life as did this distance between them.

Perhaps, then, it would be best if she gathered what her mother had already packed and just left. Taylor felt as wooden as the floor under her feet, but she forced herself into motion. With her first step, her boots made a scuffing sound.

Her mother whirled around. Tears streaked her face. She dropped the tin plate she'd been holding onto the tabletop and ran toward Taylor, her arms outstretched. "My child," she sobbed. "My heart, my love, my baby. I am so afraid for you."

Taylor didn't recall moving in turn, but there she was, clutching her mother into her embrace, holding her close in her arms as Tennie Nell cried for her only child—an outlaw half-breed quicker with a knife and a gun and a cutting word than any warrior of old. Braver and more dangerous, perhaps more reckless. "Don't cry for me, Mother," Taylor said softly, fighting tears she refused to shed. "I have brought you nothing but pain. I am an unworthy daughter, not deserving of your sorrow. Do not mourn the loss of such a one as me."

Tennie Nell Christie pulled back, her cheeks wet with tears, her expression a mask of anger. With an open hand, she slapped Taylor full across the face. Taylor cried out as her head snapped to one side. Her mother grabbed a handful of Taylor's long black hair and held it tightly, forcing Taylor to look down into her face. "I *will* mourn you. I *do* mourn you. For surely even now you are as lost to me as you would have been tomorrow if the council had wrongly hanged you. I know you did not kill that man for his horse. And I know that Monroe Hammer is dead. I am glad. I spit on his grave. But I will cry for you, child of my heart, until the day I die. That is how much I love you. Always remember that."

She released Taylor's hair and raised one of Taylor's hands to her lips, kissing her palm and then putting Taylor's hand to her own cheek. She looked Taylor in the eye. Despite the tears that stained her cheeks, her voice was again sure and strong. "You are the reason I have lived."

Her throat working, her heart breaking, and full of shame, Taylor knew what this show of emotion had cost her mother in pride. Taylor looked down and to one side of her mother. Her cheek stung, her ears were ringing, such was the force of her mother's slap.

"Look at me, Taylor."

Taylor did, her expression blank, no words forthcoming.

"You will leave this night, and you will go to your father in St. Louis."

Shock had Taylor jerking out of her mother's grasp. "I will not. I will make my way west to the white man's wilderness. I will—"

"No. You will do as I tell you. You will go to the town of St. Louis, in the place called Missouri, the Great Waters. There you will go to your father. I did not have my brother break you out of jail only to have you fling yourself to the wolves in a world unknown to you. For all your wild ways, Taylor, you are an innocent. Out west, your life will be hard and it will be short; this I tell you. And so you will go east. You will find your white family. They will take you in, and they will protect you."

Taylor was reeling inside. "I will not. I hate my—"

"Taylor." Her mother said only that one word, but her voice rang with parental authority. Taylor remained silent and respectful. Only then did Tennie Nell speak again. "You will go to your father." A moment's hesitation shadowed her eyes, but then she added, "And there you will find your beloved Amanda."

Amanda? The surprise of hearing that name stiffened Taylor in place. She could barely breathe. She'd had too many shocks today. Her world was spinning round and round. "Find her there? How? My cousin is dead from a pox she got as a child. You told me this years ago."

Her mother shook her head. "She is not dead."

Taylor's mind simply would not register her mother's words. "She is. You are saying this thing now to get me to go east. Amanda is—"

"Alive, Taylor. She is not dead. I told you what I had to at the time. I don't expect you to understand. Back then, it was best that you believed Amanda to be gone from this earth."

Suddenly too warm, then too cold, and sick inside, but with no outward display of her roiling emotions, Taylor stared at her mother, a virtuous woman who'd done the best she could with such a bad seed as Taylor for a daughter. A woman who'd watched her daughter grow up wild and spit in the face of the injustices of being half-white in a red world and half-red in a white world and of being an outcast bastard child in both societies. A woman, though, who'd never given up on her daughter, who'd tried to bring Taylor to her senses . . . a woman Taylor would have sworn had never told a lie in her life. And now this.

"Why?" It was the only word she could get out.

"Because there is one who would see you dead."

Taylor stood there, blinking, slowly shaking her head. "But . . . why? I was only a child. An innocent child. Who would want me dead?" Then, she knew. "This white family you would send me to. They want me dead. Am I right?"

Her mother nodded and took in a deep breath, exhaling slowly. "This is true. But not all of them, Taylor. There are those who love you. You are no longer a child, and so you deserve the truth. Now you are strong. You can face them."

Taylor stilled, her mind working, her expression stony. Sudden and sneaking suspicion, like a coiling snake, wrapped itself around her belly. "How do you know all this? And that Amanda still lives? That there is a white person who wants me dead? How do you know?"

Taylor knew there was only one way her mother could know. But she wanted to hear her say it.

Her mother's chin came up. She returned Taylor's unblinking stare. "Because over the years," she said unwaveringly, "I have kept in touch with one who loves you very much. Through letters and messages brought by friends."

"And all this you kept from me?"

"Yes. There was no reason to tell you. There was nothing you could do. Nothing any of us could do. We did what we had to do to protect you."

Taylor looked at her mother, seeing her now in a new light. What other sacrifices had she made that Taylor remained unaware of? What was truly in her heart? What did she think of the white man she'd loved but who had abandoned them both, Taylor and her mother? Then, something else occurred to Taylor, something she couldn't stop herself from asking. "The man whose bastard I am . . . is he the one who writes you?"

Her mother's expression never changed. "Go to St. Louis, Taylor. You will be safe there."

Rising anger had Taylor fisting her hands. "You didn't answer my question."

"You are speaking harshly to me, Taylor. It is disrespectful."

Taylor gritted her teeth together until her jaw ached. What her mother said was true. For all her wild and lawless ways, Taylor had been a respectful daughter in her mother's house. But those days and those honoring ways were gone.

"Your father will be so happy—"

"Do not call him my father!" Taylor exploded into yelling and punctuating her accusations with angry gestures. "He is merely the white man who abandoned you and me, the white man who never claimed me. He left me his bastard and brought shame to you." This woman she called her mother was suddenly a stranger to Taylor. A cold hardness, for the second time this day, engulfed her heart. "This man is without honor, and now you say he is going to help me? Is that what you would have me believe?"

Tennie Nell seemed to shrink, to become old and vulnerable right before Taylor's eyes. Fear for her mother replaced the anger in Taylor's heart, leaving her ashamed and reaching out, wanting to tell Tennie Nell she was sorry.

But her mother waved her off and then clutched spasmodically at her skirt. Her black eyes again danced with tears. "It was not like that. There are things you do not know, Taylor. Things you do not have the time to hear from me. The deputies could already be on their way back here."

"Mother, I do not care about the deputies. I want to know—"

"No. Please. No more questions. I will pack your food and some money, and you will leave. You must go to St. Louis. There is nothing more I can do for you."

Taylor couldn't bear the thought of leaving her mother here alone. "Then come with me. There is nothing holding you here."

Tennie Nell shook her head. "No, I cannot go. You must do this alone, my daughter. I watched you grow up strong and beautiful. I even saw that you got your deserved freedom from the stone prison. But you are still a prisoner in our world. And I have kept you too long to myself. Go to your father. Promise me you will. You must take great care. But he and others around him can tell you the truth—a truth you must hear from them."

Taylor frowned. She had no idea what her mother meant. What truth? But with time chasing her as surely as did the deputies, the last thing she wanted to do was argue with her mother or delay here long enough to get caught again. "I hear your words, my mother. Then, this is good-bye," she said, her heart in her eyes, her arms held open to hug her mother one last time.

Chapter Three

Good God, how much was one man supposed to take in the name of a social occasion? First it had been the extensive landscaping done to the eastern portion of Forest Park. Then it was the dedication two years ago of Eads Bridge, which had finally spanned the Mississippi River here in St. Louis, and how that had changed the face of commerce. Then it was the demise of commerce's dependence upon the steamboat in the face of the railway system. And now it was the separation of "our dear city" of St. Louis from St. Louis County. Surely next would be the city's upcoming plans for the centennial celebration of nationhood.

Through gritted teeth, Greyson Howard Talbott prided himself that he held his tongue every bit as well as he did his liquor. Still, the pompous boor accosting him just now with his asinine opinions on everything St. Louis was damned lucky this was Grey's fifth stiff drink following the buffet supper. Otherwise, he may have told the petty city official exactly what he thought he could do with his park and Eads Bridge, which the fellow had just pronounced as the greatest achievement in recent St. Louis history.

Boring. That's what the man's pointless chattering was. All of it. Deadly boring. Especially since Grey's family—mostly through his younger brother Franklin's visionary efforts—had been involved personally or financially in each of the transactions the man was pontificating on. As a result of being forced to listen to Franklin at family gatherings expound on these same subjects—while their dear mother harangued Grey about not being more involved and thereby putting everything on Franklin's shoulders—he knew firsthand all the inside sto-

ries and intimate details of each. And not once that Grey could
recall had this detestable little man been present at any phase
or on any level of the city's development. Who the devil was
he, anyway, that he didn't recognize the Talbott name and
philanthropy and leadership in charity and industry and government? The man was as uninformed as . . . Grey glanced
down at the simpering young female clinging to his arm . . .
as *she* was silly, in his opinion.

Oh, she was pretty enough, he supposed . . . all pink skin
and blond hair. But the devil of it was he couldn't quite remember who she was exactly. She was no relative. And he
hadn't brought her with him to this gathering of family and
friends and petty yet boring city officials. Instead, and acting
for all the world as if she knew him well, she had attached
herself to him some time ago when he'd made one of his many
forays over to the punch bowl. Despite the buzz of conversation all around him, which vied with the pleasant whiskey
buzz in his head, Grey mentally scrolled through the names
and faces of young ladies known to him. But no . . . nothing.
Couldn't come up with the girl's name.

Really perplexed now, he stole another sidelong glance at
the young woman. She caught him staring. He gave her a weak
smile. She giggled back at him and hugged her barely covered
breasts against his sleeve. That invitation was clear. The young
lady was of that most frightening of designations—an eligible
female. Eligible for marriage, that is. In light of that, Grey had
all he could do not to bolt from the room.

This was a perfect example, he reminded himself, of why
he much preferred the social atmosphere of one of his clubs.
There a man could have a good cigar, a decent conversation,
and a rousing game of cards without some desperate mama
tossing her daughter of a marriageable age his way. Well, no
matter. Just as he'd done with all the others, he'd soon find a
way to rid himself of this flouncing young lady who had de-
signs on him.

It was more important to him that he was pleasantly drunk
and listening with only half an ear to the conversation swirling
about him. He even managed to give every appearance of be-

ing attentive. The genial nod. The agreeable murmur of implied consent. The thoughtful expression. All that while eyeing the foyer lingeringly, wondering when he could acceptably make his escape. Why had he promised his mother—as if a man of thirty-two should have to do such a thing—that he would attend this gathering and behave? Yet he had promised. And so he would. Behave, that is. Because for all his shortcomings, he *was* a man of his infrequently given word—a laudable virtue he nonetheless was now ready to term a serious character flaw.

After all, look where living by the precepts of a virtue had landed him. Here . . . here being the celebration of his younger brother's engagement to Miss Amanda James, niece to Charles Edward James, in whose elegant mansion this little tableau among him, the clinging young woman, and the boring petty city official was taking place. A man of his word. *Ha.* The only word Grey could think of at this moment was a heated four-lettered curse he wished to fling at the pompous little toad still haranguing him with his insufferable opinions.

Wondering what would happen if he did fling the curse, Grey amused himself with picturing the general reaction among the luminaries present. The shocked looks. The outraged gasps. The widened eyes. *Wonderful.* The moment got away from him. He chuckled evilly.

"By God, sir, you find the plight of the city's orphans a laughing matter?"

Grey frowned, snapping back to the moment. *Orphans? When the devil—?* He focused on the irritating city official. The man's face was red and strained-looking above his stiff collar. His sausagelike fingers gripped his wineglass so tightly Grey was certain it would snap at any moment. While that might prove interesting . . .

Grey raised an eyebrow as he considered the speaker through narrowed eyes—and broke his word to his dear mother about manners. "No, sir, I assure you I do not. In fact, I find the orphans' plight a damned sight better than my own at this moment. I can only hope the poor children are never subjected to your long-winded harangues as I and Miss . . ."

He looked at the pink and blond grinning female still stuck to his arm. "As I and this young woman, whoever the devil she may be, have been." The young woman gasped and retracted her possessive claws from Grey's coat sleeve. "Thank you, miss," he told her, turning his attention back to the apoplectic man he was insulting. "If one of your speeches were to befall the orphans, I fear you'd have the hapless children jumping in droves off that much-vaunted Eads Bridge of yours."

Just Grey's luck . . . he'd lost his decorum on the last note of the musicians' current piece. And apparently he'd spoken into the ensuing silence more loudly than he'd realized. The room was stone quiet, and all eyes were on him. From a distance, he heard a muffled, "Good heavens, what now?" That would be his mother. And then everyone, including Grey, watched as the young lady beside him huffed out an insulted breath and stormed away in a cloud of sky blue chiffon . . . or damask or silk or whatever the devil young females today were wearing to catch a wealthy husband. But already some good was coming of breaking his word to his mother—the feeling was returning to his arm, which he exercised.

All eyes were on the petty city official as that man gave his own *harrumph,* turned his back to Grey, and went off, no doubt, to inflict his nattering presence on some other unfortunate cluster of heretofore happy guests. *Yet another good consequence of not being a man of one's word,* Grey reflected. *Insufferable bores learn to avoid you.* Deciding he'd done his duty, and then some, by his mother and Franklin and Amanda, Grey pronounced this a good time for him to take his leave. He felt certain that almost everyone else in attendance would probably agree.

As quickly as the room had quieted, the conversations and the music resumed. They were used to Grey's outbursts. He spied his host coming toward him, a huge grin on the man's face. "Ah, Charles, a splendid party," Grey told him, clapping the handsome and stately older man on his shoulder when he stood in front of him. "Excellent food. Fabulous music. And of course your niece Amanda. A wonderful girl. My younger brother is truly blessed to have found such a rare gem in this year's crop of eligible young misses."

Charles Edward James chuckled and shook his head. "Grey, my esteemed friend, you are decidedly drunk. And honest as a result."

Grinning, his expression alive with merriment, Grey feigned shock. "Me? Drunk and honest? What a detestable combination. Now, tell me, did my long-suffering mother send you over here?"

Charles sighed, an affected sound, as he nodded his silvering blond head. "Yes, I'm afraid she did."

"Ah. Have I been excused, then?"

"You have."

"Wonderful." Grey put a conspiratorial arm around Charles and lowered his voice almost to a whisper. "Tell me something else. Who the hell *was* that nasty little man I was talking to just now, the one I insulted?"

Charles shrugged. "Some minor dignitary in the city government. A Mr. Harnison, I believe. A relative of a friend. You know the type of thing."

Grey nodded. "I do. And the young lady with the altogether pleasant bosom and the blue dress? Who is she? And why does she act as if she knows me? I can't recall her name . . . or her attributes."

"And it's a good thing you don't . . . with regard to her attributes, that is. You see, she's Miss Henryetta Chalmers."

Grey frowned, trying to concentrate. "Chalmers, you say? I do know that name. Have I met her before?"

"Perhaps only briefly. She's just been let out of the nursery, so to speak. This is her first season. But more importantly to your continued well-being, you recognize her name because her father is a United States Senator. A powerful man. Of course, if you'd occasionally deign to socialize with the right people, you'd have seen her often and would readily remember that, my friend."

Pretending outrage, Grey released his host and pulled himself up to his full height. "A reprimand from you, Charles? Then, great Scott, I've done it now, haven't I?"

"Oh, yes. And it only gets worse, my good man—or better, however you wish to see it. Because Miss Chalmers is one of my niece's—your future sister-in-law's—bridesmaids. I feel certain you'll be seeing quite a bit of her in the next few months until the wedding."

Grey thoughtfully rubbed a hand over his clean-shaven jaw. "Well, that ought to be delightful, then." He handed his empty whiskey glass to his host. "Mind this for me while I say my good night to my widowed mother and Franklin and your sweet Amanda and her parents. I shall then depart with my tail tucked firmly between my legs."

Charles James chuckled. "It's not as bad as all that. You've done no harm. Just gave the gossips something to do with their loose tongues. But if you wish to leave, then I'm afraid my little gathering won't be the same."

"Awfully good of you to say so. Now, sir, if you would kindly have the formidable Estes retrieve my hat and call up my carriage from the mix of them outside, I will then bid my family and you a fond farewell in short order."

Her father lived on Vandeventer Place, west of Grand Avenue, in St. Louis. In a big house. That was all Taylor knew. That was all that her mother had scrawled on the piece of paper she'd tucked into Taylor's saddlebags. Taylor hadn't found the note until days later, when she'd been safely inside the United States in the state they called Missouri. Taylor had shaken her head at that. First the white man dishonored the Missouri people by taking their ancestral home from them. Then the white man named their state after them, to honor them. She would never understand the white man's way of thinking.

But she was here now, firmly among them in their city. She told herself she was undaunted to be in a city the size of St. Louis. After all, Tahlequah was sizable in its own right. And she'd made trips with her mother to cities outside the Nation. Adding to that was the schooling she'd undergone that had indoctrinated her into the ways and manners of the white man. She could pass for a white woman; she knew that. But still, her heart beat with some apprehension because the day's

light had long since faded, giving a sinister glare to the dark
streets pocked by pools of light shed from the street lamps.
Still, she was armed, and it was comforting. Her gun was
strapped to her hip, and there was a hidden knife in its sheath
inside her boot.

Taylor sat easily atop her paint gelding on the sprawling
city's western outskirts and looked over the tangle of streets
and buildings and wagons and carriages and people around
her. As she passed by, lost and having to backtrack through
the city's business section, and searching for Vandeventer
Place, she drew her share of curious stares. For the most part,
she ignored them. But that didn't mean they didn't make her
feel unwanted.

Taylor reminded herself that she could simply leave. She
hadn't promised her mother she'd come to St. Louis. In fact,
she'd told herself a month ago as she'd ridden away from
Tahlequah that she had no intention of finding her white father
or his family. Or Amanda. Why should she? She owed them
nothing. And they owed her nothing. She needed no one. She
could make her own way in the world.

Besides, if it was true that Amanda was alive, then it was
also true that she'd made no effort to contact Taylor in all
these years. This realization hurt worse than her father abandoning her. Perhaps, though, Amanda had been told that Taylor was dead, just as she'd been told that Amanda was. That
was the only explanation Taylor felt she could abide. Because
she and Amanda, as children, had been inseparable, like sisters. Constantly together, sharing secrets, laughing, playing
childhood games, sleeping in the same bed, promising always
to be together, never to be apart. And then, the day had come,
a day at the end of the War Between the States, when
Amanda's father, Stanley, brother to Taylor's father, had returned for his wife and child.

They had taken Amanda away, leaving Taylor heartbroken.
She'd been nine years old then, but she remembered the day
well. She recalled how Amanda's mother, Camilla James, a
daughter of stern Baptist missionaries, had cried and held Taylor for a long time, too. Camilla had then clung to Taylor's

mother, saying she would never forget her. And then . . . they were gone. As she'd grown, Taylor had convinced herself that they'd taken Amanda away because the white man Stanley James could not bear to see his wife and pretty pink child laughing with the dark-haired Cherokee child and her mother.

There was a part of Taylor that wanted to believe the reason was that simple and that wrong. But at her age now, and with the things her mother had told her, Taylor was certain there was more to it than that. Not all white people hated red people. But most red people hated all white people. Taylor counted herself among that group. And yet, here she was . . . up to her ears in bustling white people in one of their big and confusing cities. She should just leave.

That would be an easy enough thing to do . . . until her traitorous mind showed her the image of her mother crying and begging Taylor to be safe and to go to her father. And so, finally . . . with angry and unanswered questions driving her . . . she had turned Red Sky's head toward the northeast and had become the obedient daughter. That thought got an immediate scoffing sound out of Taylor now. Obedient? No. Vengeful? Yes. A walking reminder of her white father's sin— that was her, right down to her blue eyes, the same color as his. This her mother had told her many times . . . *"You have your father's eyes."* Taylor had never taken it as a compliment. She wanted nothing of her father's. Nothing. She was here to honor her mother . . . and to confront her father. And Amanda.

Only, now that Taylor was here, she had no idea how to go about honoring her mother's wish, on the one hand. And nettling her father, on the other. She was supposed to put herself under Charles Edward James's protection. Because there was one who wished her dead. Who? And why? Another white person, she supposed. Overall, though, and to her surprise, they were turning out to be not such a bad lot. Yes, they smelled funny. And they were loud and rude, always asking questions. But beyond that, they seemed harmless enough. And no one had bothered her thus far, or even in the past four weeks it had taken her to arrive here by horseback.

And so she was beginning to have second thoughts about all this. What if her father had another family, a white wife and children? The odds were that he would, even though her mother hadn't said. She might not know. But if he did, what would they think of Taylor? How would they treat her? More important, how should she treat them? Taylor's worst fear was that she'd like them. And how would that be honoring her mother and nettling her father?

Just then, Taylor realized where she was. Vandeventer Place. She reined her horse and looked around, laughing at herself. She'd been lost in thought and hadn't noticed the city buildings and the noisy traffic fading away. As she sat there now on a corner and under a street lamp, she half-expected to be challenged, given her appearance, so out of place in this obviously high-society residential section, given the palatial appearance of the homes. But no passerby challenged her. Or seemed even to care that she was here—lucky for them.

Taylor pulled her mother's note out of her shirt pocket. Checking the house number written on it against the numbers posted above the ornate double doors across the street told her that she had found her destination. The home of her white father. Taylor tucked the note back into her pocket. Her heart thumped leadenly, but she refused to name the emotion behind its tom-tomming beat.

Scowling, she stared at the house, a vast mansion across the street from her. Her father's mansion. A home roughly the size of the Cherokee capitol building. She thought of the one-room rough log cabin she and her mother had shared. Fronting this house was a formal lawn with a profusion of flowers rife with the blooming colors of a rainbow. She thought of the tangle of wild forest that all but swallowed up her mother's cabin. A black wrought-iron fence encircled this property. Back home, there was no need for such a fence. They had nothing worth stealing. The front gate here was open. An invitation? Or a dare?

Taylor inhaled, realizing it was painful to do so with her chest suddenly so tight. Still, she told herself that she felt nothing, sitting there on that warm early-summer evening atop her paint horse and staring at . . . her new home?

Maybe. She called this place uninviting at best to someone like her. Outside, many carriages were parked. Inside, through the open windows, she could see the house was ablaze with light and with richly garbed people walking about and talking and laughing. She also heard the faint strains of music. Obviously, this was a social gathering of some kind or a celebration of some sort. The people inside were wearing their finest clothes; of that she was certain.

From under the hard brim of her felt hat, and seated atop her paint gelding, Taylor looked down at herself, seeing the man's shirt she preferred over a woman's blouse. Seeing her long thick braid, adorned with a feather, hanging over her shoulder. Tight buckskin britches. Knee-high leather boots. A gun strapped to her hip. She wasn't dressed for a party. But neither did she care. This probably wasn't the best time to confront him, her conscience pointed out. No, it wasn't.

A grin of rebellion captured her lips. "Hello, Father," she said almost in a whisper as she dismounted. "Your half-breed daughter is home. Did you miss me?"

Grey said his last good night, this one to Charles's butler, Estes, who wished him a pleasant evening and closed the door behind him. Outside and donning his hat, fitting it low to his brow, Grey sauntered down the three wide steps and out of the circle of light cast by the lamps to either side of the doors. On the elegant and curving shrub-lined walk, which led to the opened gate and the carriages beyond, he caught sight of an approaching figure that had his steps slowing until he finally stopped. He squinted. What was that coming toward him? A creature in buckskin britches and armed with a holstered gun? Surely not.

Grey rubbed his eyes. He'd drunk more than he thought. But the apparition kept coming . . . until it got so close that Grey knew this was no apparition. This was an earthbound blood-to-the-bone woman. One hell of a woman, actually, who had the confident stride of a man and the figure of an angel encased in those tight britches and under that man's shirt. A woman also obviously intent, given her direction and despite her state of improper dress, on walking right up to the front door behind him and knocking on it. That should give poor old Estes a fainting fit.

Perhaps she was lost or had simply mistaken this address for her destination. And perhaps it was none of his business. For a second, Grey considered allowing her to pass, then turning around and following her back to the front door—back to Charles's party. Wouldn't he and his guests be shocked? No doubt, there would be some wonderfully dramatic reactions to this handsome yet outlandish sight coming toward him, reactions he didn't want to miss. But good sense finally won out. *Drat it.* If nothing else, Charles didn't deserve another scene this evening. So, calling himself a good and dutiful friend, Grey took it upon himself to intercede when the woman drew abreast of him. "Excuse me. May I help you, miss?"

She stopped and, in silence, looked him up and down as if he were of no consequence. That amused Grey, so he returned the insult by sizing her up in much the same way she did him. He couldn't get a good look at her face because of the shadows thrown across her features by her hat's brim, but he suspected she was young and not ugly. He also noted her long and dark thick braid—with a feather knotted to it by a strip of leather—that hung over her shoulder and how the top of her head was even with his chin. Tall for a woman, even an Indian woman, which he judged her to be, given the evidence of her attire.

She hadn't answered him, so Grey asked again, "May I help you, miss?"

From under the brim of her hat she looked up at him and said, "I don't require your help. Not unless you're Mr. Charles Edward James. And somehow I don't think you are. Now, if you'll excuse me."

So she wasn't lost or mistaken. Grey's next thought was that her speech held an unusual but not unpleasant cadence, one unknown to his ear.

She moved as if to step around him. There was really no reason why Grey should not have allowed her to do so. Except . . . sudden alarms of an unknown nature sounded in his head.

He squared his shoulders to her and used his imposing size to block her way. The woman's choices were either to deal with him or to hop over the knee-high hedges growing on either side of the walk and proceed on her way through the lawn—with him in implied pursuit.

She evidently realized as much, because she stayed where she was and sent him a level stare. "My business is with Mr. James. Not you. Now, step aside." He didn't. Her chin came up a notch. "I won't ask you again."

"I believe you," Grey answered. But still, he continued to block her way. For the life of him, he couldn't rid himself of a growing sense of dread, of something being so very wrong here, something that concerned others beyond her and Charles. So, until he knew better, Grey intended not to mind his own business. He decided to take another tack with her, one of concern for her. "Perhaps I *can* help you, miss. Is something wrong?"

"Only with you. You're blocking my way." Her voice was low and rich . . . and clearly threatening.

What was left of Grey's good whiskey cheer soured. "Yes, I am. And again I ask you, what is your business with Mr. James?"

Again she gave him that smooth and dismissing once-over of his person. "I have already answered that."

Rising temper made Grey's ears feel hot. "Well, I'm afraid I'm asking again. Mr. James is entertaining this evening." Grey gestured pointedly at her rustic outfit, complete with some type of carved-bone and beaded choker necklace. "And I would venture to say that you're not an invited guest."

She didn't say anything. Grey wondered if she was going to pull her gun and shoot him. But all she did was hook her thumbs in her gun belt and relax her pose, putting her weight on one leg. "You would be right on both counts, mister," she drawled. "I am not invited. And I am not a guest. I am, however, his daughter."

Shock stiffened Grey's knees but quickly turned to outrage. "The devil you say! How dare you show up here and say such a thing?" He leaned toward her, his voice no more than a hiss now. "I don't know who you are or what your game is, but I do know you are *not* Mr. James's daughter."

If he scared her, she didn't show it. "And how would you know that?"

"Because—" Stopping Grey was the sudden realization that he could not say the words that were on the tip of his tongue, not if he meant to keep his promise of silence on this issue to Charles. And he did mean to keep it. So he stepped back from her and finished in the most innocuous manner he could. "Because Charles doesn't have a daughter. That's how I know."

She nodded slowly . . . in a mocking way that left Grey feeling unsettled. But not as much as did her words that followed her nodding silence. "Is that what he told you, that he does not have a daughter?" she asked quietly. "Or did he tell you that he did, only she is now dead?"

Shock again held Grey in its grip. How could she know that? It was exactly what Charles had told him—that his only child, a daughter, had died years ago. Grey fought to keep his expression from giving him away, but here was this young woman saying—

"I should have known he would say something like that." She spoke quietly, as if to herself. Then she exhaled, a sad or resigned sound, and looked up into Grey's eyes. "I have not come this long way so I could stand here and justify myself to *you.* Now, if you will step aside, I will go greet my fath—"

"You will not. You're either completely insane or up to no good. Or both." Grey grabbed her purposely by her right arm, rendering her incapable of easily reaching for that ugly-looking six-shooter strapped to her hip. He whipped her around to be facing the same direction he'd been heading. With her in tow but tugging hard against his brutal hold on her, he marched toward the open gate and the cluster of carriages and drivers on the street.

"I see your game now. Somehow you've found out about his child," he accused. No sense denying what she obviously already knew, that Charles had a daughter at one time. "And now you think you can extort money from him to keep his secret pain private. That's it, isn't it? Well, I don't intend to

allow you to do that. I do, however, intend to toss you out
into the street where charlatans such as you belong. And make
no mistake, young lady; these men out here—the carriage
drivers—will make sure you stay out, if I tell them to see to
it. And they will call the law, Miss . . . uh . . . Miss—"

"James," she said . . . with taunting conviction. "Taylor
Christie James."

Grey stopped cold, still holding her slender arm but turning
now to face the glaring young woman. *Taylor.* Of course if
she knew Charles had a daughter, she'd know the girl's name.
But still, it was disconcerting to hear her say the very name
he'd heard Charles cry out over and over that night long ago
when drink had got the best of the man—a name Charles had
later said he'd never told anyone else but him. Grey could
barely breathe. This was quickly becoming a nightmare, one
that had his heart pounding and his senses reeling. His grip
on her tightened . . . she winced . . . as he leaned in toward her.
"How do you know that name? Tell me. Or I'll shake the truth
out of you."

A defiant and ugly expression claimed her face. "I have
already said. I know it because it is *my* name."

Outside the gate now and on the walkway, Grey stood with
her in the light thrown by the street lamps. Aware of the
glances of the curious drivers, he stared at this young woman
whose arm he gripped so tightly. He looked for evidence in
her face that would tell him she was crazy or lying . . . or even
that she was telling the truth. Her eyes, a deep blue, he could
now see, were unnervingly familiar. Then, he knew where
he'd seen them before. If he wasn't mistaken, they were the
same distinct blue as Charles's eyes.

"Oh, God." Grey rubbed his free hand over his forehead,
inadvertently pushing his hat up on his brow. Feeling slightly
sick for what all this might mean, but keeping his suspicions
to himself, Grey did the only thing he could think to do to
dislodge her from her story. He introduced himself. "Well,
then, Miss . . . uh . . . James, allow me to introduce myself. I
am Mr. Greyson Talbott, a *close* friend of . . . your father's,
one he's taken completely into his confidence."

She raised an eyebrow. "Not so completely. Not if he told you I'm dead. Do I feel dead to you?" When he didn't say anything, she continued. "Take your hand off me unless you want me to give it back to you . . . separated from your arm."

Believing she'd do it, too, Grey released her and dropped his arm to his side. She turned abruptly away from him and again began making her way up the long walk to the festively lit house. Grey watched her, noting her swinging braid and swaying hips, her long, slim legs and her confident stride. Damned if her walk wasn't a feminine version of her father's—of Charles's, he meant. No, he didn't. He didn't mean that at all. Grey rubbed agitatedly at his mouth and chin and wondered what, if any, his duty or his responsibility was here. Should he allow her to proceed or not? Did he have any right to stop her?

In no more than a moment, she would approach the front doors. He had to decide. Grey told himself that his first responsibility was to Charles, a man who'd been his close friend for more than five years. And one who, through the impending marriage of Amanda to Franklin, would be a relative of sorts. Besides that, Grey told himself, he had no reason to doubt Charles's story of his only child being dead. This made his decision easy. He had to stop this young woman again. He could not allow her to simply walk up to the unsuspecting man's house and announce she was Taylor. At this point, it didn't really matter whether she was or not. Because the shock alone of hearing her name spoken out loud would probably kill Charles.

Speaking of killing . . . Grey suspected she'd probably kill *him* if he accosted her again. He was thinking of that six-shooter strapped low on her hip. She knew how to use it. No one had to tell him that. So there was only one safe way— safe for him—to stop her. It was also a test. He would call out to her . . . by name. Would she recognize it as hers and turn around?

With only seconds to spare before she stood in front of the closed doors at the entrance to the James mansion, Grey started toward her and called out, "Miss James? Please, a moment more of your time? Miss James?"

Chapter Four

With her teeth gritted, and with the sounds of happy festivity inside the house assaulting her ears, Taylor pivoted around to face Mr. Talbott. Frustration ate at her. Only a few more feet, then up three wide steps, and she would finally be at her father's front door. But the interfering white man apparently wasn't going to allow it to happen. Instead, he seemed intent on forcing her to deal with him. "What do you want, Mr. Talbott?"

The man approached her, stopping close enough to force her to look up at him. She figured that was his intent, to intimidate her. With the added light from the lamps mounted to either side of the double doors behind her, she could now see his face and surprised herself with the realization that under any other circumstances she would have found him extremely handsome . . . for a white man.

"I want you to come away from this door right now," he said levelly. "I want you to let Mr. James be."

Anger leaped to the forefront of Taylor's already edgy emotions. She'd already given up her mother, her people, and her homeland. She'd come to terms with her betrayal by Monroe. And the ride here hadn't been easy. She was tired and dirty and hungry and apprehensive about finally meeting her father. And now this very rude man seemed intent on stopping her. "I have already told you," she began. "He is my father. And this is none of your business." She made a show of inching her hand close to her gun. "If you do not leave me be, I intend to drop you where you stand."

The big man pointed to her gun as his eyes narrowed to slits. "Pulling that would be a mistake, miss."

"Maybe. But you will not be around to say you told me so."

The man's expression hardened. "You're pretty cocksure of yourself."

She'd gotten to him. Fighting a grin of triumph, Taylor shrugged. "No more so than you."

"Is that so? How do you figure?"

"I am armed. And you are not."

"Am I not?" As if by magic, a gun appeared in his hand and he had it aimed at her heart.

Taylor's surprised intake of breath was a hiss. With widened eyes, she stared at the weapon. It was a small gun. But it was still a gun. Obviously he had some kind of holster up his sleeve. She had heard of such things. She met his eyes. The look in them said he was serious.

"You're going to come with me—now."

Taylor took an almost involuntary step back. She shook her head. "No, I will not do so."

"Oh, but this gun and I say you will."

Taylor exhaled slowly. She flexed her hand, wanting to go for her gun. "Why are you doing this?"

Mr. Talbott made a vague gesture with his free hand. "I keep asking myself that same question. And I have to say that I don't really know why. Except maybe because Mr. James is a good friend of mine. And I don't want to see him hurt."

Taylor didn't know exactly what to say to that, except, "I *am* his daughter."

He nodded. "You may well be. We'll find out soon enough. But not tonight. This isn't the right time . . . Miss James."

He kept calling her by her name, Taylor noticed. Because he believed her? Or because he had nothing else to call her? She glanced over her shoulder at the closed doors behind her. And then focused again on the gun pointing at her. Finally, she looked at Mr. Talbott's face.

"What to do," he said, grinning. "Hard to figure, isn't it? Can you draw your gun and shoot me before I shoot you? And if I wouldn't really shoot a woman—which you don't know if I would or not—can you get to the door before I stop you? Isn't that what you're thinking?"

Taylor's chin came up a notch. She didn't like one bit how easy it was for him to read her. Most people had great difficulty in assessing her intentions. Of course, she comforted herself, she'd practically given them away in this instance.

"I was right, wasn't I?" he said. "As I said before, you are to come with me. Are you willing to do that? Because I really feel like a fool standing here with a gun trained on you."

Taylor saw no way out of this. Helping her to decide, though, was her own earlier ambivalence toward facing her father for the first time with all those other people present. It really hadn't been something she was looking forward to doing, despite her bravado at being almost to his door. The closer she'd got to it, even before this man had confronted her, the less she'd been inclined to go through with an initial meeting tonight. So, finally, having thus convinced herself that this was her idea, she said, "I will go with you. As long as you do not—"

"You will? You'll go willingly?" Surprise flicked through his dark eyes.

"Willingly? No. You have your gun aimed at me. But I will go. First I want to know where you are taking me."

With his tall hat pushed back on his head, Taylor could see twin vertical lines form between his eyebrows. "That's a good question. I have no idea. I suppose to my town house several blocks away. That's the only place I can keep an eye on you and make sure you don't come back here tonight."

Relief coursed through her on one score. She'd feared he meant to take her to the law. But his intention, to take her to his home, still didn't sit well with her. She'd be at his doubtful mercy, because she figured he'd take her gun from her. Of course, he didn't know about the knife strapped in its sheath inside her boot. But that weapon wouldn't do her much good if he intended to keep her under lock and key. And that was what scared her the most. She'd already lived all she ever wanted to in a prison of any kind. "You cannot lock me up in your home."

He sent her a look that challenged her statement. "Actually, I can. And no one would know the difference. But I'll leave that up to you and your behavior."

With that, he waved his gun at her as a signal to precede him back down the walk and toward the carriages outside the open gate to her father's home.

His knees apart, his arms crossed, Grey sat on the padded seat of his enclosed elegant carriage and stared at the enigmatic young woman seated across from him. Moonlight, as well as the street lamps they passed, intermittently flooded the carriage's interior with their light and afforded him an intriguing picture of her.

Miss James, or whoever the devil she was, sat with a rigid posture, her expression impassive. She'd tied her horse, an Indian paint pony, to the back of the brougham. The dull thud of the animal's hooves on the hard-packed dirt of the street only added to the night sounds of the city, the soft noises of which followed them on their ride through St. Louis.

Grey considered that paint horse now with his Indian blanket under the saddle. The evidence was mounting. Her buckskin britches. The unusual cadence of her speech. Her dark hair and high cheekbones. Her braided hair, the feather. He'd bet she was extremely beautiful, all cleaned up. "Tell me, Miss James—and I only address you as such because I have no choice—are you, uhm, an Indian of some sort?"

Her eyes narrowed. "Of some sort?"

Grey exhaled, knowing this was tricky ground. He removed his top hat and set it on the seat next to him . . . and atop her gun, which he'd taken from her as she got into the carriage. He rubbed a hand through his hair. "I didn't mean my question to be an insult. I was only trying to ascertain if so and which tribe. You see, it's not easy to tell with you. You're dressed in a manner that suggests Indian blood, but you don't look—at least not wholly—Indian."

She gave him that level stare of hers that he wouldn't have ever admitted out loud unnerved him. "Why do you need to know?"

He shrugged. "Call it curiosity."

"Curiosity," she repeated, making of the word a mouthful of disdain. Grey didn't believe she meant to add anything, but then she said, "*Indian* is your word. We call ourselves The People. My mother is of the tribe called Tsalagi."

"Cha-la-kee" was how it sounded to his ears. Grey nodded and smiled, as if this were wonderful news. "Cherokee," he surmised. "I thought so."

She cocked her head at a questioning angle, the slight motion sending her long braid with its feathered adornment swinging slowly and sensually over the swell of her breast. Grey swallowed, meeting her eyes when she remarked, "You thought so?"

"I did. The Cherokee are a beautiful people, and you are, er, certainly . . . beautiful," he finished on a lame note. He felt like such a fool. But she was patently unfriendly, disconcertingly so. Well, what did he expect, he berated himself. He'd kept her from seeing to her own business and then had all but abducted her at the end of a gun and was even now taking her, against her will and essentially a prisoner, to his home . . . to do what with her there he had no idea. He scratched at his forehead. And had no idea how to proceed from here.

Then . . . she smirked at him. It became a leering grin that revealed a set of white and even teeth. Grey frowned, feeling insulted somehow. "Are you laughing at me?"

She shrugged. "You're afraid of me, aren't you, white man? You're twice my size and have two guns to my none. And yet, you fear me—fear the savage and what I might do, don't you?"

"Hardly, Miss . . . James. But speaking of white men, tell me about those blue eyes of yours. They aren't a Cherokee trait, are they?"

She sobered, her expression returning to that impassive mask Grey was already beginning to hate. "No. They are instead the eyes of my white father."

He'd of course known that, if her father was who she said it was. "Then you're a half-breed." The word was out before he could stop it. Damned lingering effects of the whiskey. It had loosened his normal controls.

Her eyes glittered. "Yes. I am as you say . . . a half-breed."

She said the word as if daring him to make something of it. Obviously, he'd insulted her. Grey thought to put her at ease. "Listen, the color of a person's skin or whose blood may run in their veins is neither here nor there to me. I don't judge anyone by it."

"How noble of you." She crossed her arms. "However, I do. I do not like white people."

"You don't?" Grey crossed his arms in imitation of her. "Interestingly enough, neither do I—like white people, I mean. For the most part, I think them a sorry lot. America's sad history of westward expansion will bear me out on this, I believe."

That got her. Her eyes widened, and she slumped back against the seat. "But you are one of them."

He never looked away from her face. "Yes, I know. And I am occasionally not the least bit happy about it, either."

Her eyes narrowed and her chin came up a proud notch. "You are mocking me."

"I assure you I am not. I am merely seeking some common ground with you that will help get us through our present dilemma."

"I do not know that word."

"Which word? *Dilemma?* It means a problem. In this case, the one that currently has you in my carriage, bound for my home, and with your gun on the seat next to me."

Her gaze slid down to the weapon in question, or to the hat atop it. She shifted her attention back to him. "This . . . dil-emma, then, is of your own making. You could have left me alone to complete my business."

"I could have. But I don't see it that way, Miss . . . James." He still had trouble calling her that. Because to do so was to admit, however tacitly, that she was indeed Charles's daughter. "Instead, I see your being here at all as the dilemma."

"For you? Or for my father?"

"Good question. For us both, I suppose. For him because

he believes that you—if you are indeed who you say you are—"

"I am."

"Be that as it may. Still, he believes his daughter to be dead."

A frown creased her mouth, as if she was troubled. "Are you sure that is truly what he believes? Or did he just tell you that, wanting *you* to believe it?"

Leaping to his friend's defense had Grey sitting sharply forward. "Why in God's name would he just *tell* me that? It's certainly not the sort of thing one just divulges. And it's not as if one night at dinner he said, 'By the way, Talbott, I had a daughter once by a Cherokee woman, but now she's dead. Please pass the peas.' " Grey sat back. "In truth, before he told me, I had no reason even to assume Charles had ever fathered a child."

Her brow furrowed, as if she was increasingly confused. "Then he has never taken a wife?"

Ha. Now he had her. "You mean other than your mother, of course?"

Her expression hardened. "He never married my mother. Not only did he make me a half-breed, but he also left me a bastard."

Grey was silent in the face of her harsh words. He tried to consider her revelations in light of what he knew of Charles. "I understand your anger, if this is all true. But tell me this— why would someone tell him you were dead? Because I believe, given the circumstances surrounding his telling me, that he firmly believes you are. Or his daughter is. Who would do that?"

"That is among the things I came to find out."

"I see." This was an awful mystery. A sudden coldness on this warm night crept over Grey's skin. "Let me ask you something else. What's kept you away all these years? Did you perhaps believe him to be dead?"

"No. I believed him not to care. In one's heart, it can be the same thing."

Heart-wrenching, her simple words were. Increasingly,

Grey had no idea what *he* believed. There was tragedy, and perhaps no small amount of danger, inherent in this young woman's appearance here in St. Louis; that much he knew. Suddenly he recalled the wedding that would soon unite his family with Charles's. He thought of them all. Charles. Amanda and Franklin. Camilla and Stanley James, Amanda's parents. Grey's own widowed mother. Himself. *Great Scott, two entire families.* It then occurred to Grey that he hadn't asked her the single most important question. "Why *are* you here just now?"

"Because you held a gun on me and—"

"Not that. I mean why are you here in St. Louis now, at this particular time? I am going to assume for a moment that you are Charles James's long-lost child. That being so, what has happened to cause you to come here now, if you've known all along that your father was alive? And why is it suddenly important that you discover who told your father that his daughter was lost to him? Obviously, behind that unknown 'who' is a why. There has to be a why. Why someone would do such a terrible thing."

She studied him in that placid yet intense manner that was already familiar to him. She seemed to be weighing whether or not he was worthy of being given an answer. "Why I am here now is my business, as is the rest of it."

So they were back to that. Grey took another tack. "Do you intend to harm Mr. James?"

She shook her head. "No. But why do you care so much? Why are you making this your business?"

Grey had no intention at this point of making his family vulnerable by admitting to the upcoming wedding between Amanda—this young woman's cousin, if she was telling the truth—and his brother, Franklin. Not to mention the attendant scandal that could arise because of her revelations. And scandal was the last thing Franklin needed right now, as he was preparing to run for mayor. In light of all that, Grey kept his answer simple. "Because Charles is my friend, as I've already said."

"You are a very loyal man." She made it sound as if he

were a very stupid man. Then, she crossed her arms and had a question for him. "How did you finally learn that your . . . *friend* had fathered a child?"

Grey sat up in a rigid posture. "Quite by mistake, I assure you. And I refuse to go further into the incident with you."

"Then you know how I feel, Mr. Talbott."

Grey ducked his chin. "Point taken. You keep your secrets. And I'll keep mine. But beyond that, may I suggest that you look at this on another level?" She shrugged her evident willingness to listen. "Thank you. You now know that Mr. James believes you—or his daughter—to be dead. If you are she, then obviously you're not. So even if you *are* his daughter, and even if your reason for being here *is* purely innocent, and your reunion *would* cause only great joy, we cannot simply spring you on him. The shock of just suddenly being faced with the reality that you're alive would kill a stronger man than he is."

She'd been nodding and listening closely as he spoke, but by the time he finished, something had flickered in her eyes, edging them with a strong emotion. "Then he is . . . unwell?"

That was a gratifying response. She at least seemed to care about Charles's health. "No. He's not unwell. But he is—how can I put this? *Fragile*, I suppose, is the best word. Do you know that word?" She nodded. Grey continued. "To me, Charles appears to have been deeply hurt by life. I fear it wouldn't take much to . . . end him."

She exhaled, somehow imbuing the sound with a considered thoughtfulness, as if breathing helped her draw not only air but also conclusions. "So because of this . . . fragile state, you think to protect him. From only me? Or from all of life's harsh truths?"

For a moment, Grey could only stare at her. What a quick mind she had. He admired that. This give-and-take between them, he suddenly realized, afforded him the same emotions that he experienced when he was engaged in a spirited high-stakes poker game. Challenging, rewarding . . . exciting. Finally, he answered her. "From only you. And I will do so until I know who you are in truth and what your purpose is in confronting him. Make no mistake, I assign no innocent motives to you. But even should you prove to be aboveboard, then he needs to be adequately prepared in advance to see you, face-to-face."

A mocking expression lit her features. "What things will you do to put your heart at rest with knowing that I speak the truth?"

The way she worded things. He had to really think to get at her meaning. When he had it, he still had no answer for her. Because he didn't know. So he stalled. "Why do you ask?"

"Because I am wondering how long you mean to keep me hidden in your home. You said until you know the truth. That could take a while . . . without my help."

White man. The unspoken words were there in her attitude. Grey sat back and eyed her sitting there confidently across from him. What in hell *was* he going to do with her? He already knew he'd have the very devil of a time keeping her hidden away for even a short period of time. She knew it, too. But beyond that, he had no stomach for locking a woman away in his home. The very idea was barbaric.

What he needed, then, was a good many-pronged scheme. One, he needed the time and the freedom to seek the truth about her. Two, he needed her cooperation for that. Three, he needed to keep a close eye on her in the meantime. Four . . . in order for him to achieve one, two, and three . . . she would have to move about in polite society—or he had to stay home all the time with her. And five—it remained true—Charles needed to get to know her before she was sprung on him as his daughter . . . if she was his daughter . . . so the shock didn't kill him.

Damn, what a convoluted mess. Still, thank God he *had* involved himself, now that he knew his entire family could be affected adversely, to put it mildly, by this young woman's sudden appearance in their lives with her secretive mission. But what was the solution to his current and many-pronged dilemma? Grey exhaled his resignation. There was only one solution, and he knew what it was.

Yes, he'd sooner shoot himself in the foot than implement it, but this was for the good of the family. He bit back a threatening peal of laughter. He'd be the one to put his own mother in the grave with that one. *The good of the family. Ha.* His mother always accused him of putting himself first. Maybe so. But not this time. This time the very lives of those he loved the most in the world—even if he never told them or acted as if he gave a damn—could be at stake.

He'd been quiet a long time while he thought all this through. So had she. He now met the waiting gaze of the very arousing and mysterious dark-haired young woman seated across from him. And knew that the pretense he was about to suggest was fraught with blind alleys and unforeseen dangers. Still, the plan he meant to propose should make his socially prominent mother very happy. That is, if she, as well as everyone else who knew him, didn't faint dead away at the shock of his announcement. *Now, isn't this interesting?* Grey asked himself. In order not to kill off a friend with a huge shock, he had to perpetrate a scheme that could very well kill off his own family and friends first. *Lovely.*

Grey rubbed tiredly at his temples. Outside his carriage he heard the *clip-clop* of the horses' hooves, heard a dog barking, heard someone calling out in the night, looking for someone who apparently hadn't come home. Grey pronounced himself sympathetic with that idea. Only thirty minutes ago his life hadn't been this vastly complicated. But this turn of events—admittedly, brought down on his own head by the sudden rearing of this ugly sense of familial duty in his heart—was certainly enough to send any man running for the hills.

While that remained a wishful and perhaps viable option, Grey nevertheless cloaked himself in the mantle of personal accountability and spoke at long last to his companion. "Well, it pains me to say this . . . Miss James. But I believe I have a plan. And it's actually very simple. The best ones always are. So, here it is." He took a much-needed deep breath. "Despite my better instincts, I will present you to society as my fiancée."

She sat forward, her expression itself a question mark. "Your what?"

The word was unfamiliar to her, obviously. "My fiancée. The woman I intend to marry."

The only reason Mr. Greyson Talbott lived past that moment was because Taylor had time only to stare in shock at the crazy white man before the carriage in which they were riding came to a sudden stop. Taylor jerked her gaze out the open window. Where were they? Had he taken her to his home as he'd said? Or to the law? In either case, what would happen now? Her heart thumped fearfully. Suddenly the carriage chassis rocked and a man called out orders. Taylor's eyes widened in panic. She gripped the leather seat's edge.

"That's only my driver, Miss James. He's directing the men who work for me. It's OK. They won't hurt you."

Taylor raised her chin and glared at him. "I am not afraid."

However, she didn't seem capable of not watching the scene outside. The night was lit up with lanterns and was alive with running men. They all charged toward the carriage. Instantly the vehicle was surrounded and the men set to work amid a chorus of "yessirs" to the orders tossed their way by the driver.

Taylor eyed the handle on the door. So far no one had opened it and tried to pluck her out. She tried to think what she should do, if they attempted such a thing. How could she defend herself? She remembered her knife. That comforted her a bit. Still, she shrank back against her seat and warily watched every move the men made as they passed in and out of her view, which was limited to the small square of the window opening.

Suddenly a man jerked open the door between her and Mr. Talbott. Taylor's hand edged toward her boot. The man, skinny and smiling, set down a three-step ladder on the ground and poked his head into the carriage's interior. "Good evening, sir. Welcome ho—" He stared wide-eyed at Taylor. Leaning forward, her hand poised just above her boot top, she stared back at him through dangerously slitted eyes.

Another man, outside and unseen, called out, "What do you want me to do with this horse back here?"

Taylor eyed Mr. Talbott. "If your man so much as touches my horse, Red Sky will kill him. I trained him that way."

"Good God." Mr. Talbott's eyes rounded. He snapped an order to the gaping man whose head was poked inside the carriage. "Tell Calvin to stay away from that Indian pony. Now."

"Yes, sir." The man jerked back and spoke sharply to this unseen Calvin. "Leave the horse be. The, uh, lady will have to see to it."

A chorus of, "What lady?" was heard, whereupon Mr. Talbott muttered something under his breath, grabbed up his tall hat and her gun, and edged forward, finally exiting the carriage. Once outside, he pocketed her gun, donned his hat, and stuck his hand back in. He meant to assist her in getting out, Taylor surmised. Disdaining his help, she ignored his outstretched hand, him, and the three-step ladder, instead jumping nimbly to the ground on her own power. The men—there were four of them besides Mr. Talbott—quieted and stilled. They stared at her.

Pointedly ignoring them, Taylor looked about her. She stood in the middle of an orderly coach yard behind a narrow three-story red-brick building. Mr. Talbott's home. On either side of this place were attached other homes of the same sort. *A curious way to build one's home*, she concluded. She turned her attention to the yard itself. A very large square in shape, covered with a sandy earth, surrounded by brick walls. At the yard's back gate sat two big wooden buildings. Most likely a coach barn and a horse barn. Lamps hung at various intervals, their cheery light making her study possible. She looked to her left. A back door into the house was open, showing a long wood-floored hall also awash with light . . . and inviting somehow.

She blinked and turned her attention to the struck-dumb men. "Which one of you is Calvin?"

The dead silence continued. Taylor wondered if she'd accidentally lapsed into Cherokee. Then, "I am, miss," came

from her right. Taylor turned to see a tall, well-muscled boy
dragging his cap off to reveal red hair. She had seen this coloring before on a bad white man who had done terrible things
in the Nation.

Taylor looked the boy, *a-ni-tsu* to her, up and down with
great disdain. "Come here." He began walking toward her . . .
with all the enthusiasm, it amused her to note, of someone
volunteering to have his throat slit.

"Follow me," she said, turning on her heel. She half-
expected Mr. Talbott to challenge her, but to her surprise he
waited with the rest of the men to see what she was doing. At
the back of the carriage, she took hold of Red Sky's bridle
and pulled his head down until his soft, velvety ear was close
to her mouth. She whispered some Cherokee words into the
animal's ear. Red Sky pulled back and looked at her, then at
Calvin behind her.

Taylor patted the horse's neck and turned to Calvin. "You
alone, other than me, may handle him. His name is Red Sky.
I have told him your name and that it is good with me for you
to touch him. Hear me well, *a-ni-tsu*—should anyone else try
to manage him or ride him, he will kill that person. Make this
known to the other men."

Calvin bobbed his head so severely Taylor feared it would
topple off his neck. But he was merely nodding in acknowledgment of her orders. "Yes, ma'am. I most certainly will.
You can count on me, ma'am."

"Good." She grabbed her saddlebags and tugged them off
Red Sky. Throwing them over a shoulder, she walked back to
Mr. Talbott. She looked up at the big man and said, "I am
ready."

He pointed to her saddlebags. "You won't need anything
in those."

Taylor quirked an eyebrow. "You cannot know that, for
you do not know what I have in them."

Without warning, he very rudely tugged them off her shoulder and tossed them easily to one of his men. "Go on about
your business," he told them. They did, dispersing instantly.
Then he turned back to her. "You're right. I don't know what

you have in them. Which is exactly why I said you won't need them."

Taylor controlled her temper, because she had no choice at the moment, but again felt the comfort of her hidden knife inside her boot. One day soon, she would use it, and then she would be free of this man. "Are you afraid I will scalp you in your sleep, Mr. Talbott?"

She allowed herself a smirk. White people thought every tribe scalped their enemies. She knew that sometimes they did much worse things.

But Mr. Talbott showed no fear. Instead, he took her arm and propelled her toward the back door. In its opening now stood the shadowed figure of a short and rounded man. "Actually, Miss James—if that's who you really are—I don't intend to do anything to cause you to want to scalp me."

"You have already given me plenty of reasons, Mr. Talbott. But I do not ever need a reason. I need only a sharp knife and the wish to do so."

His fingers tightened around her arm. Taylor smirked. She'd scared him. "Have you really ever scalped a man before, Miss James?"

She thought about lying but for some reason didn't. Maybe she was just tired. "No."

"Well, I have."

Taylor gasped and looked up at him. His face, shadowed by his hat's brim, had sinister planes and hollows she hadn't noticed before. He wasn't staring down at her. He was looking straight ahead. A chill swept over Taylor. She had a vision of her long braid hanging from his belt. She would keep her knife close by at all times, but for her own protection. With no small amount of trepidation on her part, for she had no idea what she would find inside a white man's home, Taylor stepped with him into the long and elegant hall.

They were greeted by the bowing figure of the short and rounded man she'd seen from a distance. "Good evening, sir," he said. "I hope you had a pleasant time of it. And may I assume, sir, judging by the lady's attire and the feather in her braid, that you've also managed to bring home an Indian with you?"

Chapter Five

Taylor gritted her teeth. *Indian.* The word was hated by the tribes and not used by them. Instead, she was Tsalagi and one of Yv-wi. The People.

Offended, Taylor drew herself up, prepared to do more than take offense. The bowing man straightened, giving Taylor her first good look at him. Her breath left her. Her knees weakened. She would have staggered had Mr. Talbott not already had a tight hold on her arm. Taylor put a hand to her chest and stared wide-eyed as a sudden vision robbed her momentarily of complete awareness of her surroundings.

In her sight now was a great and evil bird that descended on her, its hooked talons fierce and extended. It scooped her off the ground and bore her away to the sky. In the next instant, this bird of prey was suddenly attacked by another creature, a small yet determined bird, one Taylor somehow knew meant to save her even at the cost of its own life. The birds fought, their screams piercing the air and assaulting her ears. The war bird lost its grip on her. Screaming, Taylor twisted and turned and plummeted toward the hard earth below, toward the death that awaited her—

But instead she was returned to the moment, and to her body, with a jolt. Shaken but quiet, blinking yet aware, Taylor realized that the men apparently hadn't noticed that anything was amiss with her. That had to mean that not much time, if any, had passed. How could this be? They were still standing where they'd been, and the door was still open. Had time somehow stood still? Taylor fought the urge to put a hand to her brow or do anything that would alert them to her discomfiture—or her sense of wonder. She'd had a vision. That was the only explanation possible. Never before had she seen one.

She knew in an instant that she'd been wrong, all these years, to scorn the stories of The People. Rube, her guard in the penitentiary, had been right, too. Because here before her was the proof of the legends told by the old ones to explain the world. Just then, the strange and wonderful creature that had captured Taylor's attention closed the door to the outside. She watched his every move, analyzing every gesture for something of significance meant only for her.

Mr. Talbott turned to face the being, taking Taylor with him as he went. "Good evening, Bentley," he said. Taylor's breath caught—no time could have passed because Mr. Talbott was only now returning the greeting. "And yes, I did manage to bring a . . . uh, young lady home with me. May I present . . ." He looked down at her and frowned, then focused again on the spirit guide dressed in black. "Well, I don't know exactly who she is, to tell you the truth."

"I see, sir. That is most awkward then, is it not?"

Awestruck, remembering now Rube's words to be open to a spirit guide and that she would know the sign, Taylor watched as the one called Bentley now ran his gaze over her. A shiver slipped over Taylor's skin. He had seen her. Could he see inside her soul? This was a man-bird. A beaklike nose, thinning hair combed back, no chin, round little body clad in a white shirt, black cutaway coat, and dark pants over his skinny legs. He was magic. A bird changed into a man. For her. She was certain of it, just as she was certain that he could fly if he so chose. The old ones still spoke, at tribal gatherings, of the beings who could turn into birds and animals. She had heard the tales as a child and had believed them then. But as she'd grown and had been rejected by The People because of her white blood, she had rejected their ways as false and had waged war on them and their beliefs.

No longer. Because here such a creature was. But in a white man's house. How had this happened? Was Mr. Talbott magic also? She looked up at him, noting his strong jaw and high cheekbones, his deep-set dark eyes. He smiled down at her, his eyebrows raised. A thrill chased through Taylor. Had he captured this creature somehow? Or had the man-bird come to him of his own free will? Taylor's next thought narrowed her eyes with suspicion. . . . Mr. Talbott's smile faded. Was this big man next to her the evil bird? Did he hold the wondrous being prisoner here, as he did her? Would he try to kill them both if they tried to leave? She had many questions but only one answer. The man-bird was her talisman, her most special spirit animal, appearing to her in her time of need. And he had come to her in this house.

Overcome with her sudden spiritual fervor, Taylor wrenched away from Mr. Talbott's grasp. He made a sound, as if of protest, but did nothing to stop her as, in the ensuing quiet, she slowly advanced on this so-named Bentley. She didn't wish to startle him and have him fly away. As she'd suspected he might, though, he moved back, away from her outstretched hand. But the wall behind him stopped him. His eyes rounded. She had him now. With her face maybe an inch away from his, she began her close scrutiny of him, noting every pore and blotch in his skin.

The man-bird shifted his gaze from her to Mr. Talbott. "Do you suppose the, uh, young lady could favor us with her name, sir?"

The man-bird's voice was high and shaky, Taylor noted. Perhaps he was not yet used to his human form. He tried to scoot his way down the wall, his winglike arms flat against its surface. Taylor carefully matched him step for step along the way.

"She gave me her name, Bentley," Mr. Talbott said, sounding cheery. "I just don't know if it's really her name. Or if she is actually who she says she is. It's a devil of a mystery."

The man-bird Bentley appeared to be afraid as he nodded his head. If he was afraid, then it must be true—he was a captive here. "I see, Mr. Talbott." Then he gave Mr. Talbott a pleading look. "Actually, sir, I don't see at all."

Taylor gasped and pulled back. He was blind. He could not see. His vision had been stolen. Perhaps by a jealous and thieving crow? Taylor waved a hand in front of his face to see if he could see it. He stared round-eyed, his mouth open . . . but he didn't move. Taylor turned to Mr. Talbott. "What has happened to his sight? Who has stolen it?"

A frown creased Mr. Talbott's face. "His sight? Oh, old age, I suspect. He sees well enough, though, to get around."

Taylor was relieved by this and went back to noting every tiny detail of the man-bird's person. She jabbed at his cheek, noting the leathery feel of it. The creature remained still, not making a sound. He only watched her, as was right.

From behind her, and sounding as if something was funny to him, Mr. Talbott addressed the man-bird. "It seems our guest has taken quite a fancy to you, Bentley."

"Yes, sir. So it would seem. Help me, sir."

"In a moment, Bentley. Just don't make any sudden moves in the meantime. Now, what were we discussing? Ah, yes. The young lady's identity. By the way, Bentley, it might be a good idea not to call her an . . . well, you know. She doesn't seem to respond favorably to that word. At any rate, she says she is Taylor Christie James."

Taylor was busy plucking at the man-bird's garments, but she turned to Mr. Talbott. "No. I do not only say this. It is true. I *am* Taylor Christie James, daughter of Tennie Nell Christie and Charles Edward James." She leaned in to sniff the man-bird and then tugged hard at his sparse hair.

He startled her by shrieking and trying to fly. Taylor jumped back, retreating to Mr. Talbott's side. She clutched at his sleeve as the so-named Bentley creature flapped his arms wildly and made strange strangled sounds as he retreated down the long hall and fled around a corner and out of sight.

A deep quiet followed his disappearance. Taylor looked up at Mr. Talbott and saw him staring down at her. She let go of his sleeve and stepped back. Great amusement lit his face. Upset in the extreme, Taylor struggled to find the words to make the omens known to him. "You do not understand. The man-bird has had his feathers clipped. He cannot fly. And the crow has stolen his sight. This is because in the past I have scorned the ways of my ancestors, saying that their stories are not true. Rube warned me of the danger because I did not believe. This is a bad thing I have done. A very bad thing that does not bode well for those of us in this house."

Her true and serious words did not have the effect on Mr. Talbott that she desired. He grinned. "Well, I say differently, Miss James. I say this bodes very well." He looked down the hall to where the man-bird had fled . . . and then back down at her. "Very well indeed."

Taylor didn't agree with him at all. But she held her silence . . . and prayed in Cherokee for the first time in a long time.

Early that next morning, his sleep disturbed by the vexing problem that Miss James embodied, Grey lay awake and thinking in his big and comfortable bed, his hands behind his head, himself propped up on pillows and covered by a sheet. He'd already made his way mentally through the extraordinary events of last evening, starting with when he first stepped out of Charles's house. And ending with the near annihilation of every living creature in his household as the maids had run shrieking and crying away from the bedroom that he'd assigned Miss James. The bedroom attached to his own, of course, so he could keep a close eye on her—at great risk to his scalp or throat, he knew, should she decide to creep through the small dressing room that separated his door from hers. That was why it was locked and he had the key.

In any event, he'd had a devil of a time last night trying to convince her they meant her no harm or disrespect, that the two chambermaids were merely following his orders to show her how to use the plumbing in the bathroom attached to her bedroom. He'd told her in dire tones that either she could pay attention and learn and then attend to her own needs . . . or the maids would do it for her. Grey could still see Miss James's eyes narrowed menacingly. He sighed, figuring he'd be damned lucky if he had any servants left in his house this morning. No doubt, they'd probably all cleared out last night. At least, the smart ones had. It was the only thing to do when a hellcat was loose in your place of employment.

Grey chuckled, remembering how it had finally taken the frightened man-bird Bentley's personal intervention to save the day . . . or what was then left of the night. Grey shook his head every time he thought of poor Bentley being relegated to the status of a spirit animal, as Miss James had again explained to him in private. But finally, with Bentley standing by and nodding, corroborating everything Grey told her, they had calmed Miss James enough to convince her their efforts were not part of some hellish conspiracy against her. And that their actions were motivated by the simple yet fervent wish shared by them all that she wash the, uh, trail off her, don a clean nightgown, and get into bed, for heaven's sake. It had been after two in the morning before everyone had been able to each take to his or her own bed.

With all that ordered in his mind, Grey turned his thoughts to the more serious questions of the mystery that surrounded Miss James's sudden appearance in St. Louis and in his life. It was all so extraordinary. And unsettling. He had no idea who to turn to, who to talk to, about this. And why was that? Before today, he assured himself, he would have said that he had any number of family members or friends he could turn to in a time of trouble. But now? With this particular problem? No.

Grey rubbed at his forehead, certain the headache forming there had more to do with such an eye-opening revelation as that than it did with the amount of whiskey he'd consumed last night. Very troubling, that's what this was. But what exactly lay at the base of these feelings of isolation? Was it that he didn't trust anyone with the secret of who Miss James really was? And if not, why not? Well, for one thing, Grey couldn't be certain that unseen and unfriendly forces weren't close by and at work here. After all, the young woman's sudden presence here, when coupled with Charles's story, was extraordinary. And if all that was true—and if Grey wasn't simply manufacturing trouble where none existed—then he couldn't afford to take a chance on confiding in the wrong person, someone bent on doing injury or worse to Miss James.

Grey nodded and then froze in position. It was as if he had just heard himself, as if he had only now listened in on his own thoughts. *Someone hurting Miss James?* The very idea caused a burning anger in Grey's chest. His hands fisted around his covers. Grimacing hatefully, he stared at a damask-covered overstuffed chair next to his bureau as if it had offended him. *Someone will harm her only over my dead body.*

Grey forced himself to calm down. No one was going to harm Miss James. Still, he couldn't shake the feeling that his heart and mind were trying to tell him something that he was steadfastly refusing to admit to himself consciously. Then, he had it. He snapped his fingers. *Well, I'll be damned. That's it. I believe the girl.* It had to be true. He believed she was who she said she was. Otherwise, he had no reason to protect her. *Protect* her? Then he remembered. . . . *Aren't I protecting Charles by keeping her away from him?* He'd certainly thought so until now. But apparently it was the other way around. Grey shook his head, hating these doubts creeping into his heart. He refused to give them a home. *No. Charles wouldn't harm a fly.*

Of course, that was true. Then maybe, Grey reasoned, neither Charles nor his daughter was a danger to the other—unless they were brought together and it became known that she was his daughter. *Good God.* Grey sat forward on his bed, his elbows propped atop his bent knees. *A third party. Or parties. I keep coming back to that. Someone who seeks to harm them both. That has to be it.*

Strangely comforted by the idea of an evil third party, since such a villain absolved Charles and Miss James from being such, Grey shook his head, finally coming to the conclusion that on his own all he had was questions. And the only ones with answers—if he could get one or the other, or both, to talk—were Charles and Miss James. A chuckle escaped him. Last night he'd worked so hard to make sure the two didn't meet. And now here he was, only a matter of hours later, trying to figure out how best to bring them together. But beneath all that, Grey still had no earthly idea why, in the first place, he'd confronted her last evening. Why hadn't he left well enough alone and gone on about his well-liquored way, as he most certainly would have done at any other time? It wasn't as if involving himself in other people's lives and concerns was his strong suit.

That being so, what he ought to do today was bow out of this family squabble—which in all probability was all it was—and go wake her and send her on her way. *Miss James loose in St. Louis?* Seeking lightness in the midst of his troubling thoughts, Grey shook his head and chuckled. *That wouldn't be fair to the unsuspecting and innocent city my brother hopes to be mayor of.* Grey ran a hand through his sleep-tousled hair. *But isn't Charles both of those things as well . . . unsuspecting and innocent? By all accounts, yes. Even so, why am I working so hard to protect him? He's a grown man. He can handle a charlatan, if she is one.*

Grey stared hard at his sheet-covered toes as they poked at the covers. *But not the truth. Charles can't handle that.*

The thought was an unbidden and lurking one. Taken aback, Grey found himself staring at the mirror hung on the opposite wall. His frowning reflection stared back at him. *Now why do I think that? Who says Charles can't handle the truth? Aren't I jumping to a lot of presumptive conclusions here, none of which are really my business?* Immediately he dismissed that notion. *But it is my business. My own family could possibly be in the line of fire.* Then another truth blindsided him. *Great Scott. I've put them directly in the line of fire by harboring Miss James here in my home. Whatever trouble she's bringing to Charles will find her right here. I'm a sitting duck.*

Grey shook his head, watching his reflection mimic his every movement. Out loud, he said, "This is the final straw. I have got to quit drinking. And I have absolutely got to stop bringing home mysterious and beautiful Indians with me."

So he was back to the beginning. He could trust no one. Not Charles. Not the man's daughter. Or anyone else, not until he knew exactly who had told such an awful lie that had kept the two apart and why he—or she—had done so. There could be no innocent reason that someone would do such a heinous thing.

Grey shifted about irritably under the covers and went back to his original question to himself. Why in the living hell had he involved himself in the puzzle that was Taylor Christie James? This couldn't merely be a vagary of fate. This wasn't coincidence. Grey could not accept that. No, this was destiny, pure and simple. Somehow he personally was involved in this up to his eyeballs. Somehow the ramifications of her appearance would have significant effect on him and those he loved.

He didn't know how he knew that. He just knew that he did, in much the same way that he alone knew how fragile Charles James was, how broken and sad. To the world, the older man showed a brave face, a strong countenance, keeping his private sorrow just that . . . private. Only by drunken accident late one night at a men's social club gathering had Grey been the one with Charles when the man had broken down and cried for a little girl who'd been lost to him years ago.

On that night, even though Charles had not divulged many of the details or even why her very existence and then her death needed to be kept secret, Grey had sworn to Charles that his confession was safe with him. And it had been. From that bond had grown the deep friendship he now shared with Charles, despite his being so much older than Grey. And now Grey felt like a traitor to that vow just by having the man's very much alive daughter under his own roof. What he should do was get up, get dressed, and go call on Charles. Then in the quietest way possible tell him what had transpired last night, gently break the good news to him—

What if Miss James's being here and alive weren't good news to Charles? What if she was innocent of any subterfuge and merely sought a reunion with her father—and he didn't want one? What if the simple but equally devastating truth was that Charles had lied? That he'd abandoned the little girl—and evidently her mother, Grey assumed—and couldn't live with the guilt? And so had made up the story of his daughter's death in order to deal with his guilt?

In light of all that, what if finding Taylor here would push the man to violence against his daughter? Not wanting to be responsible for something that horrid, Grey couldn't simply turn her over to him at this point, now could he?

Grey rubbed at his forehead and then his temples. How irritating. He was back to doubting his friend of five years. Grey thought back to that night of the confession on Charles's part, now analyzing every gesture and word he could recall of his friend's. His conclusion was that Charles's grief had been no act, no lie. Then Grey recalled Charles's exact wording. Charles never said that he'd seen the girl dead. He said he'd been told, by a reliable source—one he hadn't named—that his daughter was dead. Well, that reliable source . . . a term indicating someone trusted by Charles . . . had obviously lied to him. Or maybe that source was innocent and only mistaken, too. Perhaps this person had simply been repeating gossip as if it were fact.

Oh, who the hell knows?

With that, Grey absolutely gave up. He threw the sheet back, his troublesome thoughts driving him out of his bed. He sat on its side, his elbows propped on his knees, his head in his hands. Disgust creased the corners of his mouth. The truth was that the possibilities here were nearly endless and just as confusing—and frightening in their implications. Uppermost in his mind was . . . who was this mysterious person who had kept Charles and his daughter apart all these years with lies?

Torturing Grey the most was the one question he'd been avoiding posing for himself, but one he was forced now to consider. The simple truth was that among the closest, most trusted people to Charles were members of Grey's own family. His mother. His brother, Franklin. It was almost too chilling even to consider, but could the person behind all the lies be someone Grey loved and trusted as well? His chest tightened. But he couldn't deny why he feared it could be true. The James family wasn't the only one with secrets and unanswered questions. Grey recalled how he and his brother had grown up amid hushed conversations and stony expressions and tense dramas. Even now, there were some things his widowed mother wouldn't talk about and questions she refused to answer.

Grey stood up, stretching and yawning. His own mother. She was one person he would have to question. He would try to be delicate, of course. But his first question would be why she had initially taken to her bed and cried when Franklin had told her of his very honorable intentions toward Charles's wonderfully sweet and innocent niece, Amanda—the daughter of Charles's older brother, Stanley, and his wife, Camilla. *Amanda.* Grey froze in place, thinking *Good God, she's another innocent to be considered.*

He put a hand to his temple, rubbing hard and thinking just as hard. *I am suddenly surrounded by people in jeopardy.* Worst of all, he had no idea who was putting them in jeopardy or even which ones of them were. Nothing made sense anymore. None of the truths he'd lived with, none of the people he loved. They were all vulnerable—and all suspect.

Grey reached for his trousers and began tugging them on. With growing certainty he knew his mother was the first person he should question . . . rather obliquely, though, without admitting that Taylor was actually here. With any luck, his mother may have all the answers and could clear this whole thing up. Grey chuckled, figuring his chances of actually getting straightforward answers out of her—a woman with an imperious manner and a backbone of steel—were about as great as they were for getting them out of Miss James.

Just then, as Grey was closing the fly opening to his pants, the door between his bedroom and Taylor's opened.

Grey was stupefied. He'd locked that door. He had the key. He spared a glance for the bedside table. There lay the key. *What the—?* He pivoted around, eyes wide, his hands still on his pants buttons as the door swung inward. *Who the devil?*

In stormed his answer. Miss James.

"How'd you do that?" He pointed to the open door behind her. "Did someone unlock it for you?"

"No." That was all she said. Obviously the little heathen had picked the lock. But no explanation was forthcoming, to all appearances. And apparently she was unabashed at his near nakedness, as well as her own. Barefoot, clad only in a high-necked and too-short white nightgown hastily donated last night by one of the terrified maids, and with her black and lustrous hair cascading all around her, she announced solemnly, "You have a thief in your home. My clothes are missing."

Grey shriveled inside. How to tell her he'd had them taken away . . . and burned. He moved his hands from his fly to his waist, planting them there. Without a shirt on, he felt at a disadvantage, whether it bothered her or not. And apparently it didn't. As he watched, she looked him up and down. She then met his gaze. Her expression never changed. Amused insult seized Grey. Last evening she'd done the same thing. Looked him up and down and dismissed him. Apparently, this morning, she had again found him wanting.

But she still awaited his answer to her pronouncement that he harbored a thief in his home. "I can assure you, Miss James, that there are no thieves here. Your clothes were not stolen. They were instead . . . taken."

She narrowed those wondrous blue eyes of hers. "It is the same thing."

Grey ran a hand through his hair and exhaled. "No, it is not. They were taken on my orders."

She met his words with silence. A staring contest ensued. Finally, she spoke. "Then you are the thief. You did not ask my permission."

White man. It was there again, in her posture, in her attitude, on her face. Grey felt his patience growing thin. He was trying to help her. Only she didn't seem to know it. Or appreciate it. Or care. "I had no need to ask your permission, Miss James. This is my house."

"And those were my clothes. I did not get them from you. They were not yours to take back. Order them to be returned."

This was getting tricky. He wondered if he'd need to call on the man-bird Bentley to restore peace—or his hair to his head—once he told her the truth. "I cannot. They were not . . . salvageable—"

"What is that word?"

"Well, in this instance it means you won't be getting them back."

Her expression soured. "Then I have nothing but this to wear." She wadded up a huge portion of the thin nightgown in her hand and held it out to one side, succeeding only in perfectly outlining her very feminine figure for him. And showing him that she had nothing on underneath.

Grey's breath caught. She was magnificent. He had to get her out of his room. Now. "I promise you, Miss James, I will straightaway find you suitable clothes for going about St. Louis with me."

Toward that end, last night he'd ordered his housekeeper to the shops this morning, armed with what his hapless chambermaids, those who'd seen Miss James unclothed, had figured were her measurements. Hopefully, Mrs. Scott could find some decent shoes and ready-mades and unmentionables, garments of that nature. And hopefully the gray-haired bossy old creature would be here damned soon with her purchases. Because, if he weren't mistaken, an Indian war was brewing right here in his own home, one he had no doubt he'd lose.

"These clothes you will buy, are they ones the woman you intend to marry would wear?"

Grey's expression crinkled in confusion. Marry? *Ah.* He'd barely thought about that in all his thinking this morning. But apparently it was uppermost in her mind. *Interesting.* "I have no idea," he hedged, "since you are not truly the woman I intend to marry. But the clothes will definitely be for you."

"Is there another woman you intend to marry?"

Grey hadn't expected that question and it gave him a bit of a start. "No," he heard himself saying . . . and then adding, "I couldn't imagine marrying anyone else."

His pronouncement startled him as much as it obviously had her. Her blue eyes widened appreciably. Grey's hands fisted. He stared at his reluctant guest, seeing her now as a woman—a softly rounded, beautiful, and desirable woman. But someone who wouldn't hesitate to slit his throat. Someone whose culture and background were totally foreign to him. Someone who hated him for the color of his skin. Defeat swept through Grey, leaving him with a feeling of futility, of emptiness. She would never accept him—on any level. So why should he try? *Why indeed.* Grey quickly amended himself. "What I meant to say, Miss James, was that I certainly would not have come up with the scheme of passing you off as my fiancée if I were already involved with another woman."

She visibly relaxed, nodding as if his words finally made sense to her. "Then . . . I am she. These clothes, I will not like them. And I will not wear them."

"But you haven't even seen them. If you're concerned about fashion, you should know that I didn't choose them. I wouldn't have the first idea how to go about it. Instead, I sent my housekeeper, a very capable woman, around to the shops this morning—"

"No. You do not understand. I *cannot* wear these clothes. I will give you no reason to call me *a-qua-da-li.*" She crossed her arms and stood there . . . stubbornly. "I have spoken."

Grey was at a loss. "Yes, you have. And I have heard you. But I have no idea what you said. That Cherokee word. I can't call you . . . what?"

" 'My wife.' You will not call me that. I am not. And I will not wear the clothes of such a woman to you."

"I agree you're not my . . . wife." The word stuck in Grey's throat. He'd never uttered it aloud in connection with himself. "But wearing the clothes—and you *will* wear the clothes—does not make you a wife in my society. Maybe it does in yours. But not in mine." Grey crossed his arms, showing her that he could be just as stubborn as she was.

She raised an eyebrow in challenge. Then her eyes narrowed to slits. "These clothes you will buy are the trappings of a white woman who has been bought by a man. I am not such a woman. I make my own way. And I will not wear them."

So it wasn't differing fashion sense or matrimonial customs at all. It was prejudice. Again. That did it. Grey had a hangover, this was his house, and he hadn't had his coffee yet . . . so naturally he roared. "You are *half*-white. And the half that is white *will* wear them, if I have to put them on you myself."

His gestures were as stabbing as his words were threatening. "Don't think I won't do it, because I will. And it has nothing to do with being bought. That's patently ridiculous. But if you choose not to cooperate, Miss James, let me assure you that you *will* sit here in *that* nightgown for *weeks* on end locked in *that* very room. . . ."

Stopping him was the realization that he was pointing at an open door. One he'd locked, one she'd opened . . . without the key. Well, then, that was no threat, was it? "Locked up somewhere," he amended weakly, his roar petering out to a peep, "until I have all my questions answered about who you are and why you are really here." He narrowed his eyes at her. "Unless, of course, you care to give me those answers yourself right now."

Her expression impassive, she silently considered him. He noticed that her gaze kept sliding to his bare chest. Far from flattered, Grey figured she was merely trying to figure out where best to stab him to do the most amount of damage. Then she spoke. "I have already told you these things. Who I am and why I am here."

"You have told me nothing. Only what you wish me to believe."

Her chin came up a notch. Her lips parted, she meant to say something. Something scathing, no doubt, Grey supposed—

The door to the hall opened. Grey jerked around. Bentley was backing into the room, a full breakfast tray in his hands. "Good morning, sir. I believed I heard you up and moving around. And since we appear this morning to be, ahem, short of staff, I took the liberty of bringing you the—great good God in heaven."

Bentley was, of course, now facing the room and its occupants . . . where, by all dictates of manners and morals, there should have only been one. The servant's mouth was a perfect *O* that matched his widened eyes.

Well, I'll be. He does look like a bird, was Grey's first thought, his anger evaporating. He roused himself, behaving as if nothing were out of the ordinary. "While I would appreciate your bringing me the great good God in heaven, Bentley, since I could use the reinforcement, I will assume you don't mean that literally. Now, don't just stand there, man. Come in. You're just in time."

As Grey watched—suddenly realizing that here in the person of Bentley was someone he could trust implicitly . . . as did Miss James; how useful would that be to have someone in both camps?—Bentley's pleading gaze flitted from him to Miss James and back to him. "I almost hesitate to ask, but in time for what, sir?"

"Well, it's nothing hair-raising. Sorry. Poor word choice. I merely meant you're in time to settle an argument between me and my distinguished guest."

Bentley's expression all but melted and slid off his face. "An argument, sir? Surely, I am not qualified—"

"But you are. Infinitely so, since you seem to hold a lot of sway with Miss James here."

Bentley's gaze flitted again to the quietly watching Miss James. "I assure you that I do not, sir." His loud whisper held a note of desperation.

Grey cheerfully ignored the man's denial. "Put the tray on the table, Bentley." He waited while the unhappy butler did so. "Now, while I have my coffee—no, I'll pour it myself— you tell Miss James why she can't go about St. Louis in her unmentionables."

A strangled sound came from Bentley. Grey turned away, making for the tray and hiding his grin. Yes, it was mean. He knew that. But he was a desperate man. And Miss James would do nothing to hurt Bentley. She revered him. Ignoring a twinge of what he refused to acknowledge as jealousy, Grey lifted lids on the various plates, looked over the choices, and then selected a piece of crisp bacon. Taking a bite and chewing, he turned curiously back to the silence in the room behind him.

Miss James was in Bentley's face. Literally. Her eyes were soft and doe-round. Everything inside Grey tightened. He stopped chewing. He couldn't swallow. He admitted it—he'd give his eyeteeth and his entire fortune to have her look at him like that. Just once.

Telling himself nothing good could come of such feelings, Grey held off rescuing Bentley just yet, instead turning back to the tray and pouring himself a cup of steaming coffee. Sipping at it, he again faced the quiet twosome across the room. Settling his gaze on Miss James, Grey narrowed his eyes thoughtfully. Perhaps if he could get her to accept one small thing from him, she'd then give in on larger matters. "Do you drink coffee, Miss James?"

She tore her adoring gaze away from the chubby and balding Bentley to look Grey's way, sending him an unmistakably dismissive expression. "Yes."

"Excellent. Would you like a cup?"

"Yes."

"How do you like it?"

"Black."

"Good." Well, that was one thing he knew about her. How she liked her coffee.

"Allow me, sir . . . please . . . for the love of God."

"You're in an awfully religious frame of mind today, Bentley. But no, stay where you are. I can manage." Grey turned, thinking to pour her a cup, only to realize there was only the one cup—his—since the staff had been expecting only him to be dining in his room. Grey sought the duo's attention. "Well, apparently, I can't manage without another cup. Here. Have mine." He held it out to her.

She looked at the cup, then at him . . . as if he were a steaming pile of something she'd stepped in out in the horse barn. "No. I won't take yours."

Grey exhaled, tiring of her unrelenting prejudice. "Which is it now? Because I'm white or because I've already drunk from it?"

"Neither. Because I am polite and it is yours. I would not take your things as you have taken mine."

"Well, that's put me soundly in my place, now hasn't it?" Grey fumed—all the more angry for being embarrassed that she was right.

"Please, sir," Bentley interrupted. "Allow me to get another cup and saucer from the kitchen. I should be most relieved—er, pleased to be of service. I—" He stopped, as if choking on his own words. The man's face paled. His eyes widened. "Oh, dear. This is most unforgivable. Perhaps it is because of the chaos downstairs. But I have forgotten until now, sir, that—oh, how awful of me. It was the shock of seeing, uhm, the young lady—"

"Bentley," Grey warned. Once started down that stammering road of his, Bentley could go on for hours and never get to the point. "I'm thirty-two years old and aging by the moment, man. Spit it out."

The butler fussed nervously with his hands. "Yes, sir. In all the excitement, you see, I forgot the true nature of my mission—besides your breakfast tray, I mean. And besides telling you that Mrs. Scott—oh, dear. I forgot that, too. Mrs. Scott has returned, sir, with the . . . items you requested. She said she would put them in . . . well, I've forgotten just where. But it's not that which is unforgivable. I—"

"Bentley, for God's sake, man, I will give you a twenty percent increase in your salary if you will but complete one thought or sentence."

"Yes, sir. But you're not going to be happy, sir."

"I'm not happy now, Bentley." Grey spoke with deadly calm.

"Yes, sir." Bentley took a deep breath. Standing next to him, Miss James monitored every move of the little man. For his part, Bentley steadfastly avoided looking her way as he kept his focus on his employer. "I regret to inform you, sir, that your mother awaits your presence downstairs in the drawing room."

Chapter Six

From the other side of her unmade bed, Taylor warily watched the heavyset and gray-haired old grandmother as the disapproving woman wrenched straight the unkempt covers of Taylor's bed. She then set about putting package after package atop her handiwork. As she unwrapped each one, revealing a breathtaking array of beautifully tailored clothing in every imaginable color and fabric—but none of which Taylor intended to wear—the older woman took great care to announce to Taylor, in a loud and stern voice, what each item was and how and when to wear it.

How rude of her to assume that Taylor would not know how to wear "proper clothes," as she'd called them. And even ruder to assume that Taylor didn't speak or understand English. Not only did she speak it; she could even read and write in it, her second language. Taylor wondered if Mrs. Scott could lay claim to the same accomplishment. Still, in the Cherokee way, Taylor said nothing, not even when the woman spoke loudly to her. Taylor was fairly certain that if one did not understand a language, one wouldn't magically understand it if it were yelled at one.

Beyond that, the woman could have smiled and been kind. She behaved as did the white missionary women who came to the Nation—the reservation, as they called it—with their God and their judgmental ways, intent on civilizing the savages and destroying The People's way of life. With all that fueling her rising temper, Taylor became less and less patient with the woman's useless chatter.

"And this, young lady . . ." Mrs. Scott held up a corset. "Are you listening to me?" With an ugly expression on her face, she shook the heavy garment in the air, as if trying to get a response from Taylor. "Do you understand anything at all of what I'm saying, you little savage?"

Taylor's eyes narrowed. She had heard enough. She spoke for the first time in the woman's presence. "I understand you. And yes, I am listening. That"—she pointed to the pretty be-ribboned garment the shocked and paling woman held in her grip—"is a corset. I do not intend to wear it because I do not need it. But if you continue to yell at me, I do intend to wrap that corset around your head and pull the strings as tight as possible and hold them that way . . . until you stop breathing." Taylor finished with a smile. "Do you understand me, *yan-sa*? In my language, that word is 'buffalo.' "

The buffalo called Mrs. Scott dropped the corset onto the bed and ran shrieking from the room. Her waddling gait jig-gled her large bottom unattractively under her brown skirt.

With barely a raised eyebrow, Taylor marked the woman's retreat. The door to the hallway slammed behind her. Taylor listened. . . . There was no sound of a key turning in the lock. This was good. It would only slow her down more to pick it open with her knife, and she didn't have a lot of time. Nor did she believe that the mean and very rude Mrs. Scott would come back soon to bother her. That was exactly as Taylor wished. She meant to make her secretive way downstairs, re-main out of sight, and listen in, if she could, to see why Mr. Talbott had said, "Son of a bitch," an insult to himself as well as to his mother, when he'd learned she was here.

Ignoring the clothes spread over her bed, Taylor sidled around the four-poster and made her barefoot way toward the closed door that opened onto an upstairs hall. Before she reached it, and out of the corner of her eye, she caught a movement. A flash of white. Gasping, she stopped and looked. She slumped in relief. It was only her. Or her reflection in a cheval glass. Taylor thought to bypass it . . . but something about the way she looked to herself stopped her. She stood in front of the glass, tilting the oval mirror up until her image was framed full-length. She tugged and picked at her night-gown. She frowned, pulled her hair back. In this gown, she looked like a child. And she had been treated as such—a young girl to be sent to her room while Mr. Talbott left to go speak with his mother.

Taylor grimaced in frustration. She hated to admit it, but she had to change her clothing to that of the white woman. Not yet ready to admit to herself that Mr. Talbott was right, Taylor convinced herself that it was the smart thing to do. One wore the clothing that would protect one from danger. It was that simple. In this place, she would wear the hated gowns and dresses that would keep her safe. She did not need to stand out now, to be noticed. She needed to blend with her surroundings, like the fawn did in the woods, like the bird did in the tree. She needed not to be seen by her enemies, so she would wear their coloration in order to move about among them.

Not be noticed? Taylor put a hand to her cheek and watched her reflection do the same. With her high cheekbones and long, straight hair of black? And her skin, normally pale— thanks to her white father's legacy—now tanned to a light gold on her face and neck and arms from the journey here? How could she not be noticed? She looked herself in the eye, seeing the blue of the sky reflected there. The color in them startled her. Sometimes she forgot about them. But her eyes, like her skin, told their own tale. A white father. Half-breed. Because of her eyes, her own people had shunned her in The Nation. And here, among the people of her father, they would do the same . . . not because of her blue eyes, but because of her Tsalagi features given her by her mother. And because of the way she spoke. She knew her sometimes halting use of the white man's language alone would cause her to stand out.

Taylor tried to tell herself that the white people's rejection of her wouldn't matter to her. She had no need to belong. She was whole within herself. And proud of who she was. She raised her chin, glared at her reflection . . . and knew that wasn't true. She wasn't proud, and it did matter. She hated who she was, hated the blood that made her an outcast. A sudden and horrible anger invaded Taylor's soul . . . an anger that cried out to be heard, saying it did matter. It mattered because she'd already had a lifetime of being different, no matter where she went. A lifetime of being called names, of being spit upon, of being thought of as less than people of a whole blood. It did matter.

The anger that she refused to call hurt erupted inside Taylor.

With jerking, slashing movements, she tore at the nightgown she wore, somehow fighting the white father who had abandoned her. Anger at Hammer for having taken her love and then abandoning her and for leaving her no choice but to now be among the white people fueled her jerking and tearing of the virginal cloth. Anger at her mother for sending her here had her stripping away every bit of fragile and delicate lacy trim across the bosom. Anger at Mr. Talbott for . . . everything—for stopping her last night, for bringing her here, for taking away her buckskins, which forced her into these clothes of a weak woman, had her heaving the innocent and now irreparably damaged garment over her head and tossing it away from her. It billowed brokenly and fell to the carpet in a lifeless heap of tattered cotton.

Dry-eyed, proud, and naked, Taylor stood in the middle of the room, her hands to her waist, each breath a heaving one, her hair wildly disarrayed about her. Only its silky length, its tickling of her bare skin, its lying smoothly against her skin, like a caress, comforted her. She again caught her reflection in the mirror . . . and assessed her naked appearance now. What she saw surprised her. It was as if . . . it weren't really her. This was no defeated girl looking back at her. No, this was a proud and mighty warrior woman watching her from the glass. She liked that. Taylor grinned. The warrior grinned back. Taylor cocked her head, eyeing this being. She knew it was her . . . but the woman did not look like her. She was thinner, harder . . . and still paler than Taylor had believed she was.

She should go downstairs like this. Taylor considered it, eyeing the door, then looking back to the bed and the waiting garments. No. She'd have no place to conceal her knife. Luckily she'd hid it under her pillow last night, or it would have been discovered when her clothes were stolen. Still, Taylor wondered what Mr. Talbott would do if she did go downstairs as she was now. Her nipples puckered, beading up to hard little nubs. A sudden tingling at the vee of her legs should have surprised her . . . but didn't. This wasn't the first time she'd had a reaction to this man. Last night, in his carriage and on the way here, she had watched him and had seen his appeal, the way he looked at her. And she'd known the craving again this morning when she stood in his bedroom and saw his bared chest and his muscled legs encased in his trousers.

Mr. Talbott was a handsome, well-built man. A mighty warrior himself. Muscled, broad-shouldered, dark-haired, and imposing. Taylor tried to tell herself it was only natural to have these feelings for such a man. Any woman would.

But the truth was . . . she knew a moment of real shame. Not for thinking of appearing downstairs naked, but for her awareness of Mr. Talbott. How could it be that a white man would make her feel desire? She had no reason to feel anything for him, or any of his kind, except hatred. He was the enemy, a friend of her father. Taylor suddenly felt the vulnerability of her nakedness. She smoothed her waist-length hair over her breasts, as if she could hide her shame and her wanting from herself. Never would she give in to this hunger. Never. She would show him only her bad nature . . . and not the womanly side, not the soft and yielding side that Hammer had known. No, for this white man, he would see only the wild side of her that had got her thrown in prison and sentenced to hang.

Her head up, her bearing proud, Taylor turned away from the mirror and took the few steps necessary to put her again at bedside. Once there, she sorted through the packages, snatching up those items that best suited her needs. She chose only the most serviceable of the decidedly feminine pieces, those that she could fasten herself, those that she felt would allow her the greatest freedom of movement . . . and those that didn't look like they would itch.

*   *   *

"Smirk all you wish, Greyson. I don't think it's the least bit funny, the way you insulted Mr. Harnison and Miss Chalmers last night. And poor Charles. He hosted such a nice gathering for your brother and Amanda. And here you didn't even stay for the official announcement of their engagement. Once again, I had to make your excuses. It's just too much. If you're not going to behave, my dear, then why bother showing up? I am so embarrassed that I hardly dare show my face in public today."

Grey's smirk broadened into a grin. "And yet bravely you did so in order to come here, Mother. And practically at first light."

Augusta Talbott pulled back, looking offended. "First light? It's ten-thirty, Greyson. And I did not show my face in public. I came in the enclosed brougham."

"How clever of you."

"How hot and stuffy of me, you mean. I nearly suffocated with the windows up and the curtains drawn. Do you see to what lengths you reduce me? You should be ashamed."

"And yet I'm not." Grey grinned as he looked into his mother's brown eyes. Steel-spined in public she may be, but she unbent a bit around him and Franklin. She could even approach warm and loving—as long as everything was going her way. Which, Grey also knew, wouldn't be true for long . . . not given whom he had secreted upstairs.

Seated next to her on the medallion-back sofa and holding her white and slender hand, Grey raised it to his lips and kissed it soundly. "Admit it, Mother. You love me for being such a scoundrel, don't you?"

Her chin came up. She withdrew her hand from his. "Of course I do not." She frowned. "I mean, of course I do love you. You are my firstborn. But I do wish that you could—"

"Allow me, Mother. You wish I could be more like my younger brother." Grey quirked his mouth irritably. "Be more involved in the family businesses and trusts and boards. Take a more active leadership role in the community and its government. Do more than sign whatever papers Franklin pushes in front of my face. Behave like the elder son and settle down with a good woman and raise a large family. Be more responsible and less of the profligate."

His mother raised her chin and met his accusing gaze. "I see I've mentioned the subject before."

Shrugging, Grey forgave her. "Maybe once or twice. But it's all right. You are just being a mother, and trying to save your firstborn from himself."

Her manner became imploring. "Greyson, you're a wonderful man. Don't think otherwise. I just feel you—how shall I put this? Ah, I have it. You need a challenge in your life. Something to stir you, to make your blood race. I don't believe anything has ever moved you, Greyson. You're too intelligent and too complacent. That's an awful combination."

Thinking of the death-defying challenge housed this very moment upstairs in his home, Grey grinned at his mother, noting the porcelainlike beauty of her face . . . and the worry lines he'd no doubt put there. "A challenge, is it? How about if you disown me, Mother? Just cut me out of the will. That would certainly challenge me, don't you think?"

"Greyson, do be serious. I simply want you to be happy."

"On your terms, though. Admit it."

She pursed her lips, became defensive. "Not mine, but polite society's."

"Oh, *hang* society, Mother, polite or otherwise. I don't give a fig for what society or even convention says I must do. I will do—" He couldn't say what he'd do . . . because he had no idea what would transpire with the enigmatic Miss James.

"Well, there, you see? You can't think of a thing you'll do, now can you?" His mother's finely arched eyebrows rose in triumph.

Grey chuckled, allowing her to believe she'd bested him. "Apparently, all I'm capable of doing is making your point for you. Evidently there's nothing I want to do."

Of course, he wanted very much to clear up the mystery and the dilemma that resided upstairs in the form of one maddening and unpredictable half-breed young woman who had every nerve ending in his body on edge. But he just couldn't think how to bring up the subject of Taylor Christie James to his mother. Earlier, he'd been burning with the desire to question her. But now he was no longer so sure he wanted to know any answers his mother may have regarding Miss James and her father. He feared the answers would have unforeseen ramifications for him and his family. It was a steadfast and even unreasonable feeling, one not based on any evidence he could point to . . . but one, nonetheless, he couldn't shake. It remained a truth in his mind and in his bones that whatever had happened in the James family, his own family had been involved in some way or another. Some unhappy way.

His mother heaved a sigh, managing to make it sound long-suffering. "Well, at any rate, I'm just glad that we have Franklin to fend for us."

A chuckle escaped Grey. Here was the subject he needed to deflect the talk away from himself. "Oh, admit it, Mother. You think Franklin a big bore."

She pulled back, her eyes wide. "Greyson Howard Talbott, do not put words in my mouth. I do *not* think Franklin a bore." She paused. Grey smirked. She fought a grin. "All right, I do. He is a terrible bore. Poor Amanda. But you . . . I truly think you're awful. You're a huge embarrassment to your mother."

Grey laughed. "I am not. I'm a disappointment, remember? I'm the profligate, the eternal bachelor, the man-about-town, never settling down, living only to gamble away my inheritance and drink and womanize—well, never mind on that score. But, tell me, what would your reaction be if I said I was thinking of becoming respectable and settling down to marry?"

He was thinking of his supposed ruse with Taylor, about presenting her as his affianced. The very notion excited him . . . and surprised him that it would.

His mother sent him an arch look. "Why, I'd think I was dying and you were saying anything you could to cheer me up. Now, don't tease me. Out with it, my son. What's this about, this sudden talk of your marrying and settling down? Have you actually met someone, and has she stolen your heart? Or have you gotten some society miss in a . . . well, family way . . . and I can expect her angry father at any moment at your door, armed with a shotgun and a preacher?"

"A charming scenario, Mother. One that does me great credit. But no, I'm more careful than that. And I don't dally with society misses. They're a singularly idiotic lot, if you ask me. Except for Amanda, of course. She's a rare gem."

Instantly troubled lines bracketed his mother's mouth. She glanced down at her hands folded together in her lap. Grey's suspicions grew. She was honestly distressed by Franklin's upcoming marriage to Amanda James, a brilliant union, politically and socially, that would blend the Talbott and the James families. His mother's precious society set was agog with the excitement—and she was upset. Grey's heart thumped heavily in his chest. She acted as if Franklin and Amanda's love for each other were about to trigger a bloodletting. Grey hated seeing his mother like this. He knew his behavior did no more than exasperate her. But this, what she was truly feeling now, appeared to be heartfelt worry. He opened his mouth, preparatory to asking her what was wrong, what lay at the basis of all this unhappiness, but she spoke first.

"Yes, Amanda is a gem. She is." She said it with such determination, as if she needed to defend Amanda from a detractor. "Amanda is a darling girl. She will make Franklin a wonderful wife. But I just cannot believe—well, never mind." She took a deep breath and turned a forced smile Grey's way. "Tell me about this young woman who has stolen *your* heart."

Grey allowed the change in subject . . . mostly because a pair of deep blue eyes set in an oval face with high cheekbones and a stubborn mouth burst into his consciousness. Stolen his heart? He chuckled, stretching his arm out across the back of the sofa. "Well, if the young woman has stolen my heart, it is so she can cut it out and eat it. But it's more likely it's my scalp she's after."

"Your scalp? Oh, Greyson, not more trouble? Not on top of everything else?"

Grey's eyes narrowed. "On top of what 'everything else,' Mother? Why aren't you happy over Franklin's engagement to Amanda? They love each other to an embarrassing degree. Her mother is your best friend. And politically, this wedding will assure Franklin of the mayoralty. And you're not happy. Why?"

She firmed her lips. "I am happy."

"You are not."

"I am if I say I am." Her tone of voice approached shrill.

Suspicion turned fearful in Grey's chest. "Of course you are," he said quietly.

His mother practically glared at him. "We were talking about your trouble and not about Camilla James being my friend or not."

Or not? That got his attention. Camilla not her friend? Since when? Still, Grey nodded and went on with the conversation at hand. "Yes. My trouble. Let me begin this way. Have you noticed anything, well, peculiar here today, Mother?"

As if defeated, she put a hand to her brow, rubbing there as she shook her head. Then she met his waiting gaze. "You'll have to be more specific. Peculiar is the normal state of affairs in your household."

Grey ducked his head regally, as if acknowledging an accolade. "Thank you, Mother. All right, to be specific, I have barely a servant left today. Bentley, Cook, and Mrs. Scott, to name a few, are still here. But I haven't completely assessed the tattered reduction-in-ranks to my chambermaid situation."

His mother sat up, straightening her spine. A look of reproval claimed her fair features. "The chambermaids? I have told you before that a gentleman does not . . . dabble among his employees, Greyson—"

"For God's sake, Mother, not that." He pulled back and stared at her. Her dark yet graying hair was impeccably coifed, her midnight blue day gown of the latest fashion, her mannerisms elegant. Somehow, he couldn't see Miss James surviving among women such as his mother. A sudden surge of protectiveness toward the Cherokee girl upstairs assailed him. He turned the unwelcome feeling into vexation with his mother. "You do think the worst of me, don't you?"

His mother clasped her hands tightly in her lap. "Of course I do not. Your father, God rest his soul, and I raised you to be a wonderful man. And I know that, underneath it all, you are. Only, Greyson, I *do* hear the rumors."

Grey was sulking now. He slouched down on the sofa cushions, his legs crossed, his hands in his pants pockets. He stared at his shoes. "They're not rumors, Mother. The stories are true. All of them."

His mother sat back. "I don't doubt it. All that's left, then, is for you to take up residence with riffraff. Don't look at me that way. Now, tell me why you don't have any maids." Her tone of voice warned that compliance was expected immediately.

Grey turned his head to look at her. "Where are my manners? Would you like some tea or coffee, Mother? Or breakfast? I could have Bentley——"

"I have had my morning meal. And you're already past rude in not having offered before now. I swear, Son, you need the deft touch of a woman to run your life."

"You mean ruin it."

"I mean run it. You're sinking into a dissolute mess right before my eyes. Now sit up and tell me about the maids, Greyson. I warn you, I won't leave until you do. Why have they fled?"

Here it was, the moment to begin his long tale of woe that had begun last night following his departure in disgrace from Charles's. And the devil hang the consequences. Grey exhaled, sat up—and caught a furtive movement out in the hall. A hem of a skirt, maybe. A flash of color. Just beyond the open door to this room. Someone was eavesdropping. Someone who had changed out of her white nightgown and into a white woman's clothes. This could be nothing but a disaster. Grey frowned.

"What is it, Son? You're frowning horribly."

He stood up, thankful for the footstep-muffling carpet under his feet. He was going to need it. He put a finger to his lips, signaling quiet . . . so he could whisper, "Keep talking."

His mother sent him a look of outrage. "What did you say? Keep talking? Greyson, I insist you tell me what is going on here. If you do not, I will have a word with your household staff myself—or with what remains of them."

"Nothing is going on here, Mother," he replied in a normal pitch. Then he whispered again, "Keep talking." He pointed toward the room's open door. "There's someone out in the hall."

Frowning, clearly confused, she looked from him to the doorway and back to him . . . and began ranting. "No one is there, Greyson. I have no idea what to make of your continued shenanigans. I came over here this morning out of motherly concern for you. I have already had a visit this day from that hateful old baggage Mrs. Stanhope. She tells me that her lady's maid told her that your housekeeper was in Miss Aldridge's Dress Shop at practically dawn this morning. She said Mrs. Scott was hurriedly buying every piece of ready-made apparel on the premises and spouting a tale of such nonsense that no sane person could give an ounce of credence to anything she said. . . ."

And so on. Her diatribe did an admirable job of covering Grey's stealthy progress toward the door. But with every word she uttered, Grey's stomach knotted more. He had to catch the eavesdropper. This certainly wasn't the way he'd planned on introducing Miss James to his mother. He hadn't even had time to come up with a false story of how he and Miss James—whom he also had to give another name—had met, when they had, why he'd kept her secret, what she was doing here in his home, things like that. But now it seemed that only the startling sight of her could stop his mother's tirade—if not her heart, when he suddenly yanked an Indian maiden into the room.

At this point, Grey was to the door and sidling along the wall, intent on leaping out and grabbing a hold of his guest, when . . .

. . . into the room she strolled, her long hair braided and pinned in a coil atop her head. She was dressed impeccably in a snowy-white shirtwaist blouse and simple skirt of garnet satin. She was magnificent. To the accompaniment of his mother's gasp, Miss James stopped short and pivoted to face him . . . plastered there along the wall, his hands flattened against its wallpapered surface, and him every inch the picture of a large insect adhered to it.

Trapped, embarrassed, Grey immediately straightened up and dusted at a tabletop, as if that had been his intent all along. He cleared his throat and tried to act nonchalant. "Oh, there you are, uh, Spotted Fawn. I was just telling Mother about you"—Miss James opened her mouth, no doubt to protest; Grey rushed on, vigorously shaking his head no—"and how you don't speak our language."

Spotted Fawn, formerly Miss James, closed her mouth so abruptly Grey was surprised he hadn't heard her lips slam shut. She glared at him.

As did his mother, who was now standing and who was not happy. "Greyson, who is this young . . . woman? What is she doing here unchaperoned? And don't think for a moment that I believe that such a lovely girl is named Spotted Fawn." She disgustedly spit the name out. "And if she doesn't speak our language, then how do you expect her to know what you just said to her? Are you lying to me?"

"That's not bad for a first guess, Mother." Grey exhaled on a sigh. He couldn't think how this scene could get more ridiculous . . . or worse, for that matter.

That is, until Bentley appeared in the doorway, bowing all around. "Excuse me, Mr. Talbott, Mrs. Talbott, and Miss . . . uh, Fawn." Obviously Miss Fawn hadn't been the only eavesdropper in the hallway. Grey raised an eyebrow, but the butler, who now faced his employer, maintained an inscrutable countenance. "I've only just put Mr. Charles James in the library, sir. He is in a state of acute distress, and says he has a matter of some urgency and delicacy he must discuss with you in private. What shall I tell him, sir?"

"Tell him?" Grey was certain he would explode into a thousand pieces. For as long as he lived he would kick himself soundly in the seat of the pants for ever stopping Miss James from announcing herself to her father last evening. "Tell Mr. James that I seem to have strayed into a French farce, Bentley. And that as soon as I can separate the players one from another, I'll be right with him."

Bentley's eyes rounded. "Excuse me, sir?"

"Oh, for the—tell him to have a drink. A stiff one. And that I'll be right there. Tell him to pour me one, too."

Her father was here. Taylor's breath caught, her heart felt squeezed into her chest. Surprising her was the realization that she didn't want to see him. Not this minute. Not this way. Not with Mr. Talbott and his disapproving mother watching. Abruptly, before anyone else could move, as Bentley the man-bird turned and left the room, Taylor did the same thing. She marched out behind him, her spirit guide and protector.

Following her was Mrs. Talbott's plaintive cry of, "Grey, what is going on?" And his response of, "Stay where you are, Mother. Please. I'll be right back."

Behind Taylor, a door closed. In the next heartbeat, her arm was grabbed. She jerked her gaze up. Mr. Talbott had a hold of her. "Oh no, you don't. Not just yet. Not until I know what is upsetting Charles."

While Bentley proceeded on his mission across the hall, Mr. Talbott abruptly turned her to the right. He walked her toward the long hallway that paralleled the staircase to the second floor and led—she knew from her entrance through it last night—out to the coach yard. Taylor made a darting look over her shoulder. The man-bird Bentley opened the door, disappearing inside the room . . . where her father was.

Taylor looked up at her tormentor. "Where are you taking me?"

Mr. Talbott stopped, looking suddenly lost. "Actually, I don't have the foggiest idea, Taylor."

He'd called her Taylor. Momentary surprise quieted her. She'd given no such permission. But at the moment, his familiar use of her name was a distant concern. Too much else here was wrong. Not giving him the benefit of her thinking, not telling him that she had no wish to confront her father right now, she made a simple announcement. "I wish to see Red Sky."

Mr. Talbott bent his head down to her, as if he wasn't sure

he'd heard her correctly. "I beg your pardon? You want to see a red sky? As in a sunset?"

Such nearness to him had Taylor swallowing and hating her weakness toward him. His clean and masculine scent was not the least bit unpleasant. That unsettled her and had her hissing, "No. My horse. His name is Red Sky. I wish to see him—unless you have had him taken away as you did my clothes."

Mr. Talbott managed to look sheepish, but his expression cleared. "Oh. Your horse. No, I haven't had anything *done* to him. He's out in the barn, and I'm sure he's fine. Go see him. In fact, stay out there until I come for you. Will you do that, Taylor?"

That was twice. She exhaled angrily. "I tell you this now— you do not have my permission to call me Taylor. And I will not go by the name of Spotted Fawn." Taylor wrenched her arm from his grasp. "I will go now to see my horse. And I will stay there or come back inside as I see fit, and not as you say. I may choose to ride him away from here, from this house of crazy people. I was wrong to come here. I do not belong."

With that, and giving him no chance to reply, she spun on her heel and started toward the back door. Expecting any moment to be stopped, she stuck her hand in her pocket, fumbling to loosen her—

"Tay—I mean, Miss James? Wait."

She pivoted around to face Mr. Talbott. This time her knife, which she had sheathed in a deep pocket of the skirt, was in her hand. She held it up threateningly, making sure he saw it. "Yes?"

He jerked back as if he'd been slapped. His breath left him in a hiss. "Damnation." He divided his attention between her and her blade. Then his dark eyes met hers . . . and held. "Don't leave. Please. I don't know how I know it, but I do know that you belong here . . . Taylor. You do."

Taylor pulled herself up to her full height and, with sure movements that didn't require her looking away from him, deftly sheathed and pocketed her knife. "I belong nowhere." Then, for some reason, and not quite sure she wasn't trying to convince only him, she added, "And to no man."

Again she turned her back to him and pushed on for the few steps it took her to reach the back door. Her booted feet on the hardwood floor made a final statement of each step. Grabbing the doorknob as if it were someone's neck, she wrenched it hard and opened the door. She crossed the threshold and found her feet on crunchy gravel and her senses assailed by warm spring air, ample sunshine, and chirping birds. With no small amount of relief and sense of freedom, she inhaled gratefully of the fresh air, just as she'd done when she'd left the penitentiary weeks ago.

But before she could close the door, something compelled her to look back inside, down the hall she'd just traveled. Mr. Talbott was not there. The space where he'd stood was empty, as if he'd simply vanished. Taylor ignored the disappointment that ate at her, focusing instead on his absence itself. Was he also magical, as was her man-bird? Because he hadn't had time, she didn't believe, to get back to the library door and go inside before she'd looked just now.

Could it be that Mr. Talbott was also a spirit creature, here to guide her on her way, here to intercede for her, instead of to interfere with her? Was *he* her sign that her old guard Rube had told her to watch for? Standing there, staring down the hall's empty length, with her hand still on the doorknob, Taylor entertained those questions, seeking answers. But only another question came to her. Could it be that she simply wanted it to be true, for Mr. Talbott to be her guide?

Taylor shook her head in an emphatic no to herself. It wasn't true. He was a rude white man who didn't know how to mind his own business and who felt he knew better than she did how to attend to her business. And that was all. Taylor instantly felt better and made a motion to close the door.

Just as she did, someone stepped into view at the other end of the hall. Taylor's breath caught, her heart picked up its rhythm. But it wasn't whom she'd thought . . . Mr. Talbott. Nor was it the other man, a virtual stranger to her but one she felt certain she would nevertheless recognize . . . her father. It wasn't even Bentley. Instead, it was a woman. Facing her was

Mrs. Talbott. The elegant older woman . . . slender, not as tall as Taylor, with her hands held in front of her at waist level . . . fixed her gaze on Taylor. She had no need of words. Taylor believed the other woman's icy expression spoke the words of hate for Taylor's kind in her heart.

An aching hurt centered itself deep in Taylor's chest. Would it ever, in her life, be any different? With her lips threatening to tremble, Taylor managed to get her chin up a proud notch. Then, not looking away from the woman, Taylor closed the door in the face of this new enemy.

Chapter Seven

The horse barn cleared unceremoniously of men as Taylor entered through its opened double doors. Somehow, their open fear of her restored her equilibrium a bit. It was easier to live life being feared than it was being rejected. Her steps as sure as her confining skirt would allow, and holding it up to keep the hem from sweeping through the dirt and the hay, she looked this way and that. Her horse was nowhere to be seen in any of the stalls she passed. Taylor finally stopped and called out a word in Cherokee. Red Sky immediately responded with a loud whinny. Taylor looked in the direction of the sound. Off to her left, around that corner there. Thus directed, and enjoying the familiar scent of horse, hay, manure, and leather tack, Taylor made her unerring way toward her fleet and long-legged steed.

In only another moment, she was standing outside the stall and staring in over the closed gate at her horse . . . and the owl-eyed and staring face of the boy from last night. Taylor searched her memory for his name, finally coming up with it. "Calvin," she said into the quiet broken only by the occasional stamp of a hoof or whinny of a horse elsewhere inside the barn.

"Y-yes, ma'am?" the boy responded, his voice breaking on the words. Then, as if he couldn't stop himself, he spilled his every thought. "Your horse is doing just fine, ma'am. He ate good today. And he rested quiet last night. I know because I slept in here. Didn't want him to have to kill somebody because he didn't know him. I was just brushing him down some for you." As if he needed proof, he held out a grooming brush for her to see. "His mane and tail was a tangled mess, but I got it all straightened out. I was fixing to walk him around some outside, just exercise him a bit in the fresh air. But now that you're out here and if you'd rather do it, then I suppose that's . . . what . . . you should do, I expect." He finally ran out of words.

Taylor didn't say anything. Adopting the impassive expression she usually showed the world, she looked the boy, the horse, and the stall over. They were clean and fresh, the horse and the stall. The boy was sweating and dusty. Everything was here. Saddle. Bridle. Saddle blanket. Her gaze lit on her saddlebags heaped in a corner. She would have thought that Mr. Talbott would have taken them, too. It amused Taylor that he'd taken them away from her. They contained nothing of a threat to anyone. A change of clothes, a bit of money, some personal items she'd needed on the way here.

"Did you want something, ma'am?"

Taylor met the boy's gaze. She had no idea why she thought of him as a boy. He was bigger and taller than she, no more than a few years younger than her at most. He was broad-shouldered but gave the appearance that he hadn't quite grown into his bones yet. He was respectful to her—out of fear of her, true. But respectful nonetheless. And he'd taken good care of Red Sky, better than she'd been able as she'd traveled here. She should thank him for that, for all he'd done. The very idea took her by surprise. Thank a white man? No. With no softening of her expression, she stared into the boy's face. "Leave us."

"Yes, ma'am." Calvin hurriedly, clumsily set the brush on a narrow shelf inside the stall. It toppled off into the hay. He picked it up and put it back on the shelf. It toppled off again. With a hissing intake of breath, he bent over to retrieve it yet again.

"Leave it."

Her words froze him in position, his big hand outstretched toward the fresh hay. Slowly, he straightened up and met her gaze. His tongue flicked out over his lips; he ran a hand over his sweating brow . . . and didn't seem capable of moving.

Usually Taylor gained satisfaction from such a response.

She had expected to experience that now. But she hadn't. She frowned, considering this red-haired stable boy. She made him nervous; that much was plain. She also made him feel unwelcome . . . unwanted . . . less than he was. Who better than her to know how that felt? The question, posed to herself, startled her. That she would see something of herself in a white boy was unthinkable. Was she losing her edge around his kind? Coming to think of them as people? She didn't know, didn't want to believe that. But still, she felt compelled to say something. She told herself that if she didn't speak, the two of them would stand here until the sun went down, because he was clearly waiting for her to make the next move.

So, quirking her mouth with self-disgust, and with every Cherokee drop of blood in her veins screaming against the very notion, Taylor spit out, "Thank you for your care of my horse. Red Sky looks better than I've ever seen him."

The boy Calvin blinked . . . and took a breath. He shifted about in the hay. He ducked his head the tiniest bit, an acknowledgment of her compliment. And then his chest swelled, as if with pride, and his face split into a wide grin. Surprising Taylor was how good it made her feel inside to make happy someone in a subservient position to her.

"You're mighty welcome, ma'am," the boy chirped. "I tried to do my best for you. Well, for him, I suppose."

With that, Calvin set himself in motion, crossing the wide stall in only a few steps, opening the gate, and stepping out. He stood to one side, allowing Taylor to pass by him. "In you go, ma'am. Uh, mind your skirt there. The hay's fresh and all, so you shouldn't step in any—well, you know. Anyway, I got some other chores to do. But I'll be close by. If you'll just let me know when you're done with your visit, I'll finish his grooming."

Taylor was capable of expressing only so much gratitude in one day. She didn't say thank you again. Neither did she smile. She simply nodded and walked past him into the stall, closed the gate, and watched him walk off. Then, holding her skirt up out of the hay, she picked her way over to Red Sky, who met her with a familiar nudge of welcome with his nose.

Grinning now, completely happy in each passing moment, Taylor stroked the horse's head and spoke softly to him in Cherokee.

"You're very familiar with that horse."

Taylor spun around. There stood Mrs. Talbott, her arms folded together atop the closed gate. She looked completely out of place here. Taylor's heartbeat picked up. The white woman had obviously followed her. "That's because he is mine," she blurted.

"I thought you might speak English." There was a note of triumph in her voice.

Taylor watched her warily. "I never said I did not. It was your son who did."

The older woman chuckled and shook her head. "Yes. My son. I also suppose your name isn't . . . What did he say it was?"

"Spotted Fawn."

"Is it?"

Taylor shook her head but said nothing. She knew the other woman expected her to supply her real name. But Taylor had no intention of doing so. In the Cherokee tradition, it was rude to ask a person's name. A person's name was private, intimate. It was given only eventually and then out of a gesture of good will and friendship. Taylor figured this white woman would not know that. But beyond that, and bothering Taylor more right now, was why had Mr. Talbott told those lies about her to his mother? Did he perhaps not trust this woman who had given him life? If he didn't, then could she? What would this woman do if she knew who Taylor really was? Comforted only by the weight of her knife in her pocket and Red Sky's protective nearness to her, Taylor turned the conversation so that she, instead of Mrs. Talbott, could get answers. "Is Mr. Talbott's . . . guest still here?"

The older woman frowned. Then her expression cleared. "Oh, you mean Mr. James. I'm sorry. It's just that Greyson has had so many guests today. Me. You. And now his friend. But I really have no idea if he is or isn't still here. I would assume so, since he apparently was in some distress over something. I cannot imagine what." Her expression became arch. "Why do you ask? Is it important for you to know?"

A thrill of foreboding swept through Taylor. To her, standing there and knowing the secret of her identity, the other woman's questions seemed barbed with extra meaning. So, very quickly, before Mrs. Talbott could draw any other conclusions, Taylor said, "No. It does not matter. Not to me."

"Of course not." The older woman stared at Taylor for a moment, then sent her an inquisitive, yet unfriendly, look. "Forgive me, but I . . . Well, how shall I put this? I understand you were an, uhm, overnight guest here at my son's?"

She was fishing for information that, to Taylor's point of view, was none of her business. Her only response was to say nothing, show nothing.

Mrs. Talbott's expression soured, as if she'd formed an opinion of Taylor on the strength of her silence. "I see. Well. Leave it to Greyson to do things the unconventional way."

Turning away from the woman's judgmental coldness, Taylor stroked Red Sky under his forelock. "I would not know."

"Oh, I think you do. I think you—your appearance and your presence here—provide ample evidence of just how unconventional my son can be."

Having an idea of the implied insult underlying the older woman's words, Taylor resettled her attention on her, this time noting how much the son resembled his mother. The same dark brown hair and eyes. The same chin. The same proud bearing. But that didn't stop her from challenging Mrs. Talbott to this time openly speak her mind. "Say what you mean. Unconventional how?"

The woman's face colored, and she huffed out her breath. "In every sense, young lady. I am merely trying to find out *who* you are and *what* you are to my son. As his mother, I believe I have the right to know."

"If your son believes as you do—that you have a right to know—he will then tell you. It is not my place."

"Well, this is just grand. It was bad enough to be awakened this morning by the city's biggest gossip, a woman who cannot wait to entertain me, and no doubt the rest of St. Louis society, with this latest example of Greyson's unthinking indiscretion—"

"That word is not known to me."

Mrs. Talbott stared at Taylor, looking her up and down, as if trying to determine if Taylor was baiting her. She then made a show of taking in her surroundings, giving the appearance of only just now having realized she was standing in a horse barn. She wrinkled her nose but focused again on Taylor. "An indiscretion. Let me see. Something one does . . . or someone one aligns oneself with . . . to embarrass one's family I suppose is the best definition."

Taylor's unblinking stare did not change. But it had struck her that the woman had just neatly defined for Taylor her entire life. It was true. She'd lived it in such a manner as to do the most harm to those she loved. She had her reasons why. But how could it be that this woman's son was apparently of the same sort? Why would he be? He had everything a man could ever want. Or did he? Taylor next asked herself why she would care what he had or didn't have in his life. She had her own problems . . . one of which faced her now. Finally, she spoke. "Then, you think me an embarrassment? An indiscretion?"

Apparently undaunted by Taylor's unfriendly stare, the woman shrugged, her smile not the least bit friendly. "I suspect you're much more than that. But I don't know yet what exactly to make of you."

That amused Taylor. "Most people do not."

Mrs. Talbott gripped the gate's rough edge. Her knuckles were white. "I see you're not going to be the least bit forthcoming. All I know is my son's housekeeper was seen this morning buying feminine apparel—clothing obviously not meant for her—at a dress shop. And now my son tells me his maids have all flown this morning. Then, quite out of the blue, he says he is thinking of settling down and getting married. I thought he was teasing me until you came into the room. And now I'm wondering if all those other things are connected somehow by the thread that is you." She leaned in over the stall gate. "*Is* it my son's intention to marry you, Miss . . . uh?"

"Mother. There you are."

Saved from answering her, Taylor turned with Mrs. Talbott to see—she tried his name out in her mind—Greyson striding their way. With his collarless white shirt still open at the throat and his dark trousers stretched taut with each step, he was an imposing figure. The man seemed to fill the entire barn with his presence. His brow was lined with the frown that claimed his mouth. His dark eyes sparked fire. He wasn't happy. And he was looking directly at Taylor. "Should you be inside that stall, dressed like that?"

He spoke to her in the reproving tone of a father or a husband. Taylor didn't like that . . . and retaliated. "What choice do I have? You took my clothes away last night."

Mrs. Talbott gasped and spit out her son's name: "Greyson!"

Greyson ignored his mother. He didn't seem capable of taking his angry gaze off Taylor. "I will need to speak with you inside the house, please."

She refused an answer, but her pulse quickened fearfully. What had he and her father discussed? Her palms suddenly felt clammy. Red Sky nudged her arm. She absently stroked his velvety nose while matching Greyson's angry stare with one of her own.

He turned away first, attending now to his mother. He took her arm. "Come, Mother. I'll escort you to your brougham. I have thoroughly enjoyed your visit. But I'm afraid you must go now. My peculiar household is about to combust, and I would not have you standing anywhere near the line of fire. You understand, of course?"

Her eyes wide, her mouth open, the older woman was clearly startled by her son's abrupt manner and his rude handling of her. "No, I do not, Greyson. Not at all. I—"

"Good." He turned her with him, stopping only to again address Taylor. "Would you be so good as to conclude your visit with your horse and return to your room upstairs, Miss James?"

He'd said her name. Taylor froze, her knees stiffening until they felt locked. Greyson's eyes widened. . . . No doubt he'd just realized his unthinking blunder.

"James? Miss *James*?" Her voice shrill, Mrs. Talbott questioned her son. "Greyson, did I hear you correctly?"

"*Damn.*" Greyson spoke through gritted teeth.

Mrs. Talbott jerked her disbelieving gaze to Taylor and raked it over her face, as if only now seeing features there she hadn't noticed before. Taylor didn't move. Mrs. Talbott evidently saw what she'd feared. She shook her head and all but whimpered out a "No." She sought her son's attention. Her expression could only be called imploring. "Don't you see? This will ruin everything. Everything. She just cannot *be*, Greyson."

Taylor actually saw Greyson's hold on his mother's arm tighten. He pulled her closer to his face. "She can't be *who*, Mother? What do you mean?"

The woman shook her head vigorously. A lock of her hair came undone from its pins and brushed her shoulder. Her face was wreathed in fear. "Nothing. I don't mean anything."

"You're lying, Mother."

A transforming calm came suddenly over Mrs. Talbott, like a mantle settling about her. She stood erect, looking cold and distant. The change was frightening for its speed and its effect. "I will not discuss this in front of a—out here. You will take your hand off me, Greyson. You're being disrespectful, and you're hurting me." He did as she asked. "Thank you. I will see myself to my carriage."

She picked up her skirts and turned an angry, disbelieving expression Taylor's way. Taylor, her chin up, her eyes narrowed to an answering glare, inhaled and stood up taller herself, refusing to look away first. Mrs. Talbott's expression broke, showing a flash of cold hatred. "You have no business being here." With that parting shot, she stalked out of the barn. Not once did she look back.

Taylor met Greyson's eyes. Her gaze locked with his. An encumbering silence enveloped them. The moments passed like heartbeats. Then Red Sky suddenly stamped a hoof and whinnied. The sound was shrill, startling. It spoke of terror, as if the animal had picked up on the human emotions and the dark secrets that lay behind them.

Alone and in a state of high agitation, Taylor paced her room. She'd only just come upstairs after leaving the barn. She believed that she and Greyson—the name was coming easier to her—would still be standing out there staring at each other had not Calvin, hearing Red Sky's whinny, as he'd said, blundered onto the scene and broken the spell that had wrapped her and Greyson in its spidery wisps.

The door to her room, the one that adjoined it to Greyson's, opened with a vengeance. Taylor pivoted, facing the doorway, waiting. As she'd expected, it was Greyson who filled the opening. Her heart felt like a heavy stone in her chest. She skirted her bed and dispensed with greetings, going immediately to the crux of her concerns: "What did my father want with you?"

Greyson stopped short, as if she'd struck him. His expression was a mask of reproach. "*If* he is your father."

Taylor gestured her frustration. "He is. You know it to be true."

Greyson's hand was still on the doorknob. "I know nothing. Only what you've told me. But earlier this morning, before Charles's appearance here, I had convinced myself that you were telling the truth. But now, I don't see how you *can* be his daughter."

Taylor went rigid with indignation. She was tired of being questioned. "I am who I say I am. You yourself said my name to your mother *after* you'd spoken with my father."

Grey exhaled sharply. "Yes, I did. For one thing, I have no other name to call you. And for another, it was an honest slip of the tongue. But one I'm glad I made."

Taylor nodded, secretly glad he had, too. Because his mother's response upon hearing him call her Miss James had screamed that she indeed knew something about Taylor . . . and why she couldn't possibly exist.

Redirecting her attention outward, Taylor noted that Greyson's attention hadn't wandered. He still stared at her and his expression had hardened. "Explain something for me, Taylor— if I may address you so? It seems more natural than 'Miss James,' given our predicament here. And I confess that addressing you as Miss James lends a validity to your story and a respect to you personally that I'm not yet willing to confer."

Taylor wasn't sure she understood everything he'd said, but she nevertheless nodded . . . and returned the insult. "You may. But know that I will call you Greyson."

His eyebrows rose as if she'd surprised him with that. "Fair enough." Then he got on with the subject at hand. "Charles— your father, so you say—only this morning received a very troubling message, one that put him on my doorstep. It said his daughter had been found guilty of murder and was hanged weeks ago in the Cherokee Nation. Now, how could that be . . . if you're her?"

Taylor felt certain her bones had just turned to water. She fisted her hands. Her nails bit into the flesh of her palms. When she spoke, it was slowly and in measured tones. "Who sent this wrong message to him?"

"He didn't say. And I don't know that it's wrong."

"It is wrong. I suspect my mother may have sent it. Maybe before she had the idea to send my uncle to break me out." It made sense. There would have been no way of recalling an already dispatched messenger. Taylor figured it was pure luck that she'd arrived here first—one day before the messenger with the incorrect news of her death.

Greyson was staring at her. A suspicious cast lit his features. "Did you send him the message, Taylor?"

She made a sound of disgust. "Did you not hear what I just said? Why would I send it? I *know* I was not hanged. And if you will recall, I meant to make myself known to my father last night—before he received this message."

Greyson absently scratched at his brow. "Well, you're right there."

"I am. But why would he come to *you* with this?"

"Because I'm his friend. Because he wanted someone to talk to, someone to help him sort this out. Remember, he believed his child died as long as eleven years ago——"

"Or so he says."

Greyson narrowed his eyes at her. "Yes, he does. And now this . . . this cruel joke. Or this hoax. Or this truth. I don't know which. I asked him again, and he told me again, that I'm the only one he's told about his daughter."

"Perhaps he meant that you were the only one outside our family he's talked to. My aunt and uncle and cousin here in St. Louis know of my existence."

Greyson considered her . . . and apparently her words. "Well, that's true enough."

Taylor nodded, moving on to another concern . . . one closer to the emotional mark. "Did you . . . did you tell him I'm *not* dead and that I'm here?"

"If I had, you would already have seen him because I would have brought him to you. However, I should tell you that I had decided to tell him before I knew the reason for his visit. But in light of what he told me, how could I explain you? As a ghost? Or an impostor . . . which means someone pretending——"

"I know what the word means. And I am neither of those things. Tell me this: if you are the only one my father has told about me, then how does your mother know? And she does know. You saw her face."

His expression hardened. "I did."

Undaunted, Taylor continued. "And you also know that here I stand in front of you. You know me to be real."

"You're a real person. No ghost. I know that. But other than that, I don't know the first thing about you." He advanced into the room, pacing now and glancing her way each time he passed her. "And furthermore, I have no idea how to find out. I have only your word. And your presence here has upset my entire household and even my mother. I don't know what to make of any of this. But I am about ready to tell you—whoever the devil you are—to pack your horse and leave. Just take your lies and get out."

"I do not lie." Taylor stiffened with pride. She raised her chin. Her eyes burned as they did when the wind dried them as she raced Red Sky across the forested lands of the Nation. "And I did not ask you to involve yourself in my life. You concerned yourself for your own reasons, reasons you have not told me beyond friendship for my father. But I will do as you say. I will gather my things and leave. I should have done so before now."

Taylor started to turn away. Greyson grabbed her arm suddenly, holding her close to him. "Do you understand that before I stupidly confronted you last night and put my nose in your business, I was a happy man? Life was wonderful. I had my friends. My clubs. The card games. It was good. Uncomplicated. The way I liked it. The way I mean for it to stay."

Taylor could only stare up at him and note for herself how almost black his eyes really were, like the inside of a cave, or the bottom of a well. He hadn't asked her a question or said anything she could respond to . . . and he didn't release her . . . so she waited for him to continue. He didn't disappoint her.

"Before last night, I knew humor, Taylor. And laughing. I had a house full of happy servants. No one was fleeing me. There was no rancor between my mother and me. And I could sleep at night. Eat. Drink. And be merry. That was my life. And then there was you. And now it is all falling apart. You've taken my world—with your very presence here and with your tales—and you've turned it upside down until I don't know what or who to believe, much less trust, anymore. How did you do that? How?"

Taylor strove desperately to keep her expression impassive, and her heart unmoved, in the face of such passion . . . which could lead to violence. Monroe Hammer had taught her that lesson. "How, you ask? By telling the truth," she said levelly. "If your happy world fell apart because of my truths, then it is because your world was a lie, one that you could not or would not see."

Greyson released her, practically shoving her away from him. He looked as if he was afraid, but he pointed accusingly at her. "Your words are the only lies in this house."

Taylor stepped into the space between them, caution thrown to the wind, her eyes narrowed to angry slits. "I do not care if you believe me. I do not need you to believe me. I did not come to St. Louis to see you or to ruin your life, Greyson. I came to see my father. And now I will go to him, as was my plan all along. This time do not try to stop me . . . or I *will* ruin your life."

His expression became mocking. "Or maybe you'll just *take* my life, like the murderer you are."

"If I wanted to take your life, you would already be dead."

"You sound awfully sure of yourself. Then you are a murderer?"

A heavy, ugly calm descended like a weight over Taylor. "I wonder if you hear your own words. Charles James has told you himself that his daughter was a murderer. So if you believe me to be a murderer, then you are saying you believe I am Charles James's daughter."

Greyson blinked, as if taken aback, but he recovered. "No. If I believed you to be Charles's daughter, then I would believe you are dead. Twice over."

"And yet I am not. I am alive . . . twice over. Ask yourself how that could be." She meant those to be her final words. She took a step, meaning to turn away from him.

"Taylor, wait." She did. "You're not the least bit shocked by that? By being called a murderer? *Are* you a murderer?"

Taylor looked him up and down, trying to decide how much to tell him. But then she realized . . . what did it matter? She could not be prosecuted here in this white man's land. Nor did she care what he thought of her. Maybe the more he knew about her, the more willing he'd be to leave her alone. "I did not kill the man for whose murder I was to hang."

A range of emotions . . . confusion, disbelief, uncertainty . . . played over his face, shadowing his expression much like a quick-moving storm did the plains darkened by its clouds. "You're so calm about this. Either you're a consummate liar, or you are telling the truth. But start here—why weren't you hanged?"

"I told you. I was broken out of the prison the day before."

"That's right. How daring. But the way you said that . . . that you didn't kill the man whose murder you were to hang for. Does that mean you have killed other men?"

"Yes. But they all deserved it."

"No one deserves to be murdered."

Taylor smirked. "You have not walked in my shoes."

He was silent a moment, his gaze roving over her face. She had no idea for what he looked. "How many?" he suddenly blurted.

"Three."

Greyson abruptly turned away, a hand planted at his waist, his other to his brow. "I've brought a murderer into my house," he muttered, more to himself than to her.

Taylor suddenly recalled something he had said to her last night. To his back she said, "You told me that you had scalped a man. Is that true?"

He pivoted just enough to be looking over his shoulder at her. "No. I just said that to . . . Well, I don't know why. Just to scare you into behaving, I suppose."

Taylor nodded . . . and fought unsuccessfully not to admit to herself that she didn't really want to leave this man's house. Nor did she want to cause him any more pain. These feelings took her by surprise, rocking her sense of who she was. She told herself she felt this way only because her man-bird spirit guide was still here. But she knew better, as she took in Greyson's strong physique, his dark hair, and how it tumbled onto his forehead. But it was more than that. He had a good heart. An innocent life. And he was right. He did not need her trouble here. Quickly, before she could change her mind, she said, "I will go now."

Greyson turned to her. His eyes showed hurt and confusion. "Where will you go? I would beg you not to go to your . . . well, to Charles."

"I have thought about that. For now, I will go to my cousin Amanda's house."

A light sparked in Greyson's eyes. He became animated . . . almost hopeful-looking. "By God, I forgot about Amanda. She would know you, wouldn't she?"

Taylor's heart pitter-patted. Greyson was still looking for proof that she was who she said she was. He wanted desper-

ately to believe her. A spark of something warm caught hold
in Taylor's heart and had her answering a little more eagerly
than she would have liked. "Maybe. We were only children,
nine years of age, when she was taken away."

He frowned. "Taken away? From where? And why was
she?"

Taylor found herself telling all she knew. "I do not know
the why. But for many years, from when we were babies until
we were nine years old, we were together every day. I loved
her as I would a sister. She and her mother lived with my
family—me, my mother and her brother, and my grandparents.
Then, one day, Amanda's father came. My father was with
him. And then, they left the Nation . . . my father, Amanda,
and her mother and father. I never saw them again."

The light dimmed in his eyes. He shook his head. "No, that
cannot be. Your story is absolutely fantastic. Unbelievable.
I've known the Jameses since I was a young lad myself. And
I've never heard any of this. Why would a white woman and
her baby live among the—" His eyes widened with what he'd
almost said.

Feeling cold inside, Taylor supplied the words that he'd
obviously meant to use. "The savages? Why would they live
among the savages? Pretty, light-skinned people sleeping and
eating with Indians?"

"I didn't mean that, Taylor. Not like that."

She retreated back into her Cherokee reticence and her impassive expression. "You call me a liar. And yet you call me
Taylor. You speak my name, but you do not respect me. You
do not know me. I will go away from here. And this time,
you will not stop me . . . white man."

Chapter Eight

G rey spent the late afternoon in seclusion in his library
downstairs. Seated in his favorite leather-upholstered
chair, his elbows propped atop his knees, his head in his hands,
he mourned. There was no other word for it. He was in mourn-
ing. No one had died. And not one thing was wrong anymore
in his world. It had all been put to rights, including his domestic situation. All was quiet out in the horse barn and the
carriage house. And inside, Mrs. Scott had somehow rounded
up the maids and got them to come back. So, by late afternoon,
the house had been depressingly clean and quiet. Bentley was
terrifyingly chipper and lucid. And Cook had prepared a wonderful lunch. But much to that autocratic and forbidding little
woman's disapproval, Grey had hardly been able to eat.

Other than that, he had bathed, paid the bills, attended to
the mail, had the tailor in to begin the fittings for the formal
wear he'd need for Franklin's wedding, and even signed a
sheaf of business papers sent by courier to him from Franklin.
Grey had surprised himself by actually reading the legal documents until he understood them. Following that, he had
turned down three social engagements—and one summons
from his mother—because tonight, this very evening, he intended to repair to his favorite club for activities he could
understand. Drinking and cards. Laughter and male camaraderie.

In fact, Franklin had sent word that he'd join Grey for a
space of time before he went round to Amanda's. The Stanley
Jameses were entertaining Franklin, as well as his and Grey's
mother, tonight, so even she was accounted for. Grey could
see that dinner now with Taylor in attendance, assuming she

would be. If she was, if she wasn't stashed in an upstairs bedroom at the Jameses', or hadn't been thrown out on her ear, then his mother could quite possibly become a candidate for an early grave. The poor woman would believe she was losing her mind. It would seem to her that Taylor was everywhere.

And poor Charles. Somehow, Franklin had talked him into joining him and Grey at the club. Admittedly, that invitation had been extended before Charles had got his upsetting message. So he may have already begged off to Franklin. Grey figured he'd find out soon enough.

Even so, with all those possibilities multiplying like rabbits, Grey determinedly declared that life . . . at least for the next few and blessed hours, until the repercussions of Taylor's presence were felt . . . was back to normal. His social calendar was full. The day had become uneventful. The sun was going down. The night's activities promised to be merry—

And Grey had never been unhappier. Or felt more empty. Taylor was gone. She'd saddled her horse and left, without taking the first things he'd bought her, except for the clothes on her back. She'd certainly made good on her promise. . . . She was gone. And he missed her.

No, he didn't. He couldn't. He refused to. It was insane. He'd only known of her existence for less than twenty-four hours. How could he miss her? Well, he didn't. What he meant, when he said he missed her—he tried to convince himself—was that he feared where she was and what havoc she was wreaking with her lies. He felt as if he'd lost control of a dangerous situation when he should have been able to quell it at its source. He felt as if he'd had it in his power to stop a tornado or an earthquake and he hadn't stood up to the challenge. Just as he hadn't done in the whole of his rich and idle life. It was as his mother had said. He'd never been challenged.

Well, look what happens when I am, he berated himself. *I completely failed to contain this disaster. And because I didn't, or couldn't, Taylor is gadding about town and spewing her lies and ruining people's lives.*

"No!" Grey jumped to his feet, his fists raised to the ceiling. He could no longer lie to himself or keep his emotions inside. "She's *not* lying. I'm lying to myself. *She's* telling the truth, and I know it. It's the only explanation that makes any sense." He was bellowing now. "I believe her. And I miss her. I let her go, and I want her back. God, it's *true*."

He took a deep breath and found himself facing row upon row of placid and innocent-looking leather-bound books stacked intimately together on their wooden shelves. He took a deep breath, trying to steady himself.

The door to the library opened. Grey jerked around. Bentley's rounded little bird-face was poked around the door. "Did you call me, sir?"

Grey stared at the old man . . . and wondered if he'd ever be able to look at Bentley without seeing the childlike wonder he'd witnessed in Taylor's expression as she'd gazed upon her man-bird. He could still hear her trying haltingly to explain to him what this event meant to her. Grey roused himself, thinking it did no good to think of such things now. "No, Bentley, I didn't call for you. Not unless your name is God."

Bentley blinked, as if startled. "Oh, I hardly think so, sir. Sorry to interrupt, then. But, sir . . ." He stopped, looked Grey over, and then began again. "There's something I'd like to say, sir. May I proceed?"

Grey waved a hand at him, giving permission. "Carry on."

"Thank you, sir. Forgive me . . . but you look a positive fright."

Amused, in a fatalistic way, Grey looked down at himself and chuckled. "A fright, eh?" He reeked of cigar smoke, and he'd already helped himself to the whiskey. His wrinkled shirt was all but untucked. His boots were scuffed from riding earlier this afternoon. And he'd been running his hands through his hair. No doubt, it stood on end. "I suppose I do." He met his butler's waiting gaze. "It's not been a good day, Bentley."

"No, sir, I don't suppose it has. Not for any of us, sir."

Then it got quiet. Grey stared at Bentley staring at him. "Was there anything else, Bentley?"

"I'm afraid so, sir. Only, first, I must say . . . it's awfully quiet around here now, isn't it, sir?"

"Except for my occasional outburst. Yes. I suppose it is." Grey hadn't meant to bring her up, but somehow talking about Taylor to Bentley, someone she had adored, seemed only natural. "I should think you'd be glad that Miss James is gone."

Bentley nodded his head emphatically. "Oh, I am that, sir. A most frightening time we've had of it. Most frightening." Then he shook his head no just as vigorously. "No. I'm not being truthful, sir. I must confess that, to my horror, I actually miss her. I rather enjoyed, in retrospect, my stint as a sacred man-bird. It does something for a man to be so looked up to. No doubt you know what I mean, sir."

Though relieved to hear that he wasn't the only one to miss her, Grey shook his head. "No. I don't know what you mean, Bentley. I can't say that anyone at all looks up to me. Nor should they."

Bentley's expression puckered, as if he was angry and not about to put up with such nonsense. He came fully into the room, closing the door behind him. Grey's eyebrows raised at this uncharacteristic behavior. "Sir, that's not true at all. Everyone in your employ looks up to you. Indeed, the entire city. You're a fine man. Philanthropic. Charitable in your nature as well as in your finances. You're also civic-minded and a real force in this city's development."

Grey made a sound of bemused protest and shook his head. "You're confusing me with my younger brother, Bentley."

Bentley stepped farther into the room. "No, sir, not at all. You're a good man in your own right. You simply choose to stay behind-the-scenes in most matters. You're the force behind the family, sir."

Increasingly amused, Grey said, "I had no idea you thought so highly of me, Bentley."

"I do, sir. I couldn't stay in your employ if I did not. And this . . . this Miss James situation has simply thrown you. As it would anyone. But you'll recover, sir, and see it through to its end. It just seems hard right now because you've never before been challenged in such a way by life, sir."

"Well, that's absolutely the truth, Bentley." Several things were obvious to Grey. One, Bentley wasn't the least bit doddering, as he sometimes gave the impression. Two, earlier this afternoon, while his mother had been here, his butler had been eavesdropping far longer than Grey had suspected. And three, judging by Bentley's last comment, Grey surmised that his butler knew the crux of the dilemma, too. "I've not been challenged. You're the second person to say that to me today." Then Grey recalled Taylor saying he'd never walked in her shoes. "Or maybe the third."

Bentley pulled himself up to his full five feet of height, his pose rigid and classically that of a proper butler. "Am I, sir? The third? I say, that can become tiresome, then. I hope I wasn't out of line."

"No. You're not out of line. I'm the one who is. Now, if that's all, Bentley?"

"Actually, sir, Mrs. Scott would like a word with you. She says there's something troubling her. And she does appear to be quite distressed."

Grey rubbed distractedly at his forehead, telling himself the last thing he wanted to hear was some petty something to do with the newly rehired maids. But, "All right. Send her in. And tell Cook I'll be eating out tonight, not to prepare anything for me."

"Yes, sir. I hope you have a wonderful evening, sir."

Grey believed his answering smile to be a weak one. "I'll try. Oh, and, Bentley?"

The older man had turned away to leave the room. But now he again faced Grey. "Yes, sir?"

"Thank you. For everything you said."

Bentley smiled and bowed formally. "You're welcome, sir. And thank you for the twenty percent increase in my salary. I shall endeavor to put it good use." With that, Bentley turned and marched, all but scurried, out of the room.

That left Grey to stand there alone and frowning. *Twenty percent increase in salary . . . ?* Then he had it. *This morning.* He'd promised Bentley a raise if he'd just spit his words out. *Why, that sly old dog intends to hold me to it, too.* Just as

Grey chuckled at that, his good spirits restored, there was a knock on the library door. "Come in, Mrs. Scott!" he called out.

The housekeeper did . . . and she'd been crying. Her eyes were red-rimmed and puffy, her cheeks and nose mottled with color. She dabbed a hankie to her eyes as she faced Grey. "Thank you for seeing me, sir."

"Good heavens, Mrs. Scott," Grey said as he strode toward her. "Are you all right?" A silly question, one not requiring an answer beyond the vigorous shake of her head in the negative. Grey took her by her stout arm and steered her toward the leather chair he'd been keeping warm all afternoon. "Here. Sit here and tell me what this is about."

Mrs. Scott again shook her head vigorously, loosening a wisp of gray hair that hung from her usually tidy bun at the back of her neck. "I've done a terrible thing, sir. And I wouldn't blame you if you simply let me go."

Frowning, again wondering when this eventful day would be over, Grey propped himself against his desk's edge and crossed his arms. He looked down at his housekeeper. "Why don't you tell me what you mean and we'll go from there? Would you like something to calm you? A brandy, perhaps?"

Mrs. Scott, a widowed and childless woman on the far side of fifty years, glanced up at him before sliding her gaze back to her hands, which knotted and twisted her hankie in her lap. "No, sir. Thank you. I'd just like to say what I came to say and get it over with."

Grey was quite concerned now. He'd never seen this efficient, no-nonsense woman be anything but calm and practical. "All right, then. Proceed. I take it this has nothing to do, then, with the maids? Or the household expenses? Have you uncovered some thievery?"

She looked up at him now. "No, sir. None of that. Well, yes, sir, I suppose it could be about the maids. In a way. Or their leaving earlier. But not really, sir."

Grey wondered if he'd have to give her the same 20-percent raise he'd been frustrated into giving Bentley to get her to speak her mind. Had Bentley passed the word among the staff and now they all, one by one, meant to employ the same tactics until he was completely mad and beggared? "I beg you, Mrs. Scott, in the interest of time and sanity . . . proceed."

She nodded. "Yes, sir." Then, heaving in a huge breath and speaking on her exhalation, she blurted, "I'm afraid that I'm partly responsible for Miss James's leaving today, sir. Upstairs, earlier, when I was with her and going through the clothes you had me purchase for her, I was . . ." She stared again at her hands, now speaking more slowly. "Well, I was less than nice, sir. In fact, I was rude and insulting. I don't know what came over me. I've never spoken that way before to anyone. In my own defense, I can only say that I was very upset with the maids' leaving and having everything thrown into my hands, as it were, sir, and I—"

Gray's hand on her shoulder stopped her. His stomach knotting, he peered down into Mrs. Scott's unhappy face. "What happened—exactly?"

"I don't quite remember, sir. I believe I said something like 'heathen savage,' not realizing she spoke our tongue, and—"

"Son of a . . . gun," Grey muttered, but loud enough for Mrs. Scott to stop her narrative and stare wide-eyed up at him. Grey ran a hand over his mouth and stared back at the woman. What could he say? How could he reprove her when he'd as much as done the same thing—and more than once? "Tell me, Mrs. Scott, are you sorry only because she understood you, or—"

"Oh, no, sir. I'm sorry because I said it at all. It was a very un-Christian-like thing to do. Why, I never suspected I was capable of saying such a thing, sir. I feel awful about this. And that poor girl. How she must feel now."

"Indeed." Grey cocked his head at a questioning angle. "What did she say when you . . . said what you did?"

To his surprise, a grin tugged at Mrs. Scott's mouth. "Well, it wasn't the least bit funny at the time, sir. But now it strikes me as so. She said she had no need of the, uh, particular undergarment I was holding. And that she would wrap the—forgive me, sir—corset around my own head and pull the strings tight until I could no longer breathe, if I didn't clear

out of her room right then. I don't suppose I need to tell you
that I did as she suggested, sir."

Grey couldn't stop his own chuckling reaction to this fantastic story. "She does have a way about her, doesn't she?"
And Taylor was right. From what he'd seen, she had no need
of corseting.

"Yes, sir. And I dare say she was quite within her rights to
make such a threat. I behaved abysmally to the poor girl. And
I fear my behavior helped drive her away. Can you forgive
me, sir? Or should I clean out my—"

Grey's raised hand had stopped her talking. "Please stay,
Mrs. Scott. If you left, I'd only have to find you and rehire
you. I do thank you for telling me of the incident when you
really didn't have to. That speaks to your character. And try
not to fret. I don't think your . . . harsh words with Miss James
had anything to do with her leaving, no more than did Bentley's undignified shrieking whenever she appeared. Or my
own behavior toward her. The truth is, I told her to leave."

Mrs. Scott's dark eyes rounded. "You, sir?"

Despite the sudden guilty flush in his cheeks, Grey wasn't
about to explain his reasons to his housekeeper. He figured
Bentley would do that. "Yes, and I'm living to regret it. We've
all learned a lesson today about employing kindness and a bit
of understanding with people unlike ourselves. All we can do
is hope they will do the same with us." Grey held a hand out,
indicating she should precede him. He followed her to the
closed door, reaching around her to open it. He then held it
for her, adding, "Let's endeavor to put the lesson to good use
from today on, shall we?"

"Yes, sir." She turned an imploring expression up to him.
"Are you certain there's nothing I can do to, well, get the
young lady back? If that would be appropriate, I mean."

Grey smiled, seeing the need for a second chance in her
eyes. He knew all too well that life did not often give one a
second chance. "I thank you, Mrs. Scott. But I'm afraid there's
nothing anybody can do."

Grey closed the door behind his despondent housekeeper.
Then he stood there, scanning the orderly library but not really

seeing it once his attention directed itself inward to his own churning thoughts. He pondered his plans for this evening and those of everyone else who mattered to him. Lost in thought, he wandered over to the narrow floor-length windows behind his desk and stared out at the twilight. He crossed his arms, rocked back on his heels, and saw the face that tormented him. Jet-black hair framed a face resplendent with jewel-like blue eyes. High cheekbones and a generous mouth mocked him . . . dared him to accept the challenge that she was.

A smile found its way to Grey's face, a smile that said he accepted that challenge. "No, Mrs. Scott," he muttered aloud in the otherwise empty room. "There's nothing anybody can do. Except for me, that is."

Suddenly galvanized by his newly made decision, with renewed energy coursing through him and reflected in his determined stride, Grey crossed the library and opened the door. He left the room that had been his self-inflicted torture chamber and stalked across the narrow foyer to the stairs and sprinted up them.

An otherwise deserted but grassy bluff overlooking the wide and mighty Mississippi River afforded Taylor a panoramic view of the riverfront activity below her. As twilight fell, so did her strength and determination for her mission in St. Louis. Dismounting from Red Sky, she stood next to the paint gelding and held the long reins loosely in her hand, allowing him to graze. While he did, she turned toward the setting sun and slowly raised a hand to it, as if she could capture in her palm the warmth and solace this eternal source of light shed on its people. Finally, she lowered her fisted hand to her side.

She then inhaled deeply of the air, holding its freshness in her lungs for as long as she could before exhaling and giving herself up to the sunset. All around her, the brilliant, cloudless western sky faded to the deepening shades of purples and reds that would precede the ritual death of day. Soon, all around her would be black. Dark black. And she would be alone. Taylor tried desperately not to give in to the despair that ate at her. She tried to tell herself that this, too, would pass. She

would find answers. There would be solutions. And her life
would go on. Still, it took an act of will for her to force her
attention outward. She turned again, toward the east, and
gazed on the marvels below.

Impressive steamboats, an alien yet exciting sight to her,
plied the river's waters. Along its shores, docks and ware-
houses and scurrying men abounded. Carriages and wagons of
every description passed one another on the hard-packed dirt
roads along the waterway's busy banks. Tall ships with sails
of white sat at port, rocking gently in the water and the day's
shadows.

Taylor was amazed at the sights . . . and somehow soothed.
Moments and heartbeats passed. Thoughts and worries were
suspended. She lost herself in the excitement that lay below
her. She shook her head with the wonder of it all and even
realized she was grinning, feeling a bit overwhelmed with the
scurrying and busyness displayed below her, none of which
had anything to do with her or her problems.

But soon enough, her worries again overtook her thoughts.
She stepped back from the bluff's rocky edge and stood
watching Red Sky doze. The poor animal was exhausted. It
was her fault. She'd ridden around all day, not able to settle
on what she should do next. In her wanderings and wonder-
ings, she'd ended up here in the easternmost part of St. Louis.
She'd been wrong to come here. She meant to St. Louis itself,
not just this deserted bluff. She should have gone out West as
she'd planned and not listened to her mother. This city her
mother had sent her to was a place of dangerous secrets. And
the people here whom she knew, and whom she loved, when
they heard her name would not want her here.

Still, with night falling, with hardly any money to her name,
and hungry and tired, where could she go? To her father, who
thought her dead, then alive, then hanged for murder? No, she
couldn't go to him. She didn't want to go to him, she told
herself. Not like this, and not after her reception by Greyson
Talbott. All the disbelief, the harsh words, the loud voices. It
would be no different with her father. Taylor pronounced herself just not up to that again today.

Then, to Amanda? Taylor shook her head. That promised
to be yet another scene, more emotion, many questions . . . and
another possible rejection. Still, earlier that afternoon, after
she'd stalked out of Greyson's house, she had gone as far as
getting directions from the stable boy Calvin to the home of
Stanley and Camilla James, Amanda's parents. Taylor had
been surprised to find that, in a city this size, they lived in a
grand house just around a few fashionable blocks from Greyson's town house, which was not far from her father's home.
All these people, suddenly so important in her life, all lived
close together . . . as if they'd been gathered for her conve-
nience in finding them. But she felt it was more likely that the
spirits had united them here against her in one city.

Either way, she'd started on her way to Amanda's earlier.
In fact, Taylor had found the place. She'd sat her horse outside
the wrought-iron gates for a long time, staring at the three-
story whitewashed-brick house with many rooms. She recalled
thinking at the time how the huge homes, this one and those
she'd passed, were unfriendly, unapproachable, like the penitentiary where she'd spent two months. The high fences made
of iron. The closed gates. The long uninviting walks up to the
doors. The unseen people who lived behind the glass of the
windows. These things said keep away. Taylor had thought all
this, and then she had turned Red Sky's head in the other
direction, away from her childhood friend, toward the river
and the anonymity it offered. Her thought at the time had been
that Amanda had most likely changed from the girl Taylor
remembered, anyway. Why wouldn't she have? After all, Taylor knew herself not to be the laughing child full of mischief
and play that Amanda had loved.

Taylor knew she'd changed even more in the past day. And
not for the better. She hated the hesitance that had crept like
a thief into her heart. Only last night she had held no fear
inside her soul. She'd been walking right up to the door of
her father's home, intending to announce herself to him, when
Greyson Talbott had stopped her. And now, today, she was
not capable of doing that. What now was stopping her from
making herself known? She refused to accept that it was fear

stopping her. No, it had more to do with old lies that had been told. Lies about Amanda being dead. And now her family here believed her to be dead. Why had these lies been necessary? Taylor thought back to her mother's parting words, about being careful, about someone here who had reason to want her dead. Why?

And what, she asked herself, did this person have to gain by her death? Was so much at stake that this enemy would kill her to keep alive the lies? Taylor could only imagine what Amanda and her family had been told over the years. She figured they, too, must have believed her already dead since her father had. But what else had he been told in that message he'd got today, besides her being a convicted murderer? And why had her own mother told her all these years that Amanda had died? Taylor had no answers. All she knew was that something horrible was behind all this.

Something horrible. Her mother had known it to be true. She had sent Taylor here, but she had cautioned her. Against whom, though? Why hadn't she told her who her enemy was? Perhaps Tennie Nell Christie did not know who it was herself. Taylor slumped, knowing only that there was danger here. She could taste it, feel it. She believed that if she listened hard enough, she would hear the whispering evil that seemed to follow her every footstep, that seemed to suck onto every breath she took. Unknown, unseen evil. Lurking. Waiting. Biding its time, watching for her to make a mistake.

The horrible truth was that Taylor had a sinking feeling she'd already made the mistake this evil wanted her to make. And eating at her was the knowledge that she wasn't quite sure what that mistake had been.

Lost in such thoughts and holding her horse's reins, Taylor had allowed herself to be tugged along absently by Red Sky. Awakened from his momentary doze, he had begun grazing, his strong teeth pulling at the grass. Taylor stopped, belatedly realizing how close they were to the woods . . . and how tight her chest felt. A sudden unreasoning fear assaulted her. It prickled her skin, raced her heart, and had her darting gaze searching the shadows all around her. Her hands tensed around the reins. She wished for the gun that Greyson Talbott had taken from her last night. Red Sky jerked his head up and stared at her. Taylor knew she'd communicated her fear to the horse. But he stared at her, not around them as if his keener senses picked up anything threatening.

Taylor slumped, feeling silly and weak, like a frightened old woman. Had she expected a beast to jump out at them? Had she expected to see red glowing eyes, a skulking form drawing nearer?

She told herself that such a beast would be easier to fight than the worries that sapped her strength from within. But the truth was, at this moment, nothing of this world threatened. Instead, her fright had come from within. That being so, she looked inside herself for its source. And found it easily enough. The truth—the horrible truth—was that with all the lies that had been told, no one had any reason to believe she was who she was. But worse than that, Taylor was beginning to wonder if *she* was who she believed herself to be. After all, too many people told her she didn't exist. Could they all be wrong? Or was she?

She shook her head. That was a crazy thought. She had always been Taylor Christie James. Always. Other people's lies could not change that.

Still, Taylor shook her head, wanting to dislodge the awful doubts from her mind. What she needed to be concentrating on, she berated herself, was reviewing all of her actions of the past day until she could know with certainty what mistake she might have made that had her so scared now. But in that same instant, as if it had awaited only an unclaimed second of her time, her answer burst into her consciousness. And she hated it, hated admitting that her mistake may have been leaving the safety and protection that was Greyson Talbott.

Taylor grimaced. She hadn't wanted to think about him. In fact, she'd all but ridden around in circles today trying not to feel his tug on her, trying not to see in her mind his dark eyes, his wide mouth, the way he looked at her. Tried not to hear his laughter, tried not to see the mirth that lurked in his eyes . . . or the smoldering heat in their depths. She didn't want to feel warm or grateful or anything toward him. She didn't want to like him, couldn't afford to respect him. And yet . . . she did. Nothing could be worse. He was a white man, and for all she knew, he was also her enemy.

But could the truth be that instead of her enemy he was her refuge? Her heart thumped dully at such a notion. Still, Taylor forced herself to consider his actions . . . and found herself nodding. At the very least, he'd been trying to understand, trying to help her, trying to put the pieces together. And even though he still did not believe her, nevertheless he had opened his home and his mind to her. She believed that he did not know the truth behind the lies that clouded her life. She also knew of no reason that he should involve himself in her troubles, but he had. It was that simple—and not at all understandable. Not from Taylor's perspective. She didn't believe, if the situation were reversed and he needed her help, that she would have extended her hand to him.

But wait—she caught herself—it wasn't her he was protecting. It was her father, his friend. A surge of relief swept over Taylor. She had no need to be beholden to Greyson Talbott. All he'd offered her, on the one hand, was a prison that kept her from her father and the truth. But on the other, he'd offered to her his assistance in opening the elegant doors for her to St. Louis society—wherein lay, she just knew it now, the answers, the truths, she so desperately sought. Then why not let him? He was one of them and this was his city, while she was an outsider and was lost in this place. Every door was closed to her. On her own, she had not the money, the clothes, or the connections. Without those things, she had no doubt that she'd be thrown off such commanding estates as she needed entry to.

A rare burst of laughter bubbled up in Taylor. Not humorous laughter but self-mocking laughter. She was lost and alone in a bustling city populated with hundreds upon hundreds of white people—and she needed a white man to survive. The skills she possessed to survive in the wild could not help her here. She could not traverse these streets and alleys on her own. She knew the Nation like the back of her hand. She knew

The People, how they thought, what their beliefs were, what made them tick. But not these people. Not the whites. Among them, even with blood kin surrounding her, she was as helpless as a baby.

Taking Red Sky with her, Taylor walked back to the bluff's edge and stared down at the roaring waters of the river. The encroaching night made it harder to pick out details, but she could make out yet another steamboat plowing its way along to a wharf. Absently she watched it, marking its progress. In only moments it would dock. The people aboard would then leave and go conduct their business or go home. They belonged here. She didn't.

With that realization, gone instantly was her renewed direction. Futility again ate at her. What difference did finding the answers of her life make? All of a sudden she didn't care if Amanda or her father believed her to be alive or dead. She didn't care what Greyson's mother knew about her or thought of her. It just didn't matter. Just as it didn't matter what the mean Mrs. Scott said to her. Or the young maids. Taylor just didn't care. About them. Or about anything. What difference did it make to her if any of them lived or died? Were happy or sad? Warm and dry, or cold and wet? These people, these white people, were nothing to her . . . just as she was nothing to them. Their lives would go on after today, just as would hers, with or without her answers.

Red Sky stamped his hoof, signaling his impatience. Taylor stroked his neck, cooing softly to him. She asked herself why she didn't just do as her horse seemed to want. Ride away. Her mother wouldn't know. Taylor hated her disrespectful thought, hated the notion that she would not honor her mother. But her mother could not have known to what she was sending her daughter. What would be so awful, Taylor now mused, about her making her way out West, as she'd originally planned? Her life lay ahead of her. The only thing she couldn't do was return to the Nation, to her mother. A prick of sadness ate at Taylor's heart. She couldn't afford to think now of all she had lost. She had made her choices with Monroe Hammer.

She had no one to blame but herself for her banishment from all she knew and loved.

This world, the white man's world, then, was now her world. She had to learn how to survive in it. An ugly grimace at such an unthinkable fate cramped Taylor's features. Then, pride welled up in her heart. She would do this. She'd never been bested. She would not be so now. Why was she thinking of leaving, of running away? What was she afraid of? Dying? No. Death would come to her one day, as it did to everyone. Dying was easy. It was living that was hard.

Then . . . Taylor asked herself *. . . I am staying?* She would learn why her mother had sent her here. Why she had told Taylor she would be safe here. Taylor felt anything but safe. She was hungry and tired and her clothes were confining. And she was alone. She was all those things. But not safe.

Safe. The word was a strange notion to Taylor. Had she ever been safe? With her mother, yes. With Monroe Hammer, no. And now, outside the Nation? She shook her head, saying she wasn't so sure. And why did she have a sudden need to be safe? To feel protected? She never had before. Even with her mother and then with Monroe, she'd made her own way, had stayed whole unto herself. Why should now, in the space of a day, be different? Why?

Again . . . quietly, unbidden and on silent paws like those of a cat . . . came the creeping image of herself in Greyson Talbott's home. She'd felt safe there. With him. Rare tears now stood in Taylor's eyes. She'd felt safe with a white man. In his home. Lying in a bed that he'd provided . . . and sleeping soundly with him only a room away. Eating his food last night. Then today, wearing clothes he'd bought for her. Again eating his food today, food she'd snatched up from the kitchen on her way out of his house this morning.

Taylor blinked, her blurred vision regarding her horse's coarse mane. She was changed. Greyson Talbott had changed her. She didn't know how . . . or when. But he had. The best evidence of that was his face swimming in her mind when she thought about leaving here. His name was the only one she hadn't dismissed when she'd said she didn't care. His and the man-bird Bentley's. Her spirit guide. She'd separated herself from him. Rube's curse suddenly pushed its way into her mind. If she ignored the signs, the old Cherokee guard had said, she would be destroyed . . . she and everyone she loved or would come to love.

The implications were more than Taylor could stand. She had to go back to Greyson Talbott. Sniffling, wiping at her eyes, Taylor took a deep breath. Night was upon her. The air was turning colder. And she had someplace to be. With that decision, and refusing to think further than that, she hitched up her red satin skirt and mounted herself atop Red Sky. She urged the tired horse to turn around and then directed him back down the dusty trail, away from the wooded bluff that overlooked the river. She would make her way back the way she had come. And she would find her answers.

Chapter Nine

Taylor didn't come here to her aunt and uncle's. Drat. Maybe she couldn't because she isn't who she says she is. Maybe I fell for the lies of an opportunistic charlatan. No, I just can't believe that. She is Taylor Christie James. She is. And she's not here. Where the devil can she be? Grey cursed himself and Taylor. Here he'd changed his, his brother's, and Charles James's early plans for the evening. Their meeting up at the men's club was out. Dinner at the senior Jameses' was in. Wanting to see them all interact with Taylor present, Grey had sent notes around to Charles and his brother, telling them to meet him here. Then he'd shamelessly set about getting himself and Charles invited to the intimate dinner party already planned for this evening.

But Taylor wasn't here. He knew that because of the tears being shed here this evening over their belief in her recent death. Real tears.

Still, foiled or not in his plans, it was a fine, starry night. A gentle breeze wafted in through the opened windows of the room, lifting the sheer draperies and cooling the air inside the formal parlor of Stanley and Camilla James's impressive mansion. They were all here, the elder Jameses and their daughter, Amanda; Grey's mother; his brother, Franklin. Charles James was present, too, and, of course, Grey. The topic of conversation, following a late supper hardly anyone had been able to eat, remained the recent death by hanging of Charles's daughter, Taylor, niece to Stanley and Camilla, cousin to Amanda.

A whiskey in his hand, Grey stood by the marbled fireplace, an elbow propped on the polished mantel. He gravely watched all faces and listened carefully to every word and

evaluated each nuance or hesitation in their speech. These people and their conversation were vital to Taylor . . . wherever
she was.

"Oh, Charles, it just cannot be true. I do not believe it."
Camilla James's voice was strident with emotion . . . honest
emotion, Grey believed. "I refuse to believe that a daughter
of . . ." She stopped, looked down at her hands folded in her
lap, took a breath, and then went on. "A daughter of yours
would do such a thing. Murdering someone. Do you think she
could?"

Grey watched Charles rub at his brow. "The truth is we
don't know how she grew up to be, Camilla. Or what she was
capable of."

"It's all so tragic, Charles. It simply cannot be true. A
young woman hanged?" Camilla's voice broke on the word
hanged. She shivered. "It's barbaric."

Grey fervently wished he could ease everyone's grief with
the truth that Taylor lived . . . but how could he? He didn't yet
know who in this room crowded with Jameses and Talbotts
he could trust with that knowledge. Perhaps the most troubling
realization to Grey was that his mother had not yet mentioned
that only today she'd met a Miss James at Grey's town house.
Grey had his own reasons for keeping quiet on that score, but
what were hers? Was she waiting to see what, if anything,
he'd say about Taylor?

Camilla sobbed, this time breaking down into tears. Stanley, her husband, turned to her, putting a comforting arm
around her shoulder. He gently squeezed her hands, which
were fisted around a tear-dampened handkerchief in her lap.
"Now, dear, don't upset yourself. You've been crying since
this afternoon when Augusta told us about Charles's unfortunate message. You'll become ill again if you don't get yourself
under control."

"I'm so sorry, Stanley. But this is all so upsetting." Camilla
James struggled for control and then pulled her hands free of
her husband's. She focused on Charles again. "Can we believe
this message? To me, it's no more than a cruel stunt. It has
to be." She dabbed at her eyes with her hankie. "What good

does it do to renew your grief after all this time? This is twice you've had to grieve for your dear Taylor."

"We all are grieving," Charles replied, looking stricken. "But I believe the message. I do."

"Why do you believe it, Charles?" Stanley asked his brother. The hardness in his voice captured Grey's attention.

Charles stared at his brother, his color heightening. "Because her . . . her mother sent it."

Just as Taylor surmised this morning, was Grey's confirming thought.

"Did she indeed?" Stanley further prodded, his voice cold.

Grey noticed that Camilla James sat rigidly quiet at her husband's side. Her face had drained of color. She stared wide-eyed at Charles . . . with a pleading expression on her face. Grey had no idea what to make of this.

"Yes, she did," Charles said, his voice just as steely as his older brother's had been. "And no, Stanley, she didn't tell me why she'd allowed me to believe all these years that Taylor was already dead. Isn't that what you were going to ask me?"

Stanley James gave a sly smirk. "Yes, of course. And how perfectly awful of her mother to let you think your daughter dead. Perfectly awful."

Camilla hadn't moved. But Charles's color heightened. He looked away and then down. What in the world was Stanley driving at? And Charles . . . was that guilt marring his features? Grey stared at the man he'd been championing through all this. Was *he* hiding something?

Just then, Charles looked up, capturing his sister-in-law's gaze. "I wanted to come tell you straightaway, Camilla. But I made it only as far as Grey's this morning. I'm sorry. I just didn't know how to tell you." His eyes widened and he added, "All of you, I mean. I didn't know how to tell all of you."

Charles's quick amendment heightened Grey's suspicions. His last words drew attention now to the fact that up until now his words had essentially been private ones to Camilla. What could that mean?

"Yes, it must have been awfully hard for you, Charles," Stanley James said, although his hard tone of voice belied his words of sympathy. "But why *did* you go to young Greyson here? I had no idea he knew anything at all about your . . . Taylor."

"It's no mystery, Stanley," Charles said stiffly. "I told Grey one night long ago at the club when I was overcome with—forgive me, ladies—drink and my continuing grief. He's been a true and faithful friend ever since."

All eyes were on Grey now. He nodded his acknowledgment of the compliment.

"Yes," Grey's mother, Augusta, added, drawing everyone's attention her way. "My elder son can be an excellent keeper of secrets."

"A trait I learned from you, Mother." Grey returned his mother's pointed stare. She referred, no doubt, to his secret harboring of Taylor Christie James in his town house. "Or at least I *thought* you could keep a secret," he amended. "That was before you apparently made your way to Charles's after leaving my place this morning. I should think you'd be exhausted this evening, Mother, what with all your gadding about. First my place. Then Charles's. And finally here with hurtful news that wasn't yours to impart."

Amid the gasps that followed his chastising speech, Grey's mother drew herself up in outrage. "First of all, I went to Charles out of concern, to see what was the matter and if I could help. He was so distraught, I told him I would come here to break the news and to offer my support at such a hard time. And furthermore, Stanley—and Camilla, of course—are dear friends who are about to become *our* family. I never meant to hurt anyone. I thought only of the scandal that would attach itself to such a revelation, if it were to get out. Of *course* we must consider Franklin and Amanda's upcoming wedding. As well as Franklin's campaign for mayor. Something like this, if it isn't handled properly, could ruin us all socially, as well as politically. And I have no intention of allowing that to happen."

"That was quite a speech, Mother." How well he knew her fervent aspirations to be the toast of St. Louis and at the very top of the social stratosphere. Franklin's upcoming brilliant marriage to Amanda James, as well as his being elected mayor, would cement that position for Augusta. Grey wondered how far she would go if anyone or anything threatened to upset those two applecarts for her. She could be ruthless. It was a chilling thought. "Forgive me for questioning your motives. I should have known you would place friendship and concern above political and social expediency."

Augusta Talbott forced tears to her eyes, which was how Grey always thought of his mother's shows of emotion. "Greyson, you always assign me the lowest of motives." She turned to the elder Jameses. "I assure you that I rushed here forthwith only out of concern for you and, as I said, to offer you my support and whatever comfort I could."

Everyone, all at once, rushed to assure her that they believed her. Everyone except Grey. Instead, he focused his attention inward as he mulled over the many unasked questions he still had for his mother, questions he couldn't ask in this company. For instance, how had *she* known about Taylor to begin with? Through her friendship with Camilla James? That made sense. After all, his mother was always over here, it seemed. More intriguing to Grey was why it had seemed his mother already hated the young woman—before she ever found out from Charles the nature of the message he'd received. Even more nagging was his original question: why hadn't she told anyone here that she had seen Taylor alive only today?

"Now, Grey, do apologize," Amanda remonstrated above the ebbing tide of indignant sputterings. Her gentle yet reproving voice quieted them all. "We're here tonight at your instigation, after all. To help Uncle Charles especially. But also to support each other through this time of grief for us all. And not to deal with our own personalities."

Grey raised his crystal glass of whiskey to Amanda in a salute. He then turned to his mother. "I do apologize, Mother, if I've upset you. I meant no harm. I will endeavor to show our family and friends that I can behave as well as the next person."

Thus sustained, Augusta Talbott regally ducked her head.

But not before Grey saw the angry gleam in her dark eyes. He was not forgiven. Nor would she forget. Neither would he.

"I agree with Amanda, Grey," Franklin suddenly put in needlessly, like a true politician. "Please exert some control over your behavior. This is a most exceptional circumstance, one requiring all our attention. There are many factors at play here, as Mother has duly and accurately pointed out. Things we need to consider in the cool light of reason, in order to form a more perfect response to any—"

"Oh, dear God, spare us the campaign rhetoric, Franklin. We're all going to vote for you, I'm sure. Besides, you're being exceedingly boring, little brother. Even Mother says so." Grey skewered his mother with a grin and a glare. "Don't you, Mother?"

Well, that got everyone talking and protesting at once. And got Grey ignored, again. That was fine with him. He spent his time sipping his whiskey and studying his family and friends. Clustered together in a C-shaped sitting arrangement facing the huge marble-inlaid fireplace sat the fair-haired and blue-eyed Stanley with his lovely wife, Camilla, a dark-haired, elegant woman and a sweet, gentle soul. In the upholstered chair next to their settee sat Amanda, their blond and beautiful daughter, who took after her father. Behind her chair, his hand resting lightly on her shoulder, stood Franklin, Grey's brother, a younger version of Grey, only a boring one. On a medallion-back sofa and opposite the elder Jameses sat Charles James— Amanda's uncle and Taylor's father. Next to him was Grey's own mother, the coolly elegant Augusta Talbott.

For his part, Grey still stood beside the fireplace, an elbow perched atop its polished mantel, a whiskey in his hand. His inspired plan, one that had come to him earlier as he'd sat in his library at home, was to get them all here where he could watch them. He had no doubt in his mind that the person or persons responsible for the troubles surrounding Taylor were sitting in this room. These people were everyone in St. Louis who knew of her existence, everyone to whom she was related, and everyone who would have a reason to love her, to hate her, or to harbor a desire to harm her. Nothing could have made Grey sicker, either. He also knew and loved every person present. But one or more of them meant harm to Taylor and maybe her father.

It had not escaped Gray's attention, either, that the one thing no one had done yet this evening was talk about Taylor herself. Not one good memory. Not one bad one. Nothing sweet or tender or loving. Nothing. Of course, they hadn't seen Taylor, according to her and borne out here this evening, since she was nine years old. But still, Grey mused, there wasn't one happy memory these people had of her as a baby, as a child? Did no one know her at all? He would have thought that Càmilla and Amanda would remember her. After all, they had lived with Taylor and her mother for several formative years of both girls' lives.

In fact, Taylor alleged that she and Amanda had been raised practically as sisters. If that was true, then this lack of sharing of memories made no sense . . . unless a reason existed for their not wanting to talk about Taylor among themselves. Could that be it? That was entirely possible. *My God, poor Taylor. What are these secrets and mysteries that surround her? Such a pretty girl.* Grey shook his head. Taylor wasn't pretty, not in the conventional sense of beauty. *Striking. Arresting. Heart-stopping.* Those were words better suited to her. Grey sighed. God, a liar or not, charlatan or not, how he missed her. How he wondered where she was tonight. Was she safe? Hungry? Warm? Dry?

"Are you all right, Grey? You look a little . . . I don't know . . . pensive, I suppose. And you're sighing."

"Not possible. I don't sigh, I assure you." Still, Grey spared a smile for Amanda. The others talked on around them. Franklin excused himself from Amanda's side to go speak with his mother.

When he did, Amanda gave Grey a gentle reproof. "You shouldn't be so mean to your brother, you scoundrel. And don't think I don't see through you. You love him."

Grey pretended shock. "I hardly think so." Then he grinned. "You won't tell him, will you?"

Amanda's dark eyes, though red-rimmed with recent tears,

sparkled with amusement. "Your secret's safe with me."

Grey leaned in toward Amanda. "Have I said lately how lucky a fellow I believe my younger brother to be? To have such a lovely and intelligent young woman such as yourself love him must mean he has some redeeming qualities."

Amanda squeezed Grey's hand affectionately. "You're too kind."

"Now that is the worst thing you could say about me. It would quite ruin my reputation." He chuckled along with her and then sobered, adding, "Amanda, if I haven't said so before now, I'm so very sorry for your, uh, loss."

Amanda sobered, too. This time she was the one to sigh. "Oh, Grey, it's so sad. I loved Taylor fiercely when I was a little girl."

Even in the face of her crumpling expression, but knowing as he did that Taylor lived, excitement sped through Grey. He swallowed and tried not to sound too fiercely interested. "That's the spirit, Amanda. Tell me something about her. I hear it's good for the bereaved to talk about the, uh, deceased."

"I would love to talk about her with someone, Grey. Mother is too distraught. Father simply won't allow her name to be brought up. And poor Franklin, he becomes too upset for me if I cry over her." Amanda stopped . . . a dawning thought evidently washing her features in a heightened color. She put a hand on Grey's arm. "Oh, how callous of me. I am so sorry. You've suffered a loss, too, and aren't comfortable talking about this, are you?"

Confused, Grey frowned and couldn't think who the devil— "Oh, you mean my father? That was seven years ago, Amanda. I assure you I've come to terms with his demise. He was elderly and sick most of my life and is now in a much better place, the old rascal. God rest his soul."

Amanda smiled sweetly. "You men. You have such a hard time admitting your feelings of a tender nature."

"We men know it's best to leave the tenderness in capable female hands." Grey returned her smile and endeavored to get them back to the subject that most interested him tonight— anything at all he could learn about Taylor, anything that would tell him she was real or even that she was playing him false. "I would love to hear you talk about your cousin, Amanda. Anything at all you remember. Like the color of her eyes."

Amanda plunked her hands together in her lap, smiling dreamily. "Blue. Like her father's."

"That's the first thing I noticed—" Grey cut his words off just in time. His heart thumped rapidly in his chest. With effort, he composed his features. "I'm sorry. Go ahead."

Amanda eyed him askance but continued. "Well, her eyes *were* blue. That bright and striking blue you can't help but notice. They just take your breath away. Even as a little girl, I envied her those eyes. Alas, mine are the same mud brown as my mother's."

"Nonsense, Amanda. You have the soft and winsome eyes of a doe. A man could lose himself in them."

Amanda pulled back and grinned. "If I didn't know better, Greyson Talbott, I'd say you were trying to turn my head. And aren't you the romantic?"

"Hardly. Now, my dear sister-in-law-to-be, what's your best memory of this little girl of Charles's?"

Amanda chuckled softly. "She was wild, Grey. Bold and strong and outspoken. Very intelligent. Mother says Taylor was reading in two languages by the time she was five. At that age, I was still at my mother's knee, but Taylor was off riding a full-grown horse bareback all over the countryside. Mother, of course, remembers her better and is always talking about her to me."

"But you must have some memories of her of your own," Grey immediately prompted. "Search your memory." The truth was, he simply wanted to hear more. He tried to convince himself that he was merely seeking the truth about Taylor. Apparently she hadn't lied about her relationship with Amanda or the living arrangement between the two women and their daughters all those years ago. Something else occurred to him. He counted backward and came up with the War Between the States. That may have had something to do with the women being alone together. But in the Cherokee Nation? "Amanda,"

Grey began, "what was your mother doing with the Indians?"

"Mostly trying to educate them and convert them, I suppose. Her parents were Baptist missionaries working amongst the Cherokee."

Grey absently rubbed at his chin. "I see. That makes sense, then."

Amanda nodded. "You should talk to Mother about her. All I can tell you is Taylor was everything I wasn't. I was quiet and timid and shy. Always in Taylor's shadow—and gladly so." Amanda clasped her hands together. Her expression was the most animated one Grey had ever seen on her lovely face. "Oh, Grey, I would give anything if I could just see her one more time. I loved her with all my soul. I did. I'll bet she was the most beautiful woman on the face of the earth. Just full of spit and passion like she was at nine when I last saw her."

Amanda suddenly tugged Grey close to her and whispered, "I confess I was terrified of her. Yet I adored her at the same time."

Once again Grey had to bite back words that had almost slipped past his lips. "I know just how you feel," he'd almost said. Still not trusting his ability to keep from blurting something provocative, Grey stood up again. And realized the room had grown quiet at some point. Everyone else present had been listening to Amanda talk to him about Taylor. Grey cleared his throat and looked at each of them in turn. He finally focused on Charles. "Your daughter sounds as if she was a magnificent girl."

The man looked as if Grey had hit him in the stomach. His expression twisted and his color heightened. "I wouldn't know, Grey," he said, giving a sad shake of his blond head. "I only saw her a few times in her entire life. And now . . . she's lost to me forever. My only child."

Camilla James immediately burst into tears. Stanley once again comforted her. Charles James crumpled. Grey's mother patted his hand comfortingly and glared at Grey. Amanda was again sobbing, her hands over her face. Franklin scurried back to her side and began uttering boring, useless little clichés about being a brave girl and so on.

And Grey felt terrible. Well, he'd certainly made a fine showing of it here tonight. What an ass he could be. But on the other hand, he'd learned quite a bit, too. Quite a revealing and interesting bit. Once again, all eyes—reproachful eyes— were on him. He bowed to the sad assemblage and said, "I am profoundly sorry for your loss. And I am sorry if I've deepened your sorrow in any way. It was never my intention. I think it would be best if I said good night now. Please, don't get up. I'll show myself out."

For as long as she lived, Taylor vowed, she would never understand white people.

Once she'd arrived back at Greyson Talbott's town house and boldly entered his property through the coach yard, just as she'd done last night, Taylor had been beset by a joyously confusing homecoming. Much to her astonishment, she'd been greeted like a victorious warrior by Calvin and the remainder of the men in the yard. They'd actually cheered when they spied her, which had caused Red Sky to rear and the men to scatter. A lesser rider than Taylor would have been unseated.

But once she'd got her horse under control and had dismounted . . . and while she'd been silently wondering what exactly was going on here . . . she'd been startled by Calvin, who'd stepped up to lead a suddenly docile Red Sky away. The stable boy had said he would brush and rub down the tired horse. Calvin assured her he would then give Red Sky a bag of oats. With that, the other men had cheerily escorted her to the back door and told her that Mr. Talbott was out for the evening. Taylor had drawn the only conclusion she could. The men were glad he was gone. Only that could account for the unfathomable high spirits that seemed to have seized Greyson Talbott's employees.

Once she'd been all but carried to the back door—and again like last night—there had stood Bentley in the open doorway. Only this time he'd been as overawed to see her as she'd been with him last night. He'd clasped her hands and then forgotten himself and hugged her tightly. He'd all but dragged her into the kitchen for Cook to make over her. And that tiny tornado of a person had shrieked happily, forced Taylor into a chair, and then proceeded to feed her to death. Silently, having not said one word since she'd arrived, so surprised was she by her reception, Taylor had eaten out of fear of what the crazy white people would do to her if she didn't.

After she'd eaten, she'd meant to slip away to her room, but that was not to be. Mrs. Scott had presented herself in the kitchen. Bentley and Cook had sobered and then had quietly slipped out of the room. Alone with the woman who'd called her names that morning and whose life Taylor had herself threatened, Taylor had slowly stood up, not knowing what to expect. She'd got her biggest surprise of all. The woman had burst into tears and had twisted her apron in her hands and had begged Taylor to forgive her for her unkind words. The stout older woman had even told Taylor she wouldn't blame her if she wanted to scalp her. She'd even said she deserved it. Taylor had assured her she was forgiven and that she didn't feel a scalping offense had been committed.

And that had led to further happy insanities. A bath had been drawn. The giggling chambermaids had unbraided and washed Taylor's hair. They'd taken away the dusty and rumpled clothes that earlier that day had been her new finery. Then they'd assisted her, against her wishes, with her actual bathing. Taylor had endured all this silently. She'd also absolved Greyson Talbott of any fault for his employees' behavior. Taylor now blamed everything on the full moon outside. It was the only explanation she could come up with for the lunacy that surrounded her.

After her bath, she'd been pulled and poked into a white cotton nightgown of her own . . . one purchased that morning by Mrs. Scott . . . and had finally been left alone in her room for the remainder of the evening. She'd locked the doors. Both of them. The one to the hall and the one that led to the dressing room between her and Greyson's bedrooms. Then, she had stayed put until she'd felt reasonably certain that the spirit-possessed people had gone to bed. Only then had she donned a wrapper and tied it around her waist. Then, and gingerly, she'd unlocked the door to the hall.

Outside her room, she'd stopped, looked, and listened. And sighed with relief. Blessedly, she appeared to be the only one about. So she'd sneaked downstairs to the library. She couldn't sleep. Perhaps she was overly tired. And her stomach still hurt from supper. She'd lit the lamp, selected a book to read from those nestled in the stacks on the shelves, and settled herself into a comfortable leather chair that faced the door.

And now, with her legs outstretched, her bare feet propped up on the big desk, she was enjoying a good book, a whiskey, and a thin cigar.

When the door across the way opened, Taylor started. She looked up, the cigar clamped between her teeth, a short crystal tumbler of whiskey in her hand, and the book propped up on her thighs. Into the room stepped the master of the house. Greyson Talbott. Taylor struggled to have no reaction at all, such as guiltily jumping up or dropping the glass or sucking air and choking cigar smoke into her lungs.

"I saw the light under the door," he said simply.

Taylor nodded slowly and stared back at him through the blue haze of the cigar smoke curling around her head.

"Calvin said you'd come back."

She nodded again, desperate to maintain her Cherokee impassivity and at the same time not choke on cigar smoke. Both things were hard to do. For one thing, she felt the least bit guilty about being caught here. Guilty and vulnerable, somehow. But wreaking the most havoc with her imperturbability was . . . the impressive man had apparently begun undressing before he'd come in here. His dark suit coat was thrown over his arm, his vest was unbuttoned, and his collar was open . . . So were the first two buttons of his white shirt. At his neck, and through the vee opening there, Taylor could see dark, crisp, and curling hair peeking out.

Pulling the cigar from her mouth, she exhaled the smoke and swallowed, refusing to acknowledge to herself that she was affected. But she was. Cherokee men didn't have much, if any, chest hair. Her traitorous mind wondered what it would feel like to run her fingers through it. But with the cigar still held between her fingers, all she could do was thoughtfully roll it . . . until she caught the drift of her thoughts. Quickly, guiltily, Taylor poked the cigar back in her mouth, clamping down on its innocent length with more force than was necessary.

She met Greyson Talbott's gaze. He'd caught her looking. There was awareness in his dark eyes now that hadn't been there a moment ago. Taylor raised her chin, daring him to say or do anything about it. He didn't. But still, silence between them reigned. She watched him scan her cozy den, fully assess the degree to which she'd encroached on his private territory, and again meet her waiting gaze.

"Thought I'd check with you. I just like to make sure my guests are comfortable. Do you have everything you need?" Amusement laced the sarcasm evident in his voice.

With every appearance of a calm she didn't feel, Taylor again unclamped the cigar from between her teeth. She glanced at it and realized she'd nearly bit it in two when he'd walked in. Expertly she exhaled the hazy blue smoke and took a sip of her—his—whiskey. She grimaced at the burning trail it made down her throat, and then considered him standing there across the way, his hand still on the doorknob.

"I have everything I need," she assured him.

Greyson Talbott quirked his mouth, as if fighting a grin, and nodded. "Good. I'd hoped you'd feel comfortable enough here to ask if you couldn't find what you wanted. But now I see I shouldn't have worried."

Taylor tried not to feel the sting of his reproof that clearly said she was the intruder here. Instead, her mind insisted on focusing on details other than manners. For one thing, this man made quite the sight standing there. Tall. Muscled. Handsome. And slightly amused . . . yet sensually aware of her. Very aware. Taylor took in a shallow breath, the only kind she could with her chest so tight. She couldn't lie to herself. She was just as affected by him. He stirred feelings inside her that she'd already acknowledged to herself, feelings she was also determined to keep to herself. She tried again for a deep calming breath . . . and didn't have to be told what kind of a sight she made. It was there on Greyson's face. He couldn't take his eyes off her legs.

Mainly because they were crossed at the ankles . . . and bared all the way up to her lap, where her gown and wrapper had pooled when she'd propped her feet up. Taylor's fingers tightened around the tumbler she still held. She had never before been so acutely aware of her limbs. Under his scrutiny, they seemed to throb with a life of their own . . . a pulsing, hot vitality that centered itself about where her bedclothes had. And yet she refused to reach out to cover them from his sight. She couldn't—her hands were full . . . and his hot stare froze her in place.

"You'd better knock your ashes off before you burn yourself."

Taylor blinked, frowning, not comprehending what he meant. He pointed to her cigar. She looked at it perched there between two of her fingers and saw that he was right. A light gray and impressive length of burning ash was about to cascade onto her. Coolly, as if she'd intended to do so all along, she did as he suggested. She tamped the cigar lightly over the ashtray and turned back to him. "Thank—"

He was closing the door behind him. Then he leaned a shoulder against its solidness, tossed his coat onto a nearby chair, and crossed his arms over his muscled chest. With a knee bent, causing the muscles of his thigh to strain against the fawn-colored fabric of his trousers, Greyson Talbott stared back at her. Several things occurred to Taylor, none of them innocent. The two of them were alone together in the same room . . . and weren't about to be interrupted. It was late at night. She was in his house willingly this time and dressed for bed . . . which was where he clearly wanted to take her.

She tilted her head at a wondering angle . . . and wondered what she'd do if he made such a suggestion. She wasn't so sure she'd refuse. She had every reason in the world to turn him down and only one to accept: she wanted to. That was all the provocation she'd ever needed before. But none of those men had been white and possibly her enemy.

Before she could digest that thought, one that had the effect of a cold splash of water in her face, Greyson started toward her. "Mind if I join you? I sometimes enjoy a good cigar and a whiskey myself before I go to bed."

The closer he came to her, the harder her heart thumped . . . and the more her body tingled. Giving nothing away, Taylor shrugged and took a nonchalant sip of her drink. "Help yourself," she said. "It's your house."

"That's right. It is." His voice held a pleasant, conversational note as he stepped past her. She caught a whiff of his masculine scent . . . which was already mixed with a hint of cool night air, liquor, and tobacco. And excitement.

Taylor couldn't see him now but knew, from her own earlier actions and from the sounds she heard behind her, what he was doing. On a small sideboard back there sat a crystal whiskey service that resided atop an ornate silver tray. He was pouring himself a splash . . . a generous splash . . . of the intoxicant. Taylor quirked her mouth, admiring the respectable amount of liquor he'd served himself. Then, the sound following that had to be him choosing a cigar from the humidor and lighting it, she surmised.

In another moment, he would join her. She blinked, concentrating now on herself. This was her chance. Gingerly holding her drink up out of her own way and sticking the thin, half-smoked cigar in the ashtray at her elbow, she lowered her feet to the floor, put the book on the desk, and pitched forward to jerk her bed gown and wrapper over her legs. Quickly she resettled herself and grabbed up the smoking tobacco.

Just then, Greyson stepped around her, coming into view holding his own whiskey and a lit cigar, of course. He stood directly in front of her, close enough for her to nudge him with a toe, if she'd been so inclined. An exaggerated expression of disappointment rode his features. "Oh, please, Taylor," he drawled, "you don't have to make yourself presentable on my account."

Unexpectedly she felt a heated blush claim her cheeks. Taylor had no idea when the last time she'd blushed had been. She'd believed herself too jaded to feel shame or chastisement strongly. But now, and with this man, she felt . . . unarmed, unsure of herself. And she hated that. It was a weakness. She made a show of setting the whiskey glass down on the small padded table next to her chair. She then crushed the cigar stub out and made as if to stand up. "I'll leave you to your late-night enjoyments."

Greyson took the cigar out of his mouth and stopped her with a single word. "No." Then he added, "Please. I want to talk to you."

Chapter Ten

Warily Taylor resettled herself in the chair and watched Greyson one-handedly tug a leather ottoman toward her, all without spilling a drop of his liquor. Despite herself, she noted the thrilling bulge of his arm muscles under his shirt as he labored. And the way his eyes squinted against the smoke from the thin cigar clamped between his teeth.

When he had the ottoman where he wanted it—directly in front of her—he mounted it like he would a horse and sat straddled atop it, his knees to either side of hers. He leaned in toward her, making her feel trapped and small. Her expression hardened, became a grim warning for him not to encroach any farther. Gone were her earlier feelings of passion for him. This was to be an inquisition. Taylor said or did nothing that would let him know she was the least bit frightened . . . because she wasn't.

All while staring at her—a clear attempt to intimidate her, she suspected—he handled the cigar, exhaled smoke, took a healthy sip of his drink, and clamped the cigar back in his mouth. She said nothing. In the next moment, he removed the cigar from his mouth and abruptly asked, "Where'd you go today? You didn't go to your aunt and uncle's. I just came from there. Or your father's. He was there, too. And everyone was sad because of your hanging."

Taylor tilted her head at an insulted angle and brushed back the long black hair that spilled forward with her movement. She sat up and tugged the heavy silken mass over her shoulders, out of her way. This motion also bought her time to formulate her answer. She wasn't about to tell him she'd done nothing but wander the city aimlessly like a frightened child, afraid to confront her white kin. When she again met his gaze, she realized from the glimmer in his dark eyes that he hadn't missed a single, apparently sensual, movement of hers.

Taylor knew how to quell that look. She narrowed her eyes and glared, much like a threatened wolf would. "I don't answer to you."

She braced herself for his reaction. Monroe Hammer would have slapped her, had she spoken to him in such a way. But all this man, this big white man, did was nod and grin. "No, you don't. And you don't have to tell me. You're right. I'm sorry for my prying question. Let me ask something more nicely. Why'd you come back here?"

He wasn't sorry, and wasn't asking nicely. She'd been fooled by his smile. Taylor's jaw worked with her rising anger and her humiliation at having to admit the truth. "I came back because I had no choice."

"I see." Again holding her gaze with the piercing strength of his own, he put the cigar to his lips, inhaled, then turned his head to blow out the smoke. Then he took a sip of his whiskey, eyeing her over the rim of his round crystal glass as he did. Lowering his drink, and with the cigar clutched expertly in his other hand, he said, pleasantly enough, "If you ask me, you had plenty of choices of places to go. If not your father's or your uncle's, then a hotel. A boardinghouse. Any of those. And probably some others I haven't thought of. So, why'd you come back here to me? The way I see it, if you're expecting me to feed and house you and your horse, then you owe me an answer. An honest answer."

He was right. She knew that. But it didn't make it any easier for her to swallow the lump of pride hurting her throat. Nor did it make her feel more kindly disposed toward him. It finally occurred to her, though, that she could save face by using his words from last night against him. "I came back here tonight for the same reason you brought me here last night. I do not know who I can trust. I do not know who is telling these lies that I am dead. Or why they would."

He exhaled gustily. "Well, you were right on one score this afternoon. Your father said this evening that your mother sent the letter regarding your hanging. So it probably happened like you said. But knowing that doesn't change anything. We may know who, but we don't know why. So I believe you're still in some sort of danger and must be careful whom you trust. But apparently, since you're here, you trust me, right?"

Taylor shrugged. "I have no reason not to. You say you care because of your friendship with my father. And that is good. It means you will seek the same answers that I am. And from the same people. For those reasons, I am here with you now, in your home."

Taylor watched him nod, watched him roll his cigar between his fingers. He suddenly looked up, sending her a sidelong glance through long, thick eyelashes. "I see. So you thought we should join forces?"

Taylor would give no quarter. "No. I did not think this. I know this. I have no choice because this is your town. These are your people. And I do not know the way of things here. You do."

"Well," he said with a chuckle, "I thought I did before last night when I met you. But let me tell you something about my evening, Taylor. From the looks of things here in my study, yours was better than mine. But before I do, do you need any further fortification?" He indicated her empty whiskey glass.

Taylor shook her head no. She believed she needed a clear head for this talk. "I am fine."

He chuckled. "Yes, Taylor, you are. You are very fine."

She took his meaning. So did her body. An unbidden thrill of desire danced along her nerve endings. But she kept her impassive expression in place.

"I spoke with Amanda James this evening," he said abruptly. "She tells me you have the bluest eyes she's ever seen. She envies you your eyes."

Surprise had Taylor dropping her stoic pose. She sat forward eagerly. "You have seen Amanda?" She forgot herself enough to clutch at his shirtsleeve. Under her hand, his arm felt hard and warm. "What is she like? How does she look? Did she ask about me?"

"Whoa there. One question at a time." He moved, dislodging her hand so he could rest his glowing cigar on the edge of his desk. He placed his drink next to it, and then surprised Taylor by taking her hand in his. Her breath caught when he slowly rubbed his thumb back and forth over her palm. With her lips parted and her breathing shallow, Taylor pronounced herself glad he wasn't looking into her eyes. Instead, he had his gaze trained on his actions with her hand.

When he spoke, soft and low, she had to lean forward to hear him. "First of all, Amanda's beautiful. She's blond and her eyes are brown. She's slender. An elegant young woman. Tender-hearted. Intelligent. No silly miss." He glanced up now, met Taylor's gaze. His expression was sober . . . and watchful. "And no, she didn't ask about you. How could she? She was crying, Taylor, because she believes you to be dead . . . again."

Taylor sat back, tugging her hand out of his. But she couldn't look away from the sharp intelligence in his eyes. "Again? Then she was also lied to? Was she told, as I was about her, that I died when still a child?"

He nodded. "Apparently. That's what everyone appeared to believe."

"Everyone?"

"Your father. My mother. Amanda. Her parents. And my brother, Franklin. We all had supper together at your aunt and uncle's. And I have to tell you, of them all only Franklin seemed to have no clue about what had happened in your and your family's pasts."

Taylor's mind flitted past the reference to his brother and mother in order to get to the other people Greyson had named. A hunger to see these people she loved ate at her, had her eyes wide and rounded with want. "You saw . . . my Aunt Camilla?"

"Yes. She's extremely upset over the news that you were hanged a month ago for murder. As is your Uncle Stanley."

Taylor exhaled her sadness. "I barely knew him, my father's brother. Or even my father. But still, I have brought shame to my family." Then she thought of something else. "You did not tell them that I am not dead, that I'm here?"

"No. I didn't. Because, well, I don't know yet who to trust, myself."

Defeat ate at Taylor. "You still don't believe I am who I say I am?"

He nodded. "Oh, yes. I do. I believe you. In fact, I'd pretty much come to the same conclusions today as you did about who to trust. No one." He looked sad and angry at the same time. "You see, the truth is that out of everyone I suspect who's involved somehow, Taylor, you're the only one I *can* trust at this point. Do you understand what that means?"

She nodded. "Yes. These same people we cannot trust are my family and your friends. It is a sad thing."

He rubbed a hand over his mouth, as if tired. But his dark eyes appeared more tortured than anything else. "Sadder than you think."

Taylor didn't know what to make of that, so she said nothing, just watched him as he . . . with slow, deliberate motions . . . picked up his cigar, puffed on it, exhaled the smoke, and then took another drink. He drained the glass and all but slammed it on the desk. The hard clunking sound it made startled Taylor. A change—and not a good one—came over Greyson. She met his ragged and angry glare. He reminded her of a wildcat bunching its muscles threateningly and hunkering down . . . right before it leaped onto its prey, its fangs and claws bared.

"There's something else you ought to know about Amanda," he said belligerently, while gesturing at her with his cigar. "Something that, in all the excitement today, I didn't realize until this evening I hadn't told you. Something that may explain to you why I care so much about what may be going on around you. Beyond my friendship with your father, that is."

Fear blossomed in Taylor's heart. She clutched at the leather chair's arms, digging her nails into the fabric. "Is something wrong with Amanda?"

"Wrong? No, nothing's wrong." He looked directly into Taylor's eyes. His piercing gaze burned with anguish. "Everything is right. And Amanda will make my brother a wonderful wife."

The strength drained right out of Taylor's body. Her bones melted. "Wife?" The word was no more than an exhalation of breath. She realized now that in her mind Amanda hadn't grown up. She was still the little girl that Taylor had spent every moment with and dragged into all her adventures. "Amanda is marrying your brother?"

Greyson soberly nodded. He reached forward to lay his cigar in the ashtray next to hers. Taylor found herself pulling back as he did. He didn't seem to notice. "Yep," he said. "I didn't tell you that part until now because . . . well, because I wasn't sure until now that I dare. But it's probably the most important detail of all right now, Taylor." He met her eyes, held her gaze. "Their upcoming marriage goes a ways toward explaining my involvement in your business. I have my own family to protect."

He knew something. Excitement, maybe dread, quickened inside Taylor. "Protect them from what?"

He sat back. "From who is more like it. And that's the part I still don't know. Now, my mother, as much as I hate to agree with her, brought up something tonight that is also important."

She'd all but forgotten his mother—and her reaction earlier when Greyson had blurted out Taylor's name. *Miss James.* Again she could hear him saying it out in the barn. Could smell the hay. And she could hear his mother's gasp and could see again the look she had given Taylor. She knew who Taylor was; that much had been evident. But did she also know more? With a quiet purring voice laced with dislike, Taylor asked, "Did she tell them that she had met a Miss James today at your home?"

"No. For whatever reason, no. And yes, I find that significant. But back to what she did say. Realizing that everyone thinks you are—forgive me—dead, she said your hanging for murder and your being part Indian are a scandal in the making, should any of it get out, along with our connection to you. I have to admit, something like that is sensational news. And she's right, Taylor. I cannot imagine why your story hasn't been in the newspapers."

Taylor chuckled, a harsh sound of resignation from a hardened heart. "I am sure it was—especially the story of my escape. But only in the Cherokee newspapers. The story happened in the Cherokee Nation and it was about an Indian woman. White people or their newspapers would not care. What's one more dead savage?"

Greyson suddenly looked ill at ease. "We're a sorry lot, aren't we? But you're right, of course. White people wouldn't care. At any rate, here you are alive. That makes you a threat—to your own family and to mine, since our two names and fortunes are to be united by this upcoming marriage between Amanda and Franklin."

"But how am I a threat? I mean no harm—"

"I know *you* don't. But *someone* does. Someone—we don't know who yet—was mighty invested all these years in lies that kept you and your white family separated. You thought Amanda dead. She and your father thought you were dead. So, whoever it is who has worked so hard to keep you away is not going to be happy that you're here."

"I know this to be true. My mother sent me here, and she warned me that there was someone here who would want me dead. She told me to go to my father and to seek out Amanda. That being so, we can trust them."

Greyson eyed her, a serious expression on his face. "You may be right. And she may be right. But that's assuming she knows the real truth. What if she was lied to, Taylor? What then? See? The danger here, so far, has only been implied. Nothing has actually happened. But someone told those lies. And for reasons we don't know. Perhaps we still shouldn't reveal who you are at this time. It may be that the only reason you are safe is because no one in St. Louis—outside of you, me, and perhaps my mother—knows you're alive."

"Why do you say perhaps? She heard you call me Miss James. There is only one other Miss James besides Amanda. And that is me. She knows who I am. I saw it in her face." Taylor hesitated but then asked the question that she felt needed to be asked. "Do you trust your mother with this knowledge that I live, Greyson?"

He gave her an odd look. Taylor realized why—she'd just said his name for the first time since telling him she would do so. But then he closed his eyes, squeezing them hard and pinching the bridge of his nose . . . giving the impression that he fought some sort of sudden pain. His mother, she believed, now filled his thoughts. When he opened his dark eyes, hurt was exposed in their depths. "No, Taylor. I don't trust her at all."

Silence passed heavily with each heartbeat as Taylor stared at Greyson. What an awful thing to have to admit, she mused. She couldn't imagine having to say the same thing about her own mother, that she couldn't trust the person who had given her life. A sudden sympathy for Greyson softened Taylor's heart toward him. This man carried much pain inside him.

Just then, Greyson exhaled and went on. "All right. So what do we know? You're here. And you're alive. And you're a convicted, uh, murderer who escaped jail. We can only hope the law doesn't find that out."

"It won't matter if they do. Not in this, your country. Only in mine. Cherokee law is not upheld here."

His expression became thoughtful. "That's right. It's not. It all makes sense now. That's why your mother sent you here, isn't it? Only in the Cherokee Nation are you wanted."

"Yes," Taylor confirmed for him.

Frowning, he shook his head, as if he was considering and turning over every eventuality and its consequences. "Well, still, should that become known, it has scandal written all over it. But even if you were the most sweet and innocent of girls, the simple fact that you are here and have Indian blood and—forgive me—are a, uh, bastard child is disastrous. Not that I care, Taylor. I'm speaking of my brother's political opponents. You see, he's running for mayor. And it looks like he has a pretty good chance of winning, too, despite his youth. So here poor Franklin has a socially brilliant marriage on the horizon and a budding political career. Everything was just dandy for both families . . . and then you arrived to upset the applecart of someone's carefully constructed lies. Hence, my fear that danger lurks."

Insulted, shamed, and yet full of pride, Taylor lifted her chin. "Then I will not remain here. I will go away now before my presence here is known. And before the truth can harm our families in any way."

Greyson held up a hand to stop her from getting up. "No. That's the last thing I want you to do. For one thing, there's no guarantee that the trouble wouldn't follow you. And for another, you may not care if you risk yourself, but I do. I feel responsible for you. And I want you to stay put. Right here. No more running off like you did today. Can you give me your word on that?"

Taylor was not about to acquiesce to such a high-handed demand. "No. I am responsible for me. Not you. And I know how to protect myself. I will not give you my word. If I have a need to leave, I will do so."

Greyson stared at her and then ran a hand over his face. He exhaled, as if disgusted or as if just trying to figure out what to say next. His expression became pleading. "Taylor, you can't leave. You need to think of my house as your fortress and me as your protector. As you said, this is my city, my people. You are a stranger here. And you are in danger. Already it's too late to leave. Don't you get it? My fear is that the person or persons who wish you harm could very well be someone in my family or yours. Maybe both."

Taylor's heart thumped painfully; her chest felt tight. Did no one want her to be alive? Would no one be happy that she was? Only now, at this moment, did she admit to herself just how much she'd wanted to be reunited with her father, even more so than she did with Amanda. Taylor had come here to see him, to know him . . . and to find out if he cared about her at all. What if he hated her and wanted her dead? She fought sudden and betraying tears.

And Greyson saw them. *"Goddammit."* He spit the word out and jumped up with a suddenness that had Taylor shrinking back. In a state of tremendous agitation, he paced over to a long window behind his desk. None too gently, he pulled the drapery aside and stood there, staring out into the night. "I have a confession, Taylor."

His voice was hard. He spared her a glance but just as quickly looked away from her, directing his gaze back outside to the night beyond the window.

"I'm not sure I wish to hear it." That she was capable of such conviction in her voice at this moment surprised Taylor.

"Well, you're going to, even though I know I shouldn't be telling you any of this. You see, all damned afternoon I kept hoping you'd come back. I kept wishing I'd stopped you from leaving. I told myself I was just concerned for your being alone on the streets here. But that's not true. Well, it's not the whole truth." He again sought her gaze. This time his eyes held hers as he continued. "I wanted you back because you—"

He muttered something under his breath. To Taylor, across the room, it sounded like "son of a bitch."

Again he turned away from her, watching the night. "I wanted you back because . . . I wanted you back. It's that simple. In the space of one day, Taylor, you made me realize everything that was lacking in my life. You showed me more excitement and meaning than I've ever known before. You showed me a world with possibilities. A chance to claim a life I never hoped to find. In short, I saw in you the possibility to save me from myself. I don't admit that lightly. But I wanted you back so bad I could taste it. I wished for it. I prayed for it. And now . . . here you are. And now that you are, with everything it can mean to our families, I don't know whether to thank you or to hate you for making me feel all that. All I know, Taylor, is that if you go away, I will die."

Taylor sat absolutely, perfectly, rigidly still. There was an air in the room. An air that glowed, that was scented with threat and promise. A gossamer-thin web of a spell weaving itself around them . . . and between them. There was nothing soft and beautiful to it. Its wisps were of jagged steel. Cutting. Tearing. It spoke of darkness. Of wanting. Yearning. Of hate. And anger. Of secrets too long kept. Of promises too soon broken. Of lies and truths. Lust and danger. Love. Death.

Rube's curse . . . again. Nothing and no one she loved would ever prosper.

Taylor came to her feet and stood there, staring his way, memorizing Greyson's back. His broad shoulders. His tapered waist, slim hips, and long legs. She exhaled. If she were strong, if she cared anything at all about this man, she would leave. She knew that what he said was not true—he would die if she stayed . . . not if she left. But the truth between them was as he had said—it was too late. For them both.

Taylor suspended thought and said nothing as she soundlessly picked her way around the furniture. She glided toward him, toward her fate. She had no idea if he could save her from the curse. Or if, one day, he would kill her when all the truths were known and her enemies were exposed. But still and steadily . . . she went to him.

She stood behind him. She knew he'd realized she was there. She'd seen her image in the window's reflective glass, heard his hissing intake of breath when he did, too. He didn't move. Didn't turn to her. Taylor wasn't so sure he could. She wasn't so sure there wasn't something alive and unseen holding him in place, just as it had her moments ago. Maybe this thing, whatever it was, resided with her, inside her. Was it good or evil? Did it matter?

Taylor reached her hands out, inching her cold and trembling fingers toward Grey. Slowly, as if it caused her great pain to do so, she wrapped her arms around his torso and held him to her. She pressed her cheek against his back, feeling his warm and muscled flesh, even through his shirt. And pronounced the thing done.

Under her hands, against her cheek, against her hips pressed to his backside, she felt him tremble.

Grey awoke the next morning holding Taylor in his arms. He lay at her back, his arms around her, his cheek resting against her head. Coal black silken strands of her hair covered his arm and flowed onto the sheet that covered them both. She was asleep . . . and as naked as he was, only more so, somehow. To Grey, it was as if her soft skin covered an underlying and luminous being. She glowed from within. How could that be? He knew all too well from last night that she was a flesh-and-blood woman—a sensually alive and responsive woman. An experienced woman. That detracted not one whit from her desirability to him. Because there was also about her an air of innocence, as well as an aura of the divine . . . a pagan goddess who was blameless, who had arisen from the very earth itself and had deigned to lie with him.

He felt honored. And he revered her. Either that or he was a besotted fool who would soon find himself spouting romantic poetry and climbing the dear lady's balcony—only to have her thoroughly scalp him for his daring and his idiocy. Grey chuckled at himself, thankful that his sense of humor was still in place when nothing else in his life was. Or would be from this day forward, he suspected, considering the woman he now held in his arms.

"Why do you laugh?"

Grey stilled. She was awake. "Because I fear I may be a silly fool."

She shifted in his arms, dislodging their covering sheet, and turned over to face him. In one smooth motion, she tugged her cascade of hair back from her face and again lay in his arms, their limbs entangled deliciously. Grey enjoyed each and every movement of hers. Her own nakedness, now exposed to him from the waist up, was of no apparent or blushing concern to her. In fact, she didn't even seem to be aware of it. "You have no need to fear," she said solemnly. "You are no fool, silly or otherwise."

Grey chuckled again, feeling alive with a world of possibilities because she was in his life and in his bed. "That's good to hear."

She ran her long slender fingers through the hair on his chest. She seemed to love doing that. And he certainly didn't mind. "Why did you think you were a fool?"

Delighting in their cocoon of intimacy here in his bed, with the draperies drawn against the morning's light, Grey peppered her high, smooth forehead with kisses. "Well, my dear, be-

cause you're here with me. And because of everything we, er
have done. And what it means, I suppose."

She stopped her tender ministrations to his chest and looke
up at him. A thrill chased through Grey. He felt certain h
could drown in those blue eyes of hers. But her expressio
was a frowning one. "What does it mean to you, these thing
we have done?"

"What does it mean? Well, let me consider." The truth wa
her question gave him pause. He hadn't thought beyond th
moments of intense desire for her last night when he'd swep
up the stairs with her holding his hand and just as eager as h
had been. As he thought now, Grey roved his appreciativ
gaze over her face, memorizing her features . . . the wide blu
eyes, the high cheekbones, the soft, firm mouth, the perfec
nose. He was suddenly overcome. "You are so very beautifu
Taylor."

With inherent grace and a surprising shyness, Taylor cas
her gaze downward. "I am as I was made. I had nothing t
do with my appearance."

Given that answer, Greyson realized he was on delicat
ground here. Their cultures were so dissimilar. What if the
were now married, according to her beliefs? Surprising hin
was the realization that such a notion did not alarm him. I
pleased him. How earth-shattering. And wonderful. Appar
ently, his bachelor days were numbered, if not over. And ho
odd was that? Only two nights ago, in his brougham, he'
proposed, as a cover only, that she pose as his affianced. Bu
now it appeared that their being a couple might very well b
real.

Well, then, that made his answer simple, didn't it?

Suddenly giddy with good cheer that he suspected coul
even include the boring Franklin and their imperial mother—
in small doses—Grey smiled down into Taylor's face an
kissed the tip of her nose. Such an endearment seemed t
startle her. He grinned, liking that he could catch her off-guar
but wishing that just once he could win a smile from her. H
didn't believe he'd seen one yet. "What does it mean, yo
asked me a moment ago. Well, I suppose in the simplest c

terms, Taylor, what transpired here, in this bed last night, means that we are, at the very least, betrothed. Do you know that word?"

Still unsmiling, Taylor stared at him. "Yes, I do." She untangled her limbs from his and pushed away, her hands flattened against his bare chest, which she used for leverage. Then, sitting naked and proud, her legs tucked under her, she assured him, "You *are* a silly fool, white man. It means no such thing. You place too much meaning on this." A dismissive sweep of her hand indicated his bed . . . and everything they'd done in it, evidently.

Stung, embarrassed, and always before now the one to disavow amorous and clinging women of their matrimonial notions, Grey pushed himself up and sat facing her. "And perhaps you, my heathen princess, don't place *enough* meaning on the intimacies we shared."

Her face reddened with a scowl. She poked his chest with a finger. "I am not a heathen, you round-eyes. I know all about your God and your Bible—enough to know that you think what we did last night with each other is a sin. Not to me. Lovemaking is not a bad thing. It is good. It is a sharing. But I give it only the meaning it deserves. You wanted me. And I wanted you." She looked him up and down in that haughty dismissive way of hers that was a clear insult. "Although right now I cannot remember why."

Grey was totally outraged. He'd never felt so cheap before in his life. Or used. That's what he'd been. Used. "In my culture, missy, this night we spent together would mean we were most definitely headed for an altar and a priest. But maybe it's nothing in the Cherokee Nation for a woman to give herself to any man she chooses any time she wants. I don't know how it is there—"

"No, you do not." Her voice was dangerously level and calm. "Cherokee women are virtuous. It is prized among my people, just as it is among yours. Do not judge them by me. But in my culture, the men are also held to that same behavior. Can your people say that? I do not think so. Because I was not the only person in this bed who knew what to do. And yet, you are unmarried."

Well, that certainly shut him up. Grey had no idea how to come back to that. Nor did she give him a chance to do so.

"Is this how you treat the women in your country? She gives herself and her most prized gift to you—and you insult her because she does? To a Cherokee man, it is the greatest honor in his life to have a woman willingly lie down with him. It is all she needs to do for him to know he has won her heart. She needs no words. Cherokee men know only the most deserving of men among them can earn a woman's love. You would throw this gift away, Greyson Talbott? You would tell me it means nothing to you? That I am vile and a heathen because I—" She stopped abruptly, her eyes wide and darting, her expression a mask of startled realization.

"Because you what, Taylor? Because you showed me how much you care about me?" Grey asked softly, wanting to reach out to her and stroke her cheek. He wanted also to take her in his arms and hold her, and comfort her. He wondered if any man in her life had ever comforted her. Certainly she'd been held and loved. But had she ever found solace in any man's arms?

Grey was no longer angry with her. Far from it. And neither was she with him. He knew that because tears escaped her eyes and she stared at him with the face of a hurting child. About halfway through her tirade, Grey had realized that she hadn't been talking to him or about him. He suspected her anger was directed at whoever had taught her the sensual delights she'd tantalized him with last night. "I'm sorry, Taylor," Grey finally said into the growing silence between them. "You are right. You gave me a beautiful gift that needs no words. And I didn't cherish your love as I should. Can you forgive me?"

Taylor wiped away her tears. A look of wonderment came over her face, a look that strongly affected Grey. As he watched, not daring to move, Taylor tilted her head at a questioning angle. She reached a hand out and did as he'd wanted only moments ago to do to her. She stroked his cheek and then his forehead. She slowly ran the tip of her finger down the bridge of his nose . . . and then over his lips. They tingled with her touch, but Grey didn't dare move. The moment was magic.

Taylor finally looked again into his eyes. "You would ask *me* for forgiveness? No one has ever . . . Why?"

As he'd suspected. Taylor had been used and run over. His heart went out to her, this unsmiling young woman who walked the earth alone, this young woman he could no more hope to hold onto than he could hope to rope the wind. His heart ached . . . but for himself. "I ask your forgiveness because I hurt you with my unthinking words," he said as softly as he could.

"And my words . . . they hurt you, did they not?"

Grey dared a smile. "Is that an apology from my heathen princess?"

She pulled back, blinking as if his question had pulled her out from under a spell. Her darting gaze traveled over him and his nakedness. She then looked down at herself. And up at him again. Back was the haughty, independent lone wolf of a woman who'd spun him on his heels two nights ago in front of her father's home. She arched a raven's wing of an eyebrow and said, "I never apologize."

And then she snaked a hand out, taking him by the back of his neck and pulling him to her. Kneeling in the bed with him, and just before his lips crushed hers, she put her fingers to his mouth and whispered, "Make love to me. And I will be your woman."

A thrill shot through Grey, hardening him in an instant. Taylor was absolutely magnificent, the veritable embodiment of Woman. A paragon of all the sensual arts of love. In a fever to possess her, Grey grabbed her up in his arms. Her legs locked around his waist, her arms around his neck. Grey cupped her firm buttocks, pressing her full against him. His mouth covered hers and hungrily sought to plunder its sweet depths. Taylor's moans and mewling and insistent raking of her nails over his back drove Grey absolutely wild. She wanted him inside her.

Grey fell forward onto the bed with Taylor beneath him. With one hand he braced their fall onto the yielding mattress. She accepted his weight with an upward thrust of her hips. Grey moaned into her mouth. She held his tongue with her teeth. Her hands never stopped their stroking quest as she scratched and kneaded the muscled flesh on his back and urged him on. Grey had never known such wild and sensual abandon. Never would he give her up. Never. In all his life, he—

With no warning, the door to the hall opened suddenly. Masculine footfalls advanced into the room, dimmed by the heavy draperies, and approached the bed . . . where the startled lovers were frozen in position atop it.

"Grey, old man? Good morning. Are you in here? It's so blamed dark, I can barely see. It's me—Franklin. Bentley said he believed he'd heard you moving around up here—"

A shocked gasp, sounding very close to the four-poster bed, preceded the steady beat of a hasty retreat toward the open door. "Great Scott! Good God, I am sorry. I had no idea—"

The door slammed closed behind Franklin Talbott.

Chapter Eleven

"Franklin, what in God's name are you doing here so early? Yesterday it was Mother. And today it's you. Tomorrow I will have run out of relatives and I suppose I should expect a parade of acquaintances to string through my home beginning at the crack of dawn." Grey, clad now in his trousers and a shirt he was tucking into his waistband, stood barefoot in his parlor and berated his brother. He'd left an unabashed Taylor upstairs attending to her bath and toilette.

"Early, you say? It's after luncheon. You've been abed all morning. And how was I to know you were, er, entertaining a, uhm, young lady?"

"It's not what you're thinking."

Franklin was grinning. "Oh, I think it was exactly what I'm thinking."

"Wipe that silly smirk off your face or I'll thrash you."

"No, you won't. We aren't children anymore, Grey. You can't go around bashing me now."

Grey stepped up. "You don't think so?"

Franklin stepped back. "Calm down, Greyson. You're a bachelor and how you choose to behave in the privacy of your own home—"

"Should not be interrupted by my younger brother or anyone else."

"I quite agree. And I do apologize. Perhaps you should take a stronger hand with your staff. It was Bentley who told me to go on up. But at any rate, I'm sorry if I've inconvenienced you or your . . . er, the young lady. But I have serious business to discuss with you. So the sooner you pay your little—*ack!*"

With one hand, Grey had him by the throat. "Don't you

even finish that thought. The *lady* is the woman I intend to marry."

Franklin's eyes bulged and his face turned an interesting shade of purple . . . right before he smashed a fist into Grey's midsection and doubled him over in agony. His hands gripping his knees, Grey tried desperately to breathe and not be sick.

The apparently undamaged Franklin good-naturedly supported his brother with a hand to Grey's arm as he patted him on the back and gave him a hearty, "Well, I certainly hope so, especially after that, er, performance I witnessed. But congratulations, old man. Won't Mother be shocked? As well as all of St. Louis. There now, that's the fellow. Breathe. In and out. You remember how. Now, tell me, who's the lucky young lady?"

Grey finally recovered enough to be able to straighten up some and glare with renewed respect at his brother, two years his junior. While Grey was tall, dark, and muscular like their father, Franklin more resembled their mother. He had her brown hair and eyes. He was about average height for a man and slightly built . . . thank God. With one hand clutching at his stomach, Grey rested his other heavily on Franklin's shoulder and concentrated again on breathing. For his part, Franklin crossed his arms over his chest and smiled back at Grey . . . as if nothing at all had just occurred.

Finally able to speak, Grey rasped out, "The lucky young lady is Miss James, you son of a bitch."

Franklin's stance stiffened. "The hell you say. *My* affianced is Miss James, and well you know it." Then his eyes widened appreciably. A dangerous red suffused his cheeks. He knocked Grey's hand off his shoulder and pointed in the direction of the stairs outside the room. "Do you mean to tell me that the woman upstairs in your bed is *my*—"

"Shut up your bellowing, you idiot," Grey hissed as he made his way over to the medallion-back sofa and sat heavily, bending himself double over his knees to ease his pain. Franklin followed him, sat next to him. Grey edged up to a sitting position and shot his brother a hard look. "Do you want her to hear you? Of course it's not Amanda. How could you even think it of me or of her? The Miss James I mean is her cousin. Taylor."

The words were out before Grey could even think. *Damn.* He hadn't meant to say that. But the words had already worked their magic.

A very pale Franklin clutched at Grey's arm. "Then it's true."

"What is?" came Grey's wary question as he shrugged away his brother's hand.

Franklin essentially ignored him, carrying on his discourse as if he were alone and were speaking aloud to himself. "But it's just not possible. I have labored under the belief that this Taylor girl was hanged, for God's sake. Certainly she's the same one Amanda and her mother were crying over last night." Only now did Franklin include his brother in the conversation. "And there you were—and Mother was—knowing the girl lived. And not one word to relieve the Jameses of their sorrow."

" 'And Mother was'?" Grey had immediately picked up on that. He didn't know how to feel about her having told someone what she suspected. What was her game? She always had one.

"Yes. Mother was," Franklin assured him. "Last night she knew that girl was alive and said nothing. How long have you known?"

"That she was alive? Less than two days. But about her existence at all? Five years. Charles told me about her."

"Charles told you? I myself had never even heard of her until last night."

Grey found that odd. "Good God, Franklin, you're going to be family. You mean the Jameses, not even Amanda, your fiancée, have never mentioned Taylor to you?"

A very hangdog expression claimed Franklin's features. "No. But I suppose if they believed the girl long dead and buried, why would they?"

That made sense. "Well, how much do you know now about her?"

Franklin became increasingly despondent. "Everything. Between Amanda and Mother, I believe I know everything that can be known. Meaning there's still a lot of mystery surrounding her. I fear it surrounds my dear Amanda's entire family, too."

Grey nodded, knowing the truth of that all too well. But he also wondered what *everything* meant. Was there more he didn't know himself? After all, his only sources were Taylor and her father. Frustration ate at Grey and had him rubbing his brow distractedly. He hated this being suspicious of everyone. Adding to Grey's frustration was his belief that with every name added to the list of those who knew Taylor's true identity, she was somehow made more vulnerable. "All right, then, so Mother told you Taylor is here," he said abruptly into the quiet that had grown between him and Franklin. "When?"

"This morning."

Relief coursed through Grey. "Then she didn't tell everyone last night after I left? When you were all together, I mean?"

"No. This morning."

"Did she say if she's told anyone else?"

"No. Yes. I mean she said she's told only me."

"Did you just come from Mother's?"

"Yes. Why?"

Grey shrugged. "Just curious. I was wondering if she's had time to gad about town shocking the Jameses with this news."

"Oh, surely she wouldn't."

Grey eyed his brother. "You've always been most naive where our mother is concerned."

"And you've always been most suspicious."

"Have I? And which one of us has had his opinion borne out most frequently?" Franklin made a face. "As I thought," Grey said. "Now, Franklin, have *you* told anyone?"

"No. I said I'd just come here." Franklin answered directly enough, but he was stroking his clean-shaven chin and looking everywhere except at Grey. "This is all most upsetting. You see," he began abruptly, "this morning I didn't believe Mother when she told me she'd seen *her* here only yesterday."

Grey didn't like one whit how Franklin said *her* but said nothing, just listened to what else Franklin had to say.

"So instantly, Grey, I came here in a rush to tell you I feared Mother was addled—"

"Mother is anything but addled, Franklin."

Franklin frowned. "I realize that now. Grey, I think you'd better explain what is going on here. This young lady . . . how *do* we know she is who she says she is? Does she have any proof? I mean, she says she's this Indian cousin of the very prominent James family. A cousin who Amanda says died in childhood. Then we find out she didn't die then but was recently hanged for murder. Only she wasn't really. What is she—a cat with nine lives? Good Lord, is it any wonder I'm so confused?"

"No. It is a very confusing situation, I admit. I've barely come to terms with it all myself."

Franklin looked askance at Grey. "Oh, I'd say you've come to quite good terms with it, if what I had the misfortune to witness upstairs is any indication. I am assuming that now you've enjoyed the honeymoon, you believe you'll have the wedding?"

Grey narrowed his eyes; his voice was no more than a growl. "It's not like you think. And I won't warn you again to leave off discussing her in such terms."

"How can I not?" Franklin jumped up, agitatedly pacing the neat and elegant room. Suddenly, to Grey, he seemed older and smarter, as if until now he'd been hiding another side of himself. "Grey, will you only think? Mother says this Taylor is a half-breed and that Charles was never married to her mother. I don't see how this could be worse. While I would hope I don't harbor any prejudices, my opponents will latch onto this very sensational information and will drag me through the mud with it. As well as Amanda, her parents, Charles, and his daughter. Even you. We'll all be tainted by her existence, if not her very heritage. Damn. We'll all be ruined."

"No. You and Mother will be, you mean." Something inside Grey hardened. He'd miscalculated the reason behind his brother's concerns regarding Taylor. It had nothing to do with people close to Franklin himself who could be hurt or killed.

It had to do with political aspirations. How charming. "I personally don't give a damn what your social or your political set thinks."

A sudden ugly gleam shone in Franklin's eyes. "Give a damn? You? Of course you don't. What exactly would you have to give a damn about? You're a kept man, and I'm the one having to keep you. Everything is in your name as the eldest, but I'm the one who does all the work. You sign documents and carry on with your clubs and your women. You've never cared one fig for the proprieties. You're already ruined. No *decent* woman would have you. Yet you delight in calling me boring and taunting me. Could it be that you're jealous of me, Grey? That you resent me for being the responsible one, the one who has always had to take care of the family businesses? Could it be that you know you'll never amount to anything and you hate me because I will? Do you look at me and see your failures?"

Following that tirade, a thick silence built between the two brothers with each heartbeat.

A sudden bone-deep anger overtook Grey. He hid it by lounging negligently on the couch, an arm flung over its spine, a leg resting on the cushions. He considered his little brother in this new light. Obviously, Franklin was not the simple, plodding fellow Grey had always thought him to be. The little bastard was as ambitious as their mother was. That made him just as dangerous as Grey suspected their mother could be. "Are you quite finished, Franklin?"

Franklin smiled and managed to look ruthless. "Finished? Hardly. I've barely begun." He made as if to leave the room.

Grey was up like a shot. He had a death grip on his brother's arm before Franklin took two steps. Grey jerked him around and growled down into his startled face, "Begun what? What are you talking about, Franklin?"

"Something responsible. So I'm sure you wouldn't understand. But specifically I mean I have to meet with my election committee. I have to tell them everything. And we will have to come up with a strategy to combat this scandal, should it get out."

"Like hell you will." Grey didn't even try to keep the disgust out of his voice. Franklin tried to shrug off Grey's hand, but Grey held on. "Look at it this way, Franklin—at least now you're interesting. You have skeletons in your closet. Well, your bride-to-be's family does, at any rate. You do remember Amanda, don't you, you little shit? The woman you love? The one most likely to be hurt by all this intrigue in her family? Amanda? Does she ring a bell in that little avaricious head of yours?"

Franklin's expression blanked, his eyes rounded.

"Exactly. Mother whipped you into a political froth, and you didn't even consider for an instant Amanda and her feelings. Much less the impact on her entire family, did you? You ought to be ashamed. She should be your first consideration, you ass. The mayoralty is merely a political office that ends in a matter of years. But she's to be your wife for a lifetime. And as it so happens, I like Amanda a lot. I have no idea what she sees in you, but her I respect."

Now Franklin did jerk himself away from Grey. "Don't you dare to presume to lecture me on duty and responsibility."

"I'm not. I'm lecturing you on affairs of the heart. I am of course assuming you have one. And that you haven't sold it to some political party. Or that you won't end your engagement to Amanda in order to distance yourself from a scandal." Grey stayed between his brother and the door, should he try to leave. "But you will listen to me about Taylor. It's quite the long and ugly story, Franklin. But she *is* who she says she is. Even Mother says she is. Ask yourself how *she* would know. But beyond that, obviously Taylor was never hanged. And she's only just recently found out that Amanda is alive. Taylor was told the same lies as they were."

Franklin grimaced and gestured impatiently, giving the impression that he felt they'd wandered off the subject—himself and his campaign. "Be all that as it may, I am sorry for the girl. But what does this have to do with—"

"It has everything to do with any of us who know Taylor or that she lives. Think, Franklin. Use those astute political sensitivities your supporters all say you have. Someone told the Jameses these lies years ago—when you were a child—to keep them separated. It didn't have anything to do with you and your aspirations to be mayor, for God's sake. But Taylor and her family are no longer separated. They are in the same city now, only blocks apart. So whoever is invested in keeping them apart, and for whatever reason, is not going to be happy. And don't ask me who this person might be. I don't know. But I do need to find out before someone gets killed."

Franklin's expression froze. "Killed? Dear God. I never even considered . . . Then you think there could be actual danger here, Grey?"

"Finally," Grey said sarcastically. "Yes, I do. Nothing has happened yet, but that may well be because only a few of us know that Taylor lives and that she is here in St. Louis."

Franklin looked genuinely troubled now. He gripped Grey's arm. "I've behaved like an ass, Grey. I've been acting as if her appearance here were nothing more than a well-devised plot on the part of my political enemies. Can you forgive me?"

A modicum of relief flooded Grey. "Yes. I will, if you will forgive me. We both behaved like asses, I suppose. And I will admit that had Taylor's appearance been as you just said, your opponents couldn't have plotted better. And I suppose it's only natural that you'd want to protect yourself in the clenches." Grey rubbed his sore stomach. "You're very capable in that regard."

Franklin grinned. "I should be. I was always having to fight you." But his grin didn't last long. "What *are* we going to do, Grey?" His gaze flitted to the doorway. "Where is she now?"

Grey turned to make sure she wasn't standing behind him. "Upstairs. Attending to her toilette."

Franklin nodded . . . and again became serious. "We have to tell them, Grey. I mean Amanda and her parents. And Charles. They have to know. Especially if you fear they're in danger. I suppose we are, too. I mean Mother, you, and me."

Grey nodded. "We are. All of us. I've been thinking about how to tell the Jameses without giving them all heart attacks. Franklin, will you allow me to tell them? I'd like to take Taylor along with me when I do. I think it will be easiest that way."

"All right. Is there anything I can do?"

Grey's answer was instantaneous. "Yes. Return to Mother's and find a pleasant way of telling her to keep her mouth shut. Perhaps the threat of social scandal can induce her to keep Taylor's existence hushed up for now. Tell her I'm trying to contain it, just keep it in the family. Tell her maybe we can stand united in this and no one's life will be ruined, politically or personally."

Franklin was now despondent. "You think there's a chance of a happy outcome, Grey?"

"I *pray* there's a chance of one, Franklin."

"I will, too." He started to step around Grey, who no longer resisted him, but stopped and looked up into his eyes. "I truly am sorry, Grey, for the things I said . . . about everything. I didn't mean them."

Grey held himself with dignity. "Of course you did. Most of what you said is true. I know that. And I will endeavor to lighten your load from this day on. I shall shoulder my share of the family responsibility."

Franklin considered Grey for a moment. "This girl has changed you."

Grey nodded. "She has. I wager she will change us all."

Looking undone, Franklin skirted Grey and made his way out of the room. In the hallway, he turned toward the front door and disappeared from view. Grey heard him taking his leave of Bentley, heard the front door open and close.

Overcome with a heavy sadness, Grey stood where he was, his arms crossed over his chest. Only thirty minutes ago, Franklin had been one of the ones Grey had meant to protect. And he still was, he supposed. But only thirty minutes ago, Grey would have shared with his brother that his biggest fear was that the danger could come from one of the very people he had to tell. Or even worse, from their own mother.

A little while ago, Grey knew he would have considered Franklin an ally. But now, following their most enlightening conversation and having seen for himself these new and un-

attractive facets of his brother's personality, Grey knew a moment of defeat. Franklin was capable of treachery against
Taylor. The most telling thing was . . . he'd never once asked
to meet her, not even after being told by Grey that he intended
to marry her. While he wasn't quite sure yet what to make of
that, he still had to admit that it seemed very unnatural. What
could Franklin have up his sleeve? What was he capable of in
the name of his political dreams? He'd already made Amanda
a distant second, and supposedly he loved her. What then
would he do to Taylor, someone he had every reason to fear
and hate?

"Son of a bitch," Grey muttered.

Just then, Bentley appeared in the doorway. Grey met the
old man's concerned stare. Obviously, Bentley had heard
everything . . . and had come to the same conclusions Grey
had. Belatedly Grey realized he was nodding at Bentley . . .
who was nodding back at him. At least here was as staunch
an ally as he and Taylor could hope to have. Or was he? Grey
suddenly realized that five years ago, when he'd hired Bentley,
it had been on his mother's recommendation. Grey's insides
curdled. Was there a spy in his own home?

Just then, there was a knock on the front door. Franklin
again? Bentley turned to go answer it, leaving Grey to reflect
on the seeming coincidences of timing in the past two days,
of his mother arriving without notice or invitation yesterday
to confront him and Taylor. And then, this morning, Bentley
had uncharacteristically sent Franklin upstairs with no warning
to Grey. Grey tried to hold his suspicions at bay, tried to believe that his overbearing kin had simply got around Bentley.
But Grey also wondered if maybe his mother knew something
unsavory about his butler and was using it to force his cooperation with her and to glean information from him. But
given Bentley's age, Grey could hardly imagine what it might
be or how it could matter.

The front door closed. Bentley reappeared in the open doorway to the parlor. Grey stared at the waiting Bentley. "Yes?
What is it?"

Thus acknowledged, the old man held his hand out. In it was a folded note. "This just arrived for you, sir. By courier."

Following a hasty luncheon, preceded by Greyson's washing up and then dressing, Taylor now found herself sitting opposite him—and the very astonished and downcast Bentley—in his brougham, the same enclosed carriage she'd ridden in two nights ago. If Greyson's face hadn't been so grim, if his manner hadn't been so forbidding . . . and if he weren't so angry with her right now because of her outright insistence that her spirit guide accompany them . . . she might have asked him what was wrong and where they were going. Not since she'd been a child had Taylor allowed anyone to shepherd her in such a manner as this.

But here in St. Louis, with its tall buildings, its crowded streets, and its throngs of people—any one of whom could be her enemy—Taylor was unsure of herself. And so, smartly, she'd allowed the handling she'd been subjected to in Greyson's home. But that didn't mean she wasn't paying attention now to every road they turned down and to every house they passed . . . as well as to every face. Was her father out there somewhere? Would she know him—or Amanda or Aunt Camilla—if she saw them? Would they know her?

It was suddenly of vital importance that they did. That was what Greyson had said. As soon as his angry brother had left—Taylor, and everyone else upstairs, had heard their raised voices—Greyson had bounded up the stairs, an unfolded note in his hand, and had interrupted her getting dressed, much to Mrs. Scott's indignant consternation. That stout lady—in her forgiven state now Taylor's staunchest defender—had already had her hackles raised by discovering that Taylor's bed had not been slept in. But Greyson had ignored the older woman's protests to tell her to arrange Taylor's hair and then dress her in a traveling costume, that they were going out. But he wouldn't say where.

"Not here," he'd said, giving her a weighty stare. "Later. When we're away in the carriage." The only conclusion Taylor could draw was that he suddenly did not trust someone in his

home. One of his servants? It had to be, because besides Greyson himself, there was only her and his servants residing there
And here she was with him. So it had to be one of the staff.

Not for the first time—or even the last time, she suspected—Taylor wished herself free of this intrigue and the
shackles it placed on her freedom. She wished for more of the
open air and the sunshine she'd stood and reveled in only
momentarily in the coach yard before she'd been whisked inside the stuffy carriage in which they now rode. With only the
small side windows opened for air and a cool cross-breeze
Taylor felt as cramped and as constrained as she actually was
This city of the white people grated. She longed for the open-
ness of her beloved Nation, for the hills, the forests, the icy
cold streams. She longed for the common language of the soft
spoken People. She yearned for her mother and the guidance
she could give . . . guidance Taylor now admitted she hadn'
listened to in the past but very much needed now.

Beyond that, she longed for her gun that Greyson had taken
away from her. She still had her knife, safely sheathed and
tucked away inside her new and fancy button-top boots. Mrs
Scott had nearly fainted when Taylor had whisked the weapon
out from under her bed pillow and slipped it down the side of
her polished leather shoes. But still, her gun was a much bette:
defense against another's bullets, she'd told Greyson. She
could take care of herself. She was an excellent shot. And he
knew that. Weren't three men dead because of her unerring
aim? Greyson had assured her, at lunch, that was exactly why
she wasn't getting her gun back. He didn't want to be the
fourth.

Taylor sighed, directing her gaze out the small window
watching the city going about its business. She was dressed in
the same manner as were the other women she saw. This upset
Taylor more than not having her gun. She wanted her own
clothes. Practical clothes like those she normally wore. A
man's britches and shirt and vest, along with her boots. The
first private opportunity she had, she assured herself, she
would speak with Calvin about obtaining such an outfit fo

her. She may need it—and soon. Something in her heart and her gut said this would be so.

Taylor looked down at herself now and almost didn't recognize that it was her underneath the sharply elegant and constraining dusky gray traveling costume with its high-necked white blouse and lacy cuffs. Mrs. Scott had proudly and gently laced and hooked and tied Taylor into the outfit . . . without corsets. Since yesterday, it was understood between her and the housekeeper, now also lady's maid to Taylor, that there would be no mention of corsets.

Mrs. Scott had then fashioned Taylor's long hair into an upswept do and plopped a small hat atop the curls. The hat, though ridiculously small, was the only item of her current apparel that Taylor hadn't minded. In fact, it had delighted her—it was adorned with feathers. Seeing them, Taylor had immediately savaged Mrs. Scott's handiwork. She'd freed from the hairpins a long tress at her temple, had plaited it into a thin braid, and then had plucked out a feather from the hat, which she'd fastened to her braid with a bit of red ribbon. It now hung provocatively over her shoulder and lay atop the swell of her breast. Eyebrows throughout the house and in the coach yard had risen, but no one . . . wisely so . . . had challenged her. Not even Greyson.

"Taylor, you look lovely dressed as you are."

Taylor jerked her gaze to Greyson's face. His countenance was sober, his voice cool. She glanced at Bentley, squashed next to Greyson on the narrow seat. His eyes wide, the man-bird sat rigidly and had his hands folded stiffly in his lap. His knuckles were white. Taylor focused again on Greyson. "I hate it," she said unceremoniously.

Bentley squeezed his eyes shut and began mumbling something under his breath. It sounded like a prayer.

"I'm sorry you hate your costume," Greyson said, his voice dramatic with mocking patience. "I'm sure Mrs. Scott would have allowed you to pick out another—"

"No. I don't hate just this dress"—she grabbed up a wad of the satin material in her fist as if to show him—"but all of them. They itch. And I must wear too many layers of them. I hate the bloomers—"

"Dear sweet God in heaven," came Bentley's suddenly loud voice.

"Hush up, Bentley," Greyson ordered testily. He leaned toward Taylor. "A lady doesn't mention her . . . underpinnings in the company of, well, anyone."

Taylor leaned toward Greyson, her nose nearly touching his. "I'm not a lady. A lady probably wouldn't have been in your bed last night, either. You didn't seem to mind then."

Bentley now all but sobbed a heartfelt prayer for deliverance. Greyson abruptly sat back, crossing his arms over his chest and glaring at Taylor. She sat back herself and impassively gazed at him, her mind all too happy to recall for her, and in intimate detail, the taste, touch, and feel of the striking man sitting across from her. A shiver of remembered pleasure slipped over Taylor's skin as each part of her recalled his kisses, recalled where he'd touched her with his mouth, where he'd drunk of her femininity, where his hands had caressed . . . her breasts, her belly, her—

"Stop that," came Greyson's sharp rebuke.

Bentley sucked in a breath. Taylor blinked back to the moment. Instantly she knew that her expression must have softened and betrayed her sensual turn of mind . . . because Greyson looked singularly uncomfortable as he shifted his position atop the brougham's leather seat. Taylor arched an eyebrow. Maybe now he'd be more open to telling her where they were going.

"Where is it you are taking me?" Her bold question broke the stinging silence that hung heavy like a sleeping bat between the three of them. "We are away from your home now. You may speak, Greyson."

"Why, thank you," he said sourly. "And I would prefer you call me Grey. All my friends do."

In light of his sarcastic tone, Taylor ducked her chin regally. "Then I will call you Grey when I come to consider you a friend."

Looking dumbfounded, Greyson dropped his hands to his lap in a limp heap. Taylor maintained her impassive and staring expression. Bentley began pleading, this time directly to Taylor. "Please, Miss James, won't you behave? You really do look quite lovely, as Mr. Talbott says. And this is a beautiful day. Here we are out for a nice drive, though God alone knows why I'm along for it. So cannot we just be grateful?"

"No, we cannot." Taylor frowned at Bentley as she searched for secret meaning in his words. The old ones had said the spirit guides sometimes spoke in such ways. But it seemed to her that only Grey—Greyson—spoke with words not said. But he was not her spirit guide. He was a man too much of this world. Bentley was the man-bird and her protector. She knew this. And he would go where she did, from this time forward.

"What are you contemplating over there, Taylor? And why do I feel I should be concerned?"

Taylor gave Greyson her attention. Ignoring his question and his comment, she again spoke her mind. "I would know where you are taking me."

"So we're back to that. Well, I suppose it's that or a discussion of your bloomers. Oh, sorry, Bentley. Your being here was not my idea, I assure you." To Taylor he said, "We have been summoned to your father's home."

Surprise had Taylor fisting her hands. Her pulse leaped as her mouth dried. "My father?" she rasped out.

"Yes. We've been summoned. You and I. By name, Taylor."

Her eyes widened. "How? He doesn't know—"

"Apparently he does know." Grey's expression was accusing as he archly cut his gaze to the oblivious Bentley beside him and then to her.

To Taylor, Greyson's actions were as plain as words. He suspected Bentley. She couldn't—wouldn't—believe it. She shook her head. "No. You're wrong. Who else could have—"

"I intend to find out; trust me." He leaned toward her as if he needed to assure himself that he had her complete attention. "Taylor, I should warn you that we won't be the only ones present. Your father wrote that your aunt and your cousin will also be in attendance."

Chapter Twelve

Taylor dragged in a shallow breath. She couldn't have said if her chest was tightening with anticipation or dread. What if the intent of this meeting was not a happy one? What if they wished to tell her to leave them be? "Aunt Camilla and Amanda?"

"Yes. Apparently they are anxious to renew their acquaintance with you."

That didn't sound bad—or wonderful. Taylor put her fingers to her mouth and absently rubbed her lips as she stared at Greyson. "Did the note say that—about them being anxious to . . . ?" She couldn't get the words out.

Greyson's expression softened. "Yes. It did. Why? Do you doubt that they would really wish to see you?"

"No." Taylor lowered her hand and stared at it there in her lap as she added, "I just . . . well, I just hope that the words are their true wishes."

"I see." Greyson's soft voice was like a balm to her soul. "So do I, Taylor. They'd be fools not to want to know you."

She looked up, meeting his warm gaze, his sincere smile. And felt afraid, as if she were losing a part of herself to him. She suddenly felt very young and in need of protection, unsure of herself . . . as if she required a hand to hold. A hand to hold? Her? The very idea was a slap to her dignity. Taylor reined in her emotions. Just because she'd made love to this man, just because she'd shared her body with him, it did not mean he held sway over her heart. No man owned her, and she owed no man anything. Taylor sat up straighter, steeling her spine and her resolve to be her own woman, to need no one.

Suddenly Bentley looked up and addressed his employer.

"I say, Mr. Talbott, I trust I will be allowed to remain in the carriage for the duration of your visit with Miss James's kin?"

"No. I need you!" Taylor yelped, leaning forward to clutch at his hand. A man was one thing, but a spirit guide was a completely other being. And she had no qualms about needing him. "You must be with me."

"Oh, dear." Bentley shrank back like a frightened child, practically wedging himself between Greyson's shoulder and the seat back. He very cautiously pulled his hand from under Taylor's. "I daresay, Miss James, you need only Mr. Talbott with you."

Taylor sat back, staring in dismay at her reluctant spirit guide.

To her surprise, Greyson took up her case. "No, she's quite right, Bentley. She'll need you with her." Irritably he reached around himself, an arm across his chest, to tug Bentley out from behind him. As Greyson settled again, he continued to speak to Bentley . . . although his gaze rested on Taylor. "Besides, I'm not certain that I'm in much of a mood today to play spirit guide to an Indian maiden who doesn't wish me to be such to her."

Staring at Greyson's insulted posture, Taylor drew in a deep breath and exhaled it slowly . . . for patience. It was never easy to explain Cherokee religion to white people. As a child, she'd certainly tried with the missionaries, but they'd met her halting statements of her beliefs with either mocking derision or angry rejection, calling her blasphemous. For many years, she hadn't known what the word meant. But still, here and now, and with Greyson, Taylor felt she needed to try again. "Greyson, it is not as I wish. It is as it is."

Greyson crossed his arms again. "Well, I won't even pretend that I understand that, Taylor."

She cut her gaze to the open window, recognized the area—her father's house was around the next corner. She had to hurry. Both men in the carriage with her needed to understand. Again she sought Greyson's eyes and saw he'd been watching her and waiting. "I cannot *choose* a spirit guide. Or even call on one. At worrisome times in a person's life, a guide will simply appear. We must recognize it as such and heed its words and actions, for in them is our answer."

"I see. And what sort of message are you getting from Bentley's words and actions?"

Taylor stared at the timid little man-bird and firmed her lips together into a straight line. She had no idea what his message was, but she wasn't about to tell Greyson that. She raised her chin, focused on Greyson, and improvised. "The need for caution."

Greyson made a disrespectful sound that scoffed at her words. "I could have told you that. We certainly didn't need a *man-bird* to tell us."

That was when she heard it, there in Greyson's voice, in his mannerisms. Taylor's lips twitched around a barely suppressed smile. Greyson was jealous of her attentions to Bentley. A sudden, startling thawing of her emotions swept over Taylor, blindsiding her, leaving her feeling warmed toward Grey. He was jealous. Not in a sexually possessive way like other men had been. But in a sweet way, a way of the heart. He wanted to be her man-bird. The only one she looked up to. The only one she turned to. How surprising. The big and muscled man who hadn't once let her down, the man who'd stuck by her side even at risk to himself and his family . . . wanted her to rely on him.

A rare grin escaped Taylor. She even chuckled, her heart full with a flash of joy that she didn't analyze or even deny.

Grey's stern expression dissolved. He sat forward, bracing his hands against his knees. He stared wide-eyed at her. "You're smiling. You even laughed. That is the first time I've seen you do so. I swear, I was beginning to think you humorless."

Taylor shook her head, not willing after all to admit anything out loud to him. As long as only she knew how he affected her, she was safe in her heart. "I am not without laughter, Grey. You have just not amused me until now. But I would speak to you of spirit guides." She sobered some. "The old ones say that a guide comes in a time of need to show the way."

Now Greyson was grinning at her. "Oh, they show the way, do they? Then I suppose we should have Bentley topside driving the brougham."

"I hardly think so, sir." Now Bentley was outraged. His weak little chin came up a proud notch; his arms flapped out at his rounded sides. Taylor watched him in fascination. Was he going to fly? "I would remind you, sir, that I am a butler. And as such I do not drive . . . *carriages.*" He spit the word out.

"Calm down, Bentley," Greyson drawled, patting Bentley's shoulder. "No one is expecting you to handle the horses. But I would also remind you that these are special and trying circumstances just now, and neither do butlers go tooling about the city with their employers—" He jerked his gaze to Taylor. "Did you call me Grey a moment ago?"

Lost in the harangue between butler and employer, Taylor popped her attention forward to Greyson's question. "Call you Grey? No, I did not."

"You *did*," he insisted.

They both appealed to Bentley, who shrank visibly and all but disappeared into the upholstery. He faced Taylor. "You did," he squeaked.

Taylor cut her chilling gaze over to Grey. He grinned. "Can't argue with the spirit guide, remember."

She didn't get a chance to prove that yes she could because, just then, the carriage drew to a stop. Taylor's pulse jumped. "We're here," she breathed, apprehension more than wonder accentuating her voice and words.

Grey reached over and covered her hand. Only then did she realize how cold her hands were, and on such a warm day. She couldn't seem to look away from his dark eyes and his reassuring expression. "It will be all right, Taylor. I'll be with you every step of the way. Remember, these are people who love you."

Taylor nodded. It was all she could do. But inside . . . where she kept everything important, the things that she never spoke of . . . she worried. *Perhaps they love me. But perhaps instead they are the ones who told the lies, the ones who said I was dead. Perhaps they will wish me to be so now.*

The door to Grey's brougham was barely open before the front door of her father's home was flung open.

As Grey stepped out of the carriage, Taylor used his body as a shield and leaned forward shyly to see who had come outside. It was Amanda, and she was blond and beautiful, just as she'd been as a child. A thrill of excitement shot through Taylor. She trembled with giddiness and feared that tears would spill out of her eyes. She would have known Amanda anywhere. It was such a comforting feeling, but strange somehow. Taylor felt as if she'd just recognized a person who was a stranger to her.

But wasn't she? Wasn't Amanda—along with her mother and Taylor's father—a stranger to her? Blood kin though they may all be, the truth was she didn't know them and they didn't know her . . . not anymore.

Disconcerted, suddenly unsure of herself, Taylor abruptly sat back, out of view of her—she swallowed—white family. But underneath her uneasiness, and growing stronger with each passing second, was the realization that she needn't have worried only moments ago as they'd driven up the circular driveway toward this imposing mansion. She was loved.

The proof of it was even now running Taylor's way, her skirts flying, her arms opened wide, and a look of pure expectant joy on her face. "Where is she, Greyson? Where? Did she come? Oh, dear me, let me see her! Let me see her!"

Taylor could see Greyson's profile and heard his chuckle. "Only a moment more, Amanda. Allow me to hand her out." He turned to Taylor, his hand outstretched to her, his eyes merry, his expression warm. "You'd best get out before your cousin throttles me for delaying this happy reunion."

He coupled his words with a wink at Taylor. She knew in that moment that she trusted him with her life. If he'd brought her here, then she was safe. He would never allow anyone to harm her. Perhaps it was a testament to her feeling a bit off-balance, or maybe it was simply a need to feel his touch, his reassurance, but whatever it was . . . Taylor did actually allow him to hand her out of the brougham. She put her hand in his. His fingers closed over hers and gently squeezed. Her gaze met his and held. Something sparked in the depth of his dark eyes, something that said how much he cared.

Taylor's breath caught. She wondered if he knew he'd revealed as much as he had. She sought Bentley's attention. He silently, sagely nodded and fluttered his little short-fingered hand at her, as if to say, "Go on from here. This is a good thing." Taylor nodded at him, smiling, thanking him.

And then the moment was over, she was out of the carriage—and Amanda had flung herself, laughing and crying, into Taylor's arms. Taylor held onto her childhood friend, her beloved Amanda, the sister of her heart, with as much fierce emotion as Amanda held her. Amanda alternately sobbed heartily and peppered Taylor's face with kisses. She held Taylor out from her at arm's length and stared at her, then shrieked happily and hugged her again. Taylor was just as happy but more reserved in showing it. Outwardly she smiled and submitted to Amanda's happy dramatics, but inside, Taylor felt certain her knees would give way and she would fall to the ground, so overwrought with emotion was she.

Amanda again pulled back and held Taylor out at arm's length. "Let me look at you again." Grinning, worshipful, she looked Taylor up and down. "I just knew it. You *are* the most beautiful woman on earth. I always knew you would be." She looked into Taylor's eyes, brown eyes meeting blue. "I love you so much, Taylor. You must never go away and leave us again. Never. I cannot lose you again. I cannot."

"Amanda?"

The quiet masculine voice at their side had Taylor turning with Amanda to face the speaker. Her father. Weakness invaded Taylor's bones. She started to slip. Amanda cried out, her grip on Taylor's arm tightening. Charles James . . . so blond and tall and of such elegant and ethereal bearing that he appeared to be held to the earth only by the weight of the clothes he wore . . . grabbed Taylor's other arm and held onto her as well. At her back, and steadying her with his hands to her waist, was a familiar touch and strength, that of Greyson.

With perhaps a show of deference for this meeting between father and child, Amanda released Taylor and stepped back, her hands folded together in front of her, her smile radiant.

"Are you all right, Taylor?" Grey whispered in her ear.

His warm breath and the timbre of his voice sent a shiver over her skin. She managed an unsteady nod, and Grey released her. Taylor stood her ground now, on her own power, but with her cold hands fisted at her sides. She felt naked and helpless. An assortment of noises surrounded her: a horse made a snuffling noise; Bentley thanked Greyson for assisting him out of the carriage; the driver alit, his footsteps crunching through the gravel. A close-by bird in some tree chirped. But eventually the mix of sounds faded into the background. All was quiet now around Taylor and her father. An air of expectancy settled over them. Even the wind settled. The world seemed to hold its breath . . . and to wait.

Taylor stood stiffly still. Her father gripped her arm. She didn't know how to feel about that. She did not know this man, the things that were in his heart, the things that he believed, or even what he thought. The little girl inside her wanted only to melt into his embrace and cry out all her fears and longings. But the hardened young woman she now was stood her ground and stared silently at this man who, with her mother, had caused her to have life.

"Hello, Taylor." His voice was low and soothing. Tears stood in his eyes, eyes every bit as blue as Taylor's.

She remembered these eyes from all those years ago, from the few times in her life before this moment that she had seen him. She'd been nine years old when she'd last seen him. After the war, he'd come to the Nation with Stanley James, his brother, to collect Amanda and her mother . . . and to leave Taylor and her mother behind. The men had been there as long as a week, and yet Charles James, though he had visited them, hadn't stayed in the cabin with her and her mother. He'd stayed with his brother . . . with the white people . . . as if ashamed of her and her mother. That was the first time Taylor

had wondered what was so wrong with her that her own father
would not want to be with her.

As she stood here now, with her father's hand on her arm,
a seed of remembered hate and hardness took root in Taylor's
heart and threatened to grow.

But then, Charles James spoke again, this time softly and
for her ears only. "My sweet precious child. I feared I would
never see you again. But thank God in heaven, you've been
returned to me. Hello and welcome home. At last . . . you are
home."

He gazed lovingly at Taylor, his eyes alight, his color
heightened. He was obviously overcome with a strong emotion. Yet he made no further move toward her . . . just held
her arm.

"Father?" The one word slipped out of her.

Charles James broke down. A sob escaped him. Around
them . . . Taylor and her father . . . she heard other sobs and a
masculine sniffle of emotion. And then she found herself in
her father's embrace. She didn't know what to do except hug
him in return and try to hold back her own tears. In her embrace, he felt thin yet strong, warm yet firm. He smelled of
cleanliness and goodness. There was nothing about him of the
hard, cruel man Taylor had forced him to be in her mind.
Instead, there was an air about him of one who was sick but
not dying, of one who was hurting . . . but in his heart and not
his body.

In that instant, Taylor feared for him and forgot to hate him
because he was white. She forgot to hate him because he had
abandoned her and her mother. Because he had never come
back to them. Because he had made her grow up without him.
She forgot all the hateful accusations she'd meant to throw in
his face. She knew in her heart that if she'd met him on her
ground, meaning at her mother's home in the Nation, she
maybe would have said those words. She maybe would have
spit at the ground at his feet and turned her back on him. But
not here and not seeing him like this.

When Charles pulled back from Taylor, he stroked her
cheek and roved his gaze over her face. Then he smiled. "You

have my eyes. I remembered that. I never forgot." Taylor's chin came up proudly. With his hand still clasping her arm, Charles pivoted to look over his shoulder and signaled to a dark-haired woman who'd stayed quietly behind him. "Camilla, come here. Say hello to Taylor. She is finally here." He turned to Taylor. "Do you remember Amanda's mother? Your Aunt Camilla?"

Trying to regain some of her hard-edged equilibrium, Taylor nodded. "I remember her more than I do you. She lived with me and my mother for many years."

Her father's sad expression said he was thinking of many things, that there were many things he wished to say to her. But all he finally said, with a smile that asked for forgiveness, was, "Yes. Yes, she did."

And then Camilla James came forward. Taylor's breath caught, her chest felt tight. She hadn't expected this rush of emotion for her aunt. She certainly had for Amanda and, yes, her father . . . but not her aunt, her father's sister-in-law, wife to his older brother. Still, Taylor had a dim recollection of having to be torn from this woman's grip when she'd left the Nation for good. Taylor remembered being frightened by the woman's cries and her struggling in her husband's arms. She had been begging for Taylor as she'd been dragged off with Amanda holding onto her skirt and sobbing, too. But all that was in the past.

This was today. And this woman was still beautiful. Slender, elegant, she had a high forehead and black, shiny hair. Her eyes were brown, and she was smiling at Taylor with all the love in her eyes that Taylor was used to seeing from her own mother. "Aunt Camilla," Taylor said, offering a tentative smile. "It has been many years. I have come a long way to see you. You are looking well. And my mother sends you her greetings."

Camilla James's chin trembled. Tears streaked down her high cheekbones. She made no move to wipe them away. "And I send mine to her. You are looking well, Taylor Christie James. It has been so long . . . too long. Many times have I cried for you." She lightly tapped her fisted hand over her heart. "Many times has my heart ached for the sight of you, my child."

Taylor blinked in surprise. Her aunt had spoken in flawless Cherokee. Only then did Taylor realize that she first had spoken in her native tongue to Amanda's mother. She had no idea why she had, but a laugh escaped her and the awkwardness was gone. Camilla James opened her arms to Taylor. Taylor stepped into her embrace. And it *was* like coming home. . . . finally.

With a shoulder slanted against the doorjamb, Grey stood with Charles James by the opened French doors of the drawing room. On the other side of the room resided a bank of windows, also opened. A wonderful spring breeze whispered about them and sensuously lifted gauzy curtains away from cream-colored walls. The men faced a terrace that overlooked neat and colorful flower beds. Several gardeners roved over the lawn, planting, weeding, and digging. Sunlight pouring into the room struck Charles James and threw shadows behind him. It seemed to Grey that the beam should have shone right through Charles. The man had the same luminous quality that his daughter possessed.

"I'm sorry, Grey, but can you tell me again why your butler is paying social calls with you today?" Charles James's high forehead was creased with his confusion. "It's highly irregular. Even for you."

Grey chuckled and tore his gaze away from the three women who sat across the room from him and Charles with their heads together and talking incessantly. At least, Amanda and her mother were talking. Taylor looked as if a gun had gone off close to her head and was merely nodding or shaking her head as she saw appropriate. Meanwhile, the butler in question sat in a far corner with his knees together and his hat perched on his lap. He stared straight ahead and made not a sound.

"His being here has nothing to do with me, Charles, I assure you. His presence is because your daughter—"

"By God, that has a nice ring to it. My daughter." Charles

was grinning like the proud papa of a newborn.

"Yes," Grey agreed, "it does. And I couldn't be happier for you all, Charles. I mean that."

Charles gripped Grey's arm and squeezed, a tight-lipped grin lighting his face. Grey acknowledged it and continued. "At any rate, your daughter decided, upon first laying eyes on the poor old fellow the other night, that he is her spirit guide sent to her in her time of need. She says he was a bird and now he is a man, he's magic, and she will go nowhere without him. We all agree it's much simpler to allow her to have her way in this. For his part, Bentley is terrified of her. She presented to us fully armed, in buckskin britches, and atop an Indian paint pony, mind you. But he's of two minds with this man-bird business. While he loves the adoration, he's terrified he'll say the wrong thing and get himself scalped."

Charles's eyebrows rose with his amusement. "That's quite the story. But still . . . poor Bentley. I can see where he would be appalled—at least as much as is my Estes."

At that moment, the James butler, Estes, made another dour pass by the open door of the elegant drawing room. He had no business to conduct in here, but he made no attempt to disguise his sniffing contempt of a servant hobnobbing with his betters. Charles sighed. "I suppose I should go call him off before Bentley dies of mortification."

Grey put a detaining hand on Charles's arm. "Even better, Charles, have Estes take Bentley around to the kitchen or to the butler's pantry, if you would. Perhaps the two can . . . talk about butler duties or something."

Charles gave Grey a look that told him he thought this a singularly odd request. Grey nodded that he understood. "I have my reasons, Charles. Let me just say that I'm not sure we can speak freely in front of him. Or if we even should, the proprieties and Taylor's belief aside."

Charles sobered, shooting a look in the direction of the women. "Is something wrong? Do you suspect him of something?"

Grey released Charles and absently ran a hand through his short-cropped hair, feigning nonchalance should any of the women be looking their way, and said quietly, "I suspect everyone, Charles. Because something *is* very wrong. And I believe you are aware of it."

Clearly insulted, Charles drew back. "If you suppose for one minute that I pose any threat to my own child—"

"She's no longer a child. But I am not supposing a thing, Charles. You misunderstand." Grey hoped he was right, that Charles wasn't behind the web of lies and intrigue that surrounded Taylor's life. But he had no way of knowing yet, warm receptions to the contrary. So he hedged a bit, casting guilt onto Bentley: "It's actually Bentley I have doubts about."

"Bentley?" Charles automatically looked in the direction of the man. Grey did, too. Bentley cut his gaze over to them but never moved, as much a stick of furniture as the upholstered chair he sat bravely perched atop.

As if catching the tension, the women quieted and stared the way of Charles and Grey. "Is anything wrong?" Camilla asked, a worried expression on her face. The two girls, Taylor and Amanda, sat to either side of her on a plush sofa. They were sipping tea from delicate china cups and saucers. Never had Taylor looked more out of place, Grey decided. The pained expression she sent him confirmed how awkward she felt. Grey suppressed a betraying grin.

"No, dear heart. I'm sorry," Charles answered Camilla. He then turned back to Grey and lowered his voice. "Sweet Camilla. She acts as if someone will come out of the woodwork and carry Taylor away."

"Someone could," Grey said levelly. "And as I said, I think you know it. Isn't that why you sent me your note today? I need to speak with you regarding it and how you knew Taylor was alive and here in St. Louis."

Charles again sent Grey a sharp look. "Will you join me on the terrace a moment, Grey?" He held a hand out as if to usher Grey in that direction. Then he turned to the women. "Feel free to roam the grounds or give Taylor a tour of the house. Grey and I are going to step outside for a bit of fresh air."

"But you're standing in the fresh air," Camilla James protested. To Grey, her drawn eyebrows betrayed deeper concerns. Did she not want to be alone with Taylor?

Charles sent Grey a look and then set himself in motion. "I'll just call Estes and have him and Bentley escort the ladies on a promenade through the gardens. Excuse me." Charles walked away from Grey with his arms spread as if he meant to gather the women up and carry them out bodily. "Come along, Bentley; let's put you to work," Charles said cheerfully.

Taylor shot Grey a look, one that showed her evident exasperation. He had no doubt she was determined to ask the hard questions of her aunt today. Grey wondered, though, just how many of them Camilla James could or would answer. Was it the fear of what Taylor could ask that lay behind her frowning countenance? *Damnation.* Grey's teeth gritted with frustration. He wanted to shout. All this subterfuge, the unspoken words, the implied threats, the undercurrents, the lies . . . it was all too much. A sudden and intense urge to strike something solid and inanimate seized Grey.

Damn this creeping subterfuge. But the truth was he was as stuck as Taylor was at the moment. He could do nothing but nod his chin in her direction to encourage her to go with her aunt and cousin for now. She sent him a blistering glare that adequately expressed her opinion of a civilized promenade through a flower garden when there were so many questions of utter importance to be answered. A grimace on his face, Grey watched her go. Frustration gnawed at him. For one thing, danger swirled around her, danger he could not pin down for the life of him. But for another—and he admitted this to himself with a sinking feeling in the area of his heart— Taylor would never be happy in his world, that of a staid and manner-riddled society.

Her spirit was that of the soaring eagle. Her scent was that of the earth and the blue sky. Just to look at her suggested open vistas, a warm wind, and the quiet of the prairie. She needed a wilder civilization, a freedom she could never have here. She needed a people whose heritage and language she knew and loved. She belonged to traditions and a religion and beliefs that would be nothing but ridiculed in Grey's world.

The terrible truth was ... he could not keep her. She would not stay here and she could not go back to the Cherokee Nation. A sudden sympathy for her plight ate at Grey. He had never felt so sorry for someone in his life. She was like a caged bird, one that would die if someone kept it in the cage, and one that would get itself killed if it was set free.

The sky was blue. The sun shone. The breeze was gentle. Grey was with her father inside somewhere. But outside in the gardens that girded the Charles Edward James estate, and with a bewildered Estes and Bentley following at a discreet distance, Taylor strolled with Amanda and Aunt Camilla. Their route carried them along gravel pathways laid out between new beds of greening shrubs and rosebushes alive with buds. Taylor sighed, pronouncing herself tired of tea and promenades and polite conversation. She was now caught up on the lives of the Jameses, and they on hers.

She knew about Amanda's schooling, who her friends were, and about her upcoming marriage to Franklin James. She'd heard all about the plans for the wedding and about Franklin's bid for the mayoralty. She knew about Aunt Camilla's strange sickness that periodically left her weak and bedridden. Thankfully, she hadn't had an episode recently. She knew that Uncle Stanley, who was off conducting some sort of business, didn't yet know she was here but would be delighted to learn she was. She also knew about Aunt Camilla's work with the various charities, what her hopes were for her daughter, and how happy she was to see Taylor.

In turn, Taylor had told them as much as she'd dared about her growing-up years in the Nation. They of course knew of her conviction on murder charges and her subsequent escape from jail, so she'd been spared going into details about those. Instead, Aunt Camilla had asked Taylor about her mother and had spoken fondly of the years she'd spent with her. And this was all good. But still, Taylor could make no sense of this conversation, which was more significant for what was not being said. She wanted answers to the real questions, the ones that had her here and possibly in danger. The moment was quiet between the women. Perhaps now was the time to begin.

"Who told you I was here, Aunt Camilla?"

Her aunt stopped, standing there in a path that led to a structure Amanda had said was called a gazebo. Perhaps it was Taylor's imagination, but her aunt appeared to have paled somewhat with Taylor's question. "Why don't we go sit inside there in the shade, girls? What do you think?"

She pointed to the round white-painted open-air structure ringed inside with benches. Along with Amanda, who supported her mother with a hand on her arm, Taylor nodded and headed for the gazebo. As they approached the shelter, Aunt Camilla turned to the two older men strolling behind them. "Estes, Bentley, you may go back inside, really. I'm sure we'll be perfectly safe out here in full sight of the house. We won't be long. Go on, now."

The butlers looked at each other, then over their shoulders toward the house—as if they thought guidance would come from that direction—but then they again faced the women. Bentley focused on Taylor, his expression sincere. "Is that as you wish, Miss James?"

Taylor's heart warmed for the little man-bird who behaved as if he thought he could defend her—she who had fearlessly killed men—in a time of trouble. "Yes. I will be fine. I carry your spirit with me."

Bentley shot the other butler, Estes, a smug look, no doubt to make sure the man understood Bentley's importance as a man-bird. Estes studiously ignored him. The two men bowed, finally taking their wordless leave of the women. Despite her brave words, Taylor watched Bentley's departure with a sense of foreboding. It was as if with each step of his, the farther away he got, the less sure of herself she felt. But those were the fears of an old woman. Taylor drew herself up and assured herself she was strong in her own right.

She entered the gazebo behind Amanda and sat on the bench built against a wall. Sitting there, Taylor had to admit that the setting was serene and innocent. With a sudden sense of well-being assailing her, she smiled at Amanda, whose heart full of love for Taylor shone in her brown eyes. Taylor then glanced at Aunt Camilla. The dark-haired woman was arranging her skirts as she sat opposite Taylor in the small structure. This was nice, Taylor decided, just the three of them. Perhaps all would be well and the answers would be simple.

"Taylor," her Aunt Camilla began, breaking the companionable silence. To Taylor, the older woman's voice sounded strained. She kept glancing at Amanda as she spoke, giving Taylor the impression that Amanda knew nothing about what was about to be said. "Coming here—and I mean to St. Louis—was not a good thing for you to do."

"Mother!" This was Amanda, who'd come to her feet. "How can you say such an awful thing? We love Taylor. We—"

"Be still, Amanda. And sit down. No one loves Taylor more than I do. No one." Camilla's voice broke on her last words.

Taken aback, all Taylor could do was watch Amanda sit down abruptly and Aunt Camilla struggle for composure. "Forgive me, Taylor. But it's true. You should not be here. I cannot imagine why your"—she took a deep breath—"mother sent you here. She and I have worked for years to keep you away from here and safe. I have money I want to give you. I want you to take it and go far, far away from here. Please. Today. Before it's too late. You must do it—for yourself and for Amanda's sake."

Chapter Thirteen

Amanda? What does Amanda have to do with this?" Taylor exchanged a glance with her cousin, who looked as if she'd just seen a ghost. Nervy excitement mixed with fear and ate at Taylor. She felt she was at last on the verge of answers, only now she wasn't so sure she wanted to hear them and the awful truths that lay at their roots. A nagging voice inside her head said hearts would be broken and people would be dead before her life was finally sorted out. Again, her Cherokee prison guard's warnings and his curse came to Taylor, leaving her breathless . . . and helpless to stop what she'd put into motion simply by being here and being alive.

Camilla James didn't answer Taylor's question. She simply sat there, staring at the wooden flooring of the gazebo and shaking her head slowly. "It's all coming undone," she murmured, speaking more to herself than to her daughter and Taylor.

Amanda sent Taylor a look of fearful confusion and then got up, going to her mother and kneeling in front of her, taking her hands in hers. "Mother, what is coming all undone? And why is Taylor not safe? Or me? Who would harm us?"

Aunt Camilla shook her head and cupped Amanda's cheek in her hand. "No one will harm you, Amanda. It's just that . . . well, I don't want you to hear what I have to say. It doesn't concern you. Not directly. Just . . . please, allow me to speak with Taylor. In private."

Taylor squelched the urge to jump up and retrieve Amanda and tell her to leave them be, as her mother had asked. But such interference on her part between mother and daughter would be considered inconceivably rude by Cherokee standards of behavior. And so Taylor sat, her heart pounding dully, her eyes wide . . . and waited.

Amanda had stilled, staring up at her mother. Silence passed like heartbeats. Suddenly she sprang to her feet. Her hands were balled into fists. "No. I won't, Mother. I can't. From what you just said I gather that you've always known Taylor was alive. And you've kept her away from me. How could you? You know how I love her. All those times I wanted to see her—and you told me she was dead. How awful of you. Tell me—and tell Taylor—what is going on."

"I cannot." Sounding strong and angry, Camilla James jumped up, advancing on her daughter as Amanda backed up. Taylor sat silent and stricken. Mother and daughter behaved as if she weren't there. "We all love Taylor. Me. You. Her Indian mother. Your Uncle Charles. It's just that . . . you don't understand."

Amanda's soft pink face contorted into a reddening mask of pain and anger. "Of course I don't. So tell me. Make me understand. Make me see why I've been separated all these years from Taylor. Tell me why you told me she'd died as a child, Mother. Tell me. What reason could be good enough?"

The low bench seat hit the back of Amanda's knees. She sat down abruptly, this time right next to Taylor, and clutched at her hands. Taylor intertwined her fingers with Amanda's. Her hands were every bit as cold as Taylor's were. With Amanda, she stared up at her Aunt Camilla. The dark-haired woman covered her face with her hands and took deep breaths. When she lowered them, she was dry-eyed. She sought Taylor's gaze. A soft smile claimed Camilla's face as she reached out to stroke Taylor's cheek. "You are indeed beautiful, Taylor. I never wanted to leave you."

Her aunt's hand was warm against her face. Taylor smiled. "I thank you and would have you know that I do not have feelings against you for going. You are my aunt. You had to go with your husband and your daughter. That is as it should be."

Camilla nodded, sending Taylor a look that said she pitied her—or perhaps pitied her lack of understanding. "Yes, darling. I did. I had to go. But I never wanted to leave you behind. It's important to me that you understand that."

Taylor frowned, again recalling the scene eleven years ago of Camilla James's leave-taking of Taylor and her mother. It had been frightful to the child she had been. It next occurred to her that her aunt could answer for her all the whys to her life. Taylor cocked her head at a questioning angle and asked the one word: "Why?"

Camilla James paled and turned her back on Taylor and Amanda, who could only look at each other and shake their heads. Into the silence came the sounds of birds chirping, of somewhere a dog barking . . . and approaching footsteps, more than one set, announced the arrival on the scene of two more people. Taylor looked toward the sound, and her heart took a thrilling leap. Grey and her father were nearing the gazebo . . . and they didn't look the least bit happy.

"What's wrong?" Grey called out, quickening his steps.

Taylor stood up, going to stand at the low railing that ringed the gazebo. "Aunt Camilla has just asked me to take money and to leave here before something bad happens to me and Amanda."

Grey gasped, but Taylor noted her father's reaction. He looked as if all the blood had been drained out of him. "Camilla, no!" he called out, hurrying forward, his hands held out to his sister-in-law. "No. We cannot—I will not—lose her again."

Taylor's aunt turned toward Charles James. "But we have to send her away. If we don't, then Stanley will—"

"Camilla!" Charles shouted her name, making of it a command for silence. His eyebrows lowered angrily. "Not another word. You're obviously distraught, and you don't know what you're saying."

Grey spoke up, drawling in a knowing manner. "I think she knows exactly what she's saying. And I believe it's time she said it."

"Wait," Amanda ordered, turning to her mother. "What does Father have to do with all this?"

Charles James answered for her. "He's my brother. We're

all family, Amanda. Your mother just meant your father would
. . . have the same feelings we do about Taylor."

Taylor stood up. "You mean about me leaving, don't you?"

No one said anything. Taylor looked from her aunt to her
father. Neither one of them would meet her eyes. She locked
gazes with Grey. He appeared every bit as angry and frustrated
as she felt. Taylor forced her attention back to her white family
and spoke again. "You cannot push me away. I will not leave
until I have the answers you can give me. Since I was nine I
have lived away from you, my father. I was told Amanda was
dead. A lie. I want only to know the why from you . . . and
then I will go."

"No," Grey said, cutting off anybody who might have been
about to speak. "We'll leave now, Taylor. Come with me,
please." He held his hand out to her.

Before she could move, her father brushed Grey's hand
aside. "No. She is my daughter, and she will stay here in my
home with me."

Grey rounded on the older man. "Like hell she will. She's
not safe in this house."

"That's twice, Grey. After everything I've confided to you,
you still believe I would harm my own child?"

"She's been harmed enough by the lies her family has told
her, my friend. She will stay with me until this nasty business
is concluded. And then she may do as she pleases, go where
she will."

Taylor's father's tone became pleading. "But it's not proper
for her to be unchaperoned in your house, Grey. I insist she
stay here."

"I'm afraid you're in no position to insist on anything,
Charles. She goes with me. Taylor?" Grey again held his hand
out to her. His dark eyes bore into hers.

In his eyes, Taylor could see a flicker of uncertainty. She
immediately alleviated it—and surprised herself—by stepping
out of the gazebo, going to him, and taking his hand. She then
turned to her family. They were knotted loosely together, a
picture of helplessness and loving concern. It wasn't lost on
Taylor that she stood apart from them with Grey, separated

from them by mere feet . . . a matter of inches, which may as
well have been miles and years. "I love you all," she began,
her head held high, her bearing proud. "And I am sorry if my
being here and alive is causing you pain."

Grey held Taylor close to him. They lay in bed, naked and
intertwined, in the middle of the afternoon and much to the
scandal of the entire Talbott household staff. Not that he cared
or that it could be helped. Taylor had needed him. She of
course hadn't said as much. In fact, she hadn't said anything
on the entire ride home. Silently she'd stared out the small
opening that was the brougham's window and kept her own
counsel. Grey had feasted on her elegant profile and his heart
had gone out to her. But she was of a proud and stoic nature
that didn't invite intimacy of the sort that would have had him
telling her how sorry he was the situation with her family had
soured.

Grey found it very curious that she gave freely of her body
to him but not of her heart or her thoughts. To Grey this said
she didn't know much of real love, of trusting someone, or of
intimacy with another soul. But when he thought of what he
knew about her and could surmise of her life—how hard it
had been, how much other people had taken from her—he
couldn't really call himself surprised. But what he could do
was vow that if she would allow it, he would be glad to teach
her how to give of herself in other ways.

But not today, not while she was emotionally exhausted.
The shocks and surprises had cast her up and down much like
a ship on troubled waters. On the ride to her father's, she'd
been excited and anxious. But on the ride home—*home,* Grey
liked how that sounded, especially when he was including
her—but on the ride home, she'd been subdued and saddened.
He had barely got more than a sniff or a shrug out of any
inquiries he'd made about her well-being. Not even the much-
vaunted man-bird Bentley had been able to draw her out. And
so the two men had let her be. When they arrived home, she'd
said nothing but had gone directly to the horse barn to see
Red Sky.

Grey had come inside. Anxiously he'd paced about in the library and waited for her, wondering if she'd come to him or if she'd hop on her horse and leave. About the time he felt certain the suspense would kill him, she'd come to him with the solemn pronouncement that her horse needed to be exercised and that she wished to go riding. Not one word about the afternoon's events, what she may have learned or even a question about what he may have found out. Her reticence hadn't really surprised him because it was just like her. She kept so much inside. As she hadn't included an invitation for him or anyone else to accompany her on her excursion, he'd quickly insisted on going with her. That outing had yet to happen because . . . well, this being in bed had happened first.

Grey shifted about under the sheet that covered them. Taylor lay at his side, an arm and a leg thrown over him. She draped her hand around his neck and held him possessively . . . but she never said a word. Not about caring for him, not about hurting because of her family, none of that. Instead, she showed her feelings in her lovemaking. She was an exquisite lover. Wild. Sensual. Exhausting. But again, it went back to her giving physically of herself when in reality he wanted more from her . . . her innermost thoughts, her wishes, her hurts. He wanted her to confide in him. He wanted, in short, for her to let him inside her heart and mind, the two aspects of herself that she guarded most tenaciously.

Still, that wasn't to say he wasn't happy about this particular interlude they'd just shared. But perhaps it could be a start, now that he reflected on how their being here in bed had come about. They'd come upstairs to change clothes into proper riding attire. But then and suddenly, she'd appeared in his doorway, the one that led to the common dressing room, half-dressed, her heart in her eyes. Her look had said she wanted him and that she needed him to hold her. Grey smiled, thinking it wasn't much, but it was something to build on. Now, if only he could get her to admit to herself and to him that she needed him, all would be well.

Except with her family and their secrets. Grey quirked his mouth in disgust. He wouldn't have blamed Taylor if she had left earlier. Her treatment here by them all—him, her family, his family—at one time or another had been deplorable. Not a one of them deserved as much as the most cursory of regard from her. She was a much finer creature, more honest and straightforward than anyone else he had ever met—with the notable exception of Amanda, who seemed to share many traits with Taylor. Indeed, Amanda also appeared to be as innocent and misused as Taylor herself was. But she was no shrinking violet of a girl—she would pursue her questions with her mother; Grey didn't doubt that. Certainly, at her end, Amanda would see this through to her own satisfaction. And no doubt would share with Taylor what she found out.

"Why are you smiling? What are you thinking about?"

Pulled back to the moment and to the woman in his arms, Grey settled her more comfortably against him and smiled down at her, planting a kiss on her forehead. "I was thinking of your cousin Amanda."

"My cousin?" Taylor rose, supporting herself on an elbow. Her motion dislodged the sheet, which slipped down her arm to settle at the curve of her slim waist. Exposed to Grey's eyes was an expanse of pink and tanned skin that covered the most wonderfully erotic curves and peaks and valleys of her body. "I am lying here naked in your arms and we have done the things together that give us much pleasure—and you are thinking of my cousin?"

Holding his hands up as if he were being robbed, Grey chuckled at the note of feminine outrage in her voice. "In only the purest of contexts, I assure you."

Taylor narrowed her eyes at him and poked a finger at his bared chest. "Name one . . . con-text, that word."

"Context? Hmm. OK. I was thinking of Amanda being such a good and brave girl and how she reminds me of you. And how we can depend on her to help us and tell us anything she finds out. Now, how's that for pure?"

Taylor eyed him, her gaze painstakingly inching across his every feature, as if she searched for a joke or a trick in his manner. Apparently not finding any, she glared at him and again lay down next to him, resting her head against his shoulder. "It is pure, this con-text."

Thoroughly delighted with her, Grey squeezed her in an abrupt hug born of an unexpected surge of deep emotion for her. She squawked her protest and cursed him—no doubt—in loud Cherokee.

"Taylor, you are an absolute delight." The words bubbled out of him.

Her answer, though, was in irritable tones. "And I am now a flattened one. Loosen me, *yo-hna.*"

Grey crooked a finger under her chin and raised her face to his. "What did you just call me? White man?"

"No. A bear. You squeeze me like one would. I should be glad you are not my *tso-tsi-da-na-wa* . . . my enemy."

The word was long and harsh-sounding, more dangerous in its tonality than the English word, which was as it should be, Grey decided, sobering. "I would never want to be your enemy, Taylor. Never."

She tightened her grip on him. It had the effect of an affectionate gesture. Moved, Grey stroked her cheek and smoothed her long hair back from her face. Looking into the liquid depths of her sky blue eyes, he felt dangerously close to declaring himself to her. He recalled their last discussion in bed and how it had ended badly, but even knowing that, he couldn't stop the words. "Taylor, I know this is sudden. But I've come to realize over the past few days just how I feel about you. I really believe I—"

She popped a hand over his mouth, shutting him up. She moved to lie atop him, her blue eyes sparking with anger. "Do not say another word. I am not of your people, your white people. They do not want me here. And I do not wish to remain here. You will say nothing that will stop me when that day comes when I will go. And that day will come. So there can be no words between us."

Now Grey was angry. He pulled her hand away and shrugged out from under her weight. Sitting up, propping himself against the piled pillows and pulling the sheet over his lap, he crossed his arms and aired his frustration. "No words between us? Words are all you're worried about? Taylor, look where you are. You are in my bed. We have been intimate together. More than intimate. Extremely intimate. I cannot believe the loving acts we performed together would mean less to you than shared words of caring. How can that be?"

Taylor sat up, innocently unconcerned as always regarding her nudity. Grey found it hard to listen to her. Her firm and full breasts bobbed seductively as she illustrated her story as much with elegant gestures as she did with words. "What two people say to each other is binding. It is heard. The words reach to the sky. Because words are sacred. They are like magic. They are ropes that can tie us together, never to be broken."

As moved as he was by her nakedness and her exotic mannerisms, Grey exhaled his exasperation and ran a hand through his hair. "So is what we do in this bed. It is more than magic. And it can bind us together, too. What we do here can also, uh, cause a baby to be."

"No. I have taken care of this. There will be no child between you and me."

Her expression was infuriatingly blank, stoic, impassive, and impenetrable. Cocksure, undoubting, and certain—and horrifying for being so. Not if his life depended on it was Grey going to ask her just how she'd seen to that detail. As it was, all he could do was sit and stare at her. They were miles apart here. Would they ever find common ground?

She was such a heartwarming and hair-raising mix of contradictions that kept him off-balance. Downstairs and in public she gave him barely a glance and a show of cool reserve. But up here in private she was a tigress and a wanton, yet warm and loving. Although, in an instant, at the wrong word, she could be the noble and stoic savage—a glaring warrior armed with a long-bladed knife. And then she could turn right around and act the prim lady to the last degree. She was a child. She was a woman. She was ancient and wise, yet young and innocent. No wonder his world was atilt, just as was his heart.

"I don't know what to make of you, Taylor."

She frowned. "Make of me? You need not make anything

of me. You must only remember that I am Indian, as your people call me, and that I am an escaped murderer. I have killed three men. I have stolen horses. I have lived in a log cabin among the trees. I have lived in a cave, bathed in streams, eaten only the food I gathered or killed myself. I am not of your cities and your white ways and laws. I came here only to please my mother. And when I have done my duty by her, I will go. And I will again wear buckskins and carry a gun. I will go my own way in this world."

He meant nothing to her. Grey felt his heart breaking. He leaned his head back, closing his eyes as he rested against the carved wood headboard behind him. His strength seemed to ebb out of him. After a quiet moment in which she neither touched him nor spoke to him, Grey lowered his head, opened his eyes, and looked into hers. Impassive blue, if that could be said to be a color. He considered her, roving his gaze over her. He then met her gaze. . . . It locked with his. He took a deep breath, exhaled, ran the tip of his tongue over his lips. Then he nodded. "All right. There will be no words between us. No words of caring. But neither can we do this again, Taylor. Making love, I mean. It obviously is nothing more to you than taking a bath or riding your horse. But to me it is so much more. A loving expression of my—I'm sorry. I said no words of caring, didn't I?"

With a flick of his wrist, he threw the sheet back and swung his legs over the side of the bed. With his hands to either side of him and gripping the mattress, Grey stared down at his feet and directed his words to them. "We'll do this your way, Taylor. I'll help you find your answers. I'll stick by you and protect you as best I can. I offer you my house, my food, and a bed of your own. But nothing more, meaning my bed. When it is time for you to go . . . you will go."

Behind him, he felt a shifting of her weight on the bed. For a moment, Grey believed—hoped, prayed—Taylor was reaching out to him, that she would take him in her arms and hold him and protest his words and call his bluff, although he really wasn't bluffing. He meant what he'd said. He could no longer hold her and love her and not have it mean something beyond a toss on the sheets. She meant so much more to him than that.

After a moment, he heard her whisper something in Cherokee.

For some reason, her soft voice ... perhaps its low pitch, its heartfelt tone ... froze him in place. He waited. But nothing ... only stillness and silence. Finally, and gathering his courage, Grey turned around, looking. His heart sank. He was alone. Across the way, the door that led from his bedroom to hers was open ... but was slowly closing from the other side.

An hour later, and from her bedroom window, Taylor observed Grey leaving. He was alone, and he rode that big black horse of his. Taylor flew downstairs and found Bentley. But gained no satisfaction there. Not only could he not tell her where Grey had gone, but he still urged caution and waiting on her. With a sound of disgust, Taylor had then left Greyson Talbott's home herself.

With her hair hanging in a long braid down her back, and clad in a pair of loose britches and an oversize shirt she'd cajoled Mrs. Scott to find for her, she now stalked toward the horse barn. The coach yard was empty of men. This was good. Not that she thought they would try to stop her. They were smarter than that. She simply didn't wish to deal with them. So, with her knife tucked into her knee-high boot and with her gun again riding in its holster—she'd found it in a desk drawer in the library—Taylor allowed anger to guide her steps. She pulled her floppy-brimmed felt hat low over her brow, shading her eyes from the late-afternoon sun.

She'd had all she could stand in this city of white people. She would now do things on her own and for herself. Hadn't she always? Taylor felt as if everything were happening, but nothing was being done. Everything was being said, but nothing was being explained. The answers didn't go with the questions. And the questions were not the correct ones. To her, it seemed as if everyone were talking around her but not to her. As if they whispered behind their hands and stared in her direction but said nothing to her. She felt like a towering wind-devil was fast bearing down on her—only she couldn't see it for clear skies.

It was unbearable. She'd wasted enough time. She'd only been here days, but it felt like weeks. And the nights seemed an entire season of moons.

Intense frustration ate at her. But wasn't that her own fault? she asked herself. Because it didn't have to be this way. She knew where her father lived, and she knew where Amanda and Aunt Camilla lived. And they now knew she was alive and here. Beyond that—it had been obvious this afternoon—they *knew*. Knew what? Taylor couldn't even articulate it for herself. But they knew. And Aunt Camilla had wanted to tell her, but without Amanda being present. Then she would go to Aunt Camilla's and talk to her in private. It was that simple. Or maybe she would go to her father. He would know. He did know. These elders of hers had lived the lies that had kept Taylor away from them all, but especially away from Amanda, a girl she loved as a sister.

Taylor paused for a moment, on the apron of ground out front of the barn. Maybe she should go get Amanda and the two of them would leave this place of the whites. Taylor grinned . . . but then her next thought slumped her, killing that grandiose scheme. Amanda would not go. She was white, too. This was her home and she would soon marry a white man. Grey's brother.

It occurred to Taylor again that despite how close she and her cousin had been as children, they no longer were. They were both grown women who had grown apart. But still, Taylor loved her and what they had been to each other. She recalled now how she had always secretly wished she could be more like Amanda. More genteel and loving, more open and trusting. But her life in the Nation had not allowed her to be those things. Or maybe it was more that she, because of choices she had made, hadn't allowed it.

Taylor shook her head, arguing with herself as she entered the barn and called out to Red Sky, who instantly answered with a loud whinny. A few heads popped up over the stalls— men's and horses'. Once the hands recognized her, they didn't challenge her but went quickly back to their jobs. And that was good. Taylor headed in the direction of Red Sky's whinny. The sound told her he was still in the same stall. As she turned to her left and worked her way through the barn, it struck Taylor that she was as locked away in Greyson Talbott's house as Red Sky was in the barn. Her horse was not used to such restrictions. Neither was she.

It seemed, then, that she still made bad choices. She had certainly made a mistake in giving her body to Grey. Not that she hadn't enjoyed him. She had. Even now she could feel the play of his warm, hard muscles under her hands. Even now she could taste his kiss, could feel the heat of his body as he came into her and made them one. Such thrusts and power, such skill. Thinking about it now, Taylor all but whistled out her breath. Greyson Talbott knew his way around her woman's body. His touch alone shivered her in her most private places. His kiss melted her heart. And his mouth . . . oh, his mouth. He was wickedly good.

Taylor shivered, forcing herself out of the bed and the tangle of naked bodies she saw in her mind. She should never have told him she loved him. At least her parting words earlier had been in her language and he would not know what they meant. She hadn't even known she meant them, or felt them, herself until they'd slipped past her lips. So it was just as well that they'd been spoken in Cherokee. Still, she was surprised at herself. She'd never before told anyone—not even that yellow-belly dog Monroe Hammer—that she loved him. And now, after knowing this white man for no more than three days . . . she loved him? No. It wasn't true. She'd just been overcome for a moment, seized by a shard of need, one she wouldn't give in to again.

Taylor approached Red Sky and abandoned her thoughts of love. The horse greeted her excitedly, nodding his great head and stamping a hoof. Taylor whispered words of endearment in Cherokee to the great animal. Then she entered his stall, quickly saddled him, and led him outside. There, with the sun sitting low in the western sky, with the heavens streaked red and pink, Taylor mounted up and turned Red Sky toward the open coach yard gate. Digging her heels into Red Sky's sides, she urged him into a trot. They turned out of the gate and went to the left, toward the homes of her white family. She still had no idea which one she would approach first. Her father. Or her aunt.

But either way, and today, she would have answers. She was especially interested in learning why Aunt Camilla had called Taylor's mother her Indian mother. Why would this woman who had lived with The People for such a long and loving time say such a demeaning thing about her sister of the heart?

Chapter Fourteen

No spying eyes. No prying ears. That was what Grey sought. Neutral ground. Thus, the night was right for meeting at their social club. Charles had immediately answered Grey's note from late that afternoon, after Taylor had gone to her room, asking Charles to meet him here. So here they were now.

The carpeted gaming room where they had secreted themselves was shot through with masculine decor. Dark wood wainscoting graced the thick walls. The gold- and green-flecked wallpaper above it calmed the senses. But the air was close and stuffy, reminiscent of the smoke of countless cigars. The heavy velvet draperies were drawn against the dark outside. And the door was shut and locked. No one would interrupt them.

All around Grey and Charles were neat groupings of felt-topped card tables and empty chairs. Grey stood to one side of the room, leaning an elbow against an old upright piano. In his hand, he held a whiskey. The bottle and another glass sat atop a table across the way. Charles hadn't wanted a drink. The only thing he nursed right now was a tremendous anger at Grey.

"Why are you working so hard to keep my daughter from me, Grey? You alone of all people know what she means to me. You know how I feel, how broken I've been because—"

"Spare me," Grey drawled as he moved away from the piano and went to perch a hip atop a card table, leaving his leg to dangle. "I *thought* I knew what she meant to you, Charles. I really did. Until today. I really expected you to be forthcoming with me this afternoon while the women were outside. But instead you launch into some fatherly diatribe on my behavior with your daughter."

"I have every right to question you, Grey. She is a young, unmarried girl living under your roof. You're not exactly the most acceptable of chaperons."

"I hold the same high opinion of myself on that score, Charles. Still, we've already been through this. I've told you how it occurred that she came to be in my keeping. She was approaching your door the night of the party for Franklin and Amanda, I intercepted her . . . and the rest you know. Except allow me to say that you're a little late to be showing fatherly concern for her. According to her, you've made no effort to see her since she was a child."

Charles's expression contorted into one of pain. "If you'll recall, Grey, I made no effort because I believed her to be long dead. Then I find out she's been alive all this time, only to think I'd lost her again to a hanging. And this morning— for God's sake, man—I find out she's alive and here in St. Louis in your keeping. Just what in the hell do you want from me?"

"The truth, Charles."

"I *have* told you the truth, Grey—the truth as I've known it to be. I swear it. But I will say that even had I known Taylor was alive all these years, I would not have dared to acknowledge that she was. I would not have dared to try to see her."

"Now see there? What exactly does that mean . . . you wouldn't have dared? What reason could possibly be good enough to keep a loving father away from his only child? It can't be because her mother is Cherokee and Taylor's a half-breed. After all, you had a hand—as it were—in that. So it's not that. But what is it, then? Your own guilt at having such a child? Or perhaps your guilt at leaving her mother in the manner you did? Or both?"

Charles's blond coloring heightened to a fiery red. He bared his teeth in an angry grimace and fisted his hands, stalking around in a small circle before finally striking a felt tabletop. He then pointed threateningly at Grey. "Dammit, you go too far. You don't understand. And you're way out of line, my friend."

Grey stood up, leaving his whiskey glass on the table. "Friend. That's interesting. You see, when Taylor first arrived here, I kept her from you to protect *you* until I could prove or disprove *her* story. But now, I find myself in the reverse position of protecting her from you. So, dammit, Charles, help me here. Believe me, I've been your staunchest supporter in this business. But on the very day that you welcome home your daughter—after thinking her dead twice over—Camilla offers her money to go away. Can you explain that to me? And please don't be tiresome by saying you didn't know she would do that or that none of this is my business. I've made it my business."

Charles's anger seemed to melt away, leaving him looking his fifty-odd years or more. He looked down and away from Grey. With stumbling steps he pulled out a leather-cushioned chair and sat heavily. He put his elbows on the table and rubbed at his eyes with the heels of his hands. "I didn't know Camilla would do that; I swear it. I know *why* she did, though. But you have to understand, Camilla had lied to me about Taylor being alive. I truly believed my daughter to be long dead. But now, Grey, she's here . . . and she's in great danger. Great danger."

Grey felt as if his throat were closing. He could barely swallow. Grabbing up his shot glass—he felt certain he was going to need fortifying—he quickly weaved his way around the tables and went to sit facing Charles. He sat his glass on the table. "Charles, are you telling me that Camilla James has always known Taylor was alive and she kept that from you?"

"Yes." Charles had his hands over his face, so the word was muffled but adamant.

"Why would she do that?"

"Her fear that I would go get Taylor or inadvertently give away, by word or deed, that she lived."

Grey ran a hand over his mouth. "Jesus. What business would it be of hers if you did? Taylor's your child, not hers."

Charles lowered his hands from his face, which was

splotchy with emotion. "She did it to protect Taylor."

"From you?" A cold dread filled Grey. Had he perhaps missed some deep insanity here? Or a sickness of the soul that would have a father misusing his daughter?

"No, Grey. Not from me. I love my child. I would never harm her. But there is someone who could." He hit his fist against the tabletop. "I wish to God she had never come here. I fear we can't keep her safe."

Grey clutched at Charles's sleeve. "Yes, we can. And we will. But let me tell you why she's here. Her mother sent her to you."

Charles frowned. "Her mother?"

"Yes. The hard truth is, Charles—and you already know this—your daughter was sentenced to hang for murder. However, you may not know the details. She says she didn't kill the man for whose death she was supposed to hang. And she tells me she was broken out of jail by her uncle the day before she was to hang. Furthermore, your daughter *has* killed three other men. But she assures me they deserved it."

Charles stared dumbfounded at Grey. "My little girl is certainly far from an innocent young miss."

"Yes, she is. But only in some ways." Grey wasn't about to divulge in what other ways Taylor was no innocent, but he did add, "In others, she's very naive."

Charles shook his head, wonderingly. "Camilla was right to try to get Taylor to leave."

"Camilla." Grey said her name in a considering manner. "So her emotional performance last night, her crying over the long-lost Taylor was just that? A performance?"

Charles shook his head no and grimaced, rushing to Camilla's defense. "No. It was genuine. Although she knew Taylor to have been alive all these years—"

"How did she know and you didn't?"

"She never told me until today, but she's corresponded with Tennie Nell Christie."

"Christie? Taylor's . . . mother, then, I take it?"

Charles stared at Grey a moment, then nodded. "She raised her."

"I see. We were talking about Camilla."

"Yes. Her emotion was—is—genuine. She loves Taylor very much. Last night was real. At that point we had no idea Taylor had escaped hanging and was here, remember. So Camilla's sadness at her death was genuine, I assure you. But those other things Camilla said . . . well, she had to say them like that, about believing Taylor to have been dead all along. To acknowledge otherwise could have unleashed terrible trouble. Terrible."

Grey liked this conversation less and less. It was confirming too many things for him that he already had feared. "Charles, listen to me." He waited, making sure Charles was giving him his full attention. "Did Camilla have to behave that way because in that room with us last night was the person or persons who would want to see Taylor dead?"

Charles's expression could only be called bleak. "I fear so, Grey."

A hopeless, helpless rage leached Grey's strength and took all joy in being alive from him. Taylor'd been right when she'd said that if his happy world toppled with her truths, it was because his world had been built on lies. He felt sick and cold. "I've suspected as much, Charles. Believe me, I have. Just tell me what is going on and how to help. I do want to help."

Charles crossed his arms atop the table and slanted a look to Grey. For a few silent seconds, he roved his gaze—so similar to Taylor's—over Grey's features. "You do care very much for her, don't you?"

Tight-lipped, grim, Grey exhaled and nodded. "Very much, Charles. More than I should. More than I have a right to feel. I've only known her for three days, but that seems to have been enough. Because I do. I care very much."

Charles squeezed Grey's hand in a gesture of fatherly affection. "I thought so. And I'm glad. I am. She generally has that effect on people. Very quickly, almost upon meeting her, you either hate her or love her. She invites no namby-pamby feelings on anyone's part, I assure you."

That was quite the odd speech. Grey tilted his head at a

questioning angle. "How do you know, Charles, what effect she has on people? You haven't seen her in eleven years." He watched the effect of his words on Charles, saw the emotions roving over the older man's face.

"No, I haven't. But when I told Camilla today about Taylor being here, that was when she confessed that she knew Taylor was alive and showed me her letters from Tennie. That's how I know the effect my daughter has on people. It's nothing more sinister than that. I do wish you would believe me, Grey."

Grey's jaw tightened. His hands fisted. "I'm trying, Charles. But tell me, who the hell is sending all these messages flying around St. Louis about Taylor? Do you have any idea?"

Charles shook his head. "I don't. Well, except for the one about her being hanged. That came from Tennie Nell. But the one today about her being here and alive—no, I don't. I just fear that the, uh, wrong people may be behind them. And that these messages are warnings or veiled threats. I just don't know."

Grey rubbed at his temple and then considered his friend. "I think, Charles, that now may be a good time to tell me everything you know or even suspect. Your knowledge of the past, of Taylor's past, may be the only thing that will help us figure this out and keep her alive and ensure her a future."

Charles again met his gaze. "Yes. I agree." He stopped, ran a hand over his face, and sent Grey a look of alarm. "Where is Taylor now, Grey?"

"She's safe at my town house."

Charles relaxed his posture. "Well, thank God for that much."

"Yes. Go on," Grey encouraged levelly, reaching for the whiskey bottle and the extra glass sitting in front of them. He poured Charles a drink and shoved it toward him.

"Thank you." Charles closed his hands . . . so pale and long-fingered . . . around the squat crystal glass. He stared at the dark amber liquor and began talking. "This is all so hard, Grey. So hard. Until now, Taylor has been dead to me. And now I have found her again, only to possibly lose her again.

Unless we sort this out—and quickly—she is, this moment, as good as dead."

Grey stared at Charles James, a man whose friendship he had enjoyed, a man with whom he'd played cards and drunk, a man in whose home he'd been entertained . . . a man to whom he was soon to be related by virtue of his brother Franklin's marriage to Amanda. Suddenly, given all of Charles's secrets, Grey felt as if he'd never met the older man before. "I don't care for the way you phrased that. As good as dead."

Charles took a draining swig from the glass in front of him. Grey refilled it. "Don't think for a moment that I do, either. I just fear it may be the truth." Charles turned a pleading expression on Grey. "Believe me, Grey, Camilla's done everything she's done regarding Taylor to keep her as safe as you also want to keep her. I am satisfied on that score."

"You can so easily forgive Camilla for lying to you all these years? You're a bigger man than me, Charles." Grey's stare was as level as his voice. "I still cannot fathom why she would have the nerve to keep information like that from you. Was that truly the only way, do you believe?"

"Not only do I believe it; I know it. God, poor Camilla . . . having to live with that knowledge all these years. Well, at least she was able to—" Charles's gaze slid away from Grey's face. The older man took a deep breath and went on, but in a different vein. "Camilla's philosophy was the fewer people who knew the truth about Taylor's continued existence, the less chance there was of a slip-up. We have an enemy, Grey. Someone close to us—and to you—who would like nothing more than to see Taylor dead."

Grey's heart plummeted. His hand tightened around the whiskey bottle in his grip. He stared at Charles, who eyed the contents of his glass. "You've said that before. And I've thought it, too. I accept that, but I just don't know the *why* of it, or what lies behind all this. I cannot sort it out for myself, or know how to defend Taylor against whatever is coming, without reasons and a name, Charles. Especially a name. I want to get to the bottom of this."

Charles raised his head, showing Grey a bleak expression,

one devoid of hope. "You may think you do now, Grey, my friend. But I'm not so sure. You don't want to live with what I know. The best mercy I could show you now is not to tell you."

Grey fought the urge to jerk Charles bodily up out of his chair and throttle the man senseless. "Look, you son of a bitch," he settled for saying conversationally. "I'm not some child who needs protecting. I'm a man, and I love your daughter. Granted, before now, I haven't behaved like much of a man. I haven't held up my end of the responsibilities that fell to me and my brother following our father's death. You know me to drink and carouse and never think of tomorrow. Well, believe me, all of that's over. I've never felt more serious or grown-up than I do now. And I have your daughter to thank for that—or to curse; I don't know which. Even worse, I have no idea how she feels about me, if she even at the very least thinks kindly of me. But what she feels in return doesn't matter. I will keep her safe, even at the expense of my own life and that of every blessed or cursed soul on this earth whom I know or am related to. And that includes you. Do you understand me?"

Charles nodded. His chin trembled. He looked down, staring at his measure of whiskey. His shoulders shook with silent sobs and great heaving breaths.

Grey rolled his eyes at his own unkind words. He'd kicked the man when he was down. How sporting was that? He had no idea, after all, what Charles's demons were. And who was to say, Grey told himself, that once Taylor left him he wouldn't be in this same broken condition . . . not caring, crying in his whiskey, not worth the chair he sat on?

Unable finally to hold onto his burst of anger in the face of Charles's helplessness, Grey squeezed his friend's arm in a show of support. "I'm sorry, Charles. Forgive me. I just want to—I need you to . . . Oh, hell, man, just tell me what is going on, for Taylor's sake."

Charles turned to Grey, staring intently at him, as if he meant to look right into Grey's soul and assess his worth. He heaved out a sigh and awkwardly swiped at the tears that had wet his cheeks. He then drained his whiskey glass and thumped the heavy crystal tumbler onto the felt tabletop. "Taylor is—" He cut himself off, firming his lips together and inhaling deeply.

Grey's heart damned near thumped right out of his chest. He poured out another shot for Charles. "Taylor is what, Charles?"

"Taylor is not who she thinks she is, Grey. And if we don't get her to go away from here before she finds out the truth about herself, it alone could very well kill her. And I mean inside herself. She has an enemy she doesn't even know about and for reasons she can't even guess. But I fear the simple truth of who she is will do her more harm in her heart and mind than anything anyone else could do to her."

Grey sat perfectly still. "Charles, what are you saying . . . exactly?"

"I'm saying that we need to get Taylor out of St. Louis before she learns these truths—and before another who already knows the truth finds out that she is here. She could be killed. Too much is at stake for her to live. Too many old wounds best left unspoken and unseen. We have to get her to leave, Grey. And never come back. We have to. It's her only chance."

"Son of a bitch," Grey muttered, sitting forward to prop his elbows on his knees. He tented his hands over his nose and mouth. For long moments he concentrated solely on breathing in and out and staring at the carpet. The silence in the room was almost palpable. Outside the door Grey could hear the sounds of revelry, of masculine banter and camaraderie, the happy, laughing sounds that permeated the many rooms of this mansion built to cater to a man's leisurely pursuits. But inside this small and quiet room off to one side of the grand foyer, it seemed that unbearable truths were about to be told.

Grey lowered his hands, allowing them to dangle between his knees. Inside he felt as cold and exposed as a newborn tossed naked out into a raging blizzard. However, this wintry feeling inside him was a bleak and dark season of the soul. He opened his mouth to speak . . . and to set the chain of events into motion. "I cannot believe this. It appears, from what you're saying, Charles, that we will have to tell further lies to Taylor to preserve her from the truth. Amazing. You'd better start at the beginning, my friend."

Just as she'd done that first night she'd come to St. Louis, Taylor again sat her horse outside her father's home. The evening was pleasant, the sky was darkening, and behind her on the street, fancy carriages passed to and fro. As she'd ridden here, other carriages had passed by her. The elegant people inside them had suddenly sat forward, staring wide-eyed at her. Taylor had dismissed them then, and she ignored them now. She concentrated instead on thinking just what to say to her father. She'd bravely and with determination got herself this far.

But being here now, and without Grey or her aunt and cousin in attendance, Taylor realized she felt some hesitance. It wasn't that she was afraid of the answers her father might give. It was more what she should do if he refused to answer or to tell her the truth. After all, what could she do if he didn't? He was her father. She couldn't slit his throat or shoot him. Well, she could. But she felt certain she wouldn't. And this *was* St. Louis, not the Nation, where disputes were settled more directly . . . at least in her experience and with the people she'd been involved with. Outlaws, mostly. With them, justice had run a swift course.

But not here. Threats and weapons seemed to hold no sway. These white people were too civilized to suit Taylor. She yearned for the direct over the complicated, for the physical over the emotional. She didn't want to think, to care. She wanted to act, to do, and get what she needed by her own hands . . . or her gun . . . or her knife. Those she was good with. It was only when she involved her heart that she was uncertain.

Thinking of her heart and its desires paid her back with what she deserved. The image of Grey's sad face this afternoon popped into her mind. He'd said they could not lie together anymore. This was an odd thing to Taylor. Always

before, she had been the one to say when she would lie with
a man. And never before, when she had wanted a man, had
she been refused. Until Grey. Of course, he hadn't yet refused
her. They'd been in bed together when he'd taken his stand
. . . after their lovemaking. She wondered if when she next
wanted him and had the chance to show him, if he would
really turn her away.

Taylor shook her head and stroked Red Sky's neck. The
white man asked too much. He wanted her heart, he said.
Taylor's eyes narrowed. One cannot give what one does not
have. No. That wasn't right. She had a heart, but it was divided
between two nations and two people who did not want her.
Was it any wonder, then, that she kept her heart with two
halves to herself? Maybe one day, when she could make it
whole, she would feel she could bestow it on . . . someone.

Taylor sighed, tiring of such thoughts that spoke of pity
and weakness. She raised her chin, calling up her Cherokee
pride. She had no need of anyone. She would make her own
way, as she had always done. And Greyson Talbott be
damned.

Thus restored, Taylor dismounted. She looked toward her
father's mansion. The windows were dark. Perhaps he was not
home. Or perhaps he was in another part of the house with no
window on this side to reveal a light. Uncertainty gripped
Taylor, telling her that this time there would be no Greyson
Talbott to stop her. If she went up the walk, she would make
it unchallenged to the door. She wondered how different the
last three days would have been if Grey hadn't interfered.
Would she have met him at all, had he not? Her first thought
was that she most likely would have. His brother was marrying
her cousin. So, at some point, they would have met. This was
a comforting thought. Maybe they would have met here today
at her father's.

Taylor frowned, shaking her head no. Grey would have had
no reason to come with Aunt Camilla and Amanda. After all,
neither Uncle Stanley nor Franklin Talbott—both of whom
would have had much more of a reason to do so—had accompanied her aunt and cousin.

As she looped Red Sky's reins around a wrought-iron bar in the rail fencing, Taylor took a moment to ponder what she was doing, what she was thinking. What were these thoughts in her head? She frowned with the truth—she was assuring herself that she would have met Grey. Somehow, somewhere, she would have met him. But she knew it wasn't really true. She may not have. Assailing Taylor now was a sudden realization of the chance meetings that could change a life. If one thing had been done differently, they never would have met. She found the thought unsettling. But what discomfited her the most was that she was upset by the realization that she might not have met Grey had he not poked his nose in her business.

In the next instant, Taylor realized she was grinning and shaking her head. Greyson Talbott had forced their meeting— by fate or by chance—and she was glad he had. A rare peal of laughter escaped her, garnering for her the shocked stares of a fashionably dressed man and woman just then passing by. A glare from Taylor had the woman clinging to the man's arm and them hurrying on their way. Taylor grinned again at that result. She hadn't lost her toughness. *Greyson Talbott.* She shook her head. And couldn't imagine a time in her life when she hadn't known him. He was under her skin. He filled her thoughts. She could smell him when he was nowhere around, could feel his hands on her just by thinking about him—

Enough. Taylor gave herself a mental shake and looked around, realizing that she'd already started up the walk to the house. In only moments she would be at the front door. Taylor suspended doubts and fears and steadily continued on her way. She kept her gaze trained on the closed and solid front door, facing it as if it were her enemy. And then, she was standing in front of it . . . and was lifting the brass lion's-head knocker. And knocking. For a moment, nothing happened. Then, on the other side, the sounds of a lock being turned greeted her ears. Taylor swallowed, felt her heart tripping over itself. The door opened.

Taylor recognized the butler from that afternoon. Estes. The thin, starchy-looking man took one look at her and his eyes rounded with surprise. "Oh. I say. Good evening . . . Miss, uh, James." He looked all around her as if he thought someone was missing.

"Bentley is not with me."

He met her gaze . . . his face reddened. "I should hope not. Uh, I mean I hadn't supposed he would be." The man retreated to his butler pose and remembered his duties. "Forgive me. Won't you come in, Miss James?"

He was welcoming her. Relief coursed through Taylor. She'd half-expected to be sent packing. "I will if my father is here."

The butler's expression fell. "Oh, dear. He's out for the evening. He'll be so sorry he's missed you. Is there anything I can do?"

"Yes. You can tell me where he is."

The butler looked into her eyes . . . and swallowed. Taylor saw his prominent Adam's apple bob up and down. "I see. Well, he's gone to his gentlemen's club. He's to meet Mr. Greyson Talbott there, I believe."

Taylor's pulse quickened. Her father was meeting Grey? A sense of urgency seized her. "Where is this club? What is it?"

Alarm rounded the man's eyes. "As I said, Miss James, it's a gentlemen's club. Surely you're not thinking of going there?"

Taylor cocked her head in a challenge. "Is there any reason why I shouldn't?"

"Yes, miss, I'm afraid there is. Women aren't allowed on the premises."

"What are . . . premises?"

Estes blinked, looked confused . . . but then his expression cleared. "Oh, I see. You don't understand the word. Premises are . . . the grounds, I suppose. No, wait. More like inside the building. That's it. Inside." He raked her up and down with one look—not unfriendly or demeaning, just pointed. "But you're—that is, women . . . no matter their attire or station . . . are not, uh, welcomed."

Taylor nodded consideringly. "How do I find this building where women are not welcomed?"

Estes made gulping noises. To Taylor, he looked like a fish
did when it was taken out of the water. But concern of another
stripe jumped to the fore inside her—he wasn't going to tell
her where to find Grey and her father. She arched an eyebrow
at the man and edged her hand toward her gun. Estes gasped
and began a rapid babble punctuated with dramatic hand gestures that told and showed Taylor the directions. At the end
of his exertion, as he stood there with a hand on his chest,
Taylor nodded her thanks and said, "I wouldn't have killed
you. I would only have shot you in an arm or a leg."

Estes blinked rapidly and paled. Then he said, "Thank you,
miss. That's most kind of you."

Taylor nodded her head in leave-taking and turned, heading
back down the path to the street and Red Sky. Behind her,
she heard the door close—and heard the lock turn. A momentary grin rode her lips.

But as she walked on, her mind churned over what she'd
just learned. Grey was meeting her father, but not at his home.
Could it have something to do with her? She felt certain it
did. And Grey hadn't wanted anyone else to know or to hear
what was said. Taylor's eyes narrowed. She would confront
the men, and they would tell her. She would see to that. It
didn't concern her in the least that she intended to go to a
place meant only for men. What could they be doing inside
that they didn't want women there? Well, she wasn't a mere
woman. Their rules meant nothing to her. They would give
her entry. Or they would die.

Taylor blinked, bringing herself back to the moment. What
had caught her attention? She looked toward the street. Red
Sky. He was moving about agitatedly, tugging against his reins
and showing the whites of his eyes. Suddenly he whinnied his
displeasure. Then he kicked out. Fear caused Taylor's heartbeat to accelerate. She picked up her pace, sprinting toward
her horse.

In the twilight darkness, she couldn't see if anyone—there!
A man. A big man. Grey? Even if it was, she still needed to
warn him. Perhaps he'd forgotten that Red Sky responded only
to her, her mother, and, of course, Calvin. Anyone else who

tried to handle her mount would know the animal's wrath.

Taylor was running now. She cursed the long and winding path that slowed her down. Finally she jumped the low hedge and tore through the neatly trimmed lawn, heading directly for the gate. Now she was close enough to call out. She did so, only to immediately realize she'd spoken in Cherokee. Cursing herself, she repeated it in English: "You there! Stop! Get away from him!"

The man jerked around to face Taylor. His stance was the hunkering one of an angry bear. Taylor could make out only his silhouette. His features were lost in the darkness. But something about him, something like a billowing cloak that wasn't really there, seemed to surround his being. It was darker than his form, darker than the encroaching night . . . and it was threatening. Wave after wave of ill will radiated off him . . . and hit Taylor like physical blows.

Chapter Fifteen

Taylor slowed her running steps, finally stopping on the other side of the wrought-iron fence from the man. Out of breath and needing support, she grabbed two of the bars and peered at him between them. He stayed where he was—out of range of Red Sky's hooves and teeth—and stared at her . . . silently. With the aid of the street lamp off to one side of them, Taylor could see more of him now, despite his hat's brim.

But this cannot be. Startled confusion seized her, tightening her grip on the fence's cold iron bars. In only seconds, her thoughts ran through a gamut of emotions and impressions. She feared she was losing her mind. Was it playing tricks on her? Because the man standing before her now was a handsome and stately man. He was well dressed, like a rich gentleman. There was no black shroud of evil surrounding him. Still, Taylor wondered if her first sight of this man had been a warning vision, one meant to show him to her as he really was. She didn't know what to think, but she did consider herself warned.

Where had he come from? Had he just appeared here on the street? Taylor risked looking away from him for a second or two. Behind him, across the wide street, was a richly appointed buggy. One horse. No driver. Most likely—she refocused on the man—the rig belonged to him. She stared at him standing there and watching her silently. He seemed to purposely be giving her time to assess him and the situation, as if he waited for her to catch on. But catch on to what?

She had no idea. But she continued to heed her warning vision by naming this man her adversary. Well-dressed and

handsome he may be, but he was her enemy. He fairly reeked
with hatred for her, yet she had no idea why. And once again
he seemed to have changed. Now, in the smoky light cast by
the street lamp, his features appeared heavy, his nose prominent. His mouth wide and cruel. Dark eyes held an unfriendly
glitter in their depths. A shiver of recognition just beyond her
grasp slipped over Taylor's skin. There was something naggingly familiar to her about him.

She found it revealing that he had yet to say anything to
her. He only stared . . . and hated.

"Who are you?" she demanded, thankful that there was no
fearful waver in her voice—and just as thankful that the iron
bars were still between her and him, even though they brought
to her mind a prison's bars.

"Who do you think I am?" the man barked right back at
her. She noticed his hands were fisted at his sides. And something else—he wasn't as big now as he had appeared only a
moment ago. Was it yet another trick of the light or her imagination? Or was he magic, like Bentley, and so could change
his appearance? Then Taylor saw the bulge under his coat, on
his right side. No, he was not magic. He was very human—
and he was armed. But so was she. She didn't know about
him, but she did know about herself. She was a hell of a shot
. . . providing she could get to her gun first.

Ignoring his question, as he had hers, Taylor arrowed a
glance at Red Sky—he appeared unharmed—and then back at
the man. "What were you doing to my horse? Are you a horse
thief? If you are, you ought to know that so am I. And I have
killed three men already. One more won't make much difference."

The man bared his teeth, giving Taylor a start until she
realized he was grinning. "Well, you're quite the elegant little
miss, now aren't you?" His voice was low and threatening.

Taylor narrowed her eyes. "No, I am not. No more than
you are the gentleman you appear to be."

He ignored her returned insult in favor of looking her up
and down. He then shook his head as if disgusted. "I should
have known that Charles's bastard spawn would grow up like

the wild, heathen shoot you always were. He called you his little wild flower, but you were more like a weed. Something ugly to be torn up at the root and tossed away."

A start of shock rode Taylor's nerve endings. Not for the man's insults, but because of that name. Wild Flower . . . it was her Cherokee name, given to her by her father. It was private—and this man had spoken it out loud. "Who are you?" she repeated, this time more quietly. Inside, she felt chilled . . . and uncertain that she wanted to hear his answer.

He smiled again, taking a step toward her. Almost involuntarily, Taylor took a step back. Her hand inched toward her gun. The man didn't miss her actions. "You wouldn't shoot me, would you, Taylor? Not here on a crowded street, in front of all these witnesses?" He never looked away from her but gestured behind himself to the carriage traffic at his back.

"Yes, I would. And I might anyway if you don't tell me who you are and what you want with me."

"You don't remember me? I remember you. The last time I saw you, you were just a scared little girl out in the Nation, clinging to that Indian squaw's skirts. Make no mistake, sweetheart—that's where you should have stayed."

Insult warred with burning anger. Taylor's chin edged up, but everything inside her urged caution. Heaviness invaded her limbs, and a calm descended over her. She watched every move the man made, missing nothing. Not the slightest twitch or gesture. She said nothing but continued to watch him. As surreptitiously as she could, she flexed her gun hand, exercising her fingers, readying them for a fast draw . . . should it be necessary.

The man grinned, as if enjoying her uneasiness. "You don't have anything to say to me, Taylor?"

"I have plenty to say to you. And all of it has to do with you stepping away from my horse and going on about your business."

He chuckled, a humorless sound at best, and shook his head as if he was amused. "You've got guts, girl. I'll give you that much."

Taylor didn't answer. He'd said nothing requiring one. She

blanked her expression, purposely giving nothing away of what she felt inside. She hardly dared blink. Her mouth was a straight line. All her senses were trained on this man in front of her.

"Well," he said suddenly into the silence between them, "since you don't feel like talking, I will. I could hardly believe it, Taylor, when I heard you were alive. All this time I thought you were dead. And all this time I've been happy in that thought. Really happy. You should have stayed dead. And you certainly should never have come here to St. Louis."

He knew as much—and more—about her as she did herself; that much was obvious. But who could he be? And why was he naggingly familiar? She had no idea but settled for bluffing, for pretending she did know who he was. Maybe she'd say something that would cause him to stumble. "What's it to you what I do?" she all but snarled. "You never cared about me."

His expression changed, became one of deeply ingrained anger, which radiated off him in waves. "Care about you? I have no reason to care about you. And every reason to hate you, to wish you dead. Seeing you sickens me. You're a walking sin. That's what you are, girl. A walking sin. And I don't even think you know it—no more than you really know who I am, so quit pretending."

Her ploy hadn't worked. But . . . *a walking sin?* What did that mean? It suddenly occurred to Taylor that she was standing here indulging a crazy man. Her stoic pose slipped. She felt scared, vulnerable . . . fragile. And tried even harder to appear immune to his ranting. "There is nothing to know. I have listened to you long enough. You will go away now."

He put his hands to his waist, brushing his coat back enough to reveal his gun stuck into the waist of his pants. "You're not in any position, girlie, to be telling me or anybody else what to do. You don't have any idea what you are, do you?"

This white man had no idea how many times in her life people had spit at her and told her what she was. She hadn't liked it then, and she didn't like it now, so she grinned . . .

threateningly. "A walking sin. Isn't that what you said? Do you just not like Indians? Is that it?"

His wide, mocking grin, like that on a skull, and his knowing nod told Taylor plainly enough that she'd just said something he'd wanted her to say.

He shook his head, looking disgusted now. "You really don't know, do you, Taylor? Well, I'll be . . . they didn't tell you. I don't suppose I should be surprised. They didn't tell me, either. No, I had to find out for myself. I had to do some snooping on my own, read some letters that weren't addressed to me. But it was worth it. Oh, it was worth it for a lot of years. Then you came back. They tried to keep that from me, too—that you were here—but I found out . . . as you can plainly see."

"I will not listen to you." Taylor was becoming very concerned. Night was rapidly falling, the streets were emptying, and she had important business to conduct. And still this man was accosting her, essentially holding her prisoner—something she'd sworn she wouldn't allow to happen ever again. But still, for the life of her, she couldn't move, not while he was so close to her and to Red Sky. Every finely honed instinct she possessed said she needed to get him to move away before she dared come out from behind the fence. "I have no more patience for you and your words. Either say who you are and what this is about, or leave me be."

Insult and anger waged a battle for supremacy in his expression. "You're pretty sure of yourself, aren't you, Taylor? You talk big now, but you won't for long."

"Is that a threat?"

"You'll find out soon enough. You sure you don't have any idea who I am? I haven't seen you in a lot of years, but I'd know you anywhere. You look a lot like your . . . your mother. Got your father's eyes, that's true enough. But mostly, you look . . . just . . . like your mother." He drew out his last words ominously.

Taylor's mouth dried. She thought of her mother alone in her cabin out in the Nation. And wondered if this man had followed her here from Tahlequah. "What have you done to my mother?"

He shook his head. "Nothing. And I don't intend to do anything to her. I love her. It's you I hate."

He loved her mother and hated her? "Why?"

"I already told you, girl. Pay attention. You're a walking sin . . . well, a reminder of a sin, I suppose. A sin I can't forgive or forget. And one I don't want walking around here and staring back at me. You can understand that, can't you?"

"No. I cannot. Tell me who you are, that you would know my family."

"Oh, I know your family, all right. Better than you do, I'd wager. And you still don't know who I am?" He rubbed thoughtfully at his chin. Every pose or stance of his struck Taylor as studied and false, as if he sought to hide his evilness behind a friendly facade. "Well, I guess you wouldn't. You did only see me that one time—when I came out to the Nation after the war to collect my wife and daughter."

His wife and daughter?

Then she knew—with the certainty of a lightning strike. How could she have not known? Now she knew why he seemed familiar. He was related by blood to her. She had to stiffen her knees to remain standing. Her heart pounded erratically. She thought of Aunt Camilla and Amanda. She thought of her father. This man was his brother. Taylor's voice, when she spoke, was that of an uncertain child. "Uncle Stanley?"

"Finally," he said . . . as he started around the fence toward her.

"Why didn't you stop her?"

"Stop her? I daresay, sir," Bentley said, "that a brick wall wielding an iron club could not stop Miss James from a course of action once she's made up her mind to do something."

"You're right; you're right. I'm sorry." Grey ran a hand through his hair and resumed his pacing. He'd never been so scared in his whole life. He'd just arrived home from the club to find Taylor gone. The things Charles had told him had sickened him. The betrayal, the abandonment. An awful tragedy ripe for danger—all of it directed at Taylor.

Grey stood in the foyer of his town house with his butler and his housekeeper essentially called on the carpet. Mrs. Scott's hands were folded together in front of her. And Bentley stood at formal attention, hands to his sides, his beaklike nose in the air.

On his next pass, Grey asked a question he'd already put to them. But he couldn't help repeating himself. After all, he was clutching at straws here. Desperate straws. "And you don't have any idea where she went from here? She didn't say anything?"

"No, sir," Mrs. Scott answered. "After she ordered me to get her some britches and a man's shirt—"

"What?" Grey stopped in his tracks and spun around to face her. "A man's shirt and britches? What on earth for?"

"For her to wear, sir, I'm sure. Miss James purely does not seem to like the clothing of a, um, lady. At any rate, seeing as how there were none to be had inside—besides yours and Bentley's . . . which simply wouldn't fit—I had to think quickly. She was in an awful hurry to be off, I don't mind saying. The poor girl. She looked very troubled. So I finally realized that—" Mrs. Scott stopped herself in mid-sentence, frowned, pursed her lips, and looked lost. "Good heavens, I've forgotten what I was saying. Where was I?"

Bentley unbent enough to say, "You were dashing outside, I believe."

Grey gritted his teeth—to keep from roaring in frustrated anger. He needed only a direction from them, Taylor's route, a destination, a name, anything. He couldn't just go haring off into the night, wildly calling out for her. In a city the size of St. Louis, where would he even begin? All he needed was a starting point. He had to find her before, in her innocence, she got herself killed.

"Oh, that's right," Mrs. Scott was saying. "Thank you, Bentley. At any rate, I dashed outside to the men's quarters. They're over the coach barn—"

"I know where the men's quarters are, Mrs. Scott. Please get on with it."

Mrs. Scott's lips pursed and her chin came up a notch. "Yes, sir. At any rate, as I was saying, I dashed out to the men's quarters over the coach barn and looked for Albert. Do you know him, sir?"

Grey fisted his hands at his sides—to keep from reaching for his housekeeper's throat. "I do. I hired him. Will you, for the love of God, Mrs. Scott, get to the point? This is extremely important."

"I understand that, sir. And I am trying. At any rate, he's a slim young lad, not a lot bigger than Miss James, so I supposed his clothes would come closest to fitting her without being, well, revealing. Ahem. Anyway, it took me a while, but I finally found the young rascal. He was smoking out behind the property—not that I'm a one to tell on a person. I only mention it because that is where I found him. At any rate, a discussion followed in which he said his work was done and he wasn't doing anything wrong. I told him I was sure I didn't care; he was not my concern. Then I told him to take his clothes off."

If Grey was shocked, it was nothing compared to Bentley. The butler's sniffing intake of air through his nose had a whistling quality about it. He turned fully to the housekeeper. "And I should hope he did not, Mrs. Scott."

"I should say he did," she assured Bentley. "But up in his room. I marched him up there and waited outside while he changed. The britches and shirt he had on were clean enough. So then I took the bundle to Miss James." Mrs. Scott's face wrinkled with concern. "Was I wrong to do that, sir?"

"No," Grey said distractedly, rubbing at his temple. "I'm sure your cooperation with her at that point is the only reason you still have your hair."

His housekeeper gasped and put a hand to her bun. She patted it as if assuring herself that it was indeed still there.

"Did she say anything to you, Mrs. Scott, about where she was going, what she intended to do?"

"No, sir. No more than you did before you left on that black horse of yours. And she asked me the same thing—if you'd said where you were going before you left. And I told her I was not privy to my employer's plans for the evening."

Grey exhaled, ignoring his housekeeper and butler for the moment while he tried to think like Taylor. He recalled their afternoon of lovemaking . . . and how it had ended. A sudden fear had him once again focusing all his attention on Mrs. Scott and Bentley. His gaze flitted from one to the other of them. "What did she take with her? Did she say she'd be coming back?"

The two looked at each other and then at Grey. Bentley spoke first. "Not specifically. But when I checked out in the barn, her saddlebags were still there. That's a good sign, I believe. But, oh dear, I didn't want to upset you further, sir, but she, uh, found her gun in your desk drawer . . . and took it with her."

Right on the heels of that potentially disastrous news, and while Grey was still reeling with its implications, came Mrs. Scott's report. "As Bentley said, she didn't say as much, Mr. Talbott, but I think she'll return. After all, she didn't pack anything, and she left the lovely dresses you bought her. Any young lady would want them if she was going away for good."

That didn't comfort Grey in the least. Taylor was not anyone's idea of an ordinary young lady. Then he had another question—for Bentley. "She didn't want you with her? After this afternoon, I find that strange. She's insisted before now that you go everywhere she does. What did she say to you?"

"Nothing, sir. As I've told you, I had no idea she was gone"—he turned an accusatory expression on the guilty-looking Mrs. Scott—"until you told me, sir. Which is when I checked the barn, as you know. But I really should report, sir, that as silly as it may seem and as hesitant as I am to mention it for fear of—"

"Bentley, for the love of God . . ."

"Yes, sir. A bit earlier in the evening, I had the oddest premonition of danger. I was passing through the dining room when suddenly I stopped and looked into the mirror over the buffet. I could see Miss James, but it was as if everything went black around her until she, too, faded out of the picture. It was most upsetting. It was only fleeting, but I must say it completely unnerved me. And then I—Sir! Where are you going?"

Grey had taken off at a run for the back door. He heard footsteps running after him, but he ignored them. His mind was totally absorbed with details. He'd handed his horse to Smith out in the coach yard only minutes ago, so maybe it wasn't yet unsaddled. Even if it was, he'd ride it bareback. And where he was going, what direction he should head, he still had no idea. All he knew was that Bentley the man-bird, the spirit guide, had experienced an awful vision. That much was clear. It wasn't until this moment that Grey realized how great Taylor's influence on him had been. He believed her totally about Bentley. And Grey no longer believed that Bentley was a threat or a spy. The very notion, in light of the older man's vision and his steadfast loyalty on all other occasions, now seemed ridiculous.

Grey hit the door, almost running through it before he had it open. The cool night air hit him the moment he stepped outside—and ran right into Taylor, knocking her flat into the dirt. She yelped and spit out something in Cherokee that needed no translation. Grey staggered and cursed and jumped over her so as not to fall atop her and crush her under his weight. He had a glimpse, no more than a fleeting peripheral impression, of Calvin frozen in his tracks, staring their way, and holding the reins to Taylor's horse. The animal's ears pricked forward. His wild-eyed start of surprise matched Calvin's expression.

They were forgotten as instantly as they'd been noticed. Almost before Taylor hit the ground in a rolling tumble, Grey had righted himself and jerked around and grabbed her up off the ground and into his arms. "Taylor! Thank God. I thought . . . I feared—"

All he saw was widened blue eyes staring up at him. Grey lowered his head to hers, taking her mouth in a crushing, hungry, bruising, relieved kiss. He was out of control and he knew it. He could not stop himself. His tongue sought hers—his hand was at the back of her head; his other was wrapped around her waist. He'd thought he'd lost her; it was all he could think. And now she was here and alive. He needed to feel her against him, to taste her, to know she was real, that she was truly more than his imagination—

Taylor suddenly pushed against his chest and twisted her mouth away from his. She shoved herself out of his arms and stepped back, swiping the back of her hand over her mouth. Her stare was hard and glinting . . . and her strung-together angry Cherokee litany put Grey exactly in his place. And he couldn't have been happier. He grinned to show it.

Taylor abruptly stopped talking . . . cursing. She frowned, her finely arched eyebrows lowered dangerously. "What the hell are you grinning at, white man?"

White man. Never had he loved hearing two words so much before in his life. Taylor was alive and intact emotionally, so it seemed. "You. I'm grinning at you. I thought you were dead."

She cocked her head at a disbelieving angle. "And now you know I am not. Why did you think I was dead?"

"Because . . . well, Bentley had a vision. A dark one involving you."

Taylor's stiffening stance told its own story. She opened her mouth but didn't say anything. She looked frightened.

"Something did happen, didn't it?" Grey asked, watching her carefully, looking for any sign that she . . . knew. He very much wanted to go inside. He felt too vulnerable out here, as if he feared the sharp crack of a gun being fired . . . and of its bullet finding its mark. But for the life of him, he couldn't make his feet move. He fisted his hands at his sides and waited for whatever she had to say.

"Yes. Something happened. Maybe. I don't know. I thought . . ." Her voice trailed off. Grey had never seen her indecisive before. It didn't bode well. She put a distracted hand to her temple, frowned, felt for her hat on her head, and then looked around for it.

Grey spied it by his feet and snatched it up, handing it to her. Such a simple gesture for a man who was dying a thousand deaths inside, each one with her name on it. "Where'd you go, Taylor? And why? What happened?"

She looked at him as if she hadn't understood him or couldn't decide what to answer first. "My uncle," she said. "I met my uncle. He was at my father's."

Grey's muscles tensed. "Your father's? But he was—"

"With you. I know. Estes told me. And then my Uncle Stanley was there. At the gate by Red Sky. And he . . ." Again her voice trailed off. She looked confused and indeed gestured helplessly with her hands.

"If he so much as put a hand on you, Taylor, I swear I will—"

"If he had, there would be no need for you to do so. I would have killed him myself," she haughtily assured him, sounding more like her confident self again. "Why would you think he would harm me?"

Grey scrutinized Taylor. If Stanley James hadn't told her the truth, then Grey certainly wasn't going to. He agreed with Charles on that score. And since Taylor didn't appear to know at this point, Grey decided to hedge his answer. "I didn't think he would, Taylor. Maybe it was the way you said it. But what did your uncle do . . . exactly?"

She shook her head, as if she couldn't believe her own words or her own experience. "He . . . hugged me and kissed me on my cheek. And then he left. I thought he meant to harm me. But then, it was as if he couldn't. At first he spoke meanly to me of when I was a child. He seemed evil. When I saw him from a distance, I saw a great blackness around him. A bad thing that was a part of him, but then it was gone."

Grey gasped. He heard another one behind him and whipped around to see Bentley and Mrs. Scott crowded into the open doorway. His housekeeper's eyes were rounded. She hurriedly crossed herself. Grey's gaze locked with Bentley's frightened one.

Taylor recaptured Grey's attention when she cried out, "Is that what the man-bird saw? The evil blackness surrounding my uncle?"

"Yes, it is." There was no sense denying it, Grey knew.

Taylor spared Grey no more than a glance before she sought Bentley's form in the doorway. "It's true, Miss James.

I saw it. In the dining room mirror. But what I didn't get to tell Mr. Talbott yet is what I did next. I . . . I thought good thoughts. I prayed. I called upon goodness to dispel the blackness. I . . . well, I tried to protect you, miss. And it worked. I know it sounds silly—"

"No," Grey cut in. "It doesn't sound silly. It sounds perfect, Bentley." He turned to Taylor. "I will never again doubt you. Never. I have doubted you from the moment you arrived. But never again, Taylor. From now on, you have my undying support and my unflagging faith. They are yours."

For a space of two heartbeats, Taylor did not respond. Then she said, "I have always had them, Grey. And I cherish them in my heart."

The evening air seemed to warm, yet a shiver slipped over Grey's skin as he stared into Taylor's sincere face. She was all he could see. They'd just stepped across some threshold together. Their relationship had passed onto another level, another plane. It was more a sense, a certainty, than it was a tangible something he could hold in his hand. It was beautiful . . . and it was the worst thing that had ever happened to Grey.

Keeping his sadness to himself, Grey held his hand out to Taylor. She stared at it, then at him. He suspended thought, not wanting to know if he hoped she would take it or if she wouldn't. Then, as if she'd been prodded physically from behind, she rushed toward him, grabbing for his hand as if it were a lifeline. His fingers closed around hers and squeezed. A tingling energy raced up Grey's arm, an energy that caught at his breath . . . and his heart. She was utter magic. And for the first time, she trusted him.

To Grey, this was heaven and this was hell. She trusted him. She was opening up to him—or would soon. And all he could do was lie to her from here on out in an effort to preserve her. It was so unfair. He'd already promised her father that he would do his best to ensure that Taylor did not find out the truth of her life. Grey recalled his pact that he would work with Charles to get Taylor to leave here and never come back. Grey had agreed, even knowing his promise meant giving up the one woman he would always love, the only one who could save him from himself.

But it was too late. In order to save her, he would have to destroy himself. How laughable and how stupidly noble. "Come, Taylor," Grey said, smiling at her, but sad on the inside with the irony of it all. He signaled, with a nod of his head, for Calvin to take Red Sky to the barn, then turned his attention back to Taylor. "It's time we all went inside."

Later that night, clad in a ridiculously feminine white cotton bed gown trimmed in pink satin and with her heart in her throat, Taylor padded barefoot through the adjoining dressing room and opened the door to Grey's bedroom. The room was dark. She started to back out but stopped, instantly chiding herself for such weakness. She was Taylor Christie James, daughter of Tennie Nell Christie and Charles Edward James. Half-breed. Outlaw. A killer of men. And she wasn't afraid of anything—not even of what she was about to do. Bare her heart and soul to a man.

She was lying. She was terrified. But still, she drew in a deep breath, forcing it past the tightening in her chest. "Grey?" she softly called out.

She heard bed linens rustling. Then, in a whisper that was not sleepy, that said he'd been lying here awake, he called out, "Taylor? Is that you? What are you doing?"

"Grey . . ." She fiddled with the doorknob, calling herself fourteen kinds of coward. "I . . . I would lay with you."

Silence met her words. Seconds ticked by ponderously. Then she heard a chuckle . . . but not of mirth. It sounded tortured. "Taylor, don't do this. Please. Go back to bed."

She could not understand. Why would he not want her? He had declared himself only a few hours ago out in the coach yard. And she had given him her hand. They were as one. And now he sent her away? Feeling foolish for being turned down became sudden vexation inside her. She stepped fully into his room and shut the door behind her. She stood in the pitch-black, her back against the closed door. She heard Grey sigh as if he was relieved. He thought she'd left.

"No. I will not go away," she said loudly.

A sudden thrashing around of linens mixed with Grey's startled outburst. "*Son of a*—Taylor! You scared the hell out of me." The room was suddenly flooded with light. He'd lit the lamp beside his bed. He turned the wick down until the room was in gray shadows and then propped himself up on an elbow, giving her his attention. His muscled chest was bared to her. A sheet covered his lower half. His expression was a mishmash of emotions . . . vexation, sadness, a crushing desire. Want. Need.

An answering desire flared in Taylor, puckering her nipples, causing a tingling tightness low in her belly. It made her bold. She stepped away from the door and turned to face him. She'd never done this before, this consciously seducing a man. Always before, she had simply agreed or had made a mere gesture . . . and the man had taken her. She had enjoyed their time together and then she had left, her heart and her emotions intact.

But this time and this man were different because for the first time she was giving herself. She was offering up so much more than her body. She was pulling away the armor that encased her heart. For the first time she understood risk in a way she never had before. She caught a glimpse of the awful vulnerability that came with intimacy, with a baring of one's self to another. The risk that one could give all of one's self . . . and still lose. She was taking a chance and staking her heart . . . and still, he may not want her.

With her heart pounding, with her limbs weak, and feeling as if she stood on shifting sands instead of a solid floor, Taylor . . . silently, holding Grey's gaze . . . undid the laces that held her gown. He watched her every move intently. With a single motion, Taylor shrugged out of her garment. The gown pooled at her feet, showing to him that she was naked underneath.

Grey sucked in a breath, which almost immediately left him in a gasp. "Oh, Taylor, don't. Please. I beg you. It would be so wrong."

Taylor shook her head, swishing her black silky-feeling hair over the bare skin of her shoulders and breasts. "No. It will be right. I will make it so." She stepped out of the pool of fabric at her feet and slowly, with gliding steps, walked toward him. Then she stood beside his bed, looking down at him. His heart was in his eyes. He wanted her very much; she could see that. He couldn't look away from her. Then why did he tell her no? Was it because of what he'd said this morning, about needing her to give him her heart, as well as her body?

"Grey," she began, reaching out to softly, sensually stroke the planes and angles of his face, "do you remember this morning when I left your bed, when you told me we could not do this again?"

He closed his eyes, swallowing hard, a look of tortured rapture on his face as she brushed his full and firm lips with her fingertips. "Yes," he rasped out.

"And do you remember that just before I left you, I spoke to you in Cherokee?"

He opened his eyes and captured her fingers, putting them to his lips, holding them there, and nodding.

"I said then—and I've never said this before to any other man—that I love you." She felt him freeze, his gaze locked with hers. Some deep fire lit his brown eyes, emboldening Taylor. "It does not matter that we have only met this week. Time is nothing to the heart. I loved you before I ever met you. I prayed all my life to find you. I dreamed of you. I knew your touch before I knew your name. I gave you my heart before I knew your face. I was yours before I ever came here. It is written on the wind. My mother did not send me here to my father, as she thinks, Grey. I know that now. She sent me here to find you. And now that I have, you cannot send me away. I may choose to go when it is time, but you cannot send me away. Even should I go, my heart will rest with yours."

"Taylor." It was all he said. But it was there in his voice. The love he felt for her . . . and the awful something that tortured him.

Still, Taylor pulled the sheet from him, seeing his nakedness and the evidence of his desire. She smiled at him and lifted the sheet, slipping into his bed, absolutely certain that she could make that tortured look leave his eyes forever . . . if only he would love her.

Chapter Sixteen

I n this place will I make my stand. I will not leave here. You will stop trying to give me money and telling me to go. I will not. There are dangers here to me; I know this. But I will stay and I will face them. To leave now would be the way of the coward. That is not my way. And were I to leave, these dangers . . . they would follow me and for the same reasons they stalk me here. Someone wants me dead. So all my life, if I left here, I would be looking over my shoulder. I will not live so. And so I say, if he wants me, he will find me here. In this place I will fight him. This person who would harm me—though I do not know his name—he is close to me. I feel that. I believe also that he shares my blood. And so I say . . . let him show himself."

That speech of Taylor's was given in Grey's and her father's presence. She'd given them no recourse but to deal with her stubborn determination to see the secrets that surrounded her exposed—as well as the person behind them. But it was the strangest thing. After that, nothing remotely threatening happened. A week passed. Two. Indolent days lengthened, leaching the dark from the shortened nights. And still no angry confrontations erupted. Not even the barest hint of danger surfaced. It was as if Taylor's giving her heart and her trust to Grey, as well as her brave words of courage, held at bay the old wounds and the ancient resentments. Could it be that easy? No one truly believed it could. But since nothing happened and there was no one to accuse or confront, life was forced to proceed as if nothing were wrong. Go on with life, but stay vigilant. Let sleeping dogs lie. And that was what they did.

Even Mother Earth seemed to applaud Taylor's courage.

She gave her approval by bestowing the colors of summer on
St. Louis. The greens and reds and yellows and blues of the
flowers and the shrubs were almost too bright to the eye. And
though commerce bustled, life along the Mississippi River,
just like its waters, slowed, became sluggish. The spring rains
ceased and the sun smiled warmly on the citizens. The winds
blew soft and sweet. Butterflies flitted and birds sang.

And nerves were stretched taut. The question arose . . .
what to do about Taylor? Either present her to society or hide
her unfairly. A decision was finally reached that satisfied both
the political and social ramifications of having a half-breed
outlaw in one's family. Taylor's father, with the wholehearted
endorsement of the prominent Talbotts, would proudly present
her to society and dare anyone to say different. This was a
good plan because the truth was that it was not the public who
posed the danger to Taylor's life. Sadly, as she'd realized, the
threat to her lay closer to home. But if they all needed to be
out and about, then she needed to be out and about with them.
How better to protect her?

Taylor saw the sense in the plan, but still it surprised her
to be celebrated instead of denied, made known instead of
hidden. With Grey constantly at her side, she found herself
swept up in the whirlwind activities that were so foreign to
her. Civic commitment. Charitable responsibility. Social prom-
inence. She hated it . . . at first. But guided by Aunt Camilla
and Amanda, she was nevertheless thrust into the forefront of
her white family's lives. Life, then, with all its undercurrents,
did indeed go on. There were committees to organize, money
to be raised, speeches to be written, and debates to be attended.
Banners to be printed and hung, ribbons and buttons and slo-
gans to adopt for Franklin Talbott's election campaign. And,
too, this summer, on July Fourth, would see America's centennial celebration.

Despite her usually aloof self, Taylor was finally affected
by the excitement of it all. This was what it was like to be
accepted, to be a part of a thriving family. It was indeed an
enchanted time, but not one free of the implied danger. She
always looked over her shoulder. And yet . . . nothing hap-

pened. Life went on unimpeded. Its very serenity somehow seemed sinister after a point. Like waiting for water to boil. A watched pot never seemed to do so . . . but you knew it would—the moment you looked away.

Taylor, and everyone else, was forced repeatedly to look away. The round of parties, soirees, and receptions for Amanda James and Franklin Talbott, preceding their upcoming nuptials at the end of June, had everyone in a dither. It was hard not to get caught up. Taylor was no exception. Publicly, she was the honored and cherished visiting relative. Publicly, she was a celebrated sidelight to the giddiness of the summer of 1876 in St. Louis, Missouri. Privately, those closest to her worried and watched . . . and waited.

While they did, Taylor carried on as exactly who she was . . . the daughter of Mr. Charles James, niece of Mr. and Mrs. Stanley James, and cousin to the lovely Amanda James, fiancée to Mr. Franklin Talbott. While Grey hadn't had to implement his plan to present Taylor as his affianced, he did let it be known—in no uncertain terms—that the lady's affections were spoken for. That in itself—Greyson Talbott making a commitment—was fodder enough for the gossips. They spoke in low and excited tones behind their fans as their gazes sought the happy couple dancing or strolling along the path in a moonlit garden.

But there was more. There was the titillating scandal—one no one dared voice to the Jameses or the Talbotts—of Charles's long-ago indiscretion and of the resulting young lady's bloodlines. Add to that her residing unchaperoned in Mr. Greyson Talbott's town house, instead of in her father's home as propriety demanded, and one had all the necessary elements of a long day's gossip into night. "That Grey," they said, "he is such a charming villain." Why, the girl was ruined now. All she could hope for was a quick marriage and the short memories of the people who mattered. But far from being ostracized and her family alienated, she was—to her utter disbelief—much in demand. No dinner, no party, no tea, no soiree, was complete or any hostess deemed a success unless

Mr. Greyson Talbott escorted the lovely Cherokee maiden
Miss Taylor Christie James to her event.

But Taylor was not fooled. She knew she was an oddity to
these people. Yes, they were kind enough to her face and even
in the newspaper stories printed about her. Her every coming
and going was reported. On the street, men doffed their hats.
And young women imitated her style of dress, thereby scan-
dalizing their mothers by abandoning corsets and other underpinnings. Why, if Miss Taylor Christie James deemed them
unnecessary, then they were. Half the girls had adopted a tiny
braid like hers adorned with a feather. Taylor tried not to be
insulted by their imitation. Grey assured her the young ladies
meant it as a compliment and not a mockery. Though not
convinced, she allowed it to pass.

But beneath it all . . . the social whirl, the acceptance, the
friendships, the notoriety . . . Taylor knew that everything was
not as it seemed. She couldn't deny the undercurrent, like a
river's strong undertow, of danger that lurked just around a
corner, just behind a smile. To her, it still seemed that the
shadow of threat crept closer and closer with each bright and
happy day that dawned. She couldn't put a finger on it, or
give it a face or a name. Grey did not discount her fears.
Neither did Bentley. Grey told her to suspect trouble, but he
didn't really have to—it was all she'd ever known. Of most
concern to Taylor was that Grey knew something—something
he wasn't telling her. She could see it in his eyes. He watched
her like a hawk, most especially during family gatherings.

And so, she stayed prepared. She did not lower her guard,
not even in this city of swirling skirts and formal top hats.
She watched over her shoulder, even while dancing—she was
getting better at that, by the way. She no longer crushed her
partner's toes. But still, under the ball gowns Grey had purchased for her she kept her knife secured to her calf, and she
kept her gun in her reticule . . . a silly velvet handbag with
drawstrings. She may become civilized, she told herself and
Grey—whose eyebrows had raised at the sight of her startling
accessories, as Mrs. Scott termed them—but she would not

become soft. She would not be caught unaware. And she had her suspicions.

Augusta Talbott. Stanley James. They'd both raised her hackles on first sight, but now they paid her only the kindest of attentions. They watched her; she was aware of that. A time or two, she'd inadvertently caught their hard looks directed her way. But not once, by word or deed, did they give Taylor any reason to question them or to act against them. It was most disconcerting. She was sure they hated her for whatever reasons they harbored in their hearts. But they spoke kindly of her and to her. It was like being aware of being in the presence of evil, but having it cleverly disguised as innocence and goodness—and only you knew it, but still you doubted your instincts. So what could she do? Nothing.

Uncle Stanley had even explained away his confrontation with her that night at her father's by saying it was the shock of seeing her. Though not convinced, she couldn't dispute it. Except to believe that danger was merely biding its time . . . like a rattler coiled and poised to strike, but hidden by shadows, awaiting only the misstep of its hapless victim before sinking its venom-laden fangs into innocent flesh.

Taylor and Grey had rehashed all that this morning—and had moved on to another source of irritation . . . Taylor's behavior.

"Why do you ask me this?" she said, buttering a biscuit at breakfast in the dining room. "I must carry my gun. Someone will try to kill me."

Grey all but tossed his knife onto his plate of eggs and bacon. He leaned forward, bracing his forearms against the sturdy walnut table's edge. His brown eyes danced with angry lights. "And it will be me, I assure you, if you do not stop carrying that gun around in your handbag. People are still talking about it going off at the Chalmerses' supper-dance last weekend."

Taylor narrowed her eyes at Grey as she took a bite out of her biscuit and chewed it, all the while staring at him. Once she'd swallowed, she said, "My gun did not just go off. I fired it." She sipped at her coffee and then added, "That silly yellow-hair girl should not have been hanging onto you like she was. She was rubbing her big cow's breasts on your arm."

Over in his corner of the room, where he stood when not attending to the happy couple, Bentley choked and coughed. With Grey, Taylor spared the man-bird a glance, and then they went on with their disagreement.

"I couldn't agree more, Taylor, about Henryetta Chalmers. She is a silly girl. But we don't speak of . . . women's chests at the breakfast table, dear. But as regards Henryetta, she is one of Amanda's friends and a bridesmaid for her. I'd think the least you could do is refrain from killing your cousin's friends just because they happen to annoy you."

"I was not annoyed. I was jealous."

Grey chuckled. "You are also very candid, my dear."

"Does that mean 'truthful'?" When Grey nodded, she continued. "Good. Then here is another candid thing. Amanda does not mind that I tried to shoot the girl. She doesn't like her. She is not a friend."

Grey exhaled, a sound laden with exasperation. "Then why is she—no, don't tell me. I don't want to hear about Franklin's political expediencies making their way into the bridal party. Instead, I will just remind you that I am paying for the repairs done to the wall in Senator Chalmers's ballroom. You are very lucky no one was injured or killed. Now, what *are* we going to do about your carrying a loaded pistol to parties, Taylor? As it is, I fear that all the fashionable young ladies will be doing so because you are."

Taylor grinned. She knew of three such young ladies who now had guns on their persons . . . but no corsets. In a good mood, she suddenly relented and offered a compromise. "I will stop carrying the gun. But I will keep my knife with me."

Grey looked defeated. "Is that all I can hope for? An exchange of one weapon for another?"

"Unless you wish me to be unarmed when someone tries to kill me. You won't allow Bentley to be with me anymore."

"Bentley was quickly becoming a laughingstock—" Grey nodded to the reddening butler. "My pardons, Bentley." Then

he focused again on Taylor. "Bentley has duties here. If yo
need protecting, I will do it, Taylor."

She raised her eyebrows at him . . . and popped the last o
her biscuit in her mouth. Slowly she chewed while eyeing him

His grimace was one of exasperation. "All right, yes, yo
are a better shot than me. And I couldn't hope to best yo
with a knife. Or a bow and arrow. And you can outride me
Outdrink. Outsmoke. All that. And I do appreciate all the, uh
wrestling holds you've taught me." He cut his gaze to Bentley
who was discreetly coughing, and back to Taylor. "But it i
still my place to protect you."

Taylor swallowed her food and, bland of expression, asked
"Who would you be protecting me from?"

Grey jumped up and paced about, gesturing broadly in hi
anger. "We have been over this, Taylor. I don't have a nam
I can give you."

Taylor wiped her mouth and laid her napkin beside he
plate. "You mean you don't have a name you *will* give me.
believe you know who it is who would do me harm." She cu
her gaze Bentley's way, wanting to include his guilty presenc
in this. "Both of you do. The troubles did not end when Bent
ley worked his magic on the bad shadow two weeks ago. Th
troubles are only more cautious now. I know it. And you know
it. Otherwise, why would you have your men following me
I see the men when I'm out riding, Grey—"

He'd shot to her side and was clutching at her hand. Hi
expression bared his fear. "What men? I have no men follow
ing you."

Taylor's mouth dried with the shock. "You do not?
thought they were yours. I never would have put my knife t
the throat of one—"

Grey cried out hoarsely, letting go of her and jumping back
"Sweet Jesus! You confronted one of them?"

Taylor calmly shook her head. "I did not confront him.
was behind him. He was following me while I rode wit
Amanda and Franklin in the park. I made an excuse to the
and doubled back, catching the man unaware. He was behin

a tree. I put my knife to his neck and told him to stop following me or I would slit his throat."

Grey collapsed onto his chair and covered his face with his hands. While he mumbled into his palms, Taylor sought Bentley's gaze and shrugged at him. For his part, Bentley . . . who stood openmouthed . . . said nothing.

At last, Grey lowered his hands, resting his arms on his chair. He looked as if his favorite pet had just died. "And did he, Taylor? Did he quit following you?"

"Yes. But I have seen others."

"When did this start, these men following you? And how do you know they are following you?"

"They are. And it started about a week ago."

"What do they look like?"

"White men."

"I see. Was there anything at all about them that would distinguish one from another for you?"

"No. They all look alike to me."

"Of course. As you've said before." He sighed dramatically. "What am I going to do with you?"

Taylor shrugged. "There is not much you haven't already done with me."

Bentley again made choking sounds and coughed horribly.

Grey turned on him. "For heaven's sake, Bentley, will you please go get a drink of water? Or better yet, whiskey. And bring me one. And her. In fact, everyone. I'm sure the entire staff could stand a rousing all-out drunk about now." He eyed Taylor accusingly.

"Because of me, you mean?"

"Yes, I do."

"Did you really wish me to get you a whiskey, sir?" Bentley's voice was strangled.

"No, Bentley. Just go get some water or something, will you?"

"Yes, sir." Bentley exited by way of the door that led to the kitchen.

Taylor figured she was next. And she was right. Grey was eyeing her as if he'd just caught her stealing the silver.

"What do you have planned for your day, Taylor? No more dress fittings or ladies' rallies, I hope?"

"No. I mean to exercise Red Sky. Outside of the city. By the river. I have found a place there that I like."

He nodded . . . as if he knew her secret. "By yourself, then, I take it?"

Taylor raised her chin defiantly. "Yes."

Grey leaned forward in his chair, bracing his elbows on his knees as he reached out and took her hands in his. "You mean to draw these men out by going out alone, don't you?"

Taylor never even blinked. "Yes."

"I see." His voice was dangerously calm. "And what if there were more than one?"

"I have fought more than one man at a time before, and I have lived."

Grey's expression changed. He appeared to be awash in a swamp of emotions that had him shaking his head and grinning at her. "You are one wild little hellion, aren't you? You make every day shine, every night sing. You fill my heart with your love and you scare the living hell out of me—all in the same day."

Taylor smiled. "I suppose you wish to come riding with me?"

He nodded. "You suppose correctly."

They sat on a blanket atop a bluff overlooking the Mississippi River. Between them were the remains of their picnic lunch packed by Cook. A bottle of wine was empty and lying on its side . . . no doubt knocked over somehow when they'd made love. The day was beautiful, the river idyllic, the sun bright, the breeze warm and barely strong enough to ruffle the leaves of a nearby stand of oaks and elms. Out here, free of the city's congestion, free of the interference of other people, it was hard to believe that anyone would wish them ill. Well, wish Taylor ill . . . or harm.

Grey looked over at her. Her long black hair hung down her back in a thick braid. Armed with her six-shooter and dressed again in the men's clothing that Mrs. Scott had procured for her from Albert the stable hand a few weeks back, she sat in profile to him and cross-legged, her hands folded loosely in her lap. She stared intently at the ships clogging the harbor, her gaze flitting hither and yon as she watched everything at once. No movement escaped her intelligent inspection.

Attired in a white shirt, brown vest, buff-colored riding pants, and knee-high polished black-leather boots, Grey sat with his legs stretched out in front of him and his ankles crossed. He leaned back a bit and braced his hands on the blanket underneath him. Filling his thoughts was just how little he really knew about Taylor's life before she'd come here. Her day-to-day life. He felt he knew the high points—if the hair-raising details of murder and prison escapes could be called high points. Even so, there was so little he could broach, because of the truths that he knew about her, but she didn't. He feared how one thing could lead to another in such a discussion.

Still, there was one point he wanted to make. "I didn't see anyone following us out here, Taylor. Did you?"

She shook her head. "No. We would not have made love had we been followed. Or had I felt we were threatened."

"Exactly. But I still believe we would have seen anyone who had, what with the open trail and no place, really, to hide."

"Perhaps."

He grinned. She wouldn't give an inch. "Perhaps your threatening to slit that one man's throat did the trick, if he was even following you."

"He was."

"So you've said." He let it go at that, fairly certain now that she'd attacked some innocent rider because she always felt watched. She didn't really trust white people, anyway. Grey groped for something a little more innocuous to talk about. "Had you ever seen ships before you came here, Taylor? I mean to St. Louis."

She spared him a glance and a brief smile. "Not like these. And not so many. It is why I like this place. The ships. The sky. The water. It is nice here. Red Sky likes it here, too. It must remind him of home."

A pang of star-crossed love tore at Grey. He wished she could think of St. Louis—his home—as her home. But he knew better. Still, at the mention of the horse, they both turned their heads to see the big paint gelding grazing peacefully alongside Grey's equally tall black steed. "They both seem to like it here," Grey said quietly, finally looking back on the ships below. "I own quite a few ships like those, Taylor. Maybe some of those very ones down there. I can't tell from here."

"You do?" Her inquisitive expression pleased Grey inordinately. "My mother said many times that my father owned great sailing ships such as these. I used to try to imagine what they looked like."

Grey willed away his momentary confusion when she spoke of her mother. Catching up to her train of thought, he added, "Yes. Your uncle and father and my father—well, my brother and I now—have some holdings in common, actually. Our money is tied together in one business venture or another."

"I see."

Grey grinned. . . . She was starting to sound like him.

"So this is why the marriage of Franklin to Amanda is such a good thing. The money stays in the family and strengthens these bonds of business."

Grey was impressed. Her quick intelligence had picked up on the more intricate aspects of his statement. "Yes. That's true. But it was never a consideration. I mean, nothing was arranged between them. They genuinely fell in love." . . . He hoped.

"I like Franklin," Taylor said. This was the first time she'd ever mentioned his brother. "He is good for Amanda. I am glad she has him."

Grey thought he could hear an undercurrent in her words. "Why do you say it like that, as if there's something wrong with Amanda?"

Taylor's expression hardened. "Not Amanda. Her father. My father's brother. I do not like him."

She was as disconcertingly honest as a child. What she didn't know was that Grey had never liked the man, either. Even before Charles's far-reaching confession at the club two weeks ago, Grey had always felt an unnatural tension between Stanley and Camilla, one he now knew actually existed. So, very carefully, Grey asked, "Why don't you like him, Taylor— besides his behavior that evening at your father's? Has he said anything else to you? Or treated you harshly?"

"No. But he does not have to." She looked genuinely distressed now.

"What do you mean? You can tell me anything, Taylor." He wasn't sure he meant that because of everything he knew and therefore how he would be forced to respond. With lies.

"I do not wish to speak of him. I would hear of your father instead."

"My father?" Surprised, Grey chuckled and leaned back on his side, facing her, a knee bent, and supporting his weight on an elbow. He plucked a blade of grass and picked at it. "Well, he was a rich old man—shipping, mining, railroads, banking, things like that—when my mother, still a young woman, married him. But the old rascal proved not to be too old to father two sons. Franklin and me, of course." Grey rooted around in his memories for what to say of the man. "Let's see; he was very formal and distant in his role as father. Franklin and I hardly ever saw him when we were boys. As I grew up, and despite his sudden illness and decline, the old man never let me forget what a disappointment I was to him. But he doted on Franklin. Let's see. . . . He died seven years ago of a weak heart."

Taylor had listened quietly, only nodding as he'd spoken. Now she asked, "And with your mother . . . how was he?"

Grey thought her question singularly odd, but nevertheless he answered it. "With my mother? Well, I don't have the first idea what type of husband he was to her." He laughed. "Actually I do. He was the perfect husband. Meaning, he gave her the means and the name to gain the social stature she wanted. And then had the good sense to die."

Taylor frowned . . . and stared worriedly at him.

A prick of concern stabbed at Grey. "Taylor, why do you ask? Do you know something I should hear?" He tried to remember how they'd got onto this subject. All he'd done was remark on the ships down below.

"Yes. Amanda told me something."

Grey's insides felt cold. He paid studious attention to the blade of grass in his hand. "I see. What did she say?"

"I will tell you. But first I will say that I only speak of this because of what it can mean now. To me. To us."

"I understand. Go on." Even though he'd encouraged her to speak, Grey found he couldn't look at her. He felt certain the reason for all the hushed conversations and the tense family moments he'd been aware of growing up was about to be revealed to him—and by the most unlikely of sources. His hands stilled, and he waited.

"Amanda told me what Aunt Camilla recently told her. That before your mother married your father . . . she was in love with my Uncle Stanley. And was heartbroken when he married my Aunt Camilla. Only then did your mother marry your father. You and your brother came quickly, but it was many years before my aunt bore Amanda."

Shocked, feeling betrayed somehow, Grey riveted his gaze on Taylor's face. "I've never heard any of this before. Never. Why would Amanda tell you that? And why would your aunt tell her now, even if it is true?"

Taylor looked away from him, staring out over the waters of the Mississippi. She could have been carved in stone. "She did not mean it as idle talk. And I am sorry if I hurt you with this truth."

"I'm not hurt," Grey all but barked. Taylor gave him her attention again. Grey forced a calm reasonableness on himself that he didn't feel. "I'm sorry I spoke harshly to you. Please blame it on the shock. But even if what you've said is true— and I suppose I have no reason to believe Camilla James would lie—then I see what you mean about it having consequences for us all. After all, there's nothing like old jealousies, given a shift in circumstances, to cause people to erupt in ways they might not have otherwise."

"That is how Amanda sees it, too. And I agree. Grey, my uncle told me, when I saw him at my father's two weeks ago, that there were old hurts I made people think of again. He said I had the face of a sin he could not forgive or forget."

"Good God." Grey's fears escalated. No sane—or innocent—person said things like that.

Taylor continued. "I am not accusing anyone, but your mother and my uncle . . . they watch me. I know they do not like me, even though they pretend they do. I can feel their hatred."

"Taylor, surely you don't think—"

"Please." She held a hand up to stop him from speaking. "There is more." She took a deep breath. "Aunt Camilla has again been sick. Amanda is afraid for her, that someone is trying to harm her."

"What?" Grey abruptly sat up and grabbed Taylor's arm. "Harm her? Who would—how?"

Taylor calmly looked at his hand gripping her arm and then met his gaze. "Amanda fears her mother's sudden illness may not be an illness . . . but poisoning. A slow poisoning."

Grey's blood ran cold. "How could Amanda know that, that it would be poisoning?"

"She spoke in private with her mother's doctor. He told her he could not explain Aunt Camilla's illness. But he said he'd seen the same symptoms as hers in only one other patient, and that patient had died a lingering death." She put her hand over his and squeezed it reassuringly. Sympathy shone in her blue eyes. "Grey, the doctor said the other patient was . . . your father."

Her words hit him like a physical blow. "But it was his heart that killed him. The doctor said—" The words had been automatic . . . until a sudden memory assailed Grey, leaving him feeling sick and weak. "Oh, no. The *doctor* didn't say that at all. Not to me, at any rate. It was *Mother* who said he'd told her that."

This was too much. The world around him, even Taylor, seemed to recede for Grey as he struggled internally with the awful possibilities she had just presented him. Could his mother and Stanley James truly be murderers? Were they killing their spouses slowly so as not to be suspected and in order to be together? Grey fought hard not to believe it of them. He assured himself that if it were true, he would certainly have heard of his mother and Stanley's liaison from the gossips in St. Louis.

Then he remembered some awful truths he knew of his own. Both families were originally from Boston. Stanley and Charles had moved here first. And then Grey's father had moved them here from Boston at his mother's insistence. That meant that no one here knew of their past together. And if they were careful, then no one would suspect them of . . . being lovers.

But if they were so in love, why hadn't his mother and Stanley James married each other to begin with? But he knew. Money. The James fortune stemmed from Camilla's inheritance, just as Grey's own fortune had come from his father. His mother had none of her own before her marriage. *Money. Filthy money. What would people not do for money?* As if it were in answer to his question, it popped into Grey's mind that his father had not been ill until they'd moved here. *Oh, God, it's true.*

Tormented beyond belief, Grey shook his head. It was too much to take in all at once, that his mother could possibly be so evil. His mind simply refused to register the notion. *No. Not the woman who gave me life and raised me. Impossible. It has to be.* But what if it was true? What then should he do, think, believe? Adding to Grey's concern was Stanley's confrontation of Taylor and the names he'd called her. Her uncle evidently knew the truth about Taylor. So where would this treachery end? When they were all dead? Or just when Camilla James, Charles James, and Taylor were?

Grey exhaled sharply and ran a hand through his hair. He blinked, coming back to the moment and realizing he was still staring at Taylor. On an impulse, he reached out and stroked her smooth cheek. Her blue eyes sparked with questions. A sad smile came to Grey's face, all the way from his heart. Her beautiful face, so close to his, a face he already loved with every bit of his being, looked like that of a vulnerable child. That's exactly what she was, too. Charles James's vulnerable child. Because if what Amanda suspected was true, no wonder Charles wanted his daughter gone from here as fast as possible. She'd most likely be next—and probably not by intermittent poisonings.

"I have hurt you," she said quietly. "It is in your eyes."

He shook his head and took her hand in his, holding it tightly. "No. You didn't hurt me. Instead, the things that you had to tell me did." Just then, resolve solidified inside Grey as he stared at Taylor's slender hand. She had to leave here. To hell with her talk of the ways of a coward and staying to face the danger here. To hell with it all. He'd make her go. He'd give her no choice in the matter. In essence, he had to love her enough to send her away.

"Taylor," he began, raising his head to look into her blue eyes. "I want you to leave now. Just go away from here. I will give you all the money you need. Just . . . go. And I don't want you to tell anyone where you're going. Not even me."

Withdrawing her hand from his, Taylor stared at him, her expression inscrutable. Not a muscle twitched in her face. She was dry-eyed, breathing calmly. Then, still sitting crosslegged, she rose in one willowy motion, leveraging herself up by the strength in her legs. She stood there, looking down at him.

Grey wanted to die. He put a hand out to her, but she drew back . . . away from his touch. Defeated, he lowered his hand. "Taylor, listen to me. I'm not angry with you. And this has nothing to do with what you said about my mother. I swear it. It's just that you need to leave now for the same reason you needed to leave before. Your life is in danger. You know it is. We all do."

Grey knew she would never know what a kindness he had just done her. But he hated himself—and wasn't too sure he wouldn't leap off this very bluff behind him once she rode away.

"If you wish me to go, then I will go." Her expression was stony. "And I do not want your money. I will go to my father or to Aunt Camilla."

A sense of urgency seized Grey. "No, that won't do. You know better—"

Red Sky whinnied loudly, sounding an alarm. Taylor jerked around. Grey did the same. Both horses had their heads up, their ears pricked forward. They stared toward the woods. Frowning, fearful, his heart suddenly pounding, Grey searched the tree line for whatever might have—

There! Off to their right . . . what was that?

In less than a fraction of a second, Grey recognized what he was seeing. A gasp from Taylor told him she did, as well.

Sunlight glinted off gunmetal.

"Get down!" Grey yelled, snaking his arm out and hitting Taylor hard behind her knees. He knocked her feet out from under her. She was too perfect a target standing there. Just as she hit the blanket on her back and her breath left her in a pained grunt, a shot rang out. Searing pain ripped into Grey— and the world went black.

Chapter Seventeen

Still on her back, Taylor lay there on the blanket, stunned. Grey had been hit. There was nothing she could do for him—not while they were still under fire. The high-pitched whine of two more shots had already rung out. One exploded the empty wine bottle on the blanket, sending shards of glass flying in all directions. Taylor curled defensively but got nicked on a cheek. She felt blood trickling down her face. The other bullet pinged into the ground just to one side of her and shot a clod of grass and dirt out of the ground. And still she couldn't get her breath back from Grey knocking her down.

Still another shot rang out. A bullet flew by about an inch above her head.

To hell with breathing. Taylor rolled onto her belly and ripped her gun out of its holster. Bracing her elbows on the ground, she held her six-shooter in both hands and began firing. The horses had shied back and were now at a distance but still in the clearing. Taylor aimed for the spot where she'd last seen the sunlight on the gunmetal glare—and began shooting, systematically aiming her shots along the trees in a straight line, first to one side of where she'd seen the rifle barrel and then to the other. Her reasoning was that whoever was out there—she believed there was only one man—most likely had moved by now. But in which direction she had no way of knowing. So she did all she could to keep him moving, keep him from getting another shot off.

On her fifth shot, she heard what she'd been listening . . . praying, hoping . . . for—a grunt and a cry of pain. She stopped shooting and . . . listened and watched. Seconds ticked by. She saw nothing, heard nothing. But she didn't move, didn't relax her guard. The shooter's grunt of pain could be a ploy, meant to get her to do just that. But she believed she had hit him. Where and how bad, she didn't know. So she had to assume that, though wounded and now more dangerous, he remained capable of firing his gun. So, with the blood from the glass and the sweat of fear mingling with that of the day's heat and running down her face, she waited.

It was the hardest thing she'd ever done. Her heart pounded with fear for Grey. Every instinct in her begged for her to turn to him, to see where he was hit, to see if he was alive or dead, to see if and how she could help him. He was so quiet and still, it was scary. But she didn't dare give in to those urges right now. She'd certainly be no good to him dead.

"Come on, you rotten son of a bitch," Taylor muttered, aiming her comment at her unknown assailant hidden among the trees. She directed her trained gaze in a sweep of the sun-dappled shadows before her. "Show yourself, you fu—"

A movement in the trees, no more than a flash of color, alerted Taylor. She riveted her gaze to the spot. The shooter staggered out of the woods. Taylor licked nervously at her lips as she flexed her hands around her gun. She had one more bullet before she'd have to reload. She wasn't about to be stupid now and waste it. Blood poured down the man's shirt-front. *Good.* He was clutching at his chest as he reeled a few steps toward her. Taylor pulled the hammer back on her gun. The man went to his knees . . . and then keeled over, face-first, onto the ground. For long moments, he didn't move. Neither did Taylor. She'd hadn't lived this long, given the life of an outlaw she'd chosen for herself, by being rash or stupid in past situations exactly like this one. Caution was the key. That and a well-trained horse.

Taylor called out sharply in Cherokee to Red Sky and then whistled. The paint stared her way for a split second, gave a high-pitched whinny that shied Grey's horse, and then burst into a thundering gallop toward the downed man. If the man was alive and heard all that coming his way, he'd give up his game quickly enough. He didn't move. Red Sky sailed easily over him, no more than if he'd been a felled log, and circled back toward Taylor in a canter. Just as her horse stopped beside the blanket, Taylor released her gun's hammer and stood up, satisfied the man was dead. Quickly she holstered her gun and bent over Grey, her heart in her throat as she gently turned him toward her.

"Oh no," she breathed out in a ragged whisper.

His face and the side of his head were covered in blood that still trickled down his cheek and neck. Taylor put a hand to her mouth, as much to stifle a scream of despair as to keep back the bile that rose in her throat. Grey had been shot in the head. Taking a deep breath, forcing a calm on herself she didn't feel, she put her hand on his chest, pressing down hard enough to detect his heartbeat . . . if there was one. There was. . . . A good, steady beat pumped under her hand. Weak with relief, Taylor said a silent thank-you and quickly pulled out her shirttail from her pants. She unbuttoned it enough to give her a length she could use to wipe away what blood she could from his face. She told herself she'd give anything right now for a good bottle of liquor—to use to clean the wound. She then looked closely at the wound and probed its edges.

Another thank-you was sent upward to the heavens. Grey had been grazed just above his left temple, nothing more. The wound was not deep or even long but had packed enough punch to knock him out cold—and to scare her out of ten years' growth. He'd have one hell of a headache for a few days and a scar to show his grandchildren. Amused and disheartened by that thought—his grandchildren would not be hers—she set about cleaning him up as best she could. She unsheathed her knife, tugged his clean, white shirttail out, and cut it into narrow strips, which she then fashioned into a bandage around his head. Done with that, she tried to wake him, smacking his cheeks and calling his name.

Finally he stirred, flailing his arms, fighting, and calling out, "No! Taylor!" and generally sounding confused and in pain.

She dodged his awkward blows and held his arms down— or tried to. "Grey! Stop it. It is me—Taylor. You've been shot. Be still. You will cause your wound to bleed, stupid white man. Do not fight me." Only when a tear splashed onto his face did she realize she was crying . . . out of relief and love. Instantly she dragged her shirtsleeve across her eyes, denying the tears that wet the fabric. Only weak old women cried.

Grey jerked and then tensed. His eyes popped open. "Taylor?" he called out hoarsely, searching for her, trying to sit up.

Taylor instantly leaned over him, using her weight and her hands pressed against his chest to hold him down. "Be still. You will cause your wound to bleed."

"My wound?" He looked at her as if he had no idea who she was.

Taylor had seen this before. For a time after a blow to the head, a person could talk and act crazy. At least, Monroe had done so after she'd hit him with the butt of her gun because he'd backhanded her for saying no to his sexual advances. Thankfully, the next day, when he'd again become himself, he hadn't remembered what had happened—and she hadn't reminded him. "Yes. Your wound, Grey. You were shot. Do you remember?"

His eyes cleared, his gaze focused—and he gasped, grabbing for her, tugging her atop him, holding her close. "My God, Taylor, someone shot at us. Are you OK?" He held her back from him, frantically looking her over. His eyes widened. "There's blood on your face."

She grabbed his searching hand and put it to his own head, to the bandages there. "Yes. It is nothing. But you, Grey— you were shot. Not me. I am fine. And so are you. Do you understand me?" She watched him search her face and then nod that he did. "Good. Stay here. I have to go see—"

Grey grabbed her by her shirtfront. "The man who shot at us. Where is he? Did he get away?"

Taylor cupped his fisted hand in hers and held it to her chest. "No, he did not. He shot you, and so I killed him."

Grey stared at her soberly. She wondered what he thought of her, a woman who had now killed four men and could so callously speak of taking a life. Then he smiled. "I would have done the same thing, Taylor. I would have emptied my gun into the son of a bitch."

She fought a grin of her own. "Then I am ashamed, for I have one bullet left."

He started to laugh but abruptly grimaced, putting a hand to his head. "Damn, that hurt."

"And it will for many days. Stay here." She patted his shoulder. "I wish to go see who our friend was."

Grey clutched at her arm. His expression was dead serious. "Taylor, you know he probably meant to shoot you and not me, don't you?"

"Yes."

"Help me up. I want to go with you. No—don't argue. I'm going. I want to see the bastard's face, see if I know him."

"All right." Resigned, Taylor put his arm around her shoulders and struggled with his weight as she tried to help him leverage himself upright to a stand. Then she stood with him a moment until his wave of dizziness passed. When he said he felt steadier, she slowly walked him across the clearing and toward the downed man. With Grey's muscled arm still around her slender shoulders, his long-fingered hand clutched her upper arm so tightly she had to bite her lip to keep from crying out. But she did not protest. He needed her, and she would gladly bear this pain.

Finally, they had crossed the rocky, grassy, uneven ground of the meadow and stood looking down at the man. Taylor stood in silence next to Grey. He nudged the body with the toe of his boot. The man on the ground jiggled limply. Taylor let go of Grey in order to turn the shooter over onto his back. When she did, she took a moment to note her handiwork—she'd got him right through the heart. It was as it should be. She brushed the grass and dirt off her hands onto her pants and again stood with Grey. The dead man had reddish hair and blankly staring brown eyes. Taylor's mouth curved into a grimace of anger—at herself.

"Well, I've never seen him before," Grey remarked.

"I have," Taylor said, her anger tightening her chest, making it hard to breathe.

"You? Where?"

"In the park when I was riding with Amanda and Franklin."

She pointed to the dead man on the ground. "He is the man I said was following me. I should have slit his throat right then, like I told him I would."

Taylor looked up at Grey, so tall and handsome—and bloodstained. A jagged shard of pure and deep emotion ripped through her. She'd nearly lost Grey to this coward of an assassin who now lay dead on the ground at her feet. She would never forgive herself for not dealing with him as she should have the first time. Neither would she forgive those who had hired him. They would pay.

"I just can't get over it, Son. My dear God, you could have been killed!"

"As you've said about ten times, Mother. I'm fully aware of what almost happened. Were it not for Taylor's quick thinking—"

"*Her* quick thinking?" Augusta Talbott turned to the freshly bathed and dressed Taylor, who sat quietly in a corner of Grey's parlor while his family and hers made over him and got the details of the afternoon's excitement. "It was probably *you*"—she pointed an accusing finger at Taylor—"that awful man was trying to kill when he got my son instead."

A shocked silence filled the room. Stung though she was by the woman's ungrateful rebuke, Taylor agreed. "I believe as you do."

Then she concentrated on watching everyone's reaction to this exchange. Someone in this room crowded with Jameses and Talbotts wanted her dead . . . and she wanted to know who it was and why. The only one not present was Aunt Camilla who had stayed home because she was feeling poorly again . . . according to Uncle Stanley. Taylor had exchanged a worried glance with Grey when her uncle had arrived with Amanda and made that announcement. Taylor looked now into Grey's eyes—he was smiling warmly at her, which gave her the courage to add, "I wish it *had* been me he'd shot."

"Well, I assure you I do not," Grey countered.

"Well, I assure you," his mother broke in, her face a mask of open resentment, "that had the worst happened and Grey had been . . . I can barely say the word . . . killed, I would have suspected *you,* young lady—" Now everyone protested. Grey's mother faced them, undaunted. "Well, I would have. After all, she's nothing more than a—than a *stranger* among us."

Taylor's expression hardened. The woman had obviously been thinking a word other than *stranger. Savage? Redskin? Animal?*

"That is absolutely enough, Mother." Grey's voice was raised and cold with anger. A grimace followed his outburst. He put a hand to his head. Obviously the effort had cost him. Taylor nearly came out of her seat, so badly did she want to go to him. But her uncertainty around those in this room kept her in place.

"Don't upset yourself so, Grey," his mother fussed, putting a hand over his. "You'll only make the hurt worse." She turned to Taylor and wagged a finger at her. "You're just lucky you thought to drag that dead man back here through the dirt behind your horse." She gave a delicate shudder to show her revulsion at such a barbaric act.

"I did not drag him as you say. I made a travois out of the blanket we had and put him in it. Thus did I get him back here. It was the only way. Your son was my first concern." And luck had nothing to do with it. Mrs. Talbott's statement was exactly why Taylor had made certain she hadn't come back without the dead man, whose body Grey had turned over to the police for their investigation of him and possible identification.

"Well, I for one believe you did a fine and resourceful job of it, my dear."

That was her father. His proud and smiling face made Taylor suddenly shy. She lowered her gaze, but not before noting the tiny white lines to either side of Grey's mouth and the tired look in his eyes. He was in pain and needed to lie down. She was suddenly impatient with everyone here, friend or foe. She wanted them gone so she could attend to Grey. No sooner had the thought presented itself than Taylor questioned it— was that *her* sounding so protective and loving?

"And I don't know how you can sit there, Augusta," her father had continued on, again capturing Taylor's attention as he directed his angry remarks to Grey's mother, "and disparage Taylor for saving Grey's life. I marvel that you're not singing her praises. And we"—He now included everyone in the room—"should be concerning ourselves with whoever that man was and why he would shoot at them."

Stanley James made a scoffing sound, drawing attention his way. "For God's sake, Charles. The man was obviously some sort of lowlife ruffian merely intent on robbing them, and nothing more. Must you see a conspiracy behind every act? It happened, and now it's over. Drop it."

"A pretty theory, Stanley," Grey cut in, "but it doesn't hold up. A petty thief would not have shot at us from the cover of the woods. This man meant to kill us." He looked Taylor's way, his heart in his eyes. "Or one of us."

"Hear, hear, Grey. I'm with you," Charles James offered. "This was an out-and-out attempt at murder." He then turned his angry gaze on Grey's mother. "And I will take into account, Augusta, your shock and fear for your son when I consider your remarks to Taylor. But understand this: I will *not* hear from you—or anyone else present—another disparaging word about my daughter."

"Oh, *please,* Charles," Augusta Talbott said dramatically. "A paternal note from *you* at this late date?"

"Mother," Grey snapped, his voice a low growl. "I would remind you that this is my house and these are my guests—you included."

Augusta Talbott turned to her son. She sat on a rose-damask-upholstered chair she'd pulled up next to the settee where he was reclining against piled-up pillows. "Now, Grey, what bad thing could I say about a girl who wears men's clothing and goes about with a gun holstered to her hip? A girl who rides a horse astride and parades a wounded man and a dead man through all of St. Louis for everyone to see? Why, I don't need to say anything. She brought the scandal down on all of us by her own behavior. The gossips and the newspapers will have a field day with this."

"For heaven's sake, Mrs. Talbott." Amanda came quickly to Taylor's side and to her defense. "Listen to yourself. You should be grateful, like Uncle Charles says. What did you expect Taylor to do—leave your wounded and bleeding son out there so you wouldn't be embarrassed?"

"So *I* wouldn't be? I was thinking of you, my dear, as my future daughter-in-law." Augusta Talbott's uncertain expression said she knew she'd gone too far. Her voice became wheedling. "Your wedding is upcoming, dear. And Franklin's campaign for mayor—"

"Oh, hogwash, Mother." This was Franklin. Everyone looked surprised. "I don't give a fig for any scandal. My brother's well-being comes first. I should think you'd feel the same way about your firstborn."

Augusta Talbott was under seige from all sides now. She looked Stanley James's way. Taylor noted that his expression had hardened, like stone, as he stared Augusta's way. But at whom or at what was he angry? An instant pout claimed Grey's mother's face. "Franklin, I don't believe I've ever heard you speak in such a sharp tone to me."

Taylor glanced up at Amanda, who now held one of Taylor's hands and was absently patting it. Amanda's expression was loving and proud as she stared Franklin's way. Perhaps she was seeing a decisive side of him she'd never seen before.

"I am sorry, Mother. But I felt it necessary. As Charles is willing to do, I am going to attribute your outburst at Taylor to your heightened emotion over Grey's nearly being killed."

Amanda immediately spoke up, again to her future mother-in-law and in an obvious effort to smooth things over. "I assure you, Mrs. Talbott, that once you get to know my dear cousin—"

"Your *cousin,* Amanda?" The older woman's eyes slanted like a cat's and her voice was a nasty purr. "Are you sure about that?"

Over the gasps and protests of Grey and Charles James, Taylor's Uncle Stanley spoke through gritted teeth. "That's quite enough, Augusta. Not another word."

Taylor riveted her gaze on her uncle. His heightened color

and the cruel twist to his mouth spoke of a rage barely controlled. Taylor had the distinct impression it wasn't Mrs. Talbott so much as what she'd just said that was the source of his anger. Figuring that, Taylor considered what Mrs. Talbott had said about her and Amanda being cousins but could find nothing sinister there. Everyone in this room knew they were cousins. So it had to be something other than that . . . something she wasn't aware of. Or it could just be that she was wrong and Uncle Stanley was angry with Mrs. Talbott for speaking so to *his* daughter.

At that moment, with everyone in the room at an angry impasse, the parlor door opened and in walked Bentley, pushing a silver-inlaid wheeled cart. An elaborate silver tea set reposed atop it. On its second shelf and perched on a lace doily sat a china plate piled high with small cakes. "Pardon me, but Cook thought you might enjoy a bit of refreshment while you celebrate Mr. Talbott's good fortune." He cut his gaze to Taylor and—she would swear—winked at her.

"Good fortune?" Uncle Stanley huffed. "Here now, you call a man getting shot in the head 'good fortune'?"

In what even Taylor recognized as a rare show of mettle for a domestic, Bentley faced the tall, blond, and powerful Stanley James and eyed him pointedly. "It depends on who the man was who got shot, sir. In this instance, I was referring to Mr. Talbott's and Miss James's good fortune in escaping death."

Taylor fought a grin, hiding it behind her hand and a gentle cough. Her man-bird would ever protect her.

As Stanley James made an abrupt gesture of dismissal and turned away, staring out a window, Grey smiled at Bentley. "Thank you. That will be all." Grey sat up from his sprawl on the settee. He, too, was all cleaned up, in fresh clothes, and had a more suitable bandage wrapped around his head, thanks to Mrs. Scott's efficient efforts. "And thank Cook for me," he added to Bentley. "She's outdone herself." He then turned to his mother. "Will you do us the honor of pouring? Thank you."

With everyone else thus distracted, Amanda bent over Taylor from beside her chair and whispered, "Did you get to tell Grey my suspicions about the poisonings . . . and the other?"

Taylor nodded. Amanda had already wrung the entire story of the shooting that afternoon out of Taylor . . . and had hugged Taylor and cried until Taylor had become impatient. It was only natural they would now speak of other issues. "I did. He did not want to believe it about his mother and your father or the poisonings we fear, but I think he does."

Amanda arrowed a glance her father's way. He stood possessively behind Mrs. Talbott's chair now, his hand all but on her shoulder. A sudden stricken expression overtook Amanda's features, and she turned her back on the sight. She perched a hip on the chair's arm where Taylor sat. Amanda's back was now to the room as she faced Taylor, but still she kept her voice low. "Look at them, Taylor. What are we going to do? I am so frightened for Mother. My own father. What could be more awful?"

Taylor put a cautionary hand on Amanda's arm as she checked the positions of those in the room. They'd converged congenially enough around the tea cart and were conversing in low tones as Mrs. Talbott served them. No one appeared to be paying any attention to the two girls. Satisfied that they had a few private moments before their behavior aroused notice or suspicion, Taylor put her head together with Amanda's, noting that she looked as if she were about to cry. Taylor understood Amanda's emotion all too well. To have to consider treachery on the part of a parent was an awful thing. "Hear me, Amanda. First of all, you do not know your father is responsible. Or even if your mother is being poisoned."

"Is that what you think, Taylor? That she's not and my father isn't behind it all?"

Taylor exhaled on a sigh. "No. I fear it is as you say. And so, you must protect her. Do not allow her to eat or drink anything that your father gives her."

"But that's impossible. I'm not home all the time. Neither are they. And I . . . I don't go into their bedrooms, Taylor. It's impossible for me to watch her all the time."

Exasperation ate at Taylor. "Amanda, why do you not just

tell your mother what the doctor told you? It would be better. She could protect herself."

Amanda's brown eyes were wide with emotion. "Oh, no, it wouldn't be better. Not at all. My mother may or may not believe me. Either way, I fear she would say something to my father. God alone knows what *he'd* do in that case."

"Do you mean to you? Would he harm you, Amanda?" A protective love of her cousin jumped to the fore in Taylor.

Amanda hung her head. "No."

"Then he is a good father to you?" Taylor asked this out of wistful curiosity. She had no idea how a good father, or any kind of father, behaved.

Amanda clasped her hands together tightly. "That's just it, Taylor. He's wonderful. Loving and giving. It's Mother I'm concerned about. If my father *is*"—Amanda took a deep ragged breath—"poisoning my mother and she confronts him with my suspicions and they're true . . . well, you can see what could happen. It would be even worse if I was wrong, the trouble it would cause in my family."

Amanda was right. In an effort to better gauge the likelihood of Uncle Stanley's guilt, Taylor asked, "How do your parents appear to you to get along?"

Amanda shrugged her shoulders. "It's hard to put a finger on. I've never seen them argue or even heard a fuss between them. But they're not affectionate, really. More like formal. Distant. There's a tension there when they're together. I don't know how else to explain it."

"You just did. And very well." Taylor's heart thumped woodenly—with fear for her aunt's life.

Just then, Amanda put a hand to her temple and grimaced as if she had a headache. "He's my *father,* Taylor. This is so awful. Sometimes I simply refuse to believe that he could have two so very different sides to his personality. How could he be so loving to me and so evil to my mother—his own wife?"

Knowing firsthand how Uncle Stanley could be one minute threatening and the next loving, and knowing that Amanda was not aware of that incident, Taylor grabbed her cousin's hand and stared pointedly into her eyes. "Listen to me. I want

ou to invite me to stay with you. Just do it without asking
ermission. That way I can help you watch over Aunt Ca-
nilla."

Confusion had Amanda looking from Taylor, over to Grey,
nd then back to Taylor. "But I thought Grey—"

"He asked me to leave, just before he was shot."

Amanda clutched at Taylor's hand. "Oh, Taylor, he can't
ave meant it. Tell me, had you two argued?"

Taylor's smile, an expression coming more often to her,
vas this time a rueful one. "We argue all the time. But this
ne was because of the poisonings and because he believes
ny life to be in danger."

Amanda made a scoffing sound. "Of course he does. Look
vhat happened today. Even you said you believed yourself to
e the target." She now shook her head slowly, her expression
onveying sadness and a lack of understanding. "Why would
nyone want to harm you, Taylor?"

Thinking of the way she led her life, Taylor chuckled.
There are many who would do so. I have many enemies."

"But not here, certainly? Not in St. Louis? Why, in the
vhole city you only know us, the people in this room, Taylor.
And we are all—" Amanda gasped, her eyes rounded. She put
hand to her mouth and stared in horror at Taylor.

"Exactly. We're all family. But someone in this room hates
ne very much, Amanda. I don't know why. But I do mean to
ind out."

Amanda grabbed Taylor's hands. "I'll help you, Taylor, in
ny way I can. Give me a few days—no matter what he says,
Grey needs you here with him for now—to set up your visit.
'll tell my father you're coming. Of course, Mother will
now, too. But I want to see if she suddenly gets better since
e'll know someone else will be in the home."

Taylor didn't like adding to Amanda's concerns but felt she
ad to speak her mind. "Amanda, what if she suddenly gets
vorse?"

Taylor's blond cousin, her expression pinched, took a deep
reath and closed her eyes. Then, she looked at Taylor, whose
reath caught at the wintry bleakness that shone in Amanda's

eyes. "Then I will have no choice but to call the police to my father and tell them of my suspicions."

"You'll need more than suspicions. Is there no chance you could search their rooms for the vial of poison? That would be proof enough."

Letting go of Taylor's hands, Amanda gestured helplessness. "Yes, it would, but proof only that someone was trying to kill her. It wouldn't prove who was doing it."

"It depends on where you find the poison."

Amanda was silent for a moment as she stared at Taylor. "Do you hear us? I cannot believe I am even capable of having this conversation. We sound like police detectives. This is all so far-fetched. I mean, they're my parents and your aunt and uncle. We love these people. I don't know which would be worse—if I'm wrong or if I'm right. And then there's you. With all this other going on, now someone's trying to kill you. I don't know which way to turn, what to worry about first."

Taylor frowned. Hearing the two events paired together again brought a belated realization to her mind. She hadn't latched onto this before now, a connection between her aunt's poisoning and the attempt on her own life. But earlier today, before the shooting began, Grey had also paired the two. Were they related? Certainly Uncle Stanley was the figure in common here. He'd confronted her at her father's and had been threatening. And he was the one Amanda suspected of poisoning her mother. But beyond that, Taylor had no clue as to how the two events could be related. It just didn't make any sense . . . unless Uncle Stanley had two very different reasons for wanting her and Aunt Camilla dead. That was certainly possible. Suddenly Taylor realized that Amanda was still speaking.

"Sometimes I wonder, Taylor," she said, "if I shouldn't just bundle Mother up and take her and myself to Uncle Charles's. You could join us there. After all, he's your father. And it would put a stop to all the idle gossip about your being here with Grey without benefit of a chaperone."

Taylor shook her head. "I cannot do that. There are too

many things left unsaid between my father and me. Things
perhaps best left unsaid. I don't—"

"Oh, dear, Taylor, you have to know I do not give a fig
for the gossips. I didn't mean to hurt you—"

"You did not. It's just that it would be . . . wrong. For me.
For you. And especially for your mother. Besides, your father
would not allow it."

"You're right." Amanda glanced Mrs. Talbott's way and
then looked down at Taylor. "I really do not like that woman."

"She is not very likable, I agree. But she may have a point.
I mean for your and Franklin's sake. Your wedding. His running for mayor. The further scandal of you and your mother
moving out right now would be too much. I have already done
enough to bring unwanted attention to us all."

"Oh, Taylor—as my dear Franklin so eloquently put it—
hogwash on the scandal. People will talk, no matter what. All
I know is no one had better say one word against you in my
hearing. I love you like a sister and would defend you to the
death."

A sudden evil premonition, like a great dark bird with
mighty wings, swept over Taylor, shadowing her thoughts and
shivering her with cold dread. Somehow, in some awful way,
she knew beyond a doubt Amanda's words would come back
to haunt them all.

Chapter Eighteen

The bruised-purple twilight faded into darkness. Stars winked on in the heavens. *Finally.* They were in Grey's retreat, the library, two nights following the ill-fated picnic and shoot-out. The days were exhausting with their steady stream of dignitaries, luminaries, and social gadflies coming to express their concern and outrage—but mostly to indulge their curiosity regarding Taylor's position in the Talbott household, Grey knew. But now, the sun having set, all was quiet. He and Taylor were alone together and partaking of after-dinner cigars and brandy. The very picture of lackadaisical adversaries, they sprawled in two facing leather-upholstered chairs. They'd propped their feet up on a common ottoman in the space between them.

A homey, comfortable, intimate scene. Except that, as always, the two of them were at an argumentative impasse.

In the less-than-three newsworthy weeks that had expired from the night he'd met her, Grey now admitted to himself, he'd been nothing but ambivalent in his dealings with Taylor. First he'd wanted her to go. Then he'd wanted her to stay. Then he'd wanted her to go. And now again, he wanted her to stay. Absurd was what it was. Now *she* wanted to leave. And he would not hear of it—for any reason, his heart cried out, but especially because she only wanted to leave his house, not St. Louis.

"I cannot believe you would leave me, Taylor."

"I am not leaving you. We are not married—"

"We could be so this very evening. I could call a justice of the peace and—"

"Be serious. I am going to stay with my cousin, as I should have done in the beginning."

"In the beginning you were going to stay with your father. If you must leave me, why don't you go to your father's, instead?"

"I cannot."

And that was all she'd say on the subject, the blastedly stubborn girl. Grey had his hands full. There was no way in hell he could allow her to go to Amanda's—even more important . . . to her aunt and uncle's. Worse, he had to prevent her going for reasons he had sworn not to tell her. *Damn that Charles James, anyway.*

So, stuck as he was and having to make his argument with the only weapons he could use, Grey sent her an arch look. 'All right. Your cousin. The one whose father most likely would try to kill you, according to what we believe? That cousin? You wish to go stay with her? Taylor, you heard the policeman today. That man you killed was a known hired gun and no mere robber as this same uncle of yours so elaborately claimed. Don't you wonder who could have hired him? Please go to your father's, where I know you'll be safe."

"No. I need to go stay with Amanda. For my aunt's sake."

"So you've said. And what exactly is it you could do? You'd be in a huge mansion full of rooms, all of them unfamiliar to you, and with an army of servants watching and reporting your every move. Therefore, what more . . . to ensure your aunt's safety . . . could you do that Amanda, with her greater freedom of movement and authority in the same household, could not?"

Taylor's chin came up. Grey took a deep breath. . . . Dear God, he'd wounded her pride. That would only make her more adamant.

"Amanda is timid with her father. I am not," Taylor said from behind that inscrutable Cherokee mask of hers.

"I agree. But again I ask you . . . what exactly would you do differently than she's already doing?" Grey frowned at his own question. "Come to think of it, what exactly is she doing? I don't suppose she's strapped on a gun and hauled in the police, has she?"

Through the blue haze of her cigar smoke, Taylor narrowed

her eyes at him. A shiver skittered over Grey's skin. If she ever turned that expression on him in earnest, out of genuine anger or hate, he'd need more than that gun and the police he'd just teased about. Swallowing, displaying bravado, Grey prodded her to speak. "Well?"

"She has not yet strapped on a gun or involved the police. She is watching over her mother . . . checking her food and drink and her medicines."

"Unbelievable." Grey shook his head. "How is she checking them? Is she first trying them herself? What if something is poisoned, Taylor? She's risking her life, somewhat like a king's taster."

Taylor frowned her confusion.

"A person paid to taste a king's food first in case his enemies have poisoned it." Just then, a course of action that could keep Taylor here with him, and her aunt and cousin safe, at least temporarily, popped into Grey's head. It was so simple. Feeling suddenly better, even expansive, he decided—in a diabolically good-natured way—to continue his baiting of Taylor before he proposed his plan to her. "Never mind about that. I prefer to talk about your behavior. This disloyalty toward me on your part is very eye-opening. I did take a bullet for you."

"Now you are pouting like a child. And you did not take a bullet for me. The shooter had a poor aim, that is all."

"Oh, pardon me. From where I'm sitting, with this bandage still wrapped around my head, the bastard had pretty good aim."

Taylor sipped at her brandy and eyed him over the snifter's rim. "You are the one who told me I had to leave."

"I meant St. Louis and for your own safety. I certainly never meant because I didn't want you here with me. I do. But now you wish to go merrily leap into the lion's jaws. I won't allow it."

To Grey's utter dismay, Taylor didn't say anything . . . she simply arched an eyebrow at him and grinned around the cigar she'd stuck back in her mouth. Her expression was a clear-enough answer. He could *not allow* it all he wanted. . . . She would do as she damned well pleased. On the one hand, he applauded her. She was one hell of a woman, unlike any other woman he'd ever met. He was absolutely, totally, besottedly head over heels in love with her. And on the other hand, he'd like to choke the life out of her for being so damned stubborn and willful and for scaring the hell out of him by not taking better care to keep herself alive, because she had to know that he would die without her.

Grey took a deep breath. He'd barely been able to think all that in one sentence without pausing for air. Then he realized that he hadn't really told her yet that he felt all that for her. Grey looked her in the eye. "I will die without you here."

She chuckled as she placed her cigar in the ashtray on his desk and blew smoke out the side of her mouth. "No, you will not. Your head wound is not that bad."

Well, so much for romance. His head wound, of course, was not what he'd meant. But he'd use the opening she'd given him. He wasn't above it. "Yes, it is." Employing great drama, he put a shaking hand to his head. "I fear I'm suffering a relapse."

"What does that mean . . . a re-lapse?"

Grey lowered his hand and tamped his cigar's ash into the ashtray perched on his lap. He also worked to hide his grin. Now he had her and, shamelessly, he was going to keep her. If she wasn't going to leave St. Louis altogether, then here with him was the safest place for her to stay. He sought her gaze. "A relapse means a worsening of symptoms after one first appears to be getting better. It's a very dire circumstance. I shouldn't be alone."

"You are not alone. You have ten people on your staff. Besides, it is Mrs. Scott who is now nursing your injury. Not me."

Grey grimaced and grumbled. "And how well I know that. The old harridan—that means . . . well, means 'old lady,' I suppose. At any rate, she thinks she still has to sleep in that blamed chair in my room."

Taylor's grin was a sensual tease in itself, but with her foot she poked at his. "Perhaps she, too, fears this awful re-lapse you speak of."

Trapped by his own words, Grey sulked openly.

"Ah. You are angry because it is her and not me in your bedroom." Taylor took a sip of her brandy. Above its rim, her blue eyes danced with teasing lights.

"Damned straight I am. And well you know it," Grey mock-fussed right back. But inside, his heart quickened. It was true. He missed Taylor's sweet body sleeping next to his. Her scent, the silky feel of her skin, the sweep of her thick, black hair draped over his arm, her touch, her kiss . . . her wild love-making.

"Then why don't you, uh, *remove* the chair from your room?"

Catching on to her meaning and suddenly animated by anticipation, Grey sat forward, careful of the ashtray and the cigar in it. "Would you come to me if I did?"

"No. I am done with coming to you. You must now come to me."

Grey sat back, loving this sensual innuendo between them. "What's this, my girl? You wish to be courted?"

"Perhaps."

Then he realized something else that had his pulse leaping. "I see. You're staying. You couldn't be courted, I couldn't come to you, if you weren't here. You're not leaving, are you? I've convinced you to stay, haven't I?"

"No. I have decided myself to stay. And I have come up with a better plan than leaving here."

"A better—now wait. I, too, have a plan."

"I like mine better."

"You don't even know what mine is."

"No, I do not. But mine will work better."

"Now how can you say that? Tell me what your plan is."

"First tell me yours."

"Why? So you can say it was yours when you like mine better? I hardly think so."

Taylor shrugged. "Have it your way. Tonight tell Mrs. Scott, while she prepares to sleep in the chair in your room—"

"All right, I'll tell you my plan." He lowered his eyebrows over his nose. "I cannot believe you would use, uh, bedroom blackmail on me."

Taylor grinned and shrugged and took a sip of her brandy. "It wouldn't be the first time." Then her gaze warmed, became hot and sizzling. "I'll leave my bedroom door unlocked . . . that is, if you and your head feel up to it."

The next day started very early and very disastrously. Taylor and Grey were rudely interrupted by a frantic knock on her bedroom door. Taylor's groan was no longer that of pleasure.

Grey lifted his head and shouted, "Go away!" The masterful effect was ruined by his being scooted down under the top sheet and . . . kissing Taylor. So all he'd done was tent the sheet with his head, send a muffled command to his servant, and amuse Taylor with his antics.

"I say, are you still in there, sir?" This was Bentley . . . on the other side of the door and again knocking.

From under the sheet, Grey asked, "What did he say?"

Rolling her eyes, giving up, Taylor lifted the covers and stared down at her lover, who had this morning fussily discarded the bandaging that encircled his head, saying he didn't need it or any more nursing from a gaggle of females. Taylor hadn't been offended because she hadn't been among the gaggle of females who'd insisted daily on changing his dressing and clucking like hens over him. "Bentley wants to know if you're still in here."

Grey's face was deadpan. He looked down at her nakedness, kissed her there, and then smiled up at her. "Tell him yes, my oh-so-sweet Taylor. And tell him I would like to stay in here for as long as I live. It's part of my plan, too."

"No, it is not. And I cannot tell him that. He is out in the hall, Grey, and he knows you are here."

Grey heaved a sigh. "He doesn't ever listen to me. You tell him to go away."

"Go away!" Taylor called out.

"I fear I cannot, Miss James."

Taylor looked down again at Grey. "He fears he cannot."

"The man does not yet know the meaning of fear, I assure you. But once I get at him . . ." Cursing, fighting the tangling sheet, Grey pulled himself up Taylor, stopping to kiss her skin as he went. Then, lying atop her, his weight supported on his elbows, he yelled to his butler, "Why the devil can't you go away? Are you tied to the damned doorknob, Bentley?"

"No, sir, I am not. But I have a message for you both."

Grey looked down at Taylor under him. "He has a message for us." She nodded that she'd heard. Grey turned his head toward the door and called out, "A message? Do you mean from on high, man? Angels and trumpets? That kind of message?"

There was silence . . . then, "No, sir."

Defeated, Grey lowered his head until his forehead was touching Taylor's. She arched up and kissed him with little nipping bites on his lips. "I'll give you thirty minutes to stop that," he whispered, grinning. But he duly raised his head and again shouted, "Well, spit it out, Bentley! And let me assure you that someone had better be dying!"

"Oh, sir, I'm afraid someone is. It's Mrs. James. Mrs. Camilla James. She's taken a turn for the worse."

Taylor tensed, her gaze riveted to Grey's. Her limbs felt heavy and weak, and it had nothing to do with Grey's weight atop her. "He has killed Aunt Camilla," she said through gritted teeth.

"No," Grey said, earnest now. "She's not dead. A turn for the worse, Taylor, is not the same thing as dead."

"But it is close."

"Yes, it is." He flung the sheet off them, pulled himself off her, and sat up, swinging his legs over the side of the mattress. Taylor was right behind him and already scrambling out of bed. As soon as her feet hit the carpeted floor, she headed for the bathroom.

Behind her, Grey called out to his butler, "Hold on, Bentley! I'll need you to do some things. For one, order up the brougham."

Taylor jerked around to face Grey and saw he was pulling

on his pants. "I will not need the carriage," she told him. "I will take Red Sky."

"No, you won't, so we will need the brougham. I intend to get your aunt out of that house. And I can't do it on horseback."

"Then take it. But I am going now on Red Sky. We may have to split up for some reason. If so, I want to be able to do that."

Grey's expression hardened, but he didn't argue with her. Instead, as Taylor watched, he stalked toward the door, opened it a crack, and peered out at Bentley. "Get Calvin up and have him saddle Red Sky."

"I won't need him saddled. It will take too much time."

Grey looked over his shoulder at her. He'd firmed his lips until white lines appeared at either side of his mouth. Taylor narrowed her eyes at him. Grey turned again to Bentley. "Get the brougham and Red Sky. And get us some coffee. And Mrs. Scott. Miss James will need help dressing."

"Dammit, Grey, I do not need her." Defiant and naked, already braiding her long hair, Taylor faced Grey's angry expression. "You are trying to delay me. I can dress myself in my britches and shirt."

"You're not going over there ahead of me and alone, Taylor."

She raised an eyebrow at him. "Then you need to hurry, because I will if I have to. I am also taking my gun and my knife. This is my fight and my family. I will not sit back and wait for carriages and coffee and ladies' maids. Amanda needs me now."

"Yes, she does. But we're *both* going, Taylor. Amanda will soon enough be my family, too." Grey looked as if he meant to say something else, but out in the hall Bentley spoke first.

"Excuse me, sir. But Miss Amanda's runner is down in the foyer and awaiting a reply. He says Miss Amanda said to tell Miss Taylor that her mother is calling for her."

Taylor frowned, staring Grey's way. "Aunt Amanda is calling for me?"

"It's not all that strange, Taylor . . . especially if she is as bad off as Amanda says."

"But shouldn't she instead want her own daughter, who is already there?"

Grey's expression was unreadable, as if he had carefully blanked it. "I don't know. We have to hurry, Taylor. You can get that answer for yourself when we're there." With that, he looked to Taylor for her answer to Bentley.

She grabbed a length of ribbon off her dresser and tied it around the end of her braid. "Tell Bentley to have the boy go for the doctor, if Amanda has not already had him do so. And have him tell her not to leave her mother's side, that we will be there as soon as possible. But first go ask the boy who else is with Amanda."

Grey turned to the unseen Bentley and nodded, as if only to confirm that Bentley had heard her. "Yes, miss." Bentley's muffled footsteps retreated.

Taylor grabbed up her discarded bloomers and camisole, tied herself into them, and began searching for her cotton stockings. In her search, her gaze locked suddenly with Grey's. He was shrugging into his shirt. His expression was grim. Silently they dressed and waited for Bentley's return. In what seemed like hours but was really less than a few minutes, Bentley spoke from the other side of the door. "Sir? Miss? The boy says Mr. James, her father, is present. That's good, at least."

"Oh no," Taylor said softly to Grey, hugging herself in an effort to stave off the fearful shivering that had her feeling sick.

His grim expression saying it all, Grey never looked away from her as he called out to his butler, "Thank you, Bentley! Forget the coffee and Mrs. Scott, but have the brougham and Red Sky readied, if you would."

"Yes, sir." Again Bentley's footsteps could be heard retreating down the hall toward the steps.

Grey closed the door and, in silence, he and Taylor finished dressing. Suddenly, hurrying shuffling footsteps approached the bedroom door. Taylor froze. Grey followed suit and gave her a look that said, *What now?*

The knock on the door made Taylor jump, even though she'd known it was coming. The sound barely preceded Bentley's excited, fearful voice. "Excuse me, sir, but may I please have a word with Miss James? It is extremely important."

"Of course. Hold on."

Taylor, now tucking her shirt into her britches, brushed by Grey and opened the door. "Yes, Bentley, what is it?"

The little man's face reflected great distress. "I don't know quite how to say it, miss. Or what it can mean. But I've just had the most extraordinary thought or vision—I really do not know what to call it."

Taylor's mouth dried. She gripped the door harder. "Just tell me what you saw."

The little old man inhaled deeply and then spoke rapidly. "Well, miss, it came as I passed the mirror in the hall just now. I swear to you that I am forever going to avoid looking into mirrors after this. At any rate, it was that dark shadow, like I saw before. Then it was a cloud. Then it became a big angry bird, black and gray in color. That was frightening enough, but then it was swooping down on you. And you were at Mr. Stanley James's residence. The bird, though . . . its beak was opened horribly and it had its talons bared."

Taylor's breath came in a gasping rasp of sound. She felt Grey at her back, although he hadn't touched her or said anything. She leaned back against the warm and solid support of his broad chest. He put a hand on her arm and held her protectively. "In your vision, what was I doing, Bentley?" Taylor asked, already fearing his answer.

Bentley's face drained of color. He didn't want to tell her; that much was evident. "Mind you, I only saw this for a second or two, and I am now trying to recall every detail. But you were . . . well, you were lying on the ground. Bleeding. And under you, as if you'd thrown yourself protectively over her, was Miss Amanda."

Taylor felt as if she'd been gut-punched. It was Rube's curse coming true. The old Cherokee guard had said she or those she loved would die. He'd said they would not live long lives and would not know happiness. It was coming true—and she had brought all this on them herself. By being here and by being alive. *No more.* She would do everything she could to make certain they lived—and she didn't, should it come to that.

"Son of a bitch," Grey said at her back, startling Taylor back to the moment. "Are you sure that's all you saw, Bentley? Where was I?"

"I didn't see you, sir. I'm sorry."

Grey gently squeezed Taylor's shoulders, kissing the top of her head. "It's not true. Don't you see? It can't be because I'm not there. And I won't leave you, Taylor."

She gave a shake of her head. Her chest felt very tight. Drawing in air was difficult. She had to keep her private vendetta a secret from Grey. He would tie her up and leave her here if he had any idea what she planned to do. She had no idea why Bentley hadn't seen Grey there . . . but something would happen to separate them. It would. Spirit guides were never wrong.

"I'm so sorry. But I felt I should tell you," Bentley was saying, looking from her to Grey. "I'm certain it's a warning of some sort." Then he clutched at Taylor's arm and looked into her eyes. "You will be careful, won't you, miss? We're all quite fond of you here."

Moved by his declaration, Taylor nodded and tried to speak around the lump of fear and emotion clogging her throat. "I will be careful, my man-bird. As always, you will be my talisman, and you will keep the danger from me."

She'd said it with a smile . . . but she knew she'd lied and that it was impossible. The danger would find her. And it would kill her.

Before Grey could even alight from the brougham, the front door of the Stanley James residence was jerked open. Amanda stood in the doorway. Sobbing and dressed in rumpled clothes that appeared to have been worn since yesterday, she clung to the doorjamb and to the door itself, swaying between them as if she'd been lashed to them. "Thank God you're here. I fear Mother is dying."

Grey spoke from the carriage's door he'd just opened. "Where is Dr. Meade's carriage? I told your boy to go for him."

"I haven't seen him," Amanda sobbed.

"Then where's your father?" Grey barked as his feet hit the ground. From the corner of his eye, Grey was aware of Taylor's movements. She had dismounted from Red Sky and was handing her reins over to Calvin, who'd ridden here topside and seated next to the driver.

Amanda's face contorted with another spasm of emotional pain. "Father left. I don't know where he went."

Grey frowned, exchanging a pointed look with Taylor, who now stood beside him and was pale, tight-lipped . . . and dangerously silent. "That's odd behavior for him, Amanda," Grey said, hearing the angry bark in his own voice. It wasn't directed at her but at the ugliness he felt certain the day's events would expose to them all.

With Taylor at his side, they quickly strode up the walkway that led to the opened door where the girl was. "Amanda, how is it that you're left to open the door? You must have a staff approaching fifty here. Where's your butler?"

It wasn't propriety he worried about, but chaos. Was no one in charge? Was nothing being done for Camilla? And to help Amanda?

"Grey, please, what does it matter? I was afraid!" Amanda cried, now wringing her hands together. "I heard your carriage and ran to see if it was the doctor or my father. When I saw you and Taylor from the window, I came running down myself. I sent Henry up to be with his wife, Betsy, our housekeeper. She's something of a nurse and is with Mother right now. Please, Grey, Taylor, help me."

"That's exactly what I'm trying to do, Amanda. Help you. I need to know where everyone is, though, in order to do that. I have to say I don't understand your father at all. The man's wife is dying—I'm sorry. I didn't mean—"

"It's true. She is," Amanda said, her voice breaking, a hand to her temple. She stared at the ground as she spoke, sounding as if she weren't aware she was speaking aloud. "So pale and vomiting. She's wringing wet with her own perspiration and can barely talk." Suddenly Amanda sought Grey's gaze, her own wide-eyed and nearing the precipice of panic. "I don't *know* where Father is. Do you hear me? He left in a rage, saying he would kill *her.*"

With those dire words, Amanda flung herself outside and into Grey's arms. Taylor immediately tore her cousin away from Grey and spun her to face her. "Amanda, listen to me. Kill who? Who did he mean?"

Amanda sobbed and nodded. Taylor exchanged a fearful look with Grey and then lovingly brushed Amanda's hair away from her emotion-dampened face. She gently gripped the other girl's chin. "Amanda, *who* do you think he meant?"

But Grey knew. "My mother." Even to his own ears, his voice held the ring of steel. "Goddammit," he said through gritted teeth. Both women faced him, frozen in place, their eyes wide. "Take Amanda inside, Taylor," he ordered. "Go inside now, both of you. Go on."

"Grey, your mother? Are you sure?" This was Taylor. She hadn't moved, and she still held onto Amanda, who was clinging to her.

His heart was breaking, but Grey tried his hardest not to dissolve right there. "Yes, my mother. Who else? You said so yourself not three days ago on our picnic. It's what Amanda also believes. Am I right or not?"

The women exchanged a glance and then faced him again. They didn't need to say a word, yet Taylor spoke, her heart in her eyes. "I'm sorry, Grey."

He nodded. "Me, too. For all of us."

"You have to go to her."

Grey stared stupidly at Taylor and felt certain his bones were melting. He could barely think. Stanley James had gone to kill his mother? Why? Supposedly the two were in love. Then he remembered Bentley's vision. His mind cleared. "No, Taylor. I'm not leaving you. Franklin is home with her. He'll protect her. And Bentley said we—"

"No. Bentley said only me. I can take care of myself. I always have. And Franklin may not be with your mother."

"He's not," Amanda cut in. "He's at Uncle Charles's. There's a meeting of his campaign committee. I sent a boy to get them, but to tell them to come here. So your mother is alone, Grey. And she can be the only one Father meant."

Taylor spoke next. "Go to her, Grey. She's your mother. If she's done something, no matter what it is, she's your mother and you must respect her."

Grey stared at Taylor for a long heartfelt moment. "Remember those words, Taylor. You're going to need them today. Now, go inside and take Amanda with you. Be with Camilla while you can."

With that, he pivoted to face the brougham, his gaze searching. "Calvin!" he called out impatiently. The boy sprinted around from the carriage's opposite side and gave Grey a questioning look. "Jump on Red Sky and ride for Dr. Meade's. God alone knows what's become of that James runner. After that, ride for the police. Send them to my mother's home. It's where I'll be. Go now!"

Without looking back to see if Taylor and Amanda had done as he'd said, Grey hopped back into the brougham, yelling out to his driver as he did, "To my mother's home, Edward! Hurry!"

As Edward climbed hastily onto his perch, Grey closed the door and peered out the small window, looking to where he'd left Taylor and Amanda. They were still standing there . . . holding each other and staring at him. Grey's gaze locked with Taylor's. In her blue eyes he saw everything he needed to see. Love. Regret. Sympathy. She was hurting for him and for what he may face at his mother's. Yet Grey knew that what Taylor faced here was most likely a hundred times worse. A hand held out to her, he nodded, acknowledging her silent message.

"Do you have your gun, Grey?" Taylor suddenly called out, already reaching for hers, as if she meant to throw it to him.

It wasn't what she wanted to say, Grey knew, but it was all she could say at this moment. He understood. Both of them needed not to think, not to feel. But to act. God willing, there would be time later for crushing emotion. But not now. So, hoping his expression conveyed to her the depth of his love for her, Grey shook his head. "Keep your weapon, Taylor. I have mine. And you . . . you will need yours. Be careful."

Chapter Nineteen

"Hurry, Taylor. We have to hurry."

"I'm right behind you, Amanda. Lead the way."

Under the twinkling glitter of a massive crystal chandelier hanging suspended overhead, Taylor quickly and solemnly followed Amanda's frantic form up the wide polished-wood staircase that began in the marble-tiled gallery entryway and split at a small landing about ten steps up. From there, with a grand sweep off either end of the landing, the stairs swooped upward in two directions to the second floor. Given her current frame of mind . . . uncertain, fearful, angry, seeing an omen in every word, every action . . . Taylor likened the banistered structure to the spread wings of a great bird of prey, just waiting to devour her. She swallowed and fingered her gun in its holster.

"This way." At the landing, Amanda turned left and, still holding her skirt up to keep from tripping on its rumpled length, hurried onward. "Not much farther. Oh, Taylor, I cannot believe this. I never should have told Father that you were coming."

"You mean today?"

"Yes. No. At all, I mean. Then maybe Mother wouldn't be—" Amanda gasped and jerked around to face Taylor. "I didn't mean that like it sounds. It's not because of you—"

"I know, Amanda. Just get me to her. I want to see her."

Amanda's expression crumpled. She let go of her skirt and put her hands to her face. Sympathetic yet helpless, Taylor reached a hand out to her cousin, but Amanda sank down in a crying heap on a riser. Taylor instantly sat next to her and put an arm around her, cradling her, allowing her to sob out her misery. "I'm so sorry to break down, Taylor. You always were the strong one. But we're losing her. I can't help but cry."

"Do so if you must, Amanda." What Taylor didn't say was that she was not strong, as her cousin said she was. She was hardened, but not strong. "You have been facing many sorrows these days."

Amanda lowered her hands from her face and stared heartbroken into Taylor's face. "She keeps calling for you."

Taylor nodded, frowning. "Your messenger said this also. Why me? I would think she would want you, Amanda."

Her face blotchy with emotion, Amanda stared into Taylor's eyes. "She does. She knows I'm there every second with her. But she says she has something to tell you that you should hear only from her."

Taylor's gut tightened with apprehension. She abruptly stood up. "Then we should go to her."

Still sitting, Amanda grabbed Taylor's hand and held on. "No. I'm afraid to let you talk to her. Because I fear she is waiting only to see you before she . . . lets go."

Taylor looked down into her beloved cousin's face. "We will pray that is not so. But if it is, there is nothing we can do to stop it. I should grant her wish and hear her words."

Amanda's chin quivered as she stared up into Taylor's face. Then slowly Amanda leaned forward, touching her forehead to Taylor's hand. "I love you so much, Taylor. I have thought of you so often through the years." She again looked up at Taylor. "Will you help me be strong? Will you hold my hand?"

Taylor smiled down at Amanda and stroked her face, one shaped so much like her own. "I will. But first you must show me the way." She turned to look up the stairs to the second floor.

Amanda sighed. "All right. Let's go." With Taylor still holding her hand and assisting her to stand, Amanda came to her feet.

Taylor walked quietly by her cousin's side, her hand held tightly by Amanda. In only another moment, they achieved the second floor and walked down its length, their footsteps muffled by a long woven runner. To both sides of them were closed doors that, Taylor presumed, hid the family's bedrooms. As she walked, she couldn't help but notice the gallery of family portraits adorning the walls. . . . These people were also hers. Beneath a few of the paintings were vases of fresh-cut flowers atop dark-wood tables. At the hall's very end was a tall, narrow window that allowed sunlight to cheerfully filter in. All in all, the scene was a pleasant one of exceeding wealth and domestic tranquillity . . . but a mocking one. Because behind one of these doors a woman lay on her deathbed as a result of having been repeatedly poisoned.

At least, that was what Taylor believed. Just then, a door opened about three down from where Amanda and Taylor were and on their right. Out stepped an older woman attired in a domestic's gray uniform. Her back was to Taylor as she took great care to close the door behind her. Taylor noted that the slender woman's graying hair was coming undone from its bun. Just then the woman shook her head sadly and turned around, her face a study in worry. In her hands was a basin stacked with wet and soiled cloths. She looked up and started when she saw the girls almost upon her. "Oh, you startled me, Miss James."

She was speaking to Amanda, who answered her. "I'm sorry, Betsy. This is Taylor, my cousin. She's finally here."

"Praise the Lord." The woman tugged back a wisp of the hair that had come undone and was hanging in her haggard face. She stared now at Taylor. "I'm so glad you're here. She's been asking for you."

With that, she stepped back and opened the door, giving it enough of a push to swing it open. "Go on in, honey. You, too, Amanda. She wants you both in there. I won't let anyone in until you come out. Just try not to excite her or wear her out, you hear?"

With Amanda, Taylor nodded that she heard and understood. As one, she and Amanda approached the door, turned into the room—heard the door close behind them—and walked to the bed, stopping beside it. What Taylor saw there shocked her. She stifled a gasp, reflexively squeezing

Amanda's hand. Taylor would never have known this woman
was her Aunt Camilla. The woman in the bed, clad in a white
nightgown and covered to her chest with a sheet, was pale and
sweating. She looked old. Her dark hair was lackluster; her
brown eyes glinted dully from sunken hollows of sockets. Under her eyes was limned in blue, as were her lips. She tossed
her head from one side to the other, as if in pain. But she
seemed suddenly to sense the presence of the girls. She stilled
and stared their way. She tried to smile, but it wouldn't hold.
With effort, she raised a thin clawlike hand and said, "Taylor,
you've come. I knew you would."

Her voice was whispery, feeble. Taylor's heart lurched. She
instantly stepped forward, up to the bed, and took her aunt's
hand in both of hers. It was amazingly cold and blue-veined.
Taylor jerked her gaze to Amanda, who'd appeared on the
bed's other side and now held her mother's other hand. Her
cousin nodded as if to say she knew. Taylor returned her attention to her aunt. "Of course I have come. You are my aunt,
and I love you."

Camilla James shook her head slowly from side to side,
squeezing her eyes shut as silent sobs racked her. Alarmed,
Taylor exchanged a glance with Amanda, who looked equally
distraught, and then put her free hand on her aunt's shoulder.
"Do not cry. You must not upset yourself. You must save your
strength so you can fight this and get better."

Camilla opened her eyes, showing Taylor she had knowledge of her impending death. "I have no strength. I will not
get better. It's why I sent for you." She stopped, taking in
several shallow breaths. Over the ominous rattle in the sick
woman's throat, Taylor could hear her cousin's quiet crying.
"What I have to tell you, Taylor and Amanda, you must hear
from me. Both of you." She looked to Amanda. "Don't cry,
my sweet. I have to do this."

Amanda raised her mother's hand to her lips and kissed it.
"I know, Mother. I know."

"Where is . . . Where's your father? I don't want him . . . to
hear."

Amanda met Taylor's gaze and then tenderly stroked her

mother's head. "He went—he's not here." Taylor heard the
hardness and bitterness in Amanda's voice when she spoke of
her father. But then she went on in loving, soothing tones.
"You can talk to us, Mother. No one but us will hear you."

"Good." Camilla James nodded and slowly rolled her head,
as if it took effort, until she again faced Taylor. Then, with
each girl standing on opposite sides of her bed and holding
her hands, the sick and dying woman said, "I don't have much
time." Amanda's tears flowed again. Taylor tensed her jaw,
working it, forcing a muscle in her jaw to jump . . . but she
remained dry-eyed. "I didn't want to tell you in this way. But
now I have no choice. You must know the truth."

"The truth about what, Aunt Camilla?" Taylor's stomach
was in knots and her heart thumped erratically in her chest.

Camilla's eyes filled with tears. "I am not your aunt, Taylor."

Amanda gasped at the same time as Taylor, who wondered
if maybe her aunt was a bit delirious. "Of course you are my
aunt. Uncle Stanley is my father's brother, and you are married
to him. You are my aunt. Maybe not my blood. But the aunt
of my heart."

Camilla shook her head and swallowed. Her hand in Taylor's felt limp and clammy. "No. I *am* your blood. You have
my blood, Taylor."

Taylor's heart thumped painfully. How could this be, what
her aunt was saying? She stared down into the dying woman's
imploring eyes. In a voice made high by rising emotion, Taylor asked, "What do you mean?"

Camilla James squeezed Taylor's hand. "Taylor, *I* am your
mother."

Utter and profound silence fell like a heavy curtain over
the room.

"No." The whispered word came from Amanda.

For Taylor, the room began to whirl. She felt sick, weak,
as if her bones had melted and she could no longer stand. She
clutched at the covers on the bed and pressed her thighs
against the bed's solid frame. She stared at the woman on the
bed . . . but couldn't speak. Her mind whirled with denials. *It's*

not true. She's talking out of her head. She is sick and dying. She does not know what she is saying. It's not true. It can't be true. How can it be true?

"Please believe me, Taylor. I know it is difficult," Camilla added, cutting into Taylor's shocked thoughts. "I never wanted to leave you. Never. But I had to. It was weak of me—and wrong—I know. I was a coward. But I was young and scared. I did what I had to do to keep you safe."

Amanda remained stone silent, but Taylor found her voice. "But my father . . . ? Is he—?" She could not bear to think it might be Stanley James.

"Charles is your father. We sinned, Taylor, in the eyes of the Lord. But I have always loved him, and him me. I could not help myself. Nor could he. We both knew it was wrong, our love." She turned to her daughter . . . her other daughter. "Forgive me, Amanda. I know this isn't easy for you, either."

As if horrified, Amanda drew in a deep breath and slowly breathed out her words in a whisper. "But we're the same age, Taylor and me. Mother, this cannot be. You don't know what you're saying."

"I do, my darling. I know what I'm saying. Taylor is younger than you . . . by two years. You're twenty-two, Amanda, not twenty like Taylor. I am so sorry I have allowed you to live a lie. Both of you."

Amanda's voice rose to an anguished pitch. "Oh God, Mother, what have you done?"

"I have done many wrong things. And I have paid in my heart for every one of them, I promise you. But now, I want somehow, by telling you the truth, to make them right."

"Nothing's right here, Mother," Amanda accused. "Nothing." She then caught Taylor's gaze and held it. "We're sisters, Taylor. Half-sisters. Our fathers are . . . brothers." She pulled her hand out of her mother's and stepped back from the bed. She clasped both hands over her mouth and stared in horror at her mother, repeating, "What have you done?" And then she sobbed, a wrenching sound from the heart—and ran for the door.

"Amanda!" Taylor called out, wanting to follow her. But

Camilla, showing surprising strength, gripped her hand tightly. Taylor could not get loose. She looked down at her aunt—her mother. "I must go to her."

Camilla shook her head no. "Let her be. She will come round. She loves you very much. That is not what is upsetting her. It's me and what I have done, as she said. Maybe I was wrong to say anything. But I wanted to . . . I can't . . . can *you* forgive me, Taylor?"

Taylor shook her head, not in denial of forgiveness but because she wasn't sure she could speak. She looked down on the woman in the bed but didn't really see her. Instead, she fought a battle in her head. She wanted to understand, to believe, to find forgiveness in her heart. But ugly truths, like little pitchfork-wielding demons, leaped from the corners of her mind and jabbed painfully at Taylor's consciousness. If Camilla James was telling the truth—and why would she lie, on her deathbed?—then Taylor was not who or what she'd believed herself to be all her life. Her entire life, how she thought of herself . . . it wasn't true. Then, a face popped into Taylor's mind . . . her knees stiffened, and she stared blankly at the opposite wall.

"My mother!" The two words were a cry. She was thinking of Tennie Nell Christie out in the Cherokee Nation.

"Yes," Camilla James said. Taylor blinked, seeing again the woman whose cold hand she held. "I am your mother, Taylor. And I love you. I always loved you. Tell Amanda that I'm sorry. . . ." Her last words were said on a deep exhalation of breath, followed by a lingering rattle . . . that slowly faded to nothingness.

Taylor watched helplessly. She alone knew the very moment that Camilla James no longer lived.

My mother is dead.

Taylor's strength, her will, her very soul seemed to leave her. "Mama?"

Her voice was that of a child, but there was no one to answer her. Slowly, as if dying herself, Taylor sank down beside the bed, clutching at the covers, inadvertently pulling them after her. She sat folded up on the hardwood floor,

breathing hard yet unable to catch her breath. Sightlessly she
stared at a dresser across the way. A hot sweat glazed her
skin. Her bones and muscles ached.

Then, and finally, a wail from the depths of her being rose
up inside her and tore loose. A piercing cry of too much anguish to bear filled the room and emptied Taylor's heart. She
screamed and tore at her clothes and beat her fists against the
mattress. And cried for all that she'd never known . . . and had
lost.

From the street, all appeared to be in order. No screaming
servants were fleeing down the street. The front door was innocently closed. No blood ran down the concrete steps of the
sun-dappled landing. In fact, all was quiet and normal-
appearing. Except for the sleek and muscled roan—Stanley
James's prized mount—tethered outside to a brass ring attached to an iron hitching post.

Grey shook his head, disgusted and distraught. "Why,
Mother?" he quietly asked as if she could hear him. "What
did you do?"

His brougham came to a stop. Not waiting for assistance,
and with an order to his driver, Edward, to stay put, Grey
opened the door and jumped out onto the hard-packed dirt of
the street. In only seconds he was charging up the stone steps
to the red front door of his mother's home. But with his hand
on the latch, he stopped, remaining on the wrought-iron-railed
landing. He wanted a moment to steel himself for what he
might find on the other side of this door. But he also had to
decide if he should go in shouting his presence and calling out
for his mother or sneak in quietly. He had no idea. And the
truth was, either choice could be a fatal one—for her or for
him. Or for both of them.

His heart was in his throat. Breathing was painful. What
should he do? Grey weighed his options. For one thing, he
feared walking into a chaotic scene of bloodshed. If that's
what greeted him, then . . . as evidenced by Stanley James's
horse behind him . . . a killer was still on the premises and
could be hiding in wait for Grey to walk into his trap. Or

Stanley could now, at this moment, be involved in his hideous deeds and Grey needed to rush in. He decided the first scenario was the more likely one, since he heard no gunfire or shouts coming from inside.

Still, Grey told himself to be prepared for anything. Even gunplay. He felt for his pistol in its holster at his hip. As he did, a great anger seized him. His mother might be a cold woman capable of serious wrongdoing—witness his father's poisoning—but Grey wasn't about to tolerate anyone killing her, either. Especially not her adulterous lover, whose wife was at that very moment perhaps dying.

Grey never knocked when visiting here and didn't now. Telling himself he was ready, he opened the door and stepped inside, looking and listening. Nothing. Absolute stillness and quiet greeted him. The place appeared to be in order—and abandoned. Grey quietly closed the door behind him. A fleeting and horrific scene popped into his head. Had Stanley James gone berserk and killed everyone present? Grey feared he would find the rooms littered with dead servants.

Oh, surely not, man. Surely your heightened emotions are playing havoc with your reason. That's what he wanted to believe, but the truth was no one had met him yet. Where was Caldwell? The jovial butler never allowed Grey to walk ten steps into the house before he was Johnny-on-the-spot. It was a game between them. Grey never announced himself—and the butler always knew he had arrived. But not this time.

On edge, his pulse racing, Grey walked farther into the fifteen-room city estate shared by his mother and Franklin. Feeling like an intruder, he peeked into the closest rooms . . . a drawing room, library, dining room . . . and looked around, searching for people, alive or dead, and evidence of a crime. Anything but this entombing order and silence. He then stalked purposefully through each room on the first two floors of the richly appointed Federal-style mansion his mother had bought after her husband—his and Franklin's father—had died.

His search only confirmed for him what he had already guessed. No one was in evidence. Not even in the bedrooms, for which he was infinitely thankful. The sight of his mother and Stanley rolling around in each other's arms would, at this particular moment, have put him over an edge and had him shooting them himself. In his search, Grey neglected the kitchen and the staff's quarters on the third floor. There was no reason to go search them—the two he sought would not venture into either of those places.

Giving up the search, trying to think what to do next, Grey stood at a window in the music room, which was at the back of the mansion. His mind whirling with possibilities and mysteries, he stared outside onto the manicured lawn and gardens that belonged to the house. With his attention turned inward, he rubbed absently at his stubbled jaw. Where could they be? All he wanted was to make certain that Stanley James hadn't killed his mother, or her him, and then he wanted to get the hell back to Taylor before Bentley's frightening vision came true. No one had to tell Grey who the great swooping bird with sharp talons was. It was Stanley James. And he was out for revenge today—against more than one woman.

Stanley's rage against Taylor Grey could understand—in a twisted sort of way and in light of what Charles had told him about his and Camilla's betrayal of Stanley. Taylor was the result of that betrayal so many years ago. But what Grey couldn't figure out was Stanley's apparent intent to harm his lover . . . who was, Grey now knew, his own mother, Augusta. Why would Stanley want to hurt her? Apparently, the two of them, from what Amanda had told Taylor, had been in love since their youth. Grey knew what had kept them apart back then—lack of money and social status. But their separate marriages had remedied that. So now, with Camilla dying and with Grey's father dead, the two of them would be free to be together . . . barring their being charged with the murders of their spouses. Still, all Stanley had to do was, grisly as it sounded, wait out Camilla's death, play the grief-stricken widower, and allow Augusta Talbott to comfort him.

So with such a perfect plan—perfect if one was insane—coming to fruition, why was Stanley James here? Why had he left his dying wife's bedside to come here with the expressed intent to kill his lover? Why? They were equally guilty, both in on the poisonings, so it just didn't make any sense. Grey mulled this thought for a moment, continuing to reflect on Stanley's behavior. It made no sense . . . unless—Grey's heart sank. He felt ill—unless both of them were *not* in on the treachery that surrounded Camilla and Grey's father. Unless only one of them was. His mother.

"Dear sweet God." The realization was staggering. His mother apparently was capable not only of ruining someone's life with her sharp tongue and her gossip . . . but she could also end a life, possibly two lives, by poisoning. Murder. That's what it was—if what he was thinking was true. He could be wrong. He prayed he was . . . but he didn't think he was. Grey said a brief and silent prayer for Camilla James's well-being—and for Taylor's. And yes, for his mother, too. But of them all, his heart and mind would not even allow him to think something could happen to Taylor.

Just then, Grey tensed, blinking, only now seeing the scene being played out before him in the garden. His heart picked up its pace, racing his pulse. Horror-struck, he clung to the window, his palms flat against the sun-warmed glass, and stared stupidly. Surely they hadn't been there all along. Maybe they'd been hidden by the ornamental trees or had been on the other side of the high hedges or around a corner of the house. Not that it mattered now . . . because Stanley James had just caught up to Grey's mother, who'd appeared to be fleeing from the man. And he was now choking Augusta Talbott out among her prized flowers.

"No!" Grey bellowed, beating on the glass with his open palm.

A rational part of his brain reminded him that they couldn't hear him and, even if they could, he posed no threat to Stanley James this far away and inside . . . and that if he wished to save his mother, whether she deserved it or not, he needed to go outside. Right now.

Thus galvanized into action, Grey jerked around, hurrying, skirting the piano and the settee. He jerked open the double French doors that led to a half-moon stone-paved terrace and tore across it, bellowing out as he ran. Handily he jumped over the low balusters and went sailing out onto the grass. The drop wasn't a big one, but still he staggered and had to fight to keep his feet. Every second was another one his mother was being choked.

Even as he ran, Grey could see that Stanley James still had his hands around her neck . . . but he was now, as if in a frozen tableau, staring Grey's way. It was then that Grey remembered he had a gun and he knew how to use it. He ripped his weapon out of its holster and slowed down, aiming it at Stanley James as he now walked stiff-legged toward the man. Practically out of breath, he was almost upon them. Without warning, Stanley turned Grey's mother in his arms and wrapped an arm around her neck. He pulled a gun from somewhere and stuck it against Augusta Talbott's temple. "One more step, Grey, and I'll pull the trigger."

Grey stopped, his gun still aimed their way as he held out a placating hand to Stanley. "Don't do it, Stanley."

"Then throw your gun down." Grey did. "Now kick it away from you." Again, Grey did. "That's good. Now turn around and leave. This has nothing to do with you. Get out of here."

Grey shook his head. "I can't do that, Stanley. You know I can't. She's my mother and so this has everything to do with me. Let her go, and we'll talk."

"It's too late for talking." Stanley's voice cracked. "Too late. Do you know what she did?" He tensed his arm around Augusta's neck. She cried out.

"I think I do," Grey said quickly. "And it's awful, I know. But just try to stay calm, Stanley. We can work this out."

"No, Grey, we can't. Why do you defend her? She killed your father, you know. And now she's killed Camilla. So I'm going to kill her. It's the only way."

There it was—confirmation of his worst fears. An angry side of Grey said, *Let him do it.* But Grey couldn't, not the part of him that was decent. "Don't, Stanley, I beg of you. She may deserve it, I agree with you. But . . . don't. Camilla is not dead. I was just there. She lives."

"Not for long—and because of her." Tears streamed down Stanley's face.

Grey was close enough to see that his mother's dress was ripped, her hair was undone, and she had bruising on her tear-dampened cheeks. Her widened eyes silently pleaded with Grey to save her. Grey swallowed, realized his throat was dry. Terror covered his body with the sheen of perspiration. He focused again on the insane and anguished face of his mother's lover-turned-assailant. "Just let her go. I promise you we'll get to the bottom of this and deal with it appropriately."

"How?" Stanley sobbed. "How, Grey? Can you bring Camilla back?"

"She's not dead, Stanley, I told you. Amanda and Taylor are with her now." He knew instantly it was the wrong thing to say. His heart sank.

Stanley's face reddened. It seemed to swell and change, to bloat, become unrecognizable. His expression was a snarling mask of hatred. "Don't you say that name to me. She's next. I swear to God she is. This is all her fault. I told her to leave. Did you know that? Weeks ago. I told her to leave. I saw her outside my sneaking bastard of a brother's house—and I told her to leave. She's a sin, Grey. A walking sin. And I can't allow her to live. She's next."

Somehow Grey knew the moment was here. Stanley James was ready to pull the trigger. His mother must have sensed it as well. In a flash, with everything happening at once, Grey saw his mother's bent knee poke against her morning gown, saw Stanley tense to fire his gun into her temple, and saw his mother's leg straighten sharply. Stanley James cried out—his mother had stomped Stanley's foot with the heel of her slipper. Stanley grimaced evilly, totally focused on his victim.

Grey flexed his wrist and had his wrist-holstered two-shot pistol in his hand. Cold as steel now inside, he aimed steadily at Stanley James's head and fired. And missed.

But the bullet had come sufficiently close to startle Stanley James into losing his grip on Grey's mother. She fell to the ground in a crying, shrieking heap. Grey fired again. The bullet maddeningly went wide. Stanley, now crouching, fired back, also missing . . . but not by much. Grey tossed the empty gun down and hit the ground himself, rolling in the direction of his six-shooter that Stanley had forced him to drop and kick away. He expected a bullet to take his life at any moment, but no shots were fired. All Grey heard was an anguished, pain-filled cry from his mother.

In only a second or two, Grey came up with his other weapon and rolled onto his belly in the grass. With both arms straight out in front of him and his hands fisted around his pistol, Grey looked for his target . . . who was disappearing around a corner of the house. He was getting away. Grey surged to his feet and looked to his mother. She lay in a crumpled heap on the ground. Dark red stained her silvery hair in a widening pool. It took Grey a moment to realize what he was seeing. It was blood . . . seeping from a wound to her head.

"Oh, God," Grey murmured, his voice ragged as he stared at her body. His gun dropped from his nerveless fingers. "Oh, God, what has he done?"

But Grey knew. Stanley had hit Augusta Talbott with the butt of his pistol before he'd run away. Had he killed her? "No." The one word seemed to unlock Grey's muscles. He ran to her and dropped to his knees beside her. He turned her over and gently gathered her in his arms. She was warm . . . and breathing. Grey's heart began to beat again. "Mother?" He brushed away grass and dirt and, using her skirt's hem, wiped away the blood from her face. He glimpsed her wound . . . wounds. There were two. He gently probed them with his fingers. And felt sick. An agonized groan escaped him. One of the wounds had caused a depression in her skull. He pulled his linen handkerchief out of his pocket and pressed it against the worst wound.

Looking down into his mother's face, seeing how peaceful and good she appeared, Grey closed his eyes, willing strength into his body and an end to this day's terror. "Mother, why?" came a keening cry that he only dimly realized was his own. "Why? What could be worth all this?"

Suddenly, miraculously to him, she stirred in his arms and

groaned, crying out with the mewling sound of a small, sick animal. Grey tensed, noting her spastic waking movements. He lowered her to the grass and smoothed her hair off her brow. Her poor bruised face. She was like a battered child. Grey's heart ached terribly. He tried not to cry. "Shh. Don't move, Mother. You've been hurt."

She grimaced, but from the pain or because of his words? Grey had no way of knowing. She seemed to be fighting for a consciousness that kept eluding her. Grey feared she would lapse into a coma. Attending her as best he could . . . arranging her limbs when she moved them, talking in a low voice to her . . . Grey nevertheless looked at her through the eyes of shock. Never before had his mother looked so old to him, so haggard. Sagging muscles in her face and her lined skin were amplified by the day's bright sunlight.

Then suddenly her expression cleared . . . and she spoke with a weak, thin voice. "What . . . happened?"

Relief coursed through Grey. Her words were halting, but she was coherent, not babbling. "You . . . had a knock on the head, Mother. But you're going to be all right. Just don't move."

With a restraining hand to her shoulder, with fear and urgency tearing through him, Grey looked all around for help and saw none. "Damn." He looked down at the helpless figure of his mother. He couldn't leave her like this, and there was no one else about to help him. And while he loved his mother, no matter her sins, he was also painfully, terrifyingly aware that Taylor also needed him right now . . . at this moment. What to do? He feared hurting his mother worse by moving her.

"My head. It hurts."

Grey looked down at his formerly imperious and cold and calculating mother. She was an old woman now, a child who was whimpering. "It's OK," he assured her, his voice breaking. "You'll be fine. I promise."

"Someone hit me," she said, her eyelids fluttering. "Why would he do that?"

"It doesn't matter anymore, Mother. He's gone. And he

won't be back." Hatred tensed Grey's jaw. *Not if I have anything to say about it.* That decided it for Grey. He had to risk picking her up and getting her back to the house. With any luck the servants, wherever they were, would appear, and he could turn her over to them and a doctor. Only then could he race back to Taylor's side. God alone knew what she was going through even at this moment.

With his plan in order, Grey scooped his mother up—she cried out in pain. Standing with her slight burden in his arms, Grey gritted his teeth, steeling himself against the knowledge that his actions could be worsening her injuries. "It's OK, Mother. You're going to be fine," he kept telling her.

He wondered if it was true, though. Would she be fine? Tears filled Grey's eyes. He sniffed back the emotion and started walking toward the house.

"Who are you?"

His mother's words shocked Grey into stopping. A sudden weakness leached the stiffness from his bones. "What do you mean? I'm your son. Greyson."

"I don't have children," she said with assurance if not strength. Then her head lolled against his shoulder and her eyes closed.

Grey looked down at her. She'd passed out. *Oh, God,* Grey begged. *Not this. Her memory is gone.*

Just then, a movement caught Grey's eye. He tensed . . . then relaxed. Coming toward them at a run now, from the house, were Caldwell and several of the Talbott maids. Their mouths were opened in grimaces and their coattails and apron strings flew out behind them. Had they been locked up somewhere and just now managed to free themselves? Grey didn't care. They were here now. Grey said a silent prayer of thanks for their appearance and started toward them. He wanted to run but couldn't. It was absolutely maddening, having to move so slowly now when he needed to make all haste to be away.

Taylor. Her name, that one word, was all he could think. Fear for her would not allow him to think further of her and what could be happening to her even now.

Chapter Twenty

As word got out of Camilla James's death, Taylor supposed, distant family and close friends would begin to arrive. But Camilla James had passed away less than an hour ago. So the only ones here now were those who'd been here earlier. From the upstairs bedroom window . . . her mother's bedroom window . . . Taylor stood watching events below in the circular gravel driveway.

A little earlier, a boy of about fourteen and on horseback had cantered his mount up the driveway and ahead of a black buggy. Taylor had assumed this young man to be the same messenger who'd come to Grey's this morning, only to be dispatched by him to the doctor's. Sure enough, the man in the buggy had proven to be the doctor Grey had also sent Calvin after. Taylor recognized him as the same man who had tended Grey's head wound.

Dr. Meade had rushed inside and had been escorted up to Camilla James's room by Betsy. But there had been nothing he could do. He'd next wished to see Amanda and to administer a sedative to her, to calm her. But she wouldn't allow it. And so, he'd gone downstairs to await the others who would soon be arriving.

And here they were. A fancy enclosed carriage was pulling up in front of the house. For a tense, hopeful second Taylor wondered if this was Grey returning. Then she saw Calvin behind the vehicle. He rode Red Sky bareback as had she. Disappointment wilted her posture. If Calvin was with this carriage, then it had to be that of . . . Sure enough, the door to the conveyance opened and out stepped two men. Her father and Grey's younger brother, Franklin. So they were finally here.

You are too late, my father. Numbed to the point of being dispassionate, Taylor looked behind her . . . to the body reclining in the bed, even now being arranged by Betsy. The older woman was crying softly. Taylor wasn't. She couldn't. She had no more tears. Her emotions right now were a raw wound. To do anything at all was to rub salt into the exposed wound in her soul.

She pivoted until she once again looked out the window to watch the scene below. Along with the doctor, Henry the butler—*This man is Betsy's husband*, Taylor repeated this detail to herself, as if she needed assurance that at least her rote memory survived—had come outside and was now speaking to the men. With the window closed, Taylor couldn't hear them. But she didn't have to hear to know what was being said. The doctor was telling the men that Camilla James had died. She knew this because her father suddenly buckled. Taylor tensed, stiffening her knees as she watched Henry and Franklin make a grab for him.

Finally, the men had him buttressed between them, an arm each around her father's back and a grip on each of his arms. Just then, Charles James threw his head back, his expression a distorted mask of abject sorrow. His mouth was open. Perhaps, Taylor thought, he was crying out as she had done earlier. The men moved forward and then disappeared into the house.

Taylor's first thought was that she needed to leave the room. She knew her father would want to be alone with Camilla James. But beyond that realization, her motivation was perhaps selfish. Right now, she simply did not want to see her father. Yes, he was the only one left now with the answers to the questions she had. Yes, he was the only one who could verify everything Aunt Camil—no, her mother—had told her. But right now, Taylor did not want to see him. She had no idea what to say to him.

So he could tell her the truth. So what? What need had she of his words to verify a truth? The truth needed no help. It just and simply *was*. Lies needed elaborate stories, she knew. And they had been told ... among them, that she was dead and that Amanda was dead. Other lies were that she was Cherokee and that Tennie Nell Christie was her mother. Lies. All of them. But the truth? No, it needed nothing and no one.

Neither did she. *I don't? Then why am I standing here waiting for Grey?* She was, and she knew it. A grimace of misery clutched at Taylor's features, tried to break through her control. She tensed, fisting her hands. No, she would not think further about Grey. To do so might melt the ice she had encased her heart in. Right now she did not want to speak. She did not want to feel. And she did not want to be touched. She didn't even want to breathe or to live.

But stubbornly her heart insisted on beating and her lungs continued to draw air in and push it out, almost independent of her own will. It was the oddest thing, life. One moment you possessed it ... she turned slowly again to stare at Camilla James ... and the next, you didn't. One moment you were Cherokee, one of The People—and the next, you weren't. You were white, a thing you had hated all your life. And you weren't alone in the world. You had a half-sister, a father, and a man you loved ... and one mother who was dead and another mother so many miles away who lived, yet wasn't your mother at all. But had loved you as only one could.

Tennie Nell Christie. She had sent Taylor here to learn these truths. And she had. But now she wanted to go home. The Cherokee Nation. No matter the truth of her white blood, in her heart she was Cherokee. And she wanted to go home. Now. Today. It was quiet there. Peaceful. She loved her Cherokee mother ... and so she would go. She would leave before Grey got here. Taylor frowned, not able to recall at first why he'd left and where he'd been going. Then it came to her. His mother's. He was going to his mother's to stop Stanley James and to find out if she had a hand in killing Taylor's mother.

Taylor chuckled, a self-deprecating sound. *So many mothers.*

"Are you OK, Miss James?"

Taylor jumped and turned around. There stood Betsy. Taylor had forgotten the woman was in the room. Apparently she had finished her ministrations to Camilla James and was now standing at the foot of the bed. "I'm fine," Taylor said abruptly. "My father and Mr. Franklin Talbott have arrived."

Looking weary and sad, her eyes swollen, her cheeks splotchy with color, the older woman nodded. "I'll leave you now with your aunt for a few minutes of privacy. I'm so sorry for your loss, miss."

"Thank you," Taylor managed to say, seeing no need to correct the housekeeper. What difference did it make if Betsy continued to believe Camilla James had been Taylor's aunt? In silence, she waited while Betsy left the room, gently closing the door behind her. Taylor didn't intend to be here when her father came upstairs, as he no doubt was doing at this very moment. That being so, Taylor knew she needed to tell her mother good-bye now.

Slowly, stiffly, she walked over to the bed and looked down at her . . . mother. Betsy had done wonders. Camilla James was again beautiful. She could be asleep, nothing more. Taylor fought back a sudden sob that tore at her heart. She gritted her teeth and stared through the blurring haze of her sorrow. She reached out and tenderly stroked her mother's hair . . . so long and soft and black like hers. From this woman she had got her hair, the shape of her face, her nose and mouth. This woman. Not Tennie Nell Christie. But this woman. Taylor touched Camilla's cheek. A tear splashed onto the woman's forehead. Without acknowledging to herself that it was her own tear, Taylor gently rubbed it away, feeling the cool, soft skin under her fingers.

"I love you, Mother," she whispered. "And I forgive you. I will always honor your memory. And I will try to bring honor to this life you have given me." Then she bent over and softly kissed her mother's cheek.

In the next moment—and wishing fervently she had found the courage to say those things to Camilla while she yet lived— Taylor straightened up and turned away. She would now leave the room and avoid her father. But she was too late. The door opened. Her father stood there, alone, his hand on the door-knob. Taylor's gaze locked with his. She didn't speak. Neither did he. But in his blue eyes—the same color as hers—was the truth and his recognition that Taylor now knew it, too. She now knew that this man, whose grief made him appear old, and the dead woman in the bed were her true parents. And they had left her behind, at the end of the war, in the Cherokee Nation with a woman whom she dearly loved but who was no relation to her. *Cowards.*

Bitterness welled up inside Taylor. She looked from him to her mother. She then took a deep, ragged breath and turned again to her father. "I'll leave you alone with her."

What she didn't say was that, to her, this was how he and Camilla had evidently always wanted it . . . that they would be together without her.

Shaking his head, Charles held a hand out to her in sup-plication. "Please don't leave, Taylor. Stay. I want you to stay."

Silence again ruled the distance between them. A function-ing part of Taylor's brain registered that she was hearing knocking on a door down the hall and the sound of Franklin Talbott's voice as he called out beseechingly to Amanda to please open the door and let him and the doctor in.

Again her father spoke. "Please. Stay. I . . . I don't have any right to say this, Taylor . . . but I need you."

Taylor's chin came up. She remained dry-eyed and hated herself for wanting to believe his words. In his presence she felt young, like a small girl who was uncertain of herself but more uncertain of being loved. Resentment flooded Taylor. He expected her to act the obedient child. Well, she was a woman now and did not behave as a young one would. Denying him his comfort, refusing to absolve him, Taylor looked down and away, purposely unresponsive.

After long moments of sustained silence, though, Taylor dared another glance her father's way. He no longer stood in the doorway. She looked around and found him beside the bed. His prostrating grief was too much for Taylor to bear and to witness. Now was her chance to leave. But instead, and not asking herself why, she whipped around, returning to the window where she'd stood before. She looked out on the peace and beauty of the day . . . and watched and waited. From behind her, not one sound issued forth. Her father's grief must be too deep, was Taylor's conclusion. For the briefest of seconds, she allowed herself to care and to hurt for him.

Retreating back into her hardened shell, Taylor allowed time simply to pass. To her, the seconds, the minutes, seemed to drag by as slowly as if they had been dipped in molasses and could not pull free of its sticky, syrupy hold. Her back and legs ached from remaining so still. Her eyes felt dry and scratchy, yet her vision remained clear and sharp. She watched the street and marked the passing carriages, her breath catching, then disappointment eating at her, each time one slowed down in front of the open gate to the James property but didn't turn in. Each time she would think, *Is that Grey? Is he back? What happened at his mother's? Is she alive? Is Uncle Stanley? Why would he want to kill Grey's mother? Weren't they in on this poisoning together?* So many questions and no one to answer them for her.

But those weren't the only reasons she wished and prayed for the first sight of Grey's carriage. She admitted it now. She admitted that she needed to know, with every breath she took, every beat of her heart, that he was unharmed, that he lived. If he didn't, then there was no need for her to do so. But how could she find out? What could she do? As if it had been waiting in the wings of her mind, waiting only for her to ask, the answer burst brightly into her consciousness. She could go after Grey herself.

Despite her father's wish to the contrary, she did not have to remain here. Meaning, Calvin was back with her horse. *Of course.* She could get Red Sky from Calvin, have him tell her where Grey's mother lived, and then ride there to help him. This was what she would do. But before she could turn away from the window, a black brougham did slow down at the gate and turn in. Rapidly the horses came, their hooves and the carriage's wheels churning up a cloud of dust and gravel on the long driveway. In less than a minute, the conveyance would be stopping out front.

Taylor tensed, frowning, her hands fisting. No. It couldn't be. She couldn't be seeing what she was seeing. Something was wrong. Her wondering gaze fell on Edward, the driver. He was using the whip. But that wasn't what concerned her. She shook her head, tried to clear her vision . . . but it persisted. A great dark and hovering bird of prey seemed to engulf the carriage, seemed to devour it . . . to become it. The omen. *Grey. It took him, not me.* Taylor's nails dug into her palms. "No!" she cried out, jerking around, already running for the bedroom's closed door.

From beside the bed, her father looked up, standing now. "Taylor! What is it?"

She didn't stop; she was at the door, wrenching it open. "Grey. His carriage. He has returned. And something is wrong."

"Oh, dear God, no. What else can happen today? Wait for me, Taylor."

"I cannot." She was out in the hall, running, her booted steps thudding heavily with each charging step she took. *Grey, oh God, Grey, oh God, Grey, oh God.* The litany repeated itself . . . over and over.

A door to her right jerked open. Startled, Taylor glanced its way. Franklin stood there. Amanda was at his shoulder, wide-eyed and wild-eyed. Behind her, in the room, was the doctor. But it was Amanda who called out. "Taylor, what's wrong? Why are you running?"

"It is Grey. Something is wrong with Grey." She heard their shocked protestations but had already flown by them and was at the stairs. "His carriage. It has returned!" she called out over her shoulder, aware that Amanda and Franklin were behind her now, as were probably her father and, she hoped, the doctor. Taylor attacked the stairs, all but falling down them in her haste.

Downstairs now, with no servants in sight—no doubt Henry the butler had gone to console his wife, Betsy—Taylor jerked open the door and ran outside, startling Calvin and Red

Sky. Off to one side, in front of her father's carriage and talking with his driver, Calvin called out, "Whoa, Miss James! What's wrong?"

She didn't answer, didn't have the breath or the inclination for it. She'd outpaced the others following her; that much she knew. Perhaps they'd stopped chasing her; perhaps sensibly they waited where they were, waited for the brougham to come to a stop in front of them at the front door, as it must. Or . . . as it would have, had not Taylor been running down the very middle of the driveway. Her footsteps crunched through the gravel, but still she ran, her lungs screaming for breath, her mind numb.

Obviously seeing her, Edward, the driver, yelled, "Whoa!" to the horses and sawed back on the reins and the hand brake. The lathered animals skidded and pawed. Dust and gravel filled the air in a great billowing cloud. The carriage itself, with its wheels locked, skidded sideways and shimmied to a halt . . . not fifteen feet away from where Taylor had herself finally been able to stop. She bent over, put her hands to her knees, and gasped for breath.

Just then someone from behind her grabbed her, startling a cry out of Taylor. She jerked upright and around. It was Amanda, red-faced with the heat and from running. Behind Amanda, at a distance, Taylor could see her father and Franklin and the doctor standing by his carriage with Calvin and Red Sky.

Amanda, her sister, clutched at Taylor's shirtsleeve. "I told them . . . I would see to you." Like Taylor, she gasped for breath. "I think they . . . were afraid you might . . . shoot them. My God, Taylor, what is it? What's wrong?"

"I do not know. Grey," Taylor got out, pointing to the brougham.

Just then, Edward, the driver, stood up, startling Taylor and Amanda, who clutched at Taylor as the man frantically waved his arms. Was he trying to warn them away? His words confirmed he was. "Get back, girls. Go away. Don't come any closer. It's not—"

A shot rang out. Amanda screamed; Taylor jumped. Ed-

ward grunted in pain, clutched at his shoulder, and toppled off
his perch, falling hard, bleeding, to the ground. Wide-eyed,
shocked, her mouth open, Taylor—still held in Amanda's
grip—could do no more than look to the brougham. What she
saw there made her wonder if she was addled. It was Stanley
James—not Grey—balanced in the opened door, one hand
gripping the carriage frame, a smoking gun fisted in his other.

Where's Grey? was all Taylor could think in her benumbed
state.

Amanda recovered first, letting go of Taylor and charging
toward her father. "What are you doing? Why did you shoot
him?" Her voice was a crying scream of anguish and confusion. "Father, what is going on?"

"Get back, Amanda," Stanley James said, his voice level.
With his gun, he waved his daughter away. "It's not you I
want. You're in my way. Move."

"I won't." Amanda stopped where she was . . . directly in
the line of fire between her father and Taylor. "You'll have
to shoot me first." Making of herself a bigger target, Amanda
held her arms out to either side and at shoulder height.

"I'm not going to shoot you, Amanda. I love you. You are
my daughter. It's her I want. Taylor. She's a sin I can't forgive. And this is her judgment day."

"You're not God," Amanda said quietly and firmly. "Taylor's done nothing wrong. It's you who's wrong, Father. You
can't do this."

"I can. And I will. Now move. It's the last time I'm going
to tell you."

Taylor had no intention of allowing Amanda's bravery to
get her killed. Nor did she doubt that Stanley James meant
what he'd just implied—he would shoot Amanda if she didn't
move. The man's hatred of her, Taylor knew, was stronger
than his love for his daughter.

So while they'd talked, while Amanda tried to reason with
her father, Taylor had edged her gun out of its holster, held it
at her side, and was even now taking one cautious step after
another toward Amanda's slender, vulnerable back. Taylor
prayed her father and the others stayed where they were. She

wanted nothing and no one to force Stanley's hand, because she was almost upon Amanda. Taylor herself made no sudden move to draw her uncle's attention to herself . . . just slowly and steadily advanced. She watched everything at once. Amanda. Her uncle. The horses. She heard everything. Her own rasping breath. Amanda and her father's argument. Edward's groans.

The sweat of fear and pure calculation ran down Taylor's spine. The one thing she could not do right now was wonder what this man full of hate might have already done to Grey. But he had done something. If he hadn't, he wouldn't be here in Grey's brougham, which he'd obviously taken at gunpoint. Taylor knew that if she dwelled on this, she would collapse into a ball and never stop crying. So she forced onto her very being the cold-blooded steeliness of the patient, stalking killer that her reputation said she was.

Taylor drew even with Amanda, standing on her right side as she gently put a hand on her sister's arm. Quietly, never looking her way, never taking her gaze off her uncle, who now watched Taylor much like a serpent would, Taylor said, "Get behind me, Amanda. Right now. Don't argue. Drop down into a ball and cover your head with your arms. I don't want you to see this."

"No, Taylor," Amanda sobbed. "I can't allow you to do this."

Taylor licked at her lips, tasting the salt of her sweat. "Do it, Amanda."

"Do like she says, Amanda," Stanley said, sparing only the briefest of glances for his daughter before turning an evil grin on Taylor, a grin that split his wide, cruel mouth in two like a gashing knife wound in flesh. "You don't have any part in this."

"I do," Amanda protested, straining against Taylor's tightened grip on her arm. "Why are you doing this? Stop it. Mama's dead. Nothing can bring her back. You poisoned her."

"I did not!" Stanley James screamed, his face red and contorted. "Augusta did. I never—it was all Augusta. She did it. I never loved her. Only your mother. Augusta kept trying to—

she pleaded with me, begged me to leave your mother. She threatened to tell your mother lies, that we were lovers. We weren't. I told her I didn't love her, to leave us be. But she wouldn't. She befriended your mother. She—"

"Ohmigod. Franklin. My marriage to him." Amanda stared in horror at her father.

Taylor watched her sister—yet thought of herself . . . in love with the other Talbott son, Greyson. What a terrible trickster was Fate. Terrible. It had put them all here, in this place, to face the sins of the mothers.

"That's right. You and Franklin." Stanley continued his ranting. "Augusta hated the idea of you—Camilla's daughter— loving her son. She wanted me only and not to be a part of our family through you. Then Greyson fell for Taylor, another of Camilla's daughters." Stanley's expression crumpled. "It pushed her over the edge. And she . . . killed your mother. Because of *her*." His voice a ragged roar, he pointed his gun at Taylor.

Taylor stiffened her knees. Her gun felt slippery in her hand. But she didn't dare try to wipe her hand on her britches. Fractions of seconds now were the difference between life and death.

"No!" Amanda cried out. "Not because of Taylor, Father. You have to believe me. Just put the gun down. Please. And come inside with me and see Mother."

"No." Stanley tightened his grip on the gun in his fist and descended from the carriage. He stood firmly on the ground, staring and glaring to a point somewhere behind Taylor and Amanda. "That son of a bitch is here. He betrayed me. My own brother betrayed me with your mother. She loved him, you know. Not me. Him." Stanley focused again on Amanda . . . and then Taylor. "*Your* mother," he said pointedly, "betrayed me with my own brother."

Her chin raised, Taylor said nothing. She didn't dare breathe or blink. As quietly as she could, with her gun hand still hanging at her side, but with the deft touch of long practice, she cocked back the hammer on her gun . . . and waited.

"Father," Amanda said quickly in what Taylor recognized

as a desperate attempt to divert Stanley's attention away from her, "what have you done to Augusta Talbott?"

That got a grunt of distaste out of Stanley James. "Not enough, I tell you. I used my pistol on the bitch and told her I'd never loved her, that she was trash. And crazy. Augusta has always been crazy. I knew that. I left Boston to get away from her, but she followed me here. With her husband and sons, she followed me here and made my life a living torture. But I didn't kill her, if that's what you mean. I wanted to, but that son of hers arrived before I could."

Taylor's breath caught. Amanda then asked the question Taylor dreaded: "What have you done to Grey, Father? What?"

Stanley shook his head. "Nothing."

Taylor opened her mouth, filling her lungs with air and relief. She refused to heed the doubt that asked her if she could believe this man, if she could trust him to be telling the truth. She chose to do so. She had to.

"Then where is he, Father? Why are you in his carriage? You took your horse when you left earlier."

Stanley shrugged, looking impatient and agitated now. "I don't know where he is, and I don't care. Quit talking to me, Amanda; you're confusing me." He distractedly ran a hand through his hair and shifted his weight from one leg to the other as he eyed Taylor . . . and her drawn gun.

Here we go, Taylor told herself. Her eyes narrowed with her certainty. Calm suffused her inside. Clarity came to her brain. Time slowed.

"Move, Amanda. I have unfinished business with Taylor."

His words didn't surprise Taylor. She'd expected them. But they did shock Amanda. "No. I told you I wouldn't. Taylor is my *sister*." She threw the word at her father—the wrong word.

Stanley grimaced, crouching into an ugly stance and raising his gun.

Just as he did, at a distance behind him movement caught Taylor's eye. Without having to look away from Stanley, she saw a huge roan with a big rider crouched low over his neck thunder around the gate and turn in to the James property. It was Grey. He was riding hard, urging the lathered horse to even greater speed. But he would be too late. It made Taylor sad. She said her silent good-bye to him.

As if in slow motion, Taylor watched Stanley James level his gun and cock back the hammer. She heard Amanda scream, "No!" as Taylor yanked her sister to her knees and raised her own gun, her arm stiffened with deadly accuracy as she centered her weapon on her uncle's heart . . . and fired.

But he'd jerked to one side and fired in the same instant as Taylor had. With satisfaction Taylor saw him twitch and grimace. Her bullet had caught him in the left arm, only grazing him. But his bullet had caught Taylor squarely in the shoulder. A ripping, searing pain almost took her to her knees. She staggered but kept her feet . . . saw that Grey was close enough now that she could make out his features frozen in horror and disbelief . . . and fired again at her uncle. This bullet took him high in the chest. He cried out, his gun firing almost reflexively. Again pain tore through Taylor, as the bullet ripped through the flesh in her thigh.

She went to her knees, desperately fighting the weakness that threatened to cause her to black out. Amanda clutched at her, screaming, crying. With a sudden burst of renewed strength, Taylor pushed Amanda down and threw herself on top of her. "Stay down, goddammit," she cursed. And Amanda did.

Quickly Taylor rose, firing again—just as Grey neared them and fought to bring the big roan to a stop, all the while fumbling in his effort to get his gun from its holster under his coat. He screamed out her name as Taylor watched her bullet hit her uncle again in the chest—this time almost in the center of it. Close to his heart. It wouldn't be long now, if only she could hold on. Breathing laboriously, feeling soaked with her own blood, her vision blurring, Taylor watched Stanley stare in confusion at her, as if he had no idea what had just happened. A pool of blood now stained the front of his shirt and vest.

"Why won't you die?" were her uncle's last words as he fired once again at Taylor, hit her, and then jumped and jerked and twisted as Grey, cursing and yelling, emptied his gun into Stanley James's already dead body.

The man fell to the ground, face-first. It was over.

Relieved, suddenly numb and cold, with the world around her buzzing, Taylor slumped over Amanda, who was screaming and crying under her. Stanley's third bullet had taken Taylor in her side. It was bad. Very bad.

Then hands were grabbing her, turning her over. People were all around her, all of them talking and yelling. Some were crying. It was like a nightmare. Every one of them was calling her name. They wouldn't leave her alone. Taylor tried to tell them to leave her be, but she couldn't seem to talk. Something was very wrong with her. She wanted Grey. Only Grey. Where was he? Above her—she realized she must be lying on the ground because she could see the sky above her—was her father's worried face. And Franklin's—he was holding a sobbing Amanda. And there was Calvin. And even Edward, the wounded driver, was staring down at her. But where was Grey?

Then someone brushed her hair back from her face and kissed her temple. Taylor turned her head. It took great effort. . . . She was growing steadily weaker and colder. But she did it. She looked up into Grey's face. He was sad about something . . . and crying. Or trying not to. Taylor tried to raise her hand but for some reason couldn't. She wanted to stroke his cheek.

Through the fog of a growing grayness around her, one that beckoned her away, she suddenly heard Grey's voice loud and clear. "Oh, God, Taylor. Oh, God, honey. Don't give up. Don't. You'll be OK. The doctor's right here. Just fight, baby. Fight. I love you. Please fight."

When the doctor tried to open Taylor's shirt, she pushed his hands away, telling him no. She then licked at her lips and stared up at Grey. "I can't fight, Grey," she rasped out. "It hurts too much."

"It can't hurt half as much as you leaving me. Let the doctor see to you, Taylor. Please. I love you. Do you hear me? I love you, and you have to live for me. You have to."

Taylor smiled. "I can't, Grey. I want to live. But I can't. Please don't hate me. I love you." She then looked to the ring of faces above her . . . realizing suddenly that they weren't all standing above her but were all on their knees and surrounding her. Her father stroked her forehead. Her sister held her hand. They were both sobbing quietly. "I love you, Father. And Amanda, my sister. Just know that I love you both."

Taylor felt herself slipping. She focused again on Grey. This time managing to raise a hand—it was covered in blood, her blood—to his cheek. He caught her hand there, held it, kissed her palm. Her touch left him streaked with blood. "I came here, Grey, to find you. And I did. You must go to the Nation and tell my Cherokee mother that I love her. Will you do that for me?"

Grey nodded. His tears caused wide streaks through the blood on his cheeks. "I will. But you're going with me. Do you hear me, Taylor? You're going with me."

"Yes," she said feebly, the last of her strength ebbing from her. "I will go with you. I wish to be buried there, Grey." Then she clutched at him, her body arching. "I love you, Grey."

She heard his answering words—"Oh, God, Taylor, I love you; don't leave me, please"—and then . . . all was darkness.

Her soul was adrift. The great hovering evil darkness had won . . . just as Bentley, the man-bird and spirit guide, had feared. Just as Rube, the Cherokee guard in Tahlequah, had predicted.

The day will come for you, Taylor. And you will have to make a choice. And that choice will be marked with the blood of those you love the most. Your life or theirs. The decision will be on your head and in your heart. This thing I have seen, and it will come to pass.

Epilogue

I t could not have been easy. But still, it is good that you brought her here."

They were again speaking of Taylor. Sitting on Tennie Nell Christie's rough-wood front porch with her, Grey leaned forward, bracing his elbows on his knees as he fiddled with a twig he'd scooped up a moment ago. He glanced over at Taylor's Cherokee mother. "I did only as she asked, Miss Christie."

The handsome Cherokee woman was shelling peas. Late-summer sunshine filled the day, just as the crockery bowl filled her lap. Kindness and warmth radiated from her dark eyes as she met his gaze. "Still, it is good. It is in this place that she belongs." Her hands stilled as she looked out onto the breathtaking wooded vista that was the Nation. "Here, in this place, we will keep her close to our hearts."

Grey swallowed and took a deep breath. "I'd like to stay, too. For the same reason."

Tennie Nell nodded as if she had expected him to say that and went back to her simple task. "Then you have come to like it here."

Grey couldn't get enough of watching the older woman's graceful movements with her hands. "I love it here. It's so peaceful. And quiet. Taylor said it was. She spoke to me often of the Nation's beauty. She told me of the hills and the wild game and the rivers. She was right, too."

Tennie Nell chuckled. "If my daughter were here, she would say she is always right."

Grey grinned, knowing the truth of that. "Yes, she would." He didn't know what else to say.

Without warning, Tennie Nell spoke sharply, her voice breaking. "I should never have sent Taylor to her father."

Grey sat up. They'd been through this before. "You had no choice, Miss Christie. You were trying to save Taylor's life. You did what you had to do."

"No." The word was adamant. "I knew she did not have to leave. Her white blood would save her. They could not kill a white woman in Tahlequah at their prison. I could have told her. And them. They would have had to let her go. Instead, I made my brother break her out. He is now an outlaw. And the guard Rube later died. His heart gave out."

Grey nodded. He'd heard this many times. "Miss Christie, what you say is true. You could have told Taylor she was white and had her released from prison, a free woman. If you had, what would she have done? She would have felt betrayed. And she would have gone straight to St. Louis to hunt down her father. I think you know that. So don't be so hard on yourself."

The Cherokee woman's shoulders slumped. She shook her head and continued shelling the peas. "The papers that my brother Ned threw in the prison cell with the guard told of Taylor's blood. On these papers were also written the words of that no-good Monroe Hammer. Ned forced him to tell the truth before he killed him. My daughter did not kill that man they said she did."

Grey wondered if Tennie Nell knew about the five other men her daughter—Taylor was indeed this woman's daughter, more than she'd ever been Camilla James's daughter—had killed. When he'd arrived here, he'd told her about Stanley James, that he and Taylor had killed him. But the others . . . He wondered.

"I know my daughter has killed other men, Mr. Greyson Talbott."

She always called him that. Grey's startlement was because of what she'd said. Could she read minds?

Tennie Nell grinned and shrugged. "Only sometimes. It is a gift. We call it The Sight." Then her grin faded. "I only wish

I could have seen what my Wild Flower would face in your place of the Great Waters."

Grey had no answer to that. Instead he was thinking of Wild Flower. Taylor's Cherokee name. It suited her. She was wild and free and beautiful . . . and she would grow and thrive where she was planted, no matter how difficult the terrain— or the odds.

Out of the seeming blue, Taylor's mother said, "It will not be easy for you here. You must learn our ways. But your people—what will they say about you staying here?"

Grey's heart soared. "Are you saying I can stay, Miss Christie?"

She shrugged. "It is not up to me."

Grey knew better. She hadn't wanted him to, not when he'd first brought Taylor home. Nor had Taylor's uncle, Ned Christie. Nor had anyone else of Cherokee blood. And not a one of them yet had let him forget he was a white man. But slowly, he was winning them over. Grey leaned forward again, relaxing some. "Well, there's not much they can say, Miss Christie. I already told my family I wouldn't be back. You see, whether you wanted me here or not, I already knew I wouldn't leave Taylor. Ever."

Tennie Nell nodded, her hands flying with the ease of long practice. "I know this thing you are saying. It is good. Now tell me again of your people."

Grey chuckled. Taylor's mother loved talk of the Jameses— except for Stanley—and the Talbotts. "Amanda and Franklin postponed their wedding until this fall. They want to visit here then. Charles, too." Grey sobered. "He would have come with us, but the shocks . . . the deaths. His health has never been good."

"Charles is strong. He will mend." Then she sighed. "Poor Amanda. She has lost so much."

Grey nodded, knowing the truth of that. "Yes, she has. But she's happy with my brother. It looks, too, as if he's going to be the next mayor of St. Louis."

"That is good. This brother of yours, is he anything like you?"

Grey chuckled. "Yes. Only responsible . . . and boring. I tease him about that. But he's a good man. And Amanda, whom I love like a sister already, and with the help of my former housekeeper, Mrs. Scott, is happy to take care of my mother." Grey swallowed, suddenly overcome with emotion. His mother's head injuries had changed her personality. She was a different woman . . . a sweet, simple woman who took great joy in gardening and being with Amanda. But his mother had no idea who her sons were—or what she'd done to so many lives.

"I, too, have my sorrows, Mr. Greyson Talbott." Tennie Nell spoke quietly. Grey looked over at her. "I have not told you these things before. But I will do so now, so you will understand. I have lost a sister in Camilla James's passing. Her family—the Hastings—were much like you. Very wealthy and yet very good. They came to the Nation as Baptist missionaries to open a school and an orphanage in Tahlequah. Sometimes Camilla would come and stay. And sometimes when Stanley was away on business, Charles would come see about Camilla. When the war broke out, Stanley James brought his young wife and child here to be with her family. That child was Amanda. But there was another child and that was Taylor. Charles and Camilla tried not to love, for Stanley's sake. But they could not stop their hearts. Out of their love came Taylor. We were all happy until Stanley James came to take them away after the war."

"It must have been awful for you."

She nodded. "It was. We had to keep from Stanley James the truth of Taylor's mother and father, so I took her as mine and raised her. But I always wrote Camilla, and her me. I wanted her to know of her child. Then, Stanley found a letter. Camilla wrote to tell me of this. We thought it best to tell the girls that the other one was . . . no longer alive. We also agreed that Taylor should believe her father did not want her. To keep her from going to him. And then . . . I sent her there myself." Her expression hardened. "I am a very foolish woman who never deserved Taylor."

"It's over. You can't keep blaming yourself."

"I can." Tennie Nell quickly looked away from Grey, sorting through her bowl, looking for any unshelled peas, he supposed—and also so he wouldn't see her tears.

After a quiet moment during which Tennie Nell composed herself, Grey tried another subject. "You spoke of me being very wealthy, Miss Christie. I am. And I want to do some good with my money. My brother is wiring my income to me, which I will deposit in a bank here. With it, I hope to do good things for the Nation . . . for Taylor's people."

Tennie Nell concentrated her gaze on Grey. "You are a good man, Mr. Greyson Talbott. I am certain The People will welcome your help."

Grey began to sweat. He felt nervous. He'd never asked for a woman's hand before. "And what about Taylor? Do you think she will . . . marry me?"

Tennie Nell grinned at him, her dark eyes alight with affection. "I do not know. It is not for me to say."

Just then, the sounds of crackling leaves and horses' hooves caught their attention. Riders were coming through the woods. With Taylor's mother, Grey stood up, waiting. His heart welled with love for who broke through the stand of trees and rode toward them atop Red Sky. Flanking Taylor, and atop their own mounts, were the still-terrified Bentley—he was certain he'd be scalped at any moment—and the ecstatic Calvin, who already had a Cherokee sweetheart, a lovely girl named Dahnea. The Christie cabin was crowded, but it was home.

In her hand, Taylor proudly held up two fat dead rabbits for their dinner. "I have done well for us."

"Ah, this I can see!" Tennie Nell Christie called out, smiling.

Grey grinned as well. Mother and daughter. Taylor had indeed survived her ordeal and her wounds. She had mended slowly but completely. And with Grey and these men, she had found her way back home. She never spoke of being white. In her heart and mind—and theirs—she was Cherokee. Full-blood.

"Mr. Greyson Talbott has something he would know from you." Tennie Nell turned to Grey. "Go ahead. Ask her."

Grey waited until the threesome had reined their mounts in front of the porch. Calvin dismounted first and then helped Bentley's rotund little self off his Indian pony. Taylor dismounted Red Sky by slinging a leg over the horse's neck and simply sliding down his bare side to the ground. She landed easily, still holding her kill, and looked up at Grey. "Ask me what?"

What a wild and beautiful sight she made. Courage filled him. "If you'll do me the honor of marrying me."

She grinned broadly but didn't even hesitate. "You know nothing, do you, white man? We are already married—in the way of my people. It is the woman's decision. I have given you my heart and you have moved into my family's home. And so . . . we are married as long as I say this is good with me. If you can accept that, then you can stay with me and I will love you. My heart, my life, my soul, and my body I give to you, Grey. They will always be yours. And they will have to be enough."

Despite her abrupt tone, a warm shiver slipped over Grey. Her words were vows, like a wedding ceremony, in themselves. His hands to his waist, he smiled down at her. "They and you will always be enough . . . Wild Flower."

She smiled and nodded. "Good. Then it is settled. I will make my life here with you in this place. And it shall be good, Man Who Loves Wild Flower."

DISCUSSION QUESTIONS FOR

Wild Flower

BY CHERYL ANNE PORTER

1. Cheryl Anne Porter's historical mysteries often deal with complex issues such as feminine empowerment, family relationships, prejudice, and personal growth. What issues are explored in *Wild Flower*? Why do you think these issues are still as relevant today as they were in the late 1800s?

2. Taylor's Uncle Ned suggests to her that she may not really be as tough as her reputation. Do you think that other people's perception of someone frequently differs from that individual's perception of herself/himself? How did Taylor differ from her reputation or from the perceptions people had of her?

3. The Cherokee Nation, as depicted in *Wild Flower*, reflected an evolved culture that was pretty well versed in the ways of the neighboring mostly white United States. Yet the white people Taylor encountered in the story didn't seem to know much about Cherokee ways. How do you think this discrepancy came about?

4. Thoughtful character studies and the ways in which people change are a mainstay of Cheryl Anne Porter's writing. Which character or characters do you think changed most in *Wild flower*? How did the author show these changes?

5. In *Wild Flower*, as in Cheryl Anne Porter's two previous historical mysteries, *Captive Angel* and *Prairie Song*, the heroine (and sometimes other characters, too) has to deal with the effects of unpleasant past events. How does Taylor deal with her "past baggage" in *Wild Flower*? Do you think that people can simply choose to have positive outcomes in their lives despite having to resolve painful pasts?

6. Do you think Taylor gains closure with the events of her past? If so, how does reconciling her past propel her toward her future?

7. In *Wild Flower*, Taylor reflects that she didn't know her father when she was growing up. And she asks her cousin Amanda about Amanda's father. How do you think the absence of a father affected Taylor as a child? As an adult?

8. Family themes are prevalent in Cheryl Anne Porter's writing. In *Wild Flower*, the theme of treachery within one's own family was an underlying concept. Discuss the threat of a villain within a family.

9. Taylor spoke about the prejudice white people exhibited toward Indians. What about Taylor's own feelings toward whites? How extensive do you think this so-called reverse discrimination was? Still is?

10. How was Taylor affected by learning the truth about her heritage? How did it change the way she lived her life?

Captive Angel

CHERYL ANNE PORTER

Jack Daltry came back to his father's ranch to
mend fences between them. Instead, he finds his
father dead, and a feisty, beautiful woman claiming
his dad gave her the Circle D ranch. Now a stand-
off begins between a man eaten up with anger
and a defiant beauty with emotions locked behind
a wall of self-control. But when a ruthless killer
comes after them both, Jack finds a woman of
passion and courage beside him . . . and the
chance for redemption if he can show Angel the
transforming power of love.

Read *Cheryl Anne Porter's*

BOLD NEW SERIES

About Three Passionate Sisters And The Men Who Capture Their Hearts!

HANNAH'S PROMISE
NOMINEE FOR THE BOOKSTORES THAT CARE "BEST LOVE & LAUGHTER ROMANCE" CATEGORY

After she finds her parents brutally murdered, Hannah Lawless travels to Boston, vowing revenge on their killers. When sexy Slade Garrett joins her crusade, Hannah may have found her soul-mate—or the heartless villain she seeks . . .

JACEY'S RECKLESS HEART

As Hannah heads East, Jacey Lawless makes her way to Tucson, in search of the scoundrel who left a spur behind at her parents' murder scene. When she meets up with dashing Zant Chapelo, a gunslinger whose father rode with hers, Jacey doesn't know whether to shoot . . . or surrender.

SEASONS OF GLORY

With Hannah and Jacey off to find their parents' killers, young Glory is left to tend the ranch. And with the help of handsome neighbor—and arch enemy—Riley Thorne, Glory might learn a thing or two about life . . . and love.